A KISS TO MELT HER HEART

BY
EMILY FORBES

TEMPTED BY HER ITALIAN SURGEON

BY
LOUISA GEORGE

Emily Forbes began her writing life as a partnership between two sisters who are both passionate bibliophiles. As a team, 'Emily' had ten books published. One of her proudest moments was winning the 2013 Australia Romantic Book of the Year Award for *Sydney Harbour Hospital: Bella's Wishlist*.

While Emily's love of writing remains as strong as ever, the demands of life with young families has recently made it difficult for them to work on stories together. But rather than give up her dream Emily now writes solo. The challenges may be different, but the reward of having a book published is still as sweet as ever.

Whether as a team or as an individual, Emily hopes to keep bringing stories to her readers. Her inspiration comes from everywhere, and stories she hears while travelling, at mothers' lunches, in the media and in her other career as a physiotherapist all get embellished with a large dose of imagination until they develop a life of their own.

If you would like to get in touch with Emily you can e-mail her at emilyforbes@internode.on.net

A lifelong reader of most genres, **Louisa George** discovered romance novels later than most, but immediately fell in love with the intensity of emotion, the high drama and the family focus of Mills & Boon® Medical Romance™.

With a Bachelor's Degree in Communication and a nursing qualification under her belt, writing medical romance seemed a natural progression and the perfect combination of her two interests. And making things up is a great way to spend the day!

An English ex-pat, Louisa now lives north of Auckland, New Zealand, with her husband, two teenage sons and two male cats. Writing romance is her opportunity to covertly inject a hefty dose of pink into her heavily testosterone-dominated household. When she's not writing or researching Louisa loves to spend time with her family and friends, enjoys travelling, and adores great food. She's also hopelessly addicted to Zumba®.

A KISS TO MELT HER HEART

BY

EMILY FORBES

Published in Great Britain 2015
by Mills & Boon, an imprint of Harlequin (UK) Limited,
Eton House, 18-24 Paradise Road, Richmond, Surrey, TW9 1SR

ISBN: 978-0-263-24706-0

Harlequin (UK) Limited's policy is to use papers that are natural, renewable and recyclable products and made from wood grown in sustainable forests. The logging and manufacturing processes conform to the legal environmental regulations of the country of origin.

Printed and bound in Spain
by CPI, Barcelona

Dear Reader,

This story has been floating around in my head for a while. Like so many of my ideas, it started to take shape when I got talking to a man who had just spent six months working in Antarctica. He told me some interesting tales about various accidents and emergencies that he'd encountered, and that got me thinking about what it would be like to move to the bottom of the world.

What type of people would choose to live and work in those extreme conditions, and what hardships would they face even in the twenty-first century?

I spent far too much time on research, but that gave me a very clear sense of the type of man Gabe Sullivan is. He loves a challenge, and is exactly the type of man I can imagine thriving in Antarctica—and he is the perfect man to melt Sophie's heart.

Sophie had to travel to the end of the earth to find love again, but isn't that something we would all be willing to do?

Enjoy!

Emily

Books by Emily Forbes

Tempted & Tamed!

A Doctor by Day…
Tamed by the Renegade

The Honourable Army Doc
Dare She Date the Celebrity Doc?
Breaking the Playboy's Rules
Sydney Harbour Hospital: Bella's Wishlist
Georgie's Big Greek Wedding?
Breaking Her No-Dates Rule
Navy Officer to Family Man
Dr Drop-Dead-Gorgeous
The Playboy Firefighter's Proposal

Visit the author profile page
at millsandboon.co.uk for more titles

FOR MY DAD
1935–2014
I MISS YOU

CHAPTER ONE

Hobart, Tasmania, February 26th

'ARE YOU SURE you want to do this?'

Sophie could see the concern in Luke's grey eyes and she appreciated it, but she'd made up her mind and she wasn't going change it now. She'd come too far. She *couldn't* stop now. And Luke should know that. They had been friends since they'd both been teenagers and there was only one person who knew Sophie better than Luke did—but Danny was gone now.

She squeezed his hand in what she hoped was a reassuring fashion, although she suspected she needed more reassurance than he did. His hand was warm in the chill of the hospital. Sophie didn't normally feel the cold. She had grown up in Tasmania, the wild but beautiful southern end of Australia, and cold weather was something she was used to, but the air felt frosty today. Maybe it was nervousness—not about the surgery, having her appendix out was a minor procedure—but her future plans were ambitious although she wasn't about to admit to any misgivings at this point.

She wrapped the towelling dressing gown around her body a little more firmly to ward off the chill as she said, 'I need to get away.'

'I understand that,' Luke replied, 'but why don't you take a holiday instead.'

Sophie looked at him. She wasn't in a vacation mood. 'What would I do on a holiday?' she asked.

'I don't know. Relax?'

'I don't need to relax and I don't want time to myself, I've got too much of that already. Holidays are meant to be shared with someone and we both know I have no one now. I don't want to go on a holiday but I do need to go some place where the memories won't follow me. Everywhere I look around here things remind me of Danny and I can see it in people's faces too. Every time they see me I remind them that Danny isn't here. I need to move on and I can't do that here. It's too hard. I need some space to get my head together.'

'I miss him too, Soph, but I'm not sure that spending a winter in Antarctica is necessarily the right place to get your head together.'

'It's not a whole winter, it's only seven weeks.'

'*If* the other doctor gets back. Otherwise you're there for winter. That's seven months.'

Seven months. Sophie knew that could seem like a lifetime. Danny had been dead for seven months. She knew exactly how long each day, each hour, each minute could seem.

But she also knew she couldn't stay in Hobart. She needed to get away and give her grief, and her guilt, time to fade. She knew she'd never forget, she didn't *want* to forget, but she did want to be able to live her life without memories of Danny shadowing her every move. She missed him but she missed her old self too. She wanted a chance to find the old Sophie, the one who had smiled and laughed, and she suspected it would be easier to remember how she used to be if she wasn't constantly being reminded of what she'd lost.

Her mind was made up and Luke should know that once she made up her mind she very rarely changed it. She tried to appease him. 'I appreciate your concern but it's not like I don't know what to expect.'

'Theory and practice are two very different things. I'm not pretending I understand the technicalities of your job but I do know about working in difficult environments and having to rely on others to get the job done. Working in Antarctica can't be the same as working in a city with all the support networks.'

'I know exactly what type of situations I might need to deal with,' she said. 'I admit I haven't worked in quite the same conditions but I have worked with the Antarctic Medicine Unit for two years. I have to trust everyone to do their part and they have to trust me to do mine.'

'But are you ready?'

Sophie knew what Luke was asking. It wasn't a question about her skills as a doctor, he'd have to trust her on that, it was a question about her state of mind. Sophie knew he was concerned about her and he deserved an honest answer.

'I don't know.' She'd been working towards this goal for the past six months—it had given her something to focus on since losing Danny. It had stopped her going crazy with grief and loneliness. It had seemed like a good idea but now that the moment was here, and sooner than she'd expected, she just had to hope she was making the right decision. 'I think I'm ready. The powers that be in the Antarctic programme seem to think so and I'm their best option. I *have* to be ready. They need me and I need to go.' She had to trust that the decision makers knew what they were doing. She knew her medical skills would be sufficient and she must have passed all the psych tests or they wouldn't be sending her. She had to believe she was ready.

This move would be a test for her. She knew that but she wanted to push herself, she *needed* to challenge herself. Danny had brought out the best in her, he had helped her to shine, and she was finding it hard to believe she'd be okay without him. That she *could* be okay. Danny had been her first and only love, and she'd never imagined having to live without him, but that was her reality. She needed to know if she could survive on her own.

She knew Luke was worried for her but she had to do this.

'I realise I'll either love it or hate it,' she continued, 'but I want to do something. I *have* to do something. I can't stay here and, to be honest, while I'll admit I'm nervous I'm also excited. I've been living day to day, getting up in the morning just aiming to get through one more day. This goal has given me something to look forward to. It's given me a reason to keep going.'

She knew that if the psychologists heard her last sentence they'd probably think twice about sending her to the ice. She didn't want Luke to think she was a basket case too so she tried to explain her feelings more succinctly.

'I get up in the morning and the house is quiet. There's none of Danny's stuff lying around, getting in my way. There are no piles of shoes, different ones for hiking, running, riding, paddling, abseiling and gardening. No ropes or tents or backpacks to trip over. No maps spread across the kitchen table.

'I'm never going to get that back and I miss it. I miss him. I miss listening to his big plans, listening to him plan our future and the future of the business. I felt like he took my future with him and this might be my chance to get it back. It won't be the same future, I've lost that, but perhaps it could be worth something.'

'Why haven't you told me this before? I thought you were coping.'

'I *am* coping.' She was, most days. 'But that's all I'm doing. I'm not living and I want to live again. I've lost Danny but I've also lost myself. I don't want to be sad and lonely any more. I need to get moving. I have to do *something*. This might make or break me but I have to try it.' She smiled. 'You can't pretend you're not a little bit jealous. I know this type of adventure would be right up your alley.'

Luke laughed. 'You're right. It's exactly the sort of thing I'd love to have a crack at. Danny would have too.' He paused and considered her carefully before continuing. 'Are you sure you're doing this for you and not out of some misguided tribute to Danny?'

Sophie knew that Danny was part of the reason she was going. Despite working for the Antarctic Medicine Unit for two years she hadn't ever originally intended to leave the mainland and head three thousand plus kilometres south to Antarctica. She and Danny and Luke had been inseparable since high school but the boys had been the adrenalin junkies while she had been far more conservative. Maybe this adventure was out of character for her but she wasn't foolish enough to venture out of her comfort zone without careful consideration of her reasons.

She thought Danny would be proud of her but that wasn't her main motivation. She had been going quietly mad, sitting in Hobart. There were too many memories. She hoped this adventure would be the catalyst to allow her to start again. To begin the next chapter of her life. A life without Danny.

'I think he would be proud of me for doing this,' she admitted, 'but I'm not crazy enough to take up this challenge without believing I can handle it.'

'You know I promised Danny that if anything ever happened to him I'd look after you?' Luke said.

Sophie frowned. 'You did?'

'Of course. We had to consider the possibility of things going wrong on one of our treks. We had to do risk-management assessments for every expedition and we discussed what we'd do in the worst-case situation. We had to hope for the best but prepare for the worst. Neither of us ever expected that something would happen that wasn't related to work but either way the result is the same. We planned for this and discussed it, always hoping we wouldn't need to worry about it for many years, but a promise is a promise, no matter when it's needed.'

Danny and Luke ran an adventure holiday company, catering to all the adrenalin junkies who travelled to Tasmania to explore the wilderness. Had run, she should say. The business was now Luke's. He'd bought Danny's share from her, but he was right. Every time Danny had gone off on a trek she had lived in fear of a phone call telling her something had gone wrong, but she'd never anticipated the phone call would come when he was just out for a weekend ride on the outskirts of Hobart. Danny had spent most of his days in the wilderness, living on the edge—she hadn't expected his days to come to an end in the city.

Getting knocked off his bike had been a stupid way for someone who'd spent his life trekking and white-water rafting and abseiling down cliff faces to die. He had simply gone off for a ride one morning. He'd kissed her goodbye as she'd left for work, and she hadn't seen him alive again. The driver of the car that had killed him had been overtaking a truck on a blind corner. He'd smacked head on into

Danny and the impact had been so severe that he hadn't survived the head and chest injuries he had sustained.

And just last week Sophie had learned that the driver of the car had been released from jail. He had served six months for taking Danny's life. It made her feel sick, just thinking about the unfairness of it all.

She was glad she was leaving. She couldn't imagine how she would feel if she ever came face to face with the man responsible for her husband's death. If she met him in the street she didn't think she could be held responsible for her actions. She didn't care that he'd expressed remorse. His stupidity had cost Danny his life. She knew she should try to forgive him but she hadn't been able to yet. She didn't know if she'd ever be able to.

She knew her anger at the driver was magnified by her own guilt. If she hadn't taken an extra shift that day, Danny wouldn't have been out riding. He would have been home with her.

She should have been with him. If she had been he wouldn't be dead. But guilt wasn't going to bring him back. She needed to move past that but it was difficult when everywhere she looked she saw Danny. They'd been tied together their whole lives and it was hard to move on when so many things reminded her of shared times. She knew she had to get away. That was the only way she was ever going to recover. It was the only way she was going to get over her guilt.

'I don't feel right about saying goodbye without at least checking your frame of mind,' Luke continued.

'That's why I'm doing this,' Sophie explained. 'I'm tired of people asking me how I am or, worse, saying nothing because they don't know what to say. When Danny was killed my dreams died with him. It's time for me to make some new dreams.'

For as long as she could remember she had always made three-year plans but the plans she'd made with Danny had come crashing down seven months ago and now she was a thirty-one-year-old widow. She needed a new plan.

'I feel as though I should be trying harder to stop you,' Luke said, 'but I get the impression you're not going to listen to me.'

Sophie smiled. 'You're right, but that doesn't mean I don't appreciate your concern.'

'If you can look me in the eye and promise me you know what you're doing, I'll feel like I've kept my side of the bargain with Dan.'

'I'll be fine and I like to think Danny would be proud of me.'

Luke leaned over and kissed her cheek. 'You're right, he would be proud of you, I'm proud of you too. Just make sure you don't do anything that makes me sorry I didn't try harder to talk you out of this.'

'Dr Thompson?' Their conversation was interrupted by one of the nursing staff. 'We're ready for you now.'

Sophie stood and hugged Luke. 'It'll be fine. *I'll* be fine. I promise,' she said, before she followed the nurse off to Theatre.

CHAPTER TWO

Date: March 7th
Temperature: -7°C
Hours of sunlight: 13.9

THE SEAT BELT WAS pressing into Sophie's still-tender abdomen and it was starting to irritate her now. Having had her appendix removed just a few days before her adventure wasn't ideal but she'd had no other option.

She was determined to be on this plane and she hadn't been about to let something as relatively minor as prophylactic surgery stop her. Any Australian doctor who wanted to work at one of the Antarctic stations had to have their appendix removed before they could be sent south. This clause didn't apply to anyone else—the doctor would be able to remove anyone else's troublesome appendix on the ice but the Australian Antarctic Programme didn't want to risk the station doctor. The surgery was non-negotiable but in Sophie's mind it was a relatively minor procedure and certainly something she had been happy to agree to. But she hadn't expected the tenderness to last for so many days.

She undid her belt and stood up. She could stretch her legs and her abdominals at the same time. She wandered to the cockpit, seeking company. She was the sole passenger from Hobart to the Antarctic airfield. The plane would return filled with summer expeditioners heading home for the winter but on this leg she had the entire cabin to herself.

She'd spent most of the four-and-a-half-hour flight reading the numerous documents she'd been given, trying to work out which ones were the most important. Her trip had been fast-tracked and she knew she hadn't had the same time to prepare as most others would have had. But she was tired of reading and it couldn't be too much longer before they landed. It had been dark when they'd left Hobart but the sunrise had followed them as they'd flown west, eventually catching up with them, and Sophie had watched as the sky had turned pink and lightened as they'd flown over the ocean.

She knocked on the cockpit door, eager to check with the flight crew what their ETA was. She felt like a kid on a long car trip. *'How much longer?'* She wanted to get the three-thousand-four-hundred-kilometre flight over and done with. She wanted to get to the ice.

'Perfect timing,' the pilot, said as he called her in. 'Have a seat. We've just started spotting the first icebergs.'

Sophie took a seat behind the captain and co-pilot and peered through the cockpit windows. The sea was calm and flat, a pond of dark blue dotted with white. The icebergs were stunning, crisp, pure and brilliant and all different shapes and sizes. But the ice was not pure white, like she'd expected, but lit with myriad shades of blue—turquoise, aqua, a hint of cerulean and the palest sky blue.

It was a serene, perfect vista and Sophie was mesmerised. She could hardly believe she'd done it. What at times had seemed almost impossible was now only incredible. She was almost in Antarctica.

'We should be landing in about thirty minutes.' The captain interrupted her daydreaming. 'The weather conditions look good, it should be a straightforward approach, but you should change into your survival clothing now. It will probably take you a while.'

Sophie had collected her red kitbag just prior to boarding the plane in Hobart. It contained the multiple layers she needed to wear to keep warm in the polar conditions. She'd had a brief lesson in getting dressed the previous day and she just hoped she remembered the order.

She returned to the cabin, pulled the bag out of the overhead locker and dumped the contents on her seat. She could feel the plane start its descent as she stripped off her shoes, sweatpants and jumper and pulled on thermal underwear before replacing the other layers. She stepped into her red waterproof pants, which were insulated with a down filling, making them rather cumbersome. She stuffed her shoes into the kitbag and then sat down to wrestle with the bulky insulated snow boots complete with thick rubber soles. She had some difficulty getting her feet into the boots—the puffy pants made bending awkward—but eventually she was able to lace up the white boots, which had the rather odd nickname of 'bunny boots'. She slipped her arms into the padded jacket and tugged a neck warmer over her head but decided the beanie and gloves could wait. She gathered her hair in one hand and tucked it inside her jacket, where it hung down between her shoulder blades.

By the time she'd finished and returned to her seat she could see through the window that the vast expanse of ocean was giving way to an equally vast expanse of ice and snow in the distance. She searched the horizon for signs of life, for buildings or communication towers, something, anything, to indicate that the icy plateau was inhabited. She could see miles and miles of ice, snow and ocean and eventually a few small buildings, which looked no bigger than shipping containers cobbled together, came into view. That would be the airstrip.

She knew not to expect to see a traditional tarred runway but she was nervous. She could see nothing that remotely resembled a landing strip. She knew from the mandatory flight briefing she'd had the previous day that the plane would land on a specially built pack-ice runway three kilometres long, but that didn't appease her nerves at all. She couldn't fathom how something as big and heavy as this plane could land safely on a runway made of ice. The flight briefing had covered information on the flight and the runway, as well as several topics on safety and survival in the Antarctic, but that didn't stop her from imagining the plane skidding out of control off the edge of the slippery landing strip.

She decided ignorance was bliss and turned away from the window, choosing not to watch as the plane approached the runway. She zipped up her jacket and dug her sunglasses out of her bag.

Standing at the top of the stairs, with the landing safely completed, the chill of the Antarctic autumn day took her by surprise. It was only minus seven degrees Celsius and the sun was shining, but the briskness of the wind on her face after the relative warmth of the plane was unexpected. She tugged her neck warmer up to cover the bottom half of her face and considered donning her beanie but opted just to pull the hood of her jacket over her head before she slipped her sunglasses over her eyes and made her way down the aircraft stairs.

In contrast to the relative silence on the plane, the airstrip was a hive of activity. She couldn't remember who she was supposed to look for and even if she could she doubted she'd find them. Everyone looked identical. They were all bundled up in matching government-issue red jackets, balaclavas or face masks and sunglasses as they went about their duties, making it impossible to recognise anyone.

The fluttering in her stomach, which she'd convinced herself was excitement, suddenly intensified as anticipation gave way to nervousness. Was she going to be able to handle this? All of a sudden living and working in this extraordinary environment with a group of strangers didn't seem quite so exotic and exhilarating.

But she remembered her promise to Luke and straightened her shoulders. She could do this. She *would* do it. And she'd return home stronger and surer and ready to get on with her life.

'Doc?' A thick-set man had separated himself from the bustle and was waiting for her at the bottom of the stairs. He stuck out a hand and Sophie shook it, rather awkwardly due to the thick gloves they both wore, as she took in what little she could see of him.

He was a few inches taller than her and wasn't wearing any head protection—no hat, no balaclava—just sunglasses. He was a big man but appeared to be muscular rather than fat and had hair that hung to his shoulders in thick blond ringlets. His nose was slightly hooked and his jaw was covered in a scruffy blond beard. His eyes were hidden but a cheeky smile lit up his face.

'I'm Alex, the FTO.'

From her previous dealings and background reading Sophie already thought of Antarctica as the land of acronyms but she was struggling to keep track of them all and couldn't remember what this one meant. She looked blankly at him until he qualified it for her.

'The field training officer.'

'Oh, right. It's nice to meet you.'

'I'll be driving you back to Carey Station but you've

got some time to kill first. I have to get the cargo squared away to take back with us.'

Sophie was surprised by Alex's strong Australian accent—a Queensland twang, she thought—and she realised she had expected to hear foreign accents, the kind of thing that happened when you travelled to the ski fields and the lift operators and ski instructors had European accents, even though the ski fields were in Australia. She'd been fooled by the surroundings into thinking she was in a foreign land—and she was—but this part of it was being run by Australians. It was obviously going to take her some time to adjust and she had another nervous moment as she realised that it was very likely that *nothing* would be as she'd expected.

'What do I need to do with my bags?' she asked, as she saw them being unloaded from the cargo hold. She'd been allowed three bags with a combined weight of fifty-five kilograms and, having no real concept of what she might actually need but knowing it would be impossible to get anything she'd forgotten, she'd used every ounce of her allowance. In addition to her own luggage she'd also been given the survival kit, which she had hauled down the airplane steps along with her carry-on luggage. Even though she was now wearing most of the contents of the bag, it was still bulky and she hadn't thought about the logistics of getting all her bags from the plane across the ice and snow to the buildings and to her transport. She had no idea what the procedure was.

'Is that them?' Alex pointed at her cases. Sophie nodded. 'Just the three?' She nodded again. 'I'll take care of it,' he offered. 'Give me your survival bag as well. I'll stow them in the Hägglund and I'll meet you inside the terminal when I'm done.'

Sophie didn't argue as Alex took her survival kit and

grabbed the first of her cases. She was relieved not to have to cart her heavy bags while negotiating the icy conditions.

She could see the over-snow vehicle parked a few metres from the plane. The Hägglund was an odd-looking machine and it reminded her of a childish drawing of a car crossed with a mini-tank. It looked like a box with windows set atop caterpillar treads, which Sophie knew would enable it to traverse the ice. Both the cabin and its attached trailer were square and boxy and painted bright red. Alex hoisted her bags into the attached trailer while Sophie headed for the building that he had indicated. It was difficult to walk in the cumbersome clothing, especially the heavily insulated bunny boots, and her progress felt slow and awkward.

When she finally reached the 'terminal' it turned out to be a rather makeshift building constructed out of several shipping containers, just as it had looked from the air, with a few minor modifications along the lines of some windows and a couple of doors. It also reminded her of a child's drawing and it lent a surreal air to her surroundings.

Inside, the building was full of people who, she assumed, were summer expeditioners. They were milling around, waiting to get on the plane that would fly them home for winter, but despite the crowd it wasn't any warmer inside the building. The only difference in here was that more people had their heads and faces uncovered.

'Dr Thompson?'

She turned at the sound of her name and, recognising the Scottish burr of the man's voice, she smiled as she greeted him. 'You must be John.' His accent was much more similar to what she'd expected to encounter. John was the doctor she had come to replace and while she had dealt with him before through the AMU, the Antarctic

Medicine Unit, it had only been over the phone, never in person, and it was good to be able to put a face to his name.

He was able to give her a brief handover but Sophie was relieved to hear he'd left detailed instructions for her at the station. Knowing he had more pressing things on his mind—his daughter's scheduled surgery—she insisted she would be fine. 'Just make sure you call with an update on Marianna's condition,' she said, before saying farewell to him as he made his way to the refuelled aircraft.

Alex appeared at her side as the terminal emptied of people. 'We're good to go,' he told her.

He kept up a steady stream of conversation from the moment she climbed into the Hägglund and she was grateful that he didn't appear to expect too much in the way of replies from her.

He was entertaining company, keeping her amused with stories from the ice and telling her what to expect. She was quite interested in how a rugby player from the warm climate of Queensland had adjusted to the indoor life at an Antarctic station.

'We spend more time outside than you'd think,' he responded. 'The weather is cold but it's often clear and fine. You'll be able to get out and go exploring. Do you know how to ride a quad bike?'

'No.' Sophie shook her head.

'No worries. I'll teach you. That's part of my role as the FTO. It's my job to train the other expeditioners, including you, in station safety procedures, survival skills, how to operate snowmobiles, quad bikes and the like. I'm also one of your medical support team.'

Sophie knew that some of the expeditioners had done some basic medical training and were able to assist her in an emergency situation, helping with suturing, anaesthetic monitoring and acting as scrub nurses among other things, but as Alex talked she found herself becoming increasingly nervous as it really sank in that she would be the only doctor for hundreds of miles and solely responsible for all the crew at the station.

She was feeling quite overwhelmed. She'd thought she'd be excited but everything was far more foreign than she'd anticipated, including the landscape. The pictures and videos she'd seen hadn't prepared her for the rather alien scenery that filled the windows. Vast expanses of ice stretched into the distance. She could see mountains of ice but the only thing that broke the expanse of white was the occasional rocky outcrop.

The landscape looked relatively flat but she could feel corrugations under the caterpillar treads of the Hägglund, making it seem as though they were going up and down over crests of waves. Alex told her that was exactly what happened. The wind formed the snow into drifts that then froze, making waves in the surface. In some places, where the ice rose up in thicker drifts that absorbed red light from the spectrum, the ice appeared more blue than white, but mostly it was a blinding glare that made her feel she needed to close her eyes even with her sunglasses on.

'Doc? We're almost here.'

Alex woke her as they approached the station. She hadn't meant to fall asleep but the interior of the over-snow vehicle was warm and cosy, and despite the excitement of her new surroundings she was exhausted. She hadn't slept the night before—she'd had to be at the airport by three-thirty in the morning and she hadn't seen much point in going to bed first so she'd stayed up, double-checking her packing. She'd taken out clothes and put in a few non-essential luxury items that other women who had worked on the ice suggested she take—a nice dress, decent shampoo, a thick bath towel, sheepskin boots—and as much as she hadn't wanted to miss anything on the seventy-kilometre trip from the airstrip to the station she'd been lulled to sleep by the monotonous sound of the diesel engine and the warmth of the cabin.

'I thought you might like a first glimpse of your temporary home,' Alex said, as they came over a crest in the snow.

The station was spread out before her. It was perched on the edge of a natural harbour and while Sophie had seen photos the scale still took her by surprise. Close to a dozen brightly painted buildings were scattered over the snow, as if someone had spilt a handful of children's building blocks. The buildings were a collection of shipping containers welded together to form larger structures, exactly the same as the buildings at the airstrip but on a bigger scale.

Sophie knew the bright paint scheme—red, yellow, blue and orange—was to make the buildings distinguishable from each other in blizzard conditions. The colour each 'shed' was painted depended on its function, but the brightness of the paint made the buildings look out of place, a blight on the landscape and a stark contrast to the ancient, icy plateau surrounding her.

A large dock poked out into the harbour and parked on the dock and scattered between the buildings were dozens of vehicles—trucks, graders, snowmobiles and trailers. Antennae and tanks, for water and gas storage, she suspected, sprouted out of the ground between the sheds, competing for space on the ice.

Her nervousness kicked up another notch. This was the station, her home for the next few weeks, and the little outpost of civilisation looked even more alien than the landscape.

'Welcome to Carey,' Alex said, as he brought the Hägglund to a stop in front of the largest of the buildings. This building was painted bright red and it was one thing Sophie did recognise. It was called, not surprisingly, 'the red shed', and it housed the accommodation block, the kitchen and the medical centre, and it was where she expected to spend most of her time.

Sophie pulled her gloves back on, squared her shoulders and climbed out of the cabin as she told herself everything would all be all right.

The wind whipped past her cheeks, making them ache with the cold after the warmth of the vehicle. She reached for the neck warmer and pulled it up over the lower half of her face.

'Doc, welcome.'

A tall, solidly built man greeted her as he strode across the ground without a hint of the clumsiness she herself had felt as she'd negotiated the icy conditions. This man looked completely comfortable in the alien environment. He was dressed in a bright red cold-weather suit, identical to hers, but like Alex he had his head and face uncovered and exposed to the elements. The only concession he made to the conditions was in the form of sunglasses to protect against the blinding glare of the sun. Didn't anyone else think it was cold?

He stopped in front of her and Sophie looked up, way up.

He was several inches taller than her and she stood five feet seven inches. His dark hair was cropped short and sprinkled with a little salt and pepper, and a dark, neatly trimmed beard covered the bottom half of his oval-shaped face.

'I'm Gabe Sullivan, the station leader.'

So this was the man whose job it was to run Carey Station. This was her new boss.

He took his sunglasses off and extended his hand. His eyes were a dark chocolate-brown, kind and warming, and when he smiled at her, showcasing perfect white teeth framed by the darkness of his beard, Sophie forgot about being cold. Whereas Alex looked like a weekend surfer, Gabe Sullivan looked like a pioneer. Dark, rugged and strong. He looked like an explorer who was perfectly suited to this environment. He looked confident, like a man who could easily withstand the harsh elements of this climate, and as Sophie shook his outstretched, gloved hand she felt her nervousness recede as his gaze instilled confidence in her too.

Holding Gabe's hand and looking into his dark-eyed gaze, she had an immediate sense that things would be okay. It was a bizarre feeling to get from a complete stranger, it was a ridiculous notion, but she saw something in his eyes, felt something in the strength of his grasp, that made her feel as though she had made the right decision. That this adventure would not be a huge mistake.

She could sense the strength in him and she could draw her own strength from that. In the same way that Danny had made her a stronger person she felt the same sense of security and confidence when she looked at Gabe. Standing here, looking up at him, she knew she'd be all right. She could do this. She was ready for the next stage of her life.

Alex had opened the back of the Hägglund and was removing her luggage from the trailer. Sophie forced herself to remove her hand from Gabe's glove and break eye contact as she went to help with her bags. But Gabe was there before her.

'We'll get those for you,' he offered.

'I can manage,' she said, even though she wasn't certain

that she could. Her bags were heavy and her stomach muscles complained every time she moved too quickly, let alone tried to lift something heavy.

'Alex and I will do it,' Gabe insisted. 'You'll have plenty of opportunity to help out once you get used to moving in your cold-weather gear.'

Sophie wondered if he was normally this chivalrous or whether he knew she'd recently undergone surgery but, either way, she didn't bother arguing any further. It was nice to have someone look after her for a change so rather than debating the issue she graciously accepted his offer.

She did feel awkward in the padded overclothes and she suspected it would take some time for the bulky layers to feel comfortable. But even though her movement and her vision were restricted, she was grateful for the modern comforts. She couldn't imagine surviving out here without this clothing. She was no intrepid explorer. She wasn't really any sort of explorer. While Danny would have survived and thrived in these conditions, much like she suspected Gabe did, she knew she would be quite happy to experience the wilderness provided she had some twenty-first-century comforts.

Gabe and Alex retrieved her bags from the vehicle and Sophie followed them up the metal stairs to the red shed. She needed to steady herself with one hand on the rail of the steps, which were slick with a coating of ice, and she was glad she wasn't trying to wrestle with her bags at the same time.

The two-storey building towered above her as Gabe stomped his feet on the steel grid at the top of the stairs to dislodge any snow and Sophie followed suit. Alex deposited Sophie's bags beside her and excused himself, explaining he needed to return the Hägglund to the vehicle shed.

Gabe pushed open the door. It looked heavy and exactly

like a door one would find on a freezer room. As she stepped through it she could see that was precisely what it was. As Gabe closed the door softly behind her, she noticed an immediate increase in temperature for, despite the sunshine, the outside temperature remained well below freezing. She understood the point of the freezer door now—it wasn't to keep the cold in but to keep the cold out.

She found herself in what looked like a large mud room, similar to the drying rooms she'd seen in ski lodges. Around the edge of the room were open-fronted lockers with hanging space and shelving. Gabe directed her to one with 'Doc' written above it. 'You can keep your outer layer of clothes here—boots, jackets, pants, gloves.' His voice was deep and sounded like it held a smile, Sophie felt as if she could listen to him for hours. 'The shed is heated to around twenty degrees Celsius,' he continued, 'so you don't need much more than a layer of normal clothing once you're inside. If your clothes are damp or wet, make sure you hang them with some space between them so they dry effectively. Take your linings out of your boots if they are wet. If your socks are dry leave them on, otherwise change them.'

Sophie nodded and looked around, taking in the surroundings, as Gabe brought her bags into the room and then began to strip off his outer layers of clothing. Sophie hesitated before following. She wasn't sure exactly how many layers she was supposed to discard. He had mentioned normal clothing but stripping down to one layer would leave her standing there in her thermal underwear. She didn't think that was what he'd meant.

She looked to Gabe for guidance. His waterproof jacket was hanging on a peg above his boots. His waterproof pants came off next, followed by a fleecy pullover and his long-sleeved shirt. Sophie wondered how many more layers he was going to remove until she realised he had finished and was now standing, waiting for her, dressed in a simple black T-shirt and a pair of jeans.

She could see now that her first impression of him being solidly built had been correct. It was impossible to judge people's sizes accurately when they were encased in their cold-weather gear but now that he was standing in front of her in civvies she didn't have to imagine what he looked like. His shoulders were broad, his chest was muscular and his stomach was flat. His jeans hugged his thighs, showing off his long, lean legs. He was an impressive-looking man.

Realising it was probably inappropriate to be taking stock of him like this she averted her eyes and continued removing layers until she was clothed in her sweatpants and T-shirt. She was still wearing her thermals but she wasn't about to remove another layer and stand before Gabe in her underwear. She wasn't that confident and, if the truth be told, undressing at all in front of him was making her feel a little nervous. She'd taken off enough clothing for now, she just hoped it wasn't going to be much hotter inside the shed proper. She might regret her modesty.

Once she'd finished discarding clothing, Gabe opened the next door that led further into the red shed. 'Can you hold this for me?' he asked.

His voice was deep and smooth and matched his physique. He exuded a sense of calm while looking like a man who was used to being in charge, used to being listened to, used to having people follow his instructions. She supposed that was appropriate, given that he was in charge of the station, but Sophie got the sense that he wasn't a man you wanted to disappoint.

She held the door as Gabe picked up one of her bags and slung it over his shoulder, before grabbing the two remaining bags and leading the way out of the drying room.

'Let me take one of those,' Sophie protested. All she had to carry was her virtually empty kitbag.

'I've got it,' he replied. 'I know you've only just had your appendix out. I don't want to jeopardise your recovery by letting you lift and carry things you don't need to. You're far too important on this station to put you at risk.'

Sophie didn't argue any further. Gabe was twice her size. He had removed his shoes but he was still an inch or two over six feet tall and much heavier than she was. If he was going to insist on lugging her gear, she was happy to let him. She was willing to admit relief at not having to cart her suitcases.

She didn't ask how Gabe knew about her recent surgery. As Station Leader, he would have his finger on every pulse. She knew that the Human Resources department in Hobart would have prepared a file on her and that Gabe would have read it. The file would detail everything he might need to know, from her qualifications to the results of her psych tests to her next of kin. He would know how many years' experience she had as a doctor and that she was widowed. He would have read all the reports but he didn't mention any other personal details.

She was grateful for his help and his discretion. She followed him out of the drying room into a passageway. He didn't seem bothered by the fact that he was carting over fifty kilograms of her baggage. He didn't appear to be under any strain at all. His long-legged stride ate up the corridor and Sophie had to hurry to keep up with him.

'You've missed lunch but the cook will rustle something up for you as I'm sure you're hungry, and then I'll give you a tour of the station,' Gabe said over his shoulder. 'Unless you need to rest, in which case I'll show you straight to your room.'

The aroma of freshly baked bread wafted along the

corridor, teasing her taste buds. 'Something to eat sounds good,' she said, surprising herself. She had lost her appetite since Danny's death and she couldn't remember the last time she'd actually felt like eating. But suddenly she was starving.

Gabe turned and pushed open a door. He backed into a room and when Sophie followed she found herself in the mess hall. The kitchen equipment ran along the back wall to her left. Massive serving stations filled the centre of the room and several long communal tables were arranged between the serving area and the far wall. Sophie's eyes were drawn to a series of enormous windows on the far wall and she forgot all about the smell of freshly baked bread. She forgot she was in the kitchen. She forgot Gabe had brought her here to eat. She forgot she was hungry.

The view through the windows drew her across the room. The windows looked out over the icy plateau and across the blue waters of Vincennes Bay, and she couldn't resist a closer look at the harbour. She'd only caught a quick glimpse of the station's landscape as Alex had delivered her to the red shed and she was drawn to the contrasting colours of the buildings, the ice and the water. The views were glorious.

Half a dozen armchairs with plump cushions were positioned in front of the windows and she could just imagine curling up in one and staring out across the ice. It would be a constantly changing landscape, depending on the weather conditions, and more than likely would be enough to keep her occupied for hours.

'It's incredible, isn't it?' Gabe stood beside her.

She nodded and spoke in a whisper that seemed to fit the majesty of the view. 'I can't believe I'm going to live here for the next few weeks. At the end of the earth.'

Gabe was smiling at her. 'Just wait until you see Mother

Nature in all her glory. It's beautiful today when the sun is shining but if there's a blizzard it will seem as though someone has pulled a snow curtain over the windows. Every day is different and at times the weather can, and does, change in a matter of seconds. It's a beautiful but inhospitable landscape and, while you're welcome to explore it, it's imperative we make sure you're equipped to deal with it. I'll organise for Alex to give you some survival training as we can't let you out there until we're sure you're ready, but right now I think the first order of business is getting you fed.'

Gabe introduced her to Dom, the station chef, who served her a bowl of minestrone with freshly baked rolls still warm from the oven. Sophie's stomach rumbled as she quickly gathered her brown, shoulder-length curls into one hand, pulling them into a ponytail before securing it with an elastic band that was around her wrist. She flicked her hair back over her shoulder, picked up her spoon and dipped it into the soup. She bent her head and tasted it.

'Mmm, this is fabulous, thanks, Dom. I think I'll make you my first friend.'

She lifted her head and beamed at Dom and Gabe was stunned at the way her smile lit up her face and changed her from an attractive woman into a beautiful one. How did he get her to smile like that at him? He'd been mesmerised, watching her tie her dark curls back into a ponytail—he had always loved how women could so deftly change their hairstyles—but watching her play with her hair couldn't compare to watching her face light up with a full smile. She had two dimples, one in each cheek, and the sudden flash of the matching pair completely blindsided him. She was a gorgeous woman even if, in his opinion, she was too thin. Seeing her tuck into Dom's soup was a relief.

He knew that Sophie's husband had been tragically

killed only a few months ago and he'd had reservations about the Australian Antarctic Programme sending her down here so soon after the accident, but he'd been told that she'd passed all the tests and that they didn't have any other options. She was the best choice, they'd said, and he just had to hope it worked out. The only trouble was that if things didn't go according to plan, she became his problem, not the AAP's. He was the one in charge down here. He was the one left to sort out any mess. But seeing her eat relieved some of his apprehension. That was one less thing to worry about. Maybe she was naturally thin or maybe she'd lost weight after her husband had died, but at least she was eating.

To distract himself from thoughts of her dimples, he transferred her bags to her room while she ate, before returning to help settle her into the station. Their first stop on the way to her room was the storeroom.

'This is our version of a supermarket, and you can help yourself to anything in here that you need,' he told her as he waited for her to select linen, toiletries and other essentials from the shelves. 'This floor of the shed is primarily living and rec space. We have a gym, a climbing wall, an activity centre, a library, lounge and a cinema, so there's plenty to keep you occupied for any downtime. Everything of importance as far as your role is concerned is housed in the red shed. The other sheds are for stores, machinery, that sort of thing, although there is an area set up in one shed for those who like painting or woodwork or photography, etcetera. I'll show you that another time. The medical centre and your room are down this way.

'This is your donga,' he said as he pushed open yet another door, this one leading into a bedroom. 'And the medical centre is across the corridor.'

Sophie followed Gabe into her room. It was far from

spacious. Her bags were taking up most of the free floor space, leaving just enough room for the two of them to stand side by side. The air in the room felt charged and she had a sense of anticipation but she tried to tell herself it was just the circumstances, the excitement of her new surroundings, and had nothing to do with the man standing next to her. But she was aware of how much space he took up, and as there was no room for her to move she stood beside him as she checked out her quarters.

As small as it was, it contained all the essentials. There was a single bed with built-in furniture—a tiny desk, a wardrobe and plenty of shelves and under-bed drawers for storage. It reminded her of boarding school.

'I know it's pretty basic but this is actually one of the dongas that has been recently refurbished. And we don't want to make it too comfortable because we want people to get out of their rooms and socialise—it's important in this isolated environment—but we realise people do need some privacy. You'll have internet access for emails, etcetera, but no video calls. The password and log-in details are here on your notice-board,' he said, as he pointed out a scrap of paper pinned to a board above the desk. 'All the dongas have single beds. That's not to say there aren't South Pole romances, we're not trying to deliberately make things difficult, but space is at a premium.'

'I don't think a single bed will bother me,' she said, knowing it was of little consequence to her.

'My room is next to yours. I also want to be close to the action but most of the accommodation is on the upper level. Now that most of the summer staff has left, I can arrange to move you upstairs if you'd prefer.'

'No.' Sophie shook her head. 'It makes sense for me to be close to the medical facilities.' She was the only doctor at the station so she needed to be close by, but she was also oddly comforted by the thought that Gabe would be close at hand too, especially while she familiarised herself with her strange new surroundings.

'Good decision. Staying on this floor means you'll have your own bathroom. Upstairs there are private dongas but shared facilities. You will need to keep your own bathroom clean, though. There's a roster for Saturday chores—vacuuming, cleaning common areas, shovelling snow, that sort of thing—plus everyone volunteers for a secondary position.'

'Secondary positions?'

'We all take on part-time roles in addition to normal duties. Things like librarian, firefighter, medical support team, working in the hydroponics shed or helping Dom in the kitchen. There are enough options so you should be able to choose something that interests you as long as you can do it without any extra training as we won't have time for that. But you don't need to worry about it today. I'll give you a rundown later. If you're okay, I'll leave you to get sorted. Dinner is at six and everyone will gather for a drink in the bar beforehand. Do you want me to come back for you or can you find it? It's right next to the dining hall.'

'I'll find it.'

'One last thing—it's the final bit of information for now, I promise,' he added, when Sophie suspected he'd noticed her bewildered expression. Gabe smiled at her and his dark eyes shone, and she wondered if she could think of a few questions for him, something to delay him leaving. She wasn't sure that she felt like keeping her own company but she was sure he had more important matters to attend to. 'Water is scarce over winter so we have restrictions in place.'

'Water restrictions in a place smothered in ice?' Sophie queried, thinking he had to be kidding.

'That's the problem over winter. We have plenty of ice but no water. It doesn't rain here so until the temperatures rise and the summer melt happens we have to watch our water supply. The restrictions are mainly for showers—two minutes, every second day.'

'Okay.' She hadn't been expecting that but she supposed there would be plenty more unexpected and unusual things over the next few days until she got used to her new surroundings. She closed the door behind him, letting him go. She unpacked one of her bags before deciding to explore the medical centre instead. It was her domain and she was eager to see what was in store for her.

The medical suite consisted of a consulting room, a dental and exam room, a small operating theatre, a lab, a two-bed ward, a storeroom and a bathroom. Sophie was pleasantly surprised to find the clinic so well equipped. She did a quick inventory of equipment and drugs before returning to her room. She had promised to send Luke an email to let him know she arrived safely and she figured he would have expected to hear from her by now.

She booted up her laptop and paused when the screensaver photo appeared on the display. It was a photo of Danny, taken at their wedding. The photographer had snapped it just after they'd exchanged their vows and Danny had just kissed his bride. The picture captured Danny only. He had been smiling at her, the goofy smile she had adored, and his eyes had been full of love, his dimples marking his cheeks. Sophie had loved his dimples and they had laughed about their matching genetic defects. Dimples were an inherited trait and they'd talked about passing them on to their kids. But now that wasn't to be.

She reached out and ran her fingers over the screen, tracing the angles of Danny's face, the line of his lips, the dip of his dimples. The photo stirred mixed emotions in her—love and sadness—but she couldn't bring herself to change the screensaver. She needed to see him still.

She moved her hand over the keyboard and logged onto the station's WiFi, opening up her email account before she got too maudlin. She sent Luke a quick message and promised to give more details next time when she'd had a chance to get her head around everything and had something more substantial to report or had hopefully had time to explore. It was all so different. She copied the email to the AAP division headquarters in Hobart and to her parents in Queensland to keep them in the loop. At the moment everything was very strange and new and she had no idea how to verbalise her first impressions. In a day or two things might seem less surreal.

She checked the clock and decided she had just enough time to put fresh linen on her bed and change her clothes before making her way to the bar for pre-dinner drinks. She was feeling a little homesick but knew she just needed to keep busy. She closed the laptop. She didn't need to see Danny's face right now, she needed to keep a clear head.

She eventually found her way to the bar by following the noise. It was almost full. Most of the expeditioners who hadn't left today must already be in the room. She swallowed nervously and wiped her clammy hands on her jeans. She never really liked walking into a room full of strangers.

She searched the room for a familiar face and spotted Gabe behind the bar. She headed in his direction. He saw her coming and grinned at her. Sophie returned his smile gratefully, feeling her nervousness about her new surroundings settle as she tried to fight the other butterflies that stirred in her stomach in response to Gabe's smile. She had never had such a sudden and strong reaction to any man. Danny had been familiar and comfortable. She'd never before met a stranger who could make her go weak at the knees with just a smile and a glance.

'What will you have?' he asked.

'What's on offer?'

'Most of the crew drink beer but most of that's brewed here at the station over summer so it may not be to your liking. Other than that, there's whatever we've shipped in. There's an allowance of two drinks per day, for all sorts of reasons, but you're welcome to one of Dr John's red wines or one of my Tassie beers.'

'Thanks, but I think I'll stick with something soft.' She wasn't a big drinker and while she wouldn't have minded a glass of something to relax her she thought it was more important to stay sober and focussed until she felt more at ease. She was already aware that people were looking at her with interest. She hadn't expected to be the object of dozens of pairs of eyes all at once as she came under the scrutiny of the entire crowd. She knew the number of people on base shrank over winter but there were still far more people here than she had anticipated. 'I thought most people went home for winter?'

Gabe nodded. 'They do, but there are still thirty people here for now. Another twelve will be heading home when the supply ship makes its last journey before the winter season. They've got some final packing up to do in preparation for winter and then they'll head off,' he explained.

Sophie knew the supply ship, the *Explorer Australis,* was due to dock at Carey in six or seven weeks' time after visiting the other two Australian Antarctic stations. The original plan had been for Dr John to be on board, in which case she would depart then. Until then, apparently, she would be responsible for the thirty expeditioners who remained on the base.

Gabe poured her a drink and then called the room to

attention. 'Everyone, I'd like you all to welcome, Sophie Thompson, our new doc.'

His introduction was followed by a chorus of 'G'day, Doc,' and Sophie suspected that from now on she was going to be known simply as 'Doc'. She didn't mind the idea—she was sure that being known as 'Doc' was preferable to being known as Danny's widow.

'You'll gradually meet everyone but for now let me introduce you to Finn,' Gabe said, as a tall, thin man approached the bar. 'Finn is our watercraft operator and along with me and Alex he's the third member of your medical support crew.'

Finn shook her hand. 'We're the important ones, Gabe, Alex and me,' he said, his greeting accompanied by a wide smile. 'We're the ones you need to know.'

He took her under his wing and proceeded to introduce her to more of the crew throughout dinner. Sophie knew it would take a few days before she would be able to put all the names and faces and their job roles together, but luckily no one seemed to expect too much of her in the way of conversation. She ate quietly, happy to watch the interaction between the expeditioners and get a feeling for the different personalities and listen to their stories. She was surprised to find that the majority of them had family at home. She hadn't realised so many would be in that situation and she wondered why they would choose to stay for months at a time if that was the case. But it seemed that many had been bitten by the Antarctic bug.

By the time dinner, a three-course affair that was apparently the norm, was finished and their dishes had been returned to the kitchen for the slushies to clean up, Sophie was exhausted. There had been a lot to absorb in the short time since she'd arrived and her eyelids were drooping as everyone made their way back to the bar. She listened to the plans being made around her—some of the guys decided to have a jam session, others were going to watch a movie—but Sophie just wanted to put her head down.

As soon as she thought it was polite to do so, she excused herself and went in search of her bed. Not that she expected to sleep well but it would be wise, she thought, to at least lie down. She hadn't had a good night's sleep since Danny had died and she suspected that her insomnia would be compounded by her new surroundings and a different bed.

Back in her donga she was glad she'd had the foresight to make her bed. She changed into pyjamas and unpacked a soft cashmere blanket that she had carried in her hand luggage. The blanket had once been on the bed she'd shared with Danny and she liked to think it still smelt like him. She knew that was fanciful thinking but it was something that gave her some comfort. But the blanket was as much a practical item as a comforting one. It had seemed to Sophie that she felt the cold more now that she had no one to share her bed.

She wrapped the blanket around her shoulders and climbed under the covers. She laid her head on her pillow as she thought about Danny.

She knew this experience would have been right up his alley. He had been an adrenalin junkie—not a risk-taker, any risks he'd taken had been calculated ones—and she knew he would have jumped at a chance to explore Antarctica. The company he and Luke had founded ran adventure tours all around Tasmania, offering everything from white-water rafting on the Franklin River, mountain biking down Mt Wellington, cycling the east coast, hiking on Cradle Mountain, rock-climbing and abseiling to kayaking. His job had taken him away from home, away from her, a lot but they had been planning on reorganising things to allow them to spend more time together as they'd hoped to start a family, but now it was just her and she had to make new plans. Solo plans. And today she had taken the first step on her new path.

'Doc?'

A voice disturbed Sophie and she rolled over, still half-asleep.

'Are you awake?'

'Hmm?'

'Doc.' The voice was a little louder this time. A little more insistent. 'You need to get up. There's been an accident.'

An accident? Danny?

Sophie's eyes flew open. There was a man standing beside her bed but he wasn't fair and clean-shaven, like Danny. He was tall and dark and bearded. He looked familiar but it still took her a moment to work out who it was.

'Gabe?'

What was he doing in her room?

There could only be one reason. She sat up.

'What is it?'

CHAPTER THREE

Date: March 8th
Temperature: -10°C
Hours of sunlight: 13.8

'WHAT'S HAPPENED?' SOPHIE asked, as she swung her legs out of bed. Gabe was standing right beside her and she tried to ignore the little frisson of excitement as she focussed on what he was saying rather than how close he stood.

'The Russians have lost a helicopter. We're sending out S&R and I need you to come with us.'

She mustn't be properly awake. It sounded as though he'd said 'Russians'.

'Russians? What Russians?'

'There's a Russian station not far from here. One of their helicopters has gone missing.'

'And you want me to go out on a search and rescue?'

He was nodding. 'Time is critical. I need you with me out in the field. We don't know what the situation is so we need to cover all contingencies—which means sending you out. I'll meet you in the medical centre. Get dressed, you'll need all your ECW gear and don't forget your goggles and gloves.'

She was wide awake now but she didn't bother asking

how you lost a helicopter. Whatever had happened couldn't be good and the only thing that mattered to her was what would be left for her to deal with. But she hadn't expected to have to deal with a crisis somewhere out on the ice, not on her first proper day on the job.

She got dressed in a hurry. The Antarctic motto of 'Hurry up and wait' didn't seem to apply to this station, she thought as she pulled on underwear, long thermals, socks, a shirt, pants and a fleece. She had her wedding ring, and Danny's, strung on a chain around her neck and she lifted the rings to her lips and kissed them, before tucking them inside her shirt.

'Wish me luck,' she whispered, as she stuffed a balaclava, goggles, sunglasses and gloves into the pocket of her fleecy jacket, before heading to the medical centre to prepare to venture into the great unknown.

Gabe, Finn and a third man were already in the clinic. She'd met the other man last night but she couldn't remember his name. So much of yesterday was a blur and she knew she would need time to get things straight in her head. Names, faces and routines would all need time to sink in but she feared she wasn't going to get that time today. Today she was going to be thrown straight in at the deep end.

Finn was standing beside a sack trolley that Sophie didn't remember having seen in the clinic before, and Gabe and the other man were gathering equipment. They weren't waiting for her. They had laid a stretcher on one of the treatment beds and had put a spinal board on top of it.

'Load anything you think you might need onto the stretcher or the trolley,' Gabe said to her as soon as she stepped into the room, 'and Liam, Finn and I will transport it for you.'

Liam, that was his name.

How did she know what to take? What would she need?

Sophie closed her eyes as she tried to focus. How did she know what she might need? How on earth was she supposed to figure that out? She'd been on the ice for less than twenty-four hours and she was terrified to think that perhaps she had taken on more than she could handle. Perhaps she wasn't ready for this.

'Are you okay?' Gabe asked.

She opened her eyes. 'Yes.' She might not think she was ready for this but she was all they had. She had to do her job. 'I admit I was hoping to start my stint down here with an easy emergency—frostbite, concussion, a broken finger, that sort of thing—but I'm okay, just trying to figure out what we'll need. You don't have any idea what we might be dealing with?'

Gabe shook his head. 'It could be anything from concussion to burns to fractures to internal injuries. Bring what you would need if you were waiting for an ambulance to bring in survivors from a train wreck. I imagine it will be similar.'

Oh, God. If she'd been waiting for multiple victims from a train wreck she would want to be in a modern emergency department with a team of nurses and surgeons on hand, a suite of theatres at her disposal, state-of-the-art X-ray facilities and a well-stocked blood bank and pharmacy. But instead she had herself. She was the doctor, the nurse, the radiologist, the anaesthetist and the pharmacist, and she was going to have to work in sub-zero temperatures bundled up like a mummy. It was a nightmare.

She knew she had a medical support team but she had no idea how well trained they were or whether or not they'd had any experience in this type of situation.

But Gabe hadn't finished. 'Best-case scenario you will

have patients to treat. Worst case—we won't find them in time.'

It wasn't just a nightmare, it was her *worst* nightmare.

But Gabe's comments jolted her back to reality. She needed to get her act together, she needed to concentrate. She couldn't afford any mistakes. Time was of the essence. They needed to get out of here. She looked around the clinic and started a mental inventory.

'How many people on board?' she asked.

'Only two.'

Good. She grabbed the emergency kit that she'd gone through yesterday and put it on Finn's trolley. It had sufficient supplies for two patients but she needed to add some more equipment. She grabbed extra blankets, an oxygen cylinder and bags of saline. She put a stethoscope around her neck and tucked it inside her thermals to keep it warm. It made a metallic chime against her wedding rings. She wrapped her fingers around the rings, squeezing them as she prayed for some luck.

What else would she need? In an ideal world she'd have some bags of blood to add to the pile but there was no blood stored. She knew that the crew would donate blood as needed but she was the only one who could take it. No one at Carey could donate blood if she wasn't there. She stood in the centre of the room while she tried to figure out what to do. She'd have to get some donors lined up for their return, just in case. She hoped someone at the station was O-negative.

'We're here to help. Tell us what you need,' Gabe said, and she knew he was trying to get her to hurry up but she was out of her depth. What she needed was reassurance.

'Have you done something like this before?' she asked.

'Not exactly,' he admitted. 'Major incidents are thankfully few and far between and we have stringent occupational health and safety policies, but we have trained for these situations and we are trained to work in these conditions.'

His confidence was reassuring. Sophie had no idea if he was as confident as he seemed but she chose to believe him. She looked up into his dark brown eyes, drawing strength from him again. She trusted him and she knew that as long as he was with her she'd feel better about the situation.

She took a deep breath. She was a doctor. She knew her trade and if she had to think on her feet she would. 'Okay, I think that's everything. We can go.' She picked up the bags of saline and the men carried everything else.

They got as far as the drying room before they had to put everything down again in order to get their final layers of clothing on. Her extreme cold-weather clothing was hanging where she'd left it yesterday.

Sophie emptied the pockets of her fleece as she'd need to wear the things she'd shoved in there. She stepped into her waterproof pants and grabbed her enormous white bunny boots. She pulled the balaclava over her head before shrugging into her red parka. She stuffed the bags of saline into her now-empty pockets, she had to be certain they didn't freeze. She could put them in the insulated emergency kit but she didn't know how it was going to be transported and she couldn't risk frozen saline. She didn't even want cold saline. She wanted it at body temperature.

She pulled her gloves on and picked up her goggles and sunglasses as Gabe picked up the emergency medical kit and opened the outer door. Flakes of snow blew into the drying room on a cold, whistling wind. Sophie pulled her balaclava over her mouth and nose and stretched her goggles over her head, before adjusting the hood of her parka. She followed Gabe outside but hesitated on the metal platform.

The world had completely disappeared. A blanket of white had been thrown over the plateau and Sophie couldn't see past the bottom of the steps. She hadn't been near a window to look outside since Gabe had woken her and she felt stunned, and a little scared, about how much had changed overnight. The wind was icy and strong—strong enough to whip the snow so that it blew past them horizontally.

As she trod carefully down the steps she could just make out the squat, red shape of a Hägglund parked beside the red shed. It was parked just a couple of metres from the base of the steps but Sophie knew she could only see it because of its colour. Visibility was almost nil but red did catch her eye. It seemed to be the colour of choice at the bottom of the world—red clothing, red buildings, red transport.

Sophie hadn't had time to think about the transportation logistics. The Hägglund sat on the snow on its caterpillar treads, looking like a mini-tank. Yesterday in the bright sunshine it had seemed exciting as it had shone brightly against the blue sky and white snow. Today in the gloomy surroundings, blanketed and buffeted by swirling snow, it seemed almost ominous.

She wondered how on earth they were going to find anything or anyone in these conditions. Some of Gabe's confidence that had rubbed off on her earlier vanished in an instant.

He turned to face her as she reached the bottom of the steps. His red jacket stood out in stark relief against the white background. Sophie looked around her, searching for landmarks, but she could see nothing other than Gabe and one Hägglund. He must have seen the look of panic on her face. 'What is it?'

'How on earth do you expect to find them in this?' she asked, waving one hand towards the snow. 'What if we get lost too?'

She thought Gabe was smiling but it was hard to tell when all she could see of his face were his dark eyes shielded by snow goggles.

'We can't get lost when we're not sure where we're going.'

'What?'

'The helicopter is lost. *We* are not. The last communication came when the chopper was about twenty kilometres west of here. We're the closest station but we don't have an exact location. We only have a last known location. Helicopters and planes can't fly in a whiteout so we have to go looking. But there's no need to panic, we have a pretty good idea of where to start.'

'And that's supposed to make me feel better?' she asked, as Gabe opened the rear door of the vehicle and indicated that she should climb on board. He put the emergency medical kit on the seat beside her and shut the door.

He climbed into the front, greeting Alex, who was in the driver's seat, before answering her question. 'We've got fifteen years of experience between us, not counting your years as a doctor. You do your job, we'll do ours. I promise I won't risk the lives of anyone on my team. That's not how this works. We've got GPS and radar tracking, we've got survival kits and all the right equipment, we have radio contact with our station and we've got the co-ordinates of the Russians' last transmission. We know where we're going and everyone back here will know where we are. We won't be lost.'

Sophie felt marginally better but her concerns about

their movements were now replaced with concern about the Russians' situation.

By Gabe's reckoning they were at least twenty kilometres away. She knew how long it had taken to cover the seventy kilometres from the airstrip to the station yesterday in clear and sunny conditions. She couldn't imagine how long it was going to take them to cover twenty kilometres, or more, in a blizzard. 'It's going to take us a while to find them, isn't it?'

Gabe nodded.

'How long have they been missing?'

'Only a little over an hour. They've missed one check-in and can't be raised on the radio.'

'And you think they might be able to survive out in these conditions for long enough for us to reach them?'

'We have to hope so. They have survival equipment on board. It all depends on what has happened—if they are injured and how badly, if the equipment has been damaged, if they can reach it and deploy it. There are a lot of variables—we have to plan for the worst and hope for the best.'

Now that she was out of the wind and snow, Sophie removed her goggles. Through the back window she could see that there was an enclosed trailer attached to the Hägglund. She could just make out the figures of Finn and Liam as they loaded her equipment into the trailer. They slammed the doors closed and disappeared. Moments later a second Hägglund, also with an attached trailer, crawled past her window on its caterpillar treads. She thought she could see Liam's profile as the tank-like vehicle moved past.

'Breakfast courtesy of Dom,' Alex said, as he passed a muffin and a travel mug of hot chocolate back to Sophie then pulled out behind the other vehicle.

'Are they coming with us?' Sophie asked, as she bit

into the muffin and inclined her head towards the other Hägglund, which was leading the way.

Gabe nodded. 'It's AAP policy that we always send out two vehicles or two boats or two helicopters. It's saved our people before but it seems that the Russians don't have the same policies. Liam is a mechanic and a firefighter and Finn is our watercraft operator, Alex is the survival expert and Finn, Alex and I are on your medical support team. We've got all bases covered. Ideally we'd send choppers out but the weather is against us on that, plus our choppers are kept at Douglas Station so even in good conditions they'd still be close to fifteen hundred kilometres from where the Russians were last heard from.'

Sophie hadn't got her head around the vastness of Antarctica. She knew the Russians had a research station about halfway between Carey and Douglas, two of the Australian stations, but if they had almost reached Carey that put them a long way from home. She wondered what had brought them so close. 'Do you know what the Russians were doing?'

'Apparently they were doing a check mission out over Bunger Hills but that would put them a long way off course if they're only twenty clicks from here. They must have had some sort of instrument failure that would put them at risk in these conditions.'

'What happens now?'

'Alex is in charge of the safety side of things. You're in charge of all things medical. We'll follow your orders but Alex has the overriding vote if he thinks there's any risk to the safety of our team. Fair enough?'

Sophie nodded. 'You said before that we plan for the worst and hope for the best. If they're dead, what do we do?'

'If we can get access we'll bring them back to the station

with us and the Russians will collect the bodies when the weather clears. The trailer attached to our Hägglund can function as an ambulance. We can transport casualties on stretchers in the back. Or fatalities in body bags if necessary.'

For someone without a medical background Gabe was very matter-of-fact but Sophie guessed that many of the seasoned expeditioners had faced all manner of testing situations that were well and truly out of the scope of normal workplace practices.

'Have you had to deal with deaths before?' she asked.

Gabe shook his head. 'Not me. But deaths aren't really the worst-case scenario. The worst case is two critically injured men out on the ice thousands of miles from a trauma centre.'

Terrific. A hundred different scenarios ran through Sophie's head. It was impossible to predict what she might need to deal with. It could be any number of things—hypothermia, fractures, spinal injuries, head or internal injuries, or a combination of all of these. And any treatment or even assessment of their potential injuries was going to be complicated by the conditions. The weather, the location and even the clothing they would be wearing would all increase the degree of difficulty.

She looked down at her own clothing. How was she going to treat them wearing these thick gloves? Could she take them off? How long would she have in these below freezing conditions before she suffered from frost-nip and then frostbite? Would there even be any point taking her gloves off to try to examine them when they would be wearing layers and layers of extreme cold-weather clothing?

Sophie had seen the immersion suits worn by anyone travelling in a helicopter that might be flying over water.

These suits were even bulkier than the cold-weather jacket and pants she wore as they had built-in flotation in case the chopper crashed into the sea. She would need to cut their suits away but that would expose them to the weather. In all her time at the other end of a phone line, advising the AMU doctors on medical matters, she hadn't had to deal with the concept of practising medicine in these extreme conditions. The job was suddenly much, much harder than she'd ever imagined.

To keep her mind focussed and her hands busy, she opened the medical kit and sorted through the contents, familiarising herself with where things were stored so she would be able to get quick access to whatever she needed. She closed her eyes and ran through the contents of the kit—bandages, syringes, drugs, suturing kits and needles—playing a version of the memory game as she tested her recall.

The visibility hadn't improved since they'd left Carey and they were making slow progress, but with her eyes closed Sophie felt the Hägglund slow even further. She opened her eyes, wondering if it was just her imagination. For a second she thought she saw a flash of red out to their right but then, just as quickly, it disappeared from view. Perhaps it was just the second vehicle. She kept her eyes on the spot, or where she thought the spot was, but she was only guessing.

A gust of wind blew the snow out of their way, clearing her sight line briefly. There it was again. Could it be the helicopter?

Before she could say anything the Hägglund ground to a halt. Through the swirling snow she could now make out the shape of the other Hägglund in front of them and she knew the glimpse of red out to the right wasn't Liam's vehicle.

'Is that the helicopter?' she asked Gabe.

'Looks like it.'

It looked nothing like it to her. It didn't resemble a helicopter at all. Was it just the weather and the poor visibility making it unrecognisable?

The snow cleared again and she could see now that it was a chopper. It was lying at an angle, slightly on its right side, like a beached whale. From this perspective it looked as though it had snapped into pieces and one rotor blade was sticking out of the snow several metres from the body of the helicopter.

She heard Gabe on the radio, advising the station that they had found the chopper. While she was listening to him she saw Liam climb out of the other vehicle. She could just make out his shape between the snow gusts. His red jacket was bright in the gaps in the snowfall and he held a long pole in his hand.

'What's Liam doing?' she asked Gabe as he ended his radio call. She wondered why they weren't moving. What were they waiting for?

'The chopper is resting on sea ice,' Gabe told her. 'We are right at the edge of the continent, where the sea ice meets the land ice. The two different bases can make the ice unstable. Where the two meet there are often cracks or fissures or crevasses. We need to check for stability so Liam is testing the snow and ice to make sure it's safe to proceed.'

Sophie was agitated. 'Can't we get out and walk?'

Gabe shook his head. 'No. It's further than it looks. Also it's minus ten degrees and blizzard conditions. What do you propose to do? Lug all your equipment with you? It will take fifteen minutes to cover that distance, without carrying any extra weight, and how will you treat him when you get there?'

'I don't know,' she said. Gabe was making sense but it was frustrating to have to sit and wait when she could see the chopper.

'If we can't drive over safely *then* we'll get out and walk,' he explained. 'But that means hauling the equipment on a sled.'

Alex opened his door and sprang out of the cab to help Liam. Icy wind blew into the vehicle, bringing with it a flurry of snow that blanketed Sophie's face. She was shocked at how frigid the air was. She'd felt quite warm in the Hägglund but she now realised it was only because she'd been sheltered from the wind.

She watched as Liam and Alex tested the ice. Liam was poking the pole into cracks in the ice while Alex appeared to be drilling into the icy crust. Liam was shorter than Alex with a more pronounced belly but both men were of similar build and it was difficult to tell them apart under the layers of clothing. From where Sophie sat Liam's moustache was the only differentiating factor, but once they were more than a few feet from the Hägglund they disappeared into the snow flurries to become only occasionally visible. She watched as one of them waved at the vehicle, motioning Gabe forward.

Gabe got on the radio again and this time spoke to Finn. 'Can we detach our trailer and put it behind yours? We'll leave our vehicle here, just in case we get into strife,' he said. He turned to Sophie. 'We'll have to swap vehicles. Rug up.'

Sophie pulled her goggles over her eyes and her hood over her head then clambered out of the Hägglund. Another blast of icy wind assaulted her and she bent almost double against the force of the gale as she made her way to the other tank-like vehicle and climbed into the back seat. Gabe placed her medical kit on the seat beside her before switching positions with Finn and taking over the driving. From the cab Sophie could see Alex attaching a cable from the Hägglund to Liam and a second one to himself.

'What are they doing?'

'Securing themselves to the Hägglund, just in case,' Gabe replied.

Sophie didn't ask any more questions. She didn't want to think about one of them falling through the ice. Liam and Alex continued to walk forward, testing the ice, with Gabe driving the vehicle and following closely behind them. They crept along slowly, inching across the ice.

Sophie opened the medical kit and selected a few essentials and stuffed them into her jacket pockets. She transferred surgical gloves, a torch and a thermometer, then checked that her stethoscope was still around her neck and that the saline bags hadn't frozen. She grabbed some IV tubing, a tourniquet and a needle, even though she had no idea how she would find a vein if she needed to run a drip—the cold weather and the layers of clothing were definitely going to make things difficult for her.

Their progress was slow and made even slower by a couple of stops to allow the men to swap places. Finn relieved Liam, who later relieved Alex, which gave them each a break and some respite from the sub-zero temperatures and strong winds.

Sophie tried to curb her impatience. The whole situation seemed quite surreal as the vehicle followed behind the men on foot and she had to remind herself that they were the experts and Gabe had promised to keep them all safe. She had to trust him and let them do their jobs. Her time was coming.

As they got nearer the chopper Sophie could see that it had broken into three pieces. The front and right-hand side was badly crumpled, the windscreen shattered but still mostly in position. The tail had broken off completely and one rotor blade had snapped off, probably on impact, and was sticking out of the snow, having been flung several metres from the helicopter.

Gabe stopped the Hägglund a few feet from the wreckage. As soon as he gave the all-clear Sophie leapt out of the cab.

'Can you bring the medical kit for me?' she asked. It was heavy and cumbersome and she knew she had the essentials she needed in her pockets. She also knew that by the time she had worked out what else she needed from the kit they would have brought it to her. She didn't need it to begin her assessment. It was more important just to get out of the vehicle.

Gabe had parked the vehicle on the right-hand side of the chopper, closest to the pilot. Sophie could see two men both still inside the chopper, their bright yellow immersion suits shining like twin beacons in the semi-darkness of the snow-covered cabin. She peered inside. The pilot was still strapped into his seat, his eyes closed. The other man's harness was undone, suggesting he must have moved at some point, but he was motionless too, eyes closed also.

Despite the damage to the helicopter, Sophie was just able to get her head and arms into the cabin and reach the pilot. He was slumped in his seat and the cabin had crushed around him. She grabbed the fingers of her thick padded gloves, ready to pull them off. She needed to feel for a pulse.

'You can't take your gloves off in this weather, Doc. Your fingers will freeze in minutes.' Gabe's voice startled her. She hadn't heard him come up behind her. The snow muffled all sound.

Sophie looked back at him. 'I can't work in these,' she said as she held her hands up. 'I have to feel for a pulse.'

'Doc, leave your gloves on.' Gabe's tone suggested that he wasn't making a request. 'You'll have to use your stethoscope.'

The pilot's immersion suit was tight around his face and neck. 'But he's got so many layers on,' she protested.

'Yuri is dead.'

Sophie's head whipped around as she looked across to the other Russian. His eyes were open now, his shallow breathing making his words faint.

'You speak English?'

'Da.'

'Have you checked him?' Sophie could see no evidence that the pilot had been checked or that the passenger had moved. He didn't appear to have tried to reach any of the survival gear and Sophie wondered if he'd tried to help the pilot—Yuri. What had happened?

'*Nyet*. I cannot move. My foot, it is stuck. But Yuri has not moved either.'

Sophie realised it didn't matter to her what had happened, what had gone on before they'd reached the scene. What mattered now was sorting out the casualties. She needed to prioritise but triage was a problem. She was used to casualties being brought in by ambulance. Usually the paramedics would give some indication of a patient's condition, which would make triage much easier. But out here there was no one who could tell her what the state of play was. It was up to her.

The passenger was conscious and coherent. The pilot was unresponsive. According to the passenger, the pilot was dead but Sophie wasn't prepared to accept his diagnosis. She needed to confirm that for herself. She knew he could be dead but he could also be hypothermic and, therefore, potentially in more need of help.

'Are you hurt?' she asked, directing her question to the passenger.

'My foot and my back.'

'Can you see if you can free his foot?' Sophie asked Gabe. It would buy her a few minutes with the pilot if Gabe could check out the passenger. He nodded and made his way around the front of the helicopter.

Sophie felt in her pocket for her torch while she spoke to Yuri. She wanted him to know what was going on just in case he could hear her. 'Yuri, I'm a doctor. I'm just going to open your eyes.'

Sophie tried to gently push up one of his eyelids, only to find it didn't move. It was frozen shut.

She checked the time. It was a little over two hours since the helicopter had been reported missing. In these sub-zero temperatures rigor mortis could have already started to set in and the muscles of the eyelids were one of the first to show the signs. But, then again, it could just be that Yuri's eyelids had frozen shut.

She'd heard about this happening but had never experienced it.

She opened the medical chest that Gabe had left at her side, pleased that whoever had designed it had had the foresight to make sure it could be easily opened while wearing gloves, and found the eye solution. 'Yuri, I'm going to wipe your eyes to get them open.' She poured some saline onto a gauze dressing and wiped the cloth across Yuri's eyelids. She didn't want to leave any moisture on his skin, knowing it would freeze solid again, but she needed to melt the ice that had frozen on his lids.

She flicked on the torch before lifting Yuri's eyelids, relieved to find that this time she was able to prise them open, and shone the torch briefly into first one eye and then the other. His pupils didn't react. They were fixed and dilated. It didn't help her with a diagnosis, all it told her was that his condition wasn't good.

Yuri could have a head injury but severe hypothermia could have the same affect.

Or he could be dead.

She untucked the stethoscope from her jacket and popped it in her ears. Because Yuri was slumped in his seat, she couldn't unzip his immersion suit to reach his chest. She held the stethoscope against his carotid artery listening in vain for a heart beat.

Nothing.

She took the stethoscope and held the round, silver disc under Yuri's nose, searching for condensation, looking for a sign that he was breathing.

Still nothing. But she still refused to believe it was all over for Yuri. Maybe he was just cold. She knew that in severe cases of hypothermia a person's heartbeat and respiration dropped and could be as slow as one to two per minute.

From across the cabin of the chopper she could see Gabe watching her, a question in his brown eyes.

'He could be hypothermic,' she said, refusing to give up until she'd checked Yuri more thoroughly. 'I need to get them both out.'

'We'll have to cut them out,' Gabe told her. 'Who do you want to move first?'

Sophie was nervous. She knew it was her call but the decision wasn't an easy one. Yuri's condition was potentially more critical—if he was still alive. But even if he was alive she knew that her treatment options for him were limited out here on the ice. They couldn't afford to spend precious time extricating Yuri in case the passenger's condition deteriorated. Time was valuable. She needed to get them somewhere warm. And that presented another problem.

Where could she treat them?

'Where will we put them?' she asked.

'The trailer that we brought is set up like an ambulance but you won't have much room to manoeuvre in there with two patients. The other trailer is full of safety gear,' Gabe said. 'We can set up a bivvy—a bivouac tent,' he clarified for her benefit, 'and put them in there. Who do you want moved first?' he repeated.

'Your guy.'

It was her job to save lives. There were two patients who needed her but she knew for certain that one was still alive. She couldn't afford to risk his life by making the wrong choice. She'd made her decision but still found herself looking to Gabe for confirmation. She needed his reassurance.

Gabe's brown eyes anchored her, once again settling her nerves, and she decided she preferred goggles to sunglasses. The goggles didn't hide his eyes and his eyes gave her the strength she needed. He nodded his head slightly, giving her the reassurance she sought, and she could see why he held the position of Station Leader. His quiet, calm manner would get the best out of his people.

Alex, Finn and Liam sprang into action. They had assembled a pile of gear in the snow beside the chopper. Sophie recognised metal cutters, stretchers and tarpaulins amongst the other paraphernalia.

She moved around to the other side of the chopper while the men got things organised. She let them do their jobs. There was nothing more she could do with Yuri until he was freed.

'I'm the doctor,' she said to the other man. She didn't bother to give her name. The new nickname was giving her the chance to escape the past. A chance to be someone other than Sophie, Danny's widow. 'What is your name?'

'Nikolai.'

She desperately wanted to check Nikolai's vital signs. She wanted to take his blood pressure and check his heart rate and oxygen sats, but in order to do that she needed access to his arm, wrist and fingers, and she couldn't risk exposing him to the hostile elements. She had to be content with the fact that he was alert and responsive and assume that any injuries he'd sustained weren't life-threatening. She'd need to be patient and wait until the guys had freed him from the wreckage so she resigned herself to keeping conversation going instead, making sure she kept Nikolai focussed and awake. 'Do you remember what happened?'

'Nyet.'

'Did you hit your head? Lose consciousness at all?' He looked at her blankly until she added, 'Did you black out?'

'Maybe,' he replied, and Sophie gave up her questioning. Between his possible memory loss and their language incompatibility she figured she wasn't going to get anywhere.

She stepped aside as Alex cut part of the chopper away to free Nikolai's foot. Finn was spreading a tarp on the ground as Liam and Alex pulled at the metal, twisting it out of the way and opening up some space around Nikolai's legs.

'We're clear,' Alex said.

'Ready to lift?' Gabe asked.

Sophie looked around. 'Wait! Where are you going to put him? The tent isn't up.'

'Don't worry, Doc, the bivvy will go up around you,' Gabe told her, then turned back to Alex. 'On three.'

'It's going to hurt,' Sophie told Nikolai as Gabe counted them down to the lift.

'Is okay,' the Russian replied.

'One, two, three.'

Gabe and Alex lifted Nikolai out of the chopper and Sophie saw what little colour he'd had drain from his face. Finn had placed a space blanket and the medical chest on the tarpaulin and Gabe and Alex laid Nikolai down then immediately returned to the chopper to finish cutting Yuri out.

Sophie knelt beside Nikolai and before she could ask any more questions or wonder about the wisdom of moving her patient before the tent was erected Finn had pulled a tent over the top of them all. Within seconds he had cocooned them from the wind and snow, sheltering them from the elements.

Sophie was amazed. There wasn't room to stand in the tent but it served as a perfectly adequate shelter. In order to keep its shape it needed someone to lean against the sides but Finn was able to do that while she turned her attention to Nikolai.

She barely had time to open the medical chest and begin to assess Nikolai when Gabe crawled into the tent through the small door. Sophie was immediately aware of his presence and it wasn't just because of the way he filled the space inside the tent. There was enough room in there for half a dozen bodies but his presence seemed to charge the air around her. She could feel the air shift and stir as Gabe moved, almost as though it breathed with him. It made no sense to be so aware of him, she knew nothing about him, he was just a man, yet she was far more aware of him than she was of anyone else out there today.

'Yuri is almost out,' he told her. 'We'll put him in the Hägglund when he's freed.'

'Shouldn't I check him in here ?' she asked, but Gabe's expression told her he thought she was wasting her time and for a moment she figured he probably knew more about Yuri's chances than she did. She'd only ever dealt with mild cases of hypothermia before but she still wasn't prepared to write him off just yet. 'Just in case? There's more space.'

Gabe shook his head. 'There was no chance of saving him, he was dead before we got here.'

Sophie knew Gabe was trying to make her feel better about the choices she'd made but she still felt her chest contract with guilt. A man was dead.

But she couldn't afford to dwell on Yuri now. She'd deal with that later. Right now she needed to concentrate on Nikolai.

Gabe was squatting beside her and his proximity was distracting her. She tried to block out her awareness of him, she needed to focus, but she didn't want to ignore him completely. Having him nearby made her feel positive. His presence gave her confidence and let her think that maybe things would be okay.

Now that she was shielded from the worst of the weather she could feel her body temperature begin to rise and she was willing to risk removing her gloves. She tucked them into her pocket and swapped them for a pair of surgical gloves. She opened the medical chest and rummaged for a pair of scissors, placing them on the top of the chest.

She turned to Gabe. 'Have we got spare clothes?' she asked.

He nodded. 'There'll be a survival kit in the helicopter if I can get to it.'

'And if you can't?'

'We have sleeping bags. They are just as effective at maintaining heat and easier to use. I'll bring you whatever I can find,' he said, starting to crawl back out of the tent.

'Can you bring the oxygen cylinder too?' she called after him.

Sophie didn't want to undress Nikolai too much until

Gabe had brought things to keep him warm, but she needed to start with the basics. She took one of his gloves off and popped an oximeter on his finger and took his temperature using a tympanic thermometer. She spoke to him quietly, explaining what she was doing. He didn't say much and she had no idea whether he understood anything she told him or if he was in shock and unable to comprehend what was going on.

His oxygen sats were low and so was his core temperature. She picked up the scissors and slit his immersion suit from his wrist to his elbow and wrapped a blood-pressure cuff around his arm. His pulse rate was fast and his blood pressure was low. Sophie opened the top of his suit and lifted his shirt to expose his chest. She put her stethoscope on his skin and listened for equal air entry, relieved to find his chest sounds were normal.

If asked for a diagnosis she knew he had sustained orthopaedic injuries and she suspected he had internal injuries as well, coupled with hypothermia, but she couldn't assess much more without better access. She took comfort from the fact that his vital signs, while not great, weren't critical yet, and unless he did have severe internal injuries her gut feeling was that he would probably pull through.

She palpated his abdomen while she waited for Gabe. Nikolai didn't report any tenderness with that but he did complain of back pain. She couldn't examine his back without moving him and she was reluctant to do that until she'd assessed his leg. It was a bit of a Catch-22 situation but, knowing that hypothermic patients should be kept as still as possible, she erred on the side of caution and pulled his shirt down again, trying to keep him warm.

She heard rustling as someone crawled back in through the opening of the tent. She felt the air stir and knew it was Gabe. Now she could check Nikolai's leg. Using the scissors, she slit the rubber immersion suit from his ankle to his groin.

'Doc!'

Sophie glanced across at Gabe. 'What?' she asked, as she peeled open the leg of Nikolai's suit.

Gabe gestured at Nikolai's now destroyed suit. 'Those suits cost thousands of dollars.'

Sophie shrugged. It was too late to worry about that. Even if she'd known their value she wouldn't have cared—her patient came first. 'There's more to worry about than the price of a suit,' she said, as she looked at Nikolai's leg. He'd fractured his tibia just above the ankle, his calf was swollen and bruised and she could see the bulge where the bone had snapped but hadn't broken through the skin. She ran her fingers gently over his leg and saw him grimace with pain at her touch. She could hear crepitus as the bone ends rubbed together, confirming her initial diagnosis. She pressed her fingers behind his ankle and was relieved to feel a pulse.

Now that Gabe was back with the sleeping bags she could risk uncovering Nikolai's chest and upper limbs to begin treating his hypothermia and finish her examination. She was just beginning to think she could work with Gabe without losing her focus when he passed her a sleeping bag and their fingers touched. He had removed his gloves and through the thin rubber of her surgical gloves Sophie could feel the heat of his hands. The warmth took her by surprise and she paused as the heat flooded through her. It was odd how she could feel it flow through her body until it pooled in her belly. She felt as though she was being wrapped in a warm hug and the sensation made her catch her breath.

But she was being ridiculous. A reaction like hers was totally out of proportion to a simple touch of a hand. She blamed the adrenalin that she knew would be coursing through her system. It was ridiculous to think what she was feeling had anything to do with Gabe. Her blood would be full of adrenalin. The whole situation was unusual and highly stressful—it was no wonder her senses and reactions were heightened.

She refocussed, concentrating hard to remember what she was about to do as she opened the sleeping bag out and laid it over Nikolai's legs. She'd come back to that fracture later. She'd need to X-ray it and set it but splinting would be the best she could do for now. Anything further would have to wait until they were back at the station. But before she attempted to splint his leg she wanted to administer some pain relief and begin trying to combat his hypothermia.

She connected tubing and an oxygen mask to the cylinder that Gabe placed beside her and slipped the mask over Nikolai's nose and mouth. She needed to get access to a vein in order to start an infusion of warm saline solution to increase his body temperature. She hoped she'd managed to keep the saline solution warm enough with her own body heat. She prepared the bag and the tubing, checking for air bubbles, before handing the bag to Gabe.

'Can you tuck this inside your suit to keep it warm and kneel up as high as you can to keep it elevated?' she asked him. They were restricted by the close confines of the tent but she needed the bag to be elevated and the saline to stay as warm as possible.

Gabe took the bag and Sophie returned her attention to the task at hand, managing to get vein access relatively easily considering the temperature. She made sure the saline was flowing before drawing up some pain relief. He would need it before they moved him.

'Are you allergic to anything?' she asked, hoping his English was good enough to understand her question.

'Anyone with allergies has to wear a MedicAlert bracelet while they're on the ice,' Gabe told her. She'd forgotten that and she hadn't noticed a bracelet when she'd cut Nikolai's suit but she double-checked to make sure as Nikolai shook his head. Satisfied, she drew up the pain relief and injected it into the IV line.

She opened a second sleeping bag and covered Nikolai's torso, making sure to cover his head as well before turning her attention to his leg. She splinted it as quickly and as best she could and had just finished when Alex stuck his head into the tent.

'Yuri is in the Hägglund. Let us know when you're ready to move Nikolai.'

There was so much going on and Sophie could only hope she was on top of it all. Thankfully the others all seemed to be taking things in their stride and doing what needed to be done. Liam, Gabe and Alex were taking care of the logistics and the evacuation and leaving her to worry about the medical aspects of the exercise. They seemed to be working smoothly with no outward sign that things were out of control and she had to trust that they knew what they were doing.

She nodded and turned to Gabe. 'Do you think you can get Nikolai onto a stretcher? I need to check Yuri, I have to confirm his condition.' She waited for a nod from him before she crawled out of the tent. She shoved her hands into her pockets to keep them warm as she left Alex to help Gabe as she made her way to the Hägglund. At some point the vehicle had been moved and was now only a few steps from the bivouac tent, but just those few steps were enough for her to feel the cold bite of the weather.

She climbed into the vehicle and knelt beside the bench seat where Alex and Liam had put Yuri. She was no longer able to open his eyes so she opened the front of his immersion suit instead. But it didn't take her long to come to the same decision as the others.

Yuri's skin was icy to touch, his core temperature was twenty-eight degrees Celsius and his limbs were stiff. Sophie knew her findings still didn't rule out severe hypothermia—unconsciousness would occur at about thirty degrees and his limb stiffness could be rigor mortis or it could just be the cold—but even she had to admit his condition didn't look promising. She found nothing to suggest that he might be able to be revived. It was too cold and it had been too long. She listened to his chest for a couple of minutes, hoping for any sound, a heartbeat, a breath, but it was in vain. There was nothing.

She hadn't wanted to believe that he was dead but she had to admit defeat.

Her first full day on the ice and she already had a death. She knew it wasn't her fault but that didn't stop the guilt.

She sat back on her heels. Lost. Beaten. Defeated.

She looked at Yuri's face as he lay unmoving before her and for a brief moment all she could see was Danny. All she could remember was the moment when she'd had to formally identify his body.

Physically Yuri didn't resemble Danny at all. Yuri was darker and older, with lined and weathered skin. Danny had still been a boy by comparison, and in Sophie's mind Danny would always be young, but he and Yuri had something in common now. They were both dead.

Deep down she knew she'd had no chance of saving either of them but that didn't stop the memories from flooding back. What if she hadn't taken the extra shift that day? What if she and Danny had gone out for breakfast as they'd planned? They'd been talking about spending more time together—why hadn't she said no to work? Why hadn't Danny been more important?

She knew why. They'd thought they would have a lifetime together. What did one day matter when you had the rest of your lives?

She wouldn't make that mistake twice.

CHAPTER FOUR

'DOC? ARE YOU OKAY?' Gabe's voice interrupted her guilty reminiscing.

She could see the worry in his eyes but she couldn't answer him. Not yet. Not until she got the image of Danny out of her head. She nodded.

'Are you sure?' he added.

Was he worried about her or concerned that she couldn't do her job? Did he think she was falling apart? Was he worried about her state of mind?

She had to reassure him. She knew she needed to push on. She couldn't sit here wallowing in the past. There were still people relying on her. Nikolai for starters.

'Yes.' She reached up and took the saline bag from Gabe and hung it on a hook that was sticking out of the Hägglund's roof as Gabe and Alex slid Nikolai's stretcher into the trailer. She needed to keep moving. She needed to keep busy. She knew from experience that if her mind was busy she didn't have time to dwell on Danny.

With an elaborate rope and pulley system, Gabe and Alex stabilised Nikolai's stretcher in the makeshift ambulance as Sophie secured the oxygen cylinder. Once they were finished there was just enough room for her to squeeze in too.

'What happens now?' she asked.

'We'll head back to Carey and when the weather clears the Russians will come to collect them. You'll be responsible for Nikolai until then. Are you going to be all right in here for the trip back?'

'Yes.' She didn't have any option. There was no room for anyone else once the medical chest and other equipment had been stowed in the trailer with her. Finn handed her a couple of energy bars and a bottle of water and Gabe showed her how to use the intercom to communicate with the front cab if she needed to, but other than one stop to let Finn and Liam out to collect the other Hägglund the return trip went without incident.

By the time they reached Carey Sophie was exhausted and she wondered if this was going to be permanent state for her while she was on the ice but, then again, her first proper day on the job had been beyond stressful. It had required massive levels of concentration and she'd had no respite. Being the sole doctor for hundreds of miles was no picnic.

There were plenty of willing hands to help unload the Hägglunds when they returned to the station but it was her Russian patients that Sophie was concerned with. Nikolai was her first priority and he was transferred immediately from the vehicle to the medical centre but she was unsure what the procedure was for the pilot.

'What happens to Yuri?' she asked Gabe. 'Do we have a morgue?' She couldn't remember seeing a morgue, there certainly wasn't one attached to the medical centre, which would have been the obvious place, but she knew she'd only seen a fraction of the red shed and who knew what was housed in some of the other station buildings.

'Not as such,' Gabe replied. 'We'll have to freeze him in a body bag and wait for the Russians to collect him.'

That sounded a bit archaic but she supposed it was the way things were done and she wasn't about to argue. She couldn't pretend to be up to speed with all the procedural ins and outs and she had other priorities. 'No post-mortem?' she queried.

Gabe shook his head. 'I'm the coroner for our station but you pronounced Yuri dead at the scene, which is out of my jurisdiction so the Russians will take care of that.'

Sophie was relieved. She didn't think her skills extended to conducting an autopsy. All she could do for Yuri now was to prepare his body. It wasn't an urgent task but she wanted to do that before he was zipped into a body bag and taken away.

'Can Yuri be brought to the medical centre too?' she asked, 'I'd like to clean him before we freeze him.'

'Sure, Doc. I'll send Alex and Finn to help you if you think that's enough hands. I need to put in a call to update the Russians on the situation.'

Sophie nodded. Nikolai was waiting for her. Yuri too. She needed to get moving.

X-rays of Nikolai's leg confirmed a slightly displaced simple tibial fracture. Sophie sedated him before realigning it and Finn had helped her to put a cast on it. Sophie wasn't too concerned about the fracture; of more concern was the blood that appeared in his urine. On examination she suspected bruised kidneys, and when Alex told her that Nikolai's seat in the chopper had snapped at the base that confirmed her diagnosis and she felt marginally happier with his condition.

Alex, Finn and Sophie worked tirelessly to get Nikolai sorted and when they eventually had him stable, fed and resting in one of the two beds in the small ward room Sophie turned her attention to Yuri. She undressed and bathed him, examining his body for signs of injury. But apart from some bruising on his chest and abdomen there were no other visible signs and she suspected he must have died from internal injuries. But it wasn't her role to determine the cause of the death or to investigate the accident. Her job was difficult enough and she had no desire to complicate it further.

When she had finished tending to Yuri Alex and Finn zipped him into a body bag and took him out of the clinic. She didn't ask where they would take him, she didn't think she needed to know, and there was enough going on in her head already.

Finding herself alone for the first time that day, she was tempted to sit down but thought she might never get up again. She could feel fatigue starting to take hold. Her legs were wobbly and her head was light. She needed to eat something but she didn't want to leave Nikolai. To distract herself and her stomach, she checked his obs and tidied the clinic. If she kept busy she wouldn't be able to fall asleep. She was putting the last few items away in a cupboard when the clinic door opened and Gabe appeared.

'How's it going?' he asked, as she straightened up and shut the cupboard door.

Her energy level lifted. Maybe it was just having some company again, someone to talk to, but she seemed to have an immediate reaction to Gabe that she didn't notice with any of the others. His energy seemed to flow to her and she felt as though it could sustain her. 'Okay,' she replied. 'I'm under control, I think. Have you spoken to the Russians?'

'I have,' he said, as he perched on the edge of her desk. 'They will come to fetch Yuri's body and Nikolai when the weather clears, if you give Nikolai the okay to travel. Their doctor has asked for an update on his condition so I told them you'd call when you can.'

'I'll talk to him now.' She may as well get it done now.

She suspected the Russian doctor would be keen to hear from her—she knew she would be sitting by the phone if the situation were reversed. She crossed to her desk, only realising as she reached for the phone that Gabe was practically sitting on it. He didn't move.

He took up a lot of room. The room was small to begin with and Gabe seemed to fill most of the available space. She could feel her stomach fluttering as she reached for the phone. Goose-bumps covered her skin, making the hairs on her arms stand up.

Gabe finally stood up as he gave Sophie the number. He waited while she'd made the call but at least he didn't remain sitting on her desk. He moved just far enough away to enable her to concentrate but she was still aware of his whereabouts as he wandered through the clinic and into the ward room. Her eyes followed his movements and even as she spoke to the Russian doctor she kept Gabe in the corner of her vision. Through the open door she saw him stop at Nikolai's bedside before he returned to the clinic room.

'Do you want to go and grab some dinner and a shower?' he asked, as she hung up the phone.

She managed a smile. 'I thought we were only allowed to shower every second day? I don't think I qualify for one yet.'

'Oh, I think you've earned it, and as the station leader I can grant favours.'

'Really?'

'Of course. There have to be some perks to the job or no one would take it on.' Gabe smiled at her, his teeth a startling white in the dark shadow of his beard, and Sophie's body sprang to attention. She'd thought he exuded a sense of calm confidence but when he smiled at her she felt anything but calm. Her heart raced in her chest, her palms sweated and her breathing was shallow. She was in equal parts nervous, excited and self-conscious. It was purely a physical reaction but thankfully Gabe didn't seem to notice her discomfort. He continued, 'I'm sure you could do with a break.'

As tempting as it was, Sophie was reluctant to go. 'It does sound good but I don't really want to leave Nikolai.' She didn't want to leave Nikolai or Gabe.

'I'll stay with him. I can call you over the intercom system if I need you. You'll only be a few steps away.'

Sophie was still finding her feet on her first proper day. She'd hate to abdicate responsibility and have something go wrong. 'Thanks for the offer but I think I'll stay here and I might put that favour in the bank for when I could really use one.'

'I'll bring dinner to you, then. What about Nikolai? Can he eat?'

Sophie glanced at the sleeping form of the Russian. He was sedated and seemed to be sleeping peacefully. 'He's had some soup,' she said. 'It's probably better to leave him sleeping.'

Gabe returned within minutes, carrying a tray of food, which he put onto her desk.

'It smells fantastic.' She was starving. She'd had nothing but a couple of energy bars since her take-away breakfast and now that she could smell dinner she could no longer distract her stomach or her brain from the idea of eating.

'Pumpkin soup and mushroom risotto,' Gabe said, as he removed the cloches covering the dishes with a flourish.

Sophie could see two servings of soup and risotto on the tray. Was he planning on eating with her?

Her earlier nervousness returned. The butterflies in her stomach had been getting a lot of exercise since she'd arrived in Antarctica. She'd expected some nerves with regard to her surroundings and the work, but her reaction to Gabe was unexpected and she wasn't sure what to do about it. And she definitely wasn't sure if spending time alone with him was a good idea. He flustered her. Actually, that wasn't quite true—her reaction to him flustered her.

She decided not to jump to conclusions. Perhaps he wasn't staying. Perhaps he had work to do. Perhaps he was going to deliver her meal and then take his to his own office. She lifted two bowls for herself off the tray and sat at her desk. Gabe grabbed a second chair, pulled it over to the desk and sat down too. It looked like he was planning on eating with her.

'You don't need to stay. Why don't you eat in the dining room with everyone else?'

'Because I thought that after the day we've had you might like some company. Was I wrong? Would you rather be alone?'

'No, not at all.' She didn't want him to go and although his presence unsettled her she preferred the idea of his company over being alone. She'd had enough of being alone.

'All right, then.' He picked up a linen napkin and shook it open before placing it gently across her lap. Sophie froze as his hand brushed her thigh. Even through the thin fabric of her scrubs she could feel his body heat and the sensation tied her tongue in knots as she struggled to make conversation. But her brain seemed to have shut down for the day, which wasn't surprising given the day she'd had, but it did leave her feeling at a distinct disadvantage.

His presence put knots in more places than just her tongue. Her stomach was doing so many somersaults she wasn't sure if she was going to be able to eat, despite the fact that she was starving. She didn't know what to think about Gabe yet or about the reaction he provoked in her. She didn't want to be so aware of him. She wanted to be neutral. She wanted to be Switzerland. She didn't want to find him attractive but that was exactly what was happening. She didn't know what it was yet—his strength? His eyes? His solidness? He seemed dependable and he gave her confidence in this unfamiliar environment. But it was more than confidence. Having him nearby heightened her senses and she realised then what it was.

He made her feel alive.

He passed her some cutlery and her fingers brushed against his as she took the silverware from his hand, sending another burst of energy through her, and this time she couldn't pass it off as adrenalin or fatigue.

It was attraction.

It was absurd. She'd known him for barely twenty-four hours, yet she couldn't deny what she was feeling. Her hands were shaking, her stomach was tied up in knots and her pulse was racing. Gabe stirred her senses.

She couldn't deny it but she could try to ignore it.

It was way too soon to find another man attractive. Even though it was obvious she wasn't getting a say in the matter—her body was making its own decisions. It wasn't her fault but it was still trouble.

She snatched her hand back and unwrapped her cutlery, breaking eye contact, and spooned up some soup as she willed her hands to quit shaking. She wasn't even sure if she could eat. It was hard to swallow when it felt like all the air was being squeezed from her lungs.

But Gabe seemed unfazed. 'You coped really well today,' he said as he stirred his soup.

'I'm not sure that Yuri would agree.' Sophie hadn't had a chance to process how she felt about Yuri's demise. She knew she couldn't have changed the outcome but that didn't seem to stop the guilt.

'Please, don't blame yourself for that. We were too

late. There was nothing you could have done. You have to agree.'

'Maybe. But that doesn't change the fact that someone died today.'

'Agreed. But it wasn't of our doing. You should focus on the things that went right. Nikolai is going to be okay, thanks to you. Today was a challenge but I thought you were remarkable.'

His comment brought a smile to her lips. How was it that he knew exactly the right thing to say?

She wanted to challenge herself and today had certainly been a challenge, both mentally and physically. She'd been worried at times about being out of her depth, and to know that Gabe thought she'd handled the situation well was reassuring. She hadn't thought she was one who looked for approval but Gabe's compliment helped to assuage her guilt.

'Although I don't imagine that's how you pictured your first day would go?' he added.

She shook her head. 'No. Please, tell me that today was out of the ordinary.' Being challenged like this on occasions was fine, but she didn't think she wanted to have days like this constantly.

'Definitely extraordinary. I've never had a day like it in the three years I've been here.'

'You all seemed to cope with it better than me.'

Gabe shrugged. 'We've had plenty of training and we're used to these conditions. Everything was new for you. I had hoped to organise some field training for you before you had to experience a real emergency but obviously that went out the window. But I promise we'll do it as soon as we get a decent day.'

'Barring any other emergencies.'

'Yes.' He smiled at her and his chocolate-brown eyes

shone and it felt like the temperature in the room rose another couple of degrees.

Sophie finished her soup and pushed it to one side, ready to make a start on the risotto. 'You've been here for three years? This is a long-term proposition for you?'

'Not three years continuously but this is my third stint and it's getting close to a total of three years. There's a saying on the ice that goes something like this. The first time you come to Antarctica is for the adventure, the second time is for the money and the third time is because you can't work anywhere else.'

'And is that right?'

'Pretty much. Although I don't know about the money part. I spent many years working on mine sites and the money is better there. And you get more time off. But I've chosen to come back here when I could easily have gone back on the mines, so I guess I must like it.'

'What do you like about it?'

'It's the last frontier. It's a beautiful place but it can be hostile. It will test your wits and your endurance but I like the challenge. Working on the mines was interesting but after a while it became mundane. Being here is definitely not about the money. It's been a huge adventure and I'm afraid it's rather addictive.'

'You don't mind being here for months at a time?'

'Not at all.'

'Do you miss your family?'

'I don't have any.'

'No one?' Everyone had someone, didn't they? But Gabe was shaking his head.

'That's another reason why this suits me. These guys are like family to me. There are a few of us who have done several stints together and you become pretty close.'

Sophie wondered how close he was with other members

of the crew. He had a lone-wolf aura about him, seeming to stand apart, but she wondered if that was something she projected onto him. Maybe it was more of an alpha-wolf thing, not a lone wolf. She'd seen how the others responded to him—the S&R team and the general crew last night when Gabe had been behind the bar—there was respect and a bond so perhaps alpha wolf was a better description. Even she was falling under his spell.

'What did you do on the mines?'

'I was a chef.'

'Really?'

'I was called a cook but I trained as a chef.'

'How long did you work there for?'

'Eight years with a year off in the middle when I went to work on a cattle station and I came here when I was twenty-eight.'

'To work as a chef?'

'No. I wanted a change and the Antarctic programme appealed to me but there wasn't a chef's position at the time so I worked as a storeman first.'

'And now you're the station leader.' Sophie suspected a lot of drive and determination lay behind his calm exterior.

'Yep.'

'How do you go from being a chef in the mines to a station leader in Antarctica? They seem like polar opposites—' Sophie broke off when Gabe raised one eyebrow and she realised what she'd said. 'Pardon the pun.'

He grinned at her and the force of his smile distracted her from thoughts of her accidental pun.

'There's a lot of downtime with mining rosters. Most mines run a two-week-on, two-week-off roster. The guys with families spend their weeks off at home, doing family things. I spent my time off studying and getting as many qualifications and certificates as I could.'

'What did you need?'

'For the storeman's job not much—a driver's licence, first aid and CPR qualifications—but my additional licences helped me get the station leader role. The AAP was more interested in people management skills and on paper I was probably overqualified for the job. I ran the kitchen at the last mine site, which was a big operation, but all the extra things might have made the difference between me and the next candidate.'

'What sort of extra things?"

'My OH&S experience, forklift and truck licences, boat licence, and now I'm the policeman, coroner and station counsellor as well.'

'Are you a type-A personality or just a regular overachiever?'

Gabe laughed and his deep, rich voice vibrated through her. 'I'm a late bloomer. It took me a while to work out what I wanted to do with my life. How about you? Did you always want to become a doctor?'

'Pretty much,' she said, as she swallowed the last mouthful of her risotto. It was creamy and full of flavour. 'That was delicious.'

'Dom's a genius in the kitchen. Good food is such a morale booster, especially over winter.'

'I didn't really expect to have fresh vegetables in my meal.'

'The mushrooms are grown in our hydroponics shed.'

'Do you grow all your vegetables here?'

'No. We couldn't keep up with the demand when the station is at capacity over the summer months but that's okay because fruit and veg can be flown in then. But we can grow enough to supply the smaller winter crew and the shed is a popular option on the volunteer roster for the winter expeditioners—it's warm and has constant light, which is a nice contrast to the winter conditions on the ice,' he said, as he picked up their plates. 'Shall I bring back some dessert or do you want to take a break and head to the mess room?'

'No, if it's okay I'll stay here, I need to take Nikolai's obs.'

Sophie pushed her chair back and went into the ward room. She could feel her eyelids drooping as she checked Nikolai and recorded her readings. The warmth of the room and the fullness of her belly was a soporific combination and the other hospital bed was beckoning. Surely it wouldn't hurt to put her head on the pillow for a couple of minutes while she waited for dessert? She stretched out on top of the sheets and closed her eyes. She just needed a few quiet moments to make sense of the day.

Alex had offered to take dessert to Sophie but Gabe had insisted that he didn't mind. Despite the mountain of paperwork that faced him after the day's events, he had no desire to sit at his desk. Sophie was like a breath of fresh air to the station. To him. And it had been a long time since he'd felt an attraction to someone. He knew it was dangerous but he was drawn to her and his desk and the pile of paperwork couldn't compete with his desire to spend a little more time in her company. He knew he wasn't thinking with his head, he knew he was headed for trouble, but he couldn't resist.

He pushed open the clinic room door, only to discover Sophie fast asleep on the spare bed in the two-bed ward. She was lying on top of the sheets and he could only assume she hadn't intended to doze off, but he wasn't surprised. Today would have been stressful for her, it was no wonder she was exhausted. But she'd coped really well with the drama. He had known she'd been nervous—that was completely reasonable—but she'd held it together. He knew from her file that she had emergency-room experience but no field experience. She hadn't been a medic in the defence force, like many other polar medicine doctors, including Dr John, had been.

He watched her as she slept. She was wearing a set of navy blue surgical scrubs that made her skin look pale and perfect and she had striped thermal socks on her feet. On one of her cheeks there was still a light dusting of powder that he suspected had come from the surgical gloves. He'd wanted to reach out and brush it off while they ate dinner but had decided against it. It was endearing to him that she hadn't noticed it and he knew that by wiping it away he was just looking for an excuse to touch her and that would have seemed far too familiar.

She had pulled her dark hair into a ponytail but some wisps had escaped from the elastic and curled around her face. He searched for signs of her dimples but they'd disappeared while she slept. She looked peaceful but, in his opinion, still too thin.

The station was heated to twenty degrees Celsius year round, a comfortable temperature usually, but he wasn't sure how warm the scrubs were and he suspected that with no meat on her bones she would feel the cold. He wondered if he should wake her and send her to bed but realised she would probably want to stay in the clinic to keep an eye on Nikolai. He grabbed a blanket instead and draped it over her, hoping she would be okay. He was reluctant to leave her but he knew it would seem odd if he stayed. There was no reason for him to keep watch over her but he felt an unusual sense of guardianship. She seemed vulnerable and delicate, although he knew she wasn't. He'd seen her strength today so it was obviously just a sense he got while she was sleeping.

She was an odd mixture of fragility and strength. Her fragility brought out his protective instincts, even though she wasn't his to protect, and she was unlikely to ever be, but he couldn't deny that he'd felt a spark of attraction today. No surprise really. She was an attractive woman, but the spark had been more than simple curiosity.

Maybe it had just been the circumstances. Maybe the drama today had served to bond them. Perhaps that connection he believed he'd felt hadn't been chemistry. Perhaps it was nothing more than a shared experience. But it didn't feel like nothing and he couldn't ignore it completely, no matter how hard he told himself to.

He needed to walk away.

Perhaps he could pretend the attraction didn't exist. Perhaps if he could ignore it, it would go away. He wasn't one to play around with anyone on the station. In his experience that was fraught with disaster. He'd been badly burnt before with a workplace romance on the mine and now he saved his romancing for other continents. He would prefer it if his crew played by the same rules but it wasn't something he could enforce, only suggest, and, let's face it, there often wasn't much else to do at the station, particularly over winter, and people got bored and fooled around.

He had been concerned about Sophie's perceived lack of experience but she'd proved herself today. It seemed she was going to be a good addition to the crew and he didn't want to jeopardise his position or hers by overstepping his self-imposed mark.

He didn't know why he was even thinking about it. Romance was probably the last thing on her mind. She had enough to deal with—she was in a foreign environment, she was exhausted and newly widowed—and it was unlikely she had the energy or desire for anything along the lines he was contemplating.

He needed to walk away.

He couldn't continue to stand there, watching her sleep. He couldn't get involved. He couldn't give in to temptation. It wasn't what either of them needed.

He was better off alone. He'd made that decision long ago and there was no reason to change his modus operandi now. He was the product of a broken home, of a father who'd lied and cheated and a mother who'd been unable to cope, and the one time he'd thought about risking everything for love he'd been spectacularly played for a fool. From then on he'd vowed never to get seriously involved in a relationship. Short-term flings, a weekend here and there, had become his way, and that worked for him. But it wouldn't work if he and Sophie were living under the same roof.

He didn't need complications.

Walk away, Gabe.

She doesn't need you to get involved. She doesn't need protecting. She's strong. She's made it here after everything she's been through. She doesn't need you.

Walk away.

Don't get involved.

Don't go looking for trouble.

He walked away.

CHAPTER FIVE

Date: March 9th
Temperature: -10°C
Hours of sunlight: 13.7

SOPHIE WOKE EARLY the next morning. She'd had an interrupted sleep, just the sound of Nikolai's breathing had been enough to disturb her. She hadn't realised she'd already grown used to the silence that came with sleeping alone.

Nikolai's condition was stable, she hadn't needed to stay in the clinic for the night but she'd been reluctant to leave him. She'd been worried his condition might deteriorate so it had been easier to stay, but she'd been surprised at how easily she'd fallen asleep. It had been the first night in a long time that she'd gone to sleep without thinking of Danny but she refused to feel guilty. That had been one reason for coming to Antarctica: she wanted to move forward. She didn't want to forget the past but she did want to put it behind her. She wanted to move on.

She closed her eyes and Gabe's soft, chocolate eyes came to mind. She could recall the easy feeling of confidence his smile gave her and the spark she'd felt when they'd touched. She'd wondered if that spark had just been adrenalin but she knew it was more than that. She was attracted to him, but was she exaggerating her reaction? Had the circumstances increased her awareness and response to him? Had the excitement of the day and her loneliness combined to make her hyper-aware? She wouldn't know until she saw him again. She wouldn't know the answer until she touched him again.

She kept one eye on the door, waiting for Gabe, but it was Finn who came to relieve her so she could shower and have breakfast. Gabe appeared only briefly later in the morning to get an update on Nikolai, but there was no reason to touch him and he seemed to be a little distant. Perhaps he had a lot on his mind but she felt silly. She must have been exaggerating the attraction, he certainly didn't seem to feel it.

Sophie attended to Nikolai and tried not to think about Gabe. The weather hadn't improved enough for Nikolai to be transferred so she would have a patient to keep her occupied for at least another twenty-four hours. She also needed to email Luke with the update she'd promised, but she didn't know where to start. How could she possibly be expected to describe her first day? She didn't think she could put yesterday's events into words. Only someone who had been through a similar experience would understand. Only someone who had been there would believe it. Someone like Gabe.

But no matter how much she tried to concentrate on other things, her mind kept returning to Gabe.

Was she betraying Danny with her thoughts?

She sighed. It was just something else to feel guilty about. Perhaps feeling guilty was something she was going to have to get used to. Unless she could block Gabe from her mind.

But she knew that was easier said than done. She had never had such a strong physical reaction to a man before. She'd always known that she and Danny were meant to be together but she didn't remember ever feeling such a strong sense that things were out of her control, that greater powers were at work. She and Danny had had a simple, straightforward relationship. She had no idea what sort of relationship she and Gabe were going to have but she had a feeling it wouldn't be simple. And until she had more time to try to work it out, she knew she needed to resist the pull of attraction.

Date: March 12th
Temperature: -8°C
Hours of sunlight: 13.3

Sophie was up with the sun. She was settling comfortably into station life and things were starting to become familiar. The weather had finally cleared and the Russians had collected Nikolai and Yuri's body, which meant she was free to leave the clinic and get out and have her first quad bike lesson with Alex. She was eager to get that ticked off because Gabe had promised to take her on an excursion once she had mastered the bike.

She had breakfast and dressed in all her layers and followed Alex outside. It was the first time she'd ventured from the red shed to one of the outbuildings and she was keen to get going, but Alex stopped her at the foot of the metal steps. He picked up a rope that was dangling from a metal pole and held it loosely in his hand. Sophie could trace the line of rope back to metal rings on the outer wall of the red shed.

'See these ropes?' he asked her. 'You'll find these between all the buildings. They're guide ropes. When the visibility is poor or in blizzard conditions these can be the only means you have of finding your way between the sheds. As long as you have hold of one of these, you can follow it from one building to the next.'

At various intervals between the red shed and the other sheds Sophie could see metal poles sticking out of the ice. Ropes were strung between the poles but she could see that they acted as guides, not barriers, as they hung low enough to rest on the ice and would allow vehicles to drive over them. It was a beautiful crisp, clear morning, much like the day she'd arrived, but now she understood just how quickly the weather could turn and she knew the guide ropes would have been invaluable in the whiteout conditions of her first full day.

She followed Alex along the line of the rope to the yellow machinery shed. It was massive and filled with an assortment of construction vehicles. Graders, trucks, forklifts, and snowmobiles were lined up inside, but Sophie was surprised to see quad bikes in the corner as well, and she realised she hadn't really imagined riding a four-wheeled motorbike over the snow.

'We're really using bikes? With wheels and tyres? We're not using the snowmobiles?' she asked.

'It's no different from driving the trucks that you see in here,' Alex said, and Sophie supposed that made sense. 'Quad bikes can be used on hard-packed snow and ice. Snowmobiles are for soft snow—powder snow. They're operated in the same way but because it's easier to tip a quad bike over I want to make sure you can handle that, but there are a few basics to understand before we can head out.'

Alex pulled a soft duffel bag from the back of a quad bike. 'Lesson one, protection. Wear the right clothing and take extra layers with you. Exposure to the weather kills more people than anything else. Always take a survival kit, you saw these the other day on our S&R. You need one between two people.' He opened the bag and proceeded to empty the contents, listing them off for Sophie's benefit as he unpacked and then repacked the kit.

'There's a tent and sleeping bags, spare clothing, a first-aid kit, spare radio, plus cooking equipment and rations for two days. *Always* make sure you've got one of these with you. You've seen how quickly the weather can change and once I've shown you how to use this equipment and set up the tent, this really can mean the difference between life and death.'

'Lesson two, communication. Always tell someone where you are going and when you expect to be back. Check in twice a day for overnight trips.' He showed her how to use the radio but this at least was familiar to her as she had used a similar system with the emergency retrieval team at the South Hobart Hospital.

'Lesson three, company. Never go out alone. That's one of Gabe's non-negotiable rules.'

'Does he have many?' she asked.

'Lots. But all for valid reasons.'

'He seems like a good leader.' Sophie couldn't resist trying to pump Alex for a little bit of information.

Alex nodded. 'He is. We have a strong team here and a lot of that is due to Gabe. It's a tough environment, unforgiving, and it presents a host of difficulties in terms of people management but Gabe handles it well. He has everyone's respect. We've become good mates over the past few years, as close as brothers in some ways. He's a great bloke but if you want to get out and about while you're here we need to forget about Gabe and make sure you're competent on a quad bike.'

'I'd better warn you, I'm a bit of a klutz.' Sophie was starting to feel a little nervous. She'd never ridden a motorbike before and now that she was standing here it was looking a little daunting.

'You can drive a car, can't you?'

'Yes, but I'm pretty well hopeless at anything that requires general co-ordination *and* balance. I don't need balance to drive a car but I'm not so sure about a quad bike.' There was a lot more to going out on a sightseeing trip in Antarctica than simply hopping into a car, but she knew that if she wanted to see anything of the icy continent she needed to pay attention and ensure she knew what to do.

'Have you ever ridden a motorbike?'

Sophie smiled and shook her head. 'I'm an emergency-room doctor. I've seen the damage people do to themselves on motorbikes.'

'Well, that's why it's important to understand the basics and the safety aspects. Can you ride a bicycle?'

'On flat ground.' She'd never been comfortable with off-road cycling because of her terrible balance and she hadn't ridden a bike since Danny's accident, and she didn't imagine she ever would again.

But this wasn't a bicycle. Balance, or lack of it, might not be such an issue and fortunately there didn't seem to be all that much that she could crash into out here. This was her adventure and she was determined to make the most of it.

She knew Danny would have loved this adventure, he would have been the first one to encourage her to have a go, but she was doing this for herself now, not for anyone else.

'We'll take it easy to begin with, Doc,' Alex promised, as he fitted her with a helmet and got her training under way.

Sophie lost track of time as she concentrated on following Alex's instructions and eventually he declared her competent. 'Now, would you like to take the lead and we can head back to the station?'

She looked around. They were out on the ice but she couldn't see the station and she knew of no landmarks. She'd lost track not only of time but also of direction. If she'd been on her own she would have been in dire straits. 'I have absolutely no idea where we are,' she admitted.

'All right, then, that means it's time for lesson four. Survival training. First step is planning—know where you plan to go, know how to use your GPS unit and have some basic navigational skills,' Alex said, and he proceeded to show her how the GPS unit worked. 'But you also need to have a back-up plan in case something does go wrong—there are several huts dotted at various distances from the station. It's important to know where the nearest hut is but, in a worst-case scenario, if you are injured or stranded away from any of the huts you need to know what to do in order to survive.'

He taught her how to set up a small bivouac tent, strung between their quad bikes and reinforced how important it was to have protection from the wind. 'Wind chill can be the killer in sub-zero temperatures. If you can get out of the wind you have a better chance of survival if it's twenty degrees below zero.'

'I have no intention of being out in those sorts of temperatures,' Sophie replied. She hoped she'd be cocooned inside the red shed if conditions were that atrocious.

'You were out in similar conditions on the search and rescue. Those conditions could have easily deteriorated and while I know you had plenty of experienced people with you we all have to be prepared for the worst, and to cope with the worst you need to be able to find food, shelter and warmth. And if you don't have shelter with you, you need to know how to build it.' He glanced at his watch and said, 'I think we have time for one final exercise before we should be heading back. Are you up for one last thing?'

Sophie had been on a steep learning curve. It had been another hectic day that had required lots of concentration but she found it exhilarating and the buzz meant she was far from tired. 'What is it?'

'I thought I'd show you how to make an ice cave.'

'Sure.'

Alex pulled some tools out of the survival kit and showed her how to dig a person-size depression in the snow, stopping after a couple of minutes to strip off his padded jacket. 'When you start to get warm you need to remove some clothing,' he told her. 'Don't allow sweat to gather inside your clothes, otherwise when you cool down again the moisture will make you cold.' Once he'd stripped down he showed her how to use a snow saw to cut blocks of ice that they laid across the hole for a ceiling.

'Why can't we just cut blocks of ice and build an igloo type structure on top of the ice?' Sophie asked. 'Why must we dig a hole first?'

'It keeps the wind out more effectively if we dig down first,' he replied. The cave was just about complete and Sophie was able to picture the finished version when they were interrupted by a radio call.

'Alex, this is Gabe, can you read me? Over.'

Alex looked at Sophie. 'You can take this one,' he said. 'See if you can remember what to do.'

Sophie picked up the handset for the two-way and depressed the 'talk' button.

'Gabe, this is Sophie. Over.'

'Doc, good. Listen, I need you back here. Dom's had an accident in the kitchen. He's sliced his finger quite badly. We can't stop the bleeding and I suspect it might need stitches. How far away are you? Over.'

Sophie turned to Alex. Despite the navigational training she really had no idea how far they were from the station, although she had a vague idea about in which direction it lay.

Alex took the handset from her and replied to Gabe. 'Twenty minutes. Over.'

'Okay. He's in the clinic. I'll meet you there. Over and out.'

Back at the station Sophie left Alex to put the quad bikes away and hurried into the red shed. She found Gabe and Dom in the clinic.

'Couldn't you find something else to use?' she asked, when she saw that Dom's left hand had been wrapped in a tea towel.

'It's a clean one,' Dom quipped.

'It's also the third one we've used and the cut is still bleeding,' Gabe added, as Sophie washed her hands and pulled on a pair of surgical gloves. Gabe's tone was calm and measured but Sophie heard the unspoken message that, despite Dom's jokes, the injury wasn't a minor one. Gabe had told Sophie that he thought the cut needed stitching and Sophie trusted his judgement.

'Which finger is it?' she asked, as she nodded in response to Gabe's comments.

'Index.'

She unwrapped Dom's bloodied hand, keeping some pressure on his index finger. Amongst the dried blood she could see several old scars, which she assumed were from previous knife cuts, and he was missing the very tip of his middle finger too. Carefully she exposed the latest injury, relieved to find that, although the cut was deep and would need stitching, the edges were at least clean and smooth. Dom had obviously been using a sharp knife.

'I will need to stitch this but it's not too difficult,' she said, as she administered a ring block anaesthetic. She didn't want him wriggling while she was trying to stitch the wound. While she waited for the anaesthetic to kick in she got a suturing kit out of the cupboard and opened it up.

'What were you cutting?' she asked, as she checked Dom's finger to see if the anaesthetic had taken effect.

'Carrots for the roast and the knife slipped.'

'Can you feel that?' she asked as she pricked the end of his finger.

Dom shook his head and Sophie threaded the needle and began stitching.

'Can I have a waterproof dressing over that, Doc?' he asked as Gabe snipped the thread for her. 'I need to finish off dinner prep.'

'You're not going back into the kitchen,' she said. 'You've got the rest of the day off. If you keep working, it's likely to keep bleeding. There must be someone else who can chop a few carrots. I can do it if necessary,' she offered.

'I'll take care of the prep,' Gabe told Dom. 'We'll see you in time for the meal.'

Dom was sent to his donga to rest and Sophie followed Gabe to the kitchen. A mountain of vegetables was piled onto the stainless-steel island. Dom didn't appear to have got very far into the pile before tragedy had struck. Sophie sat at the bench and watched Gabe chop and slice his way through the mound. There was no reason for her to stay but she was reluctant to go. She had nothing else she had to do and sitting enjoying his company was preferable to spending time alone in her room.

'How did you go with Alex?' he asked her.

'Good. He said he'll sign me off as competent on a quad bike so now I can go exploring.'

'Not alone, though.' Gabe's brown eyes were serious as he paused in his slicing and dicing to look at her.

'Don't worry, I know. I've had a thorough safety briefing too. But I would like to get out and have a look around,' she said, picking up a vegetable peeler and a potato and starting to peel. They had the kitchen to themselves and if she was going to sit there chatting she might as well work. If she didn't help, she suspected dinner would run very late.

'I'll see what I can do,' Gabe replied. 'We have Sundays off and people usually go somewhere then, weather permitting.'

'Where do they go?'

'There's a penguin colony not far from here, that's where we take most of our new expeditioners for their first trip. The quintessential Antarctic experience.' He smiled at her and Sophie felt a rush of heat through her bones. 'Sometimes a group will go off cross-country skiing or out to one of the huts just for a change of scenery.'

'What do you like to do in your spare time?'

'I don't seem to have a lot of that but I enjoy dusting off the cross-country skis in good weather and I like to potter around in the kitchen too.'

'Do you miss being a chef?'

'Not really. If I want to cook, Dom's always happy to lend me his kitchen.'

'What made you become a chef? Was your mum a good cook or did your family have a restaurant?'

'Why would you think that?'

'People seem to gravitate to what they've been exposed to.'

'So you come from a line of medicos?'

'No.' Sophie smiled. 'I grew up on a farm of sorts. My parents had an apple and pear orchard south of Hobart.'

'Had?'

'They're retired now. They sold the property and moved to Queensland.'

'But you ended up a doctor.'

'It was either that or a vet. When I was at school I always had an animal hospital, and any injured wildlife I found on the property I'd care for. Possums, sugar gliders, the occasional joey. But by the time I had almost finished school I'd decided to study medicine. My grandpa was a doctor so I guess I followed in his footsteps. The orchard was his hobby but my father's passion so I guess the medical gene just skipped a generation. I always wanted to fix animals and people. I still do.' But she hadn't been able to fix Danny. She pushed that thought aside as she finished peeling the last potato and it wasn't until much later that she realised Gabe hadn't answered her question. He hadn't told her why he'd become a chef or what had made him change careers.

Dinner had been cleared away, Dom had retired to his room and Gabe was pretending to read but in reality he was watching Sophie. Alex had challenged her to a game of Scrabble, which was interesting in itself, Gabe had never known him to have an interest in board games, but it wasn't the fact that Alex was playing Scrabble that was fascinating Gabe, it was Sophie. The new doc had really knocked him for a six. He hadn't expected her. He'd expected someone less capable, less attractive and less desirable.

He'd missed her today when she'd been away from the red shed. That in itself was ridiculous. How could he miss someone he barely knew? But already he was used to having her around, already he noticed a hole in his day when she wasn't there to fill it.

He knew he needed to keep his distance in order to keep some perspective.

He laughed to himself. What he really needed was to get laid. It had been too long between women. Maybe that would sort him out. The trouble was it was going to be several more months before he would be back in Australia. It would be several months before he would be able to scratch that itch.

So that meant more cold showers for him but, of course, he had to be living where there were water restrictions. Everything was conspiring against him.

He had deliberately avoided relationships since coming to Antarctica. His last serious relationship had ended three years ago, imploding spectacularly and precipitating his move to the ice. He'd had enough of women and Antarctica had seemed like a pretty good place to go if he wanted to avoid them. He saved his romancing for his leave, a weekend here and there, which meant he was able to avoid anything that could resemble a relationship and, to date, it had been relatively easy. In three years he hadn't met anyone who had tempted him. Until now. Until Sophie.

But if Alex was keen on Sophie too that presented a different problem. Over the past three years he and Alex had formed a strong friendship and, if anyone had asked, Gabe would have said Alex was like a brother to him. But that didn't give him the right to ask what his intentions were or to ask him to back off. Alex knew Gabe's thoughts on relationships and Gabe suspected he would give Gabe his blessing if he knew that Sophie had caught his eye but that wasn't the point.

Sophie was out of bounds. It didn't matter that since she'd arrived on the scene he hadn't been able to stop thinking about her. She had captivated his attention, crept unbidden into his thoughts and interrupted his concentration and made him contemplate breaking his self-imposed rule.

But he knew he was being ridiculous. He knew he had to walk away.

He'd only known her for five days. Surely he could resist her.

Walk away, Gabe.

She wasn't worth risking his heart for. It would only be asking for trouble. At least, that's what he tried to tell himself but every time Sophie smiled and her dimples flashed his resolve was sorely tested.

Toughen up, he told himself, *she's just a woman. There are dozens just like her.*

But as he walked away he wasn't sure that was true.

CHAPTER SIX

Date: March 15th
Temperature: -12°C
Hours of sunlight: 13.0

THE WEATHER HAD closed in again but Sophie didn't mind being cooped up inside. She'd had a couple of outdoor experiences and, while one had been far more relaxed than the other, both had left her exhausted. It was hard work, being outside in this climate. The conditions were much harsher than she'd anticipated and it required a lot of concentration to stay focussed. Indoor tasks were far more familiar to her and came much more naturally. She felt as though she had things under control while she was inside.

She'd been busy for the past couple of days, so busy that she'd even had a day when she hadn't thought about Danny, but she'd refused to feel guilty about it, which made a pleasant change. Maybe coming to the ice would be the cure she was hoping for. Maybe she would be okay.

Along with routine medical care she also needed to schedule a series of health screenings for a few of the crazier expeditioners who were planning on taking part in an outdoor swim—the annual April Fools' Day swim. Sophie couldn't understand what the attraction was in stripping down to a pair of swimmers and jumping into water that was near freezing, neither could she believe that this activity was actually on the station calendar and sanctioned by the AAP, but part of her role in occupational heath and safety meant she had to do health checks on anyone who was planning to participate.

The health checks were relatively straightforward and required her to check general fitness and heart function. There were a dozen expeditioners who had signed up, all men, not surprisingly—women had more sense—and Sophie needed to get started on their checks. Some had made an appointment to see her, others, including Gabe, hadn't as yet.

She sent a reminder email to those who hadn't booked in. To Gabe's she added a note that she'd heard from Dr John, hoping that would encourage him to come and see her. She'd been too busy to think about Danny but not too busy to notice that she hadn't crossed paths with Gabe for a day or two and she'd missed his company. She hadn't yet got to know many people, the crew on the station were busy with their own jobs and her role was relatively independent, broken only by brief periods when she needed to see a patient, but there was no one on her team as such. Alex, Dom, Finn and Gabe were the only ones she'd formed any sort of connection with and she felt most comfortable with Gabe. She liked him and she liked the way he made her feel. Just seeing him could make her smile. He made her feel happy.

Her email worked. Within half an hour Gabe stuck his head into the clinic.

'Hey, Doc.' His greeting was relaxed, no explanation as to why he was there or whether he'd even seen her email.

'Hi. Have you come for your medical check?' Sophie tried to remain calm and collected too but her spirits lifted the moment he smiled at her and her immediate reaction was one of excitement.

'No, I thought you'd be busy. I just wanted to catch up with Doc John's news about his daughter.'

'Did he email you as well?'

'He did but there was a bit of medical jargon in there that didn't make a lot of sense. I thought you could explain what it meant. If you've got time?'

'Sure.' Sophie opened John's email on her computer, thinking she'd focus better if she looked at the screen instead of at Gabe, but his next move distracted her even further. He wheeled a small stool over and sat behind her, looking over her shoulder. She could feel his breath on her neck, little puffs of warm air that made her spine tingle and made the soft hair at the base of her skull stand on end.

She was terribly conscious that he sat just inches behind her. She sat a bit straighter in her chair, trying to put some space between them so she could concentrate, but it took a lot of effort.

'Okay. Marianna's tumour is benign, which is good news. It means it won't spread into other areas of her body but it is quite large and until the surgeons operate they don't really know if they'll be able to get it all out. The question is whether they will be able to excise all of it without doing other damage.'

'If it's benign, does it have to come out?'

'Yes. If they leave it, it will continue to grow and that's not what they want, but surgery itself is a risk. There's always the chance that Marianna won't make it through, which is why John wanted the surgeons to wait until he got home before they operated. In case she doesn't make it.'

'I thought his tone was quite positive in the email he sent me.'

'There's certainly more good news than bad at this

stage, but I think he's keen to have some time at home to support both his wife and daughter while Marianna recovers.'

'The supply ship will leave Hobart around the end of March to make its final trip down here before winter,' Gabe said, 'so he has another couple of weeks to see how things play out before he needs to decide whether or not to get on the ship to come back down here.'

In two weeks she would know if John was returning. She would know if her time here would be short-lived. It was going so fast already. There was so much she wanted to experience, what if she didn't get a chance? She wanted to make the most of every opportunity and that included spending more time with Gabe. To delay him, she decided to ask about the logistics of the swim.

'Have you got time to explain the April Fools' Day swim to me?'

'Sure. What would you like to know?'

'I need to know what the routine is. What's expected of me?'

'Liam and Duncan will dig a pool down by the harbour and they usually get it ready a week or so beforehand so you'll be able to have a look at it in advance. The ice will be at least a metre thick and they'll use the excavator to rip through it to make the pool. The pool is smallish, not that the dimensions matter to you but it'll be a couple of metres wide by about four long. Just big enough to get wet in.'

'What is the water temperature?

'At this time of year it'll be between zero and two degrees Celsius.'

'That's freezing!'

'Not quite. Sea water here freezes at about minus two degrees. Don't worry,' he said with a grin, 'no one stays in for long but for the swim to count they have to put their heads under water. But before we go ahead the conditions have to be right in terms of wind speed. A sunny day with little or, better yet, no wind is ideal.'

'How do people get warm again afterwards?'

'Space blankets and fleece-lined boots,' Gabe told her. 'We set up a small hut next to the pool with a heater. It becomes like a little sauna and everyone hops in there after their dip to dry off and get dressed but there's also a tradition of defrosting in a warm spa later. It gets fired up on special occasions.'

'Has anyone ever had a medical emergency?' Sophie knew the shock of jumping into an icy-cold pool could be enough to trigger cardiac arrest in some cases.

'No, but John did take the defibrillator with him last year.'

'Great, that's reassuring.'

'Better to be safe than sorry.'

'Better not to do the swim at all, I would have thought,' Sophie retorted, and Gabe laughed. She was glad she was needed on standby and therefore not under any pressure to join in the swim.

'Where would the fun be in that?'

'It sounds like you're still planning on joining in?'

'I am.'

She raised an eyebrow. 'So shall I do your check-up now then?'

'No, I can wait. I've taken up enough of your day.'

'I've got time and I'm guessing you do too. You seem to have plenty of time to chat so let's get it out of the way.'

Gabe shrugged and gave in. 'All right, you're the boss. Where would you like me?'

'Take your shirt off and have a seat on the bed,' she said, as she turned to pull his file out of the cabinet. When she turned back she found he had done as she'd asked and was sitting on the bed, bare-chested.

She was staring straight at his broad shoulders and tanned chest. His pectoral muscles were lightly covered with dark hair that trailed down to his navel, dividing a toned six-pack and leading her eyes lower. She hadn't really thought this through. She was an experienced doctor, and so was used to seeing naked or semi-naked men, but for some reason the sight of Gabe sitting bare-chested in front of her set her pulse racing. He was very male and his hard, solid body threw her into a state of confusion.

Danny had been muscular but lean and wiry and what little chest hair he'd had had been fair. Gabe was such a contrast to what Sophie was used to and seeing him in all his glory was really confusing her. Her memories of Danny were becoming jumbled and that unsettled her.

She swallowed and tried to think of something to say that sounded professional. After all, it was just a routine physical examination. If she could just remember that.

'Any medical history that I should be aware of?'

Gabe shook his head.

'No family history of high blood pressure or cardiac problems?' she asked, as she opened out the automatic blood-pressure cuff. And that presented her with another dilemma. She hadn't thought about having to touch him. The feel of his bare skin under her fingers as she wrapped the sphygmomanometer cuff around his arm set her nerves on fire and she had to focus hard to stop her hands from shaking.

Her reaction reminded her of the first time she'd had to examine a cute, nearly naked twenty-something man when she'd been a med student. She'd blushed and stammered her way through the exam then too. But she wasn't a med student any longer, she was an experienced doctor, and she should be able to examine a man without losing her cool or her concentration.

She wasn't a student and Gabe was definitely not a twenty-year-old youth. He was all man. There was no disputing that. She needed to focus.

She was a professional. She needed to act like one.

She turned away while the blood-pressure cuff inflated. She picked up a stethoscope. She didn't need it to take his blood pressure, the machine would do that automatically, but she would need it to listen to his chest, and it gave her a reason to step away, gave her something to do while she got her hormones under control.

The machine beeped at her and she returned to Gabe's side. 'BP and pulse normal,' she told him as she switched off the machine and unwrapped the cuff.

She placed the bulb of the stethoscope onto his chest. His pecs were well defined, his chest was solid and his stomach was flat with ridges of abdominals. His physique was undoubtedly masculine but she tried to convince herself he was just another patient as she ran her eyes over his smooth, olive skin.

'Deep breaths, in and out through your nose for me,' she said, as she moved the stethoscope around and tried to ignore the fluttering in her stomach.

She bent her head as she listened to his breathing and she could feel each one of his exhalations as a soft puff of air on her cheek. She closed her eyes and found herself breathing in time with him.

When she lifted her head and opened her eyes as she finished listening she found herself staring into his chocolate-brown gaze. Their lips were millimetres apart. If she tipped her chin just the slightest fraction she would be able to taste him. She held herself still, terrified that if she moved she wouldn't be able to resist pressing her lips to his.

She held herself rigid as Gabe lifted his hands and plucked the stethoscope from her ears. His hands brushed her cheeks and Sophie held her breath as he looped the stethoscope around her neck.

He leaned towards her. Was he going to kiss her? There could only be a space the width of a butterfly wing between their lips and she swore it must be one of the butterflies that had escaped from her belly.

She knew he was about to kiss her but at the very last moment she chickened out, turning her head and stepping away. She couldn't do this. She didn't know how.

She'd never let a man take control like this. Without uttering a word, she could feel him pulling her in. Seducing her. But she didn't know how to let go. She didn't know how to let herself be seduced.

She had lost her virginity to Danny but they had been friends first. There had been nothing uncomfortable about it but there had also been no seduction. For she and Danny it had just been the next logical step and that was how it had felt. That first time had been good but hadn't set her world on fire or her heart alight, but somehow she knew that getting to close to Gabe would be different. Getting close to Gabe would be flirting with danger, playing with fire, and she would most likely get burnt.

She had no experience in this adult game of lust and desire. She'd been safe with Danny but Gabe felt dangerous. While she felt she could trust him to keep her from any physical danger, matters of the flesh were a different story.

She stepped back on shaky legs and her hands shook too as she picked up a heart-rate monitor and tried to ignore what had just passed between them.

'Time for your fitness test,' she said, and her voice

wavered and wobbled as nervousness combined with breathlessness.

She handed him the monitor. He'd have to strap it around his own chest, she wasn't game. She needed some distance, some time to gather her thoughts, and doing the fitness test now would buy her some valuable time.

'So, how'd I do?' he asked without a trace of breathlessness as she slowed the treadmill down after ten minutes.

Her heart rate had recovered while Gabe had walked on the treadmill but she suspected it would still be beating faster than his. 'Unfortunately, you're as fit as a fiddle.' If she'd been able to fail him he wouldn't have been able to take part in the swim, a result she would have been happy with.

'I'm good to go, then?'

'I guess so but that doesn't mean I condone this exercise. I'd like it on record that I think it's a stupid idea.'

'I can't say I disagree with you, Doc.'

'Then why on earth are you planning on going ahead with this?'

'It's a tradition and, as station leader, I feel I need to take part. These types of activities, while possibly stupid, are good for team bonding and morale. The sort of thing that men need to take part in, especially when we're down here for months on end with only a few people, it's important to foster team spirit.'

'But what about the safety aspect? Don't you think it's important to be mindful of that?'

'That's why it's compulsory to have these health checks first. Alex will take care of the logistics of the exercise and he takes his responsibilities very seriously. Provided he and I think the activity is safe on the day in terms of the weather conditions, the site and everyone's physical fitness, we'll consider it a low-risk activity and I'm prepared to put my hand up and join in. They're my team and I like to lead from the front.'

That fitted perfectly with what she'd surmised about Gabe's personality so far. He was someone who would have your back, someone strong and dependable. She'd seen how he treated everyone with respect and the respect they gave him in return. He was just the sort of man you'd want to have on your team.

'You'll get the final say on the day,' he reassured her. 'You'll get a chance to double-check our BPs, heart rates and anything else you want before we jump in. You'll have to trust Alex and me to take care of the rest. Deal?'

His dark brown eyes locked onto hers. He was so calm and convincing. So dependable. Everyone else at the station seemed to trust him implicitly and from everything she had seen so far she had no reason to doubt his word. Until she had reason to think otherwise, she would continue to trust him too.

She stuck out her hand. 'Deal.'

Gabe took her hand in his and as his fingers wrapped around hers she knew she could trust him, she just wasn't sure she could trust herself.

CHAPTER SEVEN

Date: March 17th
Temperature: -11°C
Hours of sunlight: 12.7

SOPHIE HID IN the clinic for the next two days, using her diary as a shield. She had appointments booked solid. Not only did she have to see the expeditioners who were planning on joining in the April Fools' Day swim but many were due for their regular bimonthly health checks as well. In order to get through all the appointments, she offered to see expeditioners in their lunchtime, giving her a reason to take a late or early lunch and therefore avoid Gabe.

She was finding it difficult to get the image of a semi-naked Gabe out of her head, and their almost-kiss, and she was worried about behaving normally around him. Her plan was to avoid him for a few days in the hope that the picture would fade and she'd be back to normal. Then she might be able to trust herself not to embarrass either of them.

She managed to fill her spare time too, either by reading or by hiding in the hydroponics shed, where she'd volunteered her time, but there was no escaping Saturday-night activities. Psychologists who had made a career of studying people who were subjected to long periods of working in isolation, including at Antarctic stations, had recommended a weekly activity as a way of breaking up the routine, or sometimes the monotony, of life on the ice. This was particularly important over the winter season when the expeditioners couldn't necessarily get outside. The Saturday-night festivities gave them all something to look forward to and a reason to socialise, and Sophie knew she'd be expected to join in.

One thing she was looking forward to after ten days on the ice was dressing in something a bit smarter than a T-shirt and leggings or scrubs. A couple of women who had worked on the ice before her had suggested that she pack a couple of skirts or dresses to be worn on Saturday nights. Everyone made a bit more of an effort, again mostly to break the monotony and differentiate the weekend from the rest of the week, but it felt good to bathe and wash her hair with a purpose in mind, rather than just because it was her turn to have a shower.

Carey station always tried to find something to celebrate on a Saturday night and this Saturday was tailor made for a celebration—it was St Patrick's Day.

Sophie dressed in a soft, emerald-green silk dress. Sleeveless with a belted waist and a skirt that fell in narrow pleats, it was one of her favourites. It made her eyes look exceptionally green and always made her feel confident. It had seemed a luxury when she'd packed it but it had rolled up so small that she'd convinced herself she had room for it and she was glad she'd brought it. She left her hair loose and it fell in thick, dark waves past her shoulders. She brushed some green eye shadow over her lids and moistened her lips with a pale pink gloss as she tried to ignore the thought that she might be dressing for Gabe.

The dining room had been decorated and Dom, who after agreeing to take one day off after his incident with the knife, was back in the kitchen, cooking up an Irish feast, which meant lots of potatoes and lamb and Guinness. Irish flags decorated the walls and someone had cut enormous four-leaf clovers out of green plastic and decorated the tables.

Everyone was expected to wear something green and everyone appeared to have made an extra effort with their outfits. Alex had a gigantic green top hat perched on his blond curls and Finn looked dapper in a green velvet smoking jacket. Where that had come from and why he'd have it in Antarctica Sophie vowed to find out, until she was distracted by Gabe and forgot all about Finn.

He was wearing snug denim jeans with a rich green polo shirt that hugged his chest and arms. He wasn't dressed up as elaborately as some of the others but he looked gorgeous. The shirt made the most of his toned physique and she could picture exactly what was underneath it. It had seemed ridiculous to pack a dress but she was glad now that she had. Gabe looked fantastic and suddenly Sophie wanted to look her best too.

Dinner was self-service and as Sophie picked up a plate and stood in line, Gabe stepped in behind her.

'Happy St Paddy's Day, Doc,' he greeted her as he reached past to grab a plate. He seemed calm and relaxed as usual and it was probably just coincidence that he was beside her but her senses were heightened. He smelt fresh and clean and Sophie had a sudden urge to lean a little closer to fully appreciate his scent.

'What category have you nominated for in the Annual Paddy's darts and pool competition?' he asked, as the line moved slowly forwards.

'Category?'

'We have a darts and billiards competition as part of

the night's festivities. The sign-up sheet has been on the notice-board for a couple of days. Haven't you seen it?'

Sophie shook her head. 'It doesn't sound like my kind of thing.'

'Everyone is expected to nominate for one or the other,' he told her. 'Finn is the current darts champion and Alex is the pool champ. Challengers play against each other to win the right to challenge the champion.'

'I can't imagine doing either. I'm hopeless at all sports.'

'You have to put your name down for something. This is what's at stake.' At the end of one of the tables were two huge trophies, which had been engraved with the names of past champions around their bases. 'So, which will it be?'

'It will have to be pool, not darts,' she told him. 'You definitely don't want to be around if I'm throwing sharp, pointy things.'

Gabe laughed and steered her past the notice-board and waited while she added her name to the list.

The competition got under way as soon as dinner was finished. The Guinness was flowing, along with plenty of red wine, and it didn't take much encouragement from the crowd to convince Liam to get his violin out and play some music to accompany the games. Liam played the violin like a fiddle and a couple of the scientists gave a reasonable demonstration of some Irish dancing as Sophie waited for her turn at the pool table.

Her opponent was Andrew, an engineer. 'Would you like to rack or break?' he asked.

'I have no idea what you're talking about.'

'Racking is just what we call it when you set the balls up at the beginning of the game, using this.' Andrew was holding a plastic triangle in his hand. 'Breaking just means having the first shot to break up the rack. If I rack, you'll break,' he explained.

That didn't make things any clearer for her but as she didn't know if there was a right and wrong way to rack the balls but thought she could probably manage to hit one if they were all grouped together, she replied, 'I think I'll break.'

Watching him rack the balls and chalk his cue, she suspected he'd done this before. She had never played and as she wondered what she'd got herself into, Gabe arrived at her side. 'Do you think I should just forfeit now and get it over with?' she asked him.

'I didn't think you'd be the type to roll over quite so easily.'

He was right. It wasn't in her nature to give up at the first hurdle. 'I'm not,' she agreed, before asking, 'So which stick do I use, then?'

'It's called a "cue",' Gabe explained as he selected one for her and rubbed a small chalk block over the end, just as Andrew had done.

'What's that for?'

'It stops the cue from slipping off the ball,' he replied as he handed her the stick.

Sophie reached for the cue, taking it before Gabe had released it. Her hand closed over the top of his and a surge of adrenalin ran through her. She could feel her hand shake and wondered how she would ever be able to hit the ball now. She swallowed hard and tried to ignore the heat that was pooling in her belly. All she could see in her mind's eye was the image of semi-naked Gabe, stripped down to his waist, bare-chested and sitting in her clinic. She stepped back and tried to focus on the green of his shirt instead of thinking back to the last image she had of him when he'd been semi-naked and about to kiss her. She turned away and tried to focus on the green felt of the pool table and concentrate on the game.

She rested her left hand on the surface of the table, like she thought she'd seen others do, and standing upright she tried to line up a shot.

'Here, do it like this.' Having relinquished the cue, Gabe was now standing behind her. 'Lean over the table and put your left hand like this.' He demonstrated the position and Sophie did as instructed, only to find that he was leaning over her shoulder and readjusting her position. 'Look down the line of the cue and take aim.'

Gabe's left arm was stretched out alongside hers. His right arm wrapped around her back and guided her hand on the cue. She tried to ignore the fact that her bottom was pressed into Gabe's groin but her silk dress was so flimsy she could feel his body heat pulsing through the thin fabric.

Once Gabe seemed confident that she had the correct stance, he stepped back. Sophie let out her breath, closed her eyes and hoped for the best. Somehow she managed to connect with the white ball and sent it crashing into the coloured balls, scattering them across the table.

'Not bad, Doc,' Gabe said.

Andrew took his shot and Sophie watched as a coloured ball fell into a corner pocket. She was wondering what she should do for her turn when Andrew lined up for a second shot.

'Isn't it my turn?' she asked Gabe.

'Not until Andrew misses,' he replied. 'If you pot a ball, you get another turn.'

Andrew's next shot missed the pocket so Sophie started to line up. The black ball looked as if it was in a good spot but Gabe stopped her. 'Stay away from the black ball.'

'Why?'

'That's the money ball but you can't sink it until you've got all your other ones in. You're smalls,' he said.

'I'm what?' She felt as though Gabe and Andrew were

speaking a foreign language. None of this made any sense. No wonder she hated sports.

'You have to try to sink the seven solid colour balls, the ones with the low numbers. If you hit one of Andrew's first or sink one of his by mistake he'll get an extra shot. If you sink the black one before all your others, Andrew wins. Aim for the yellow one.' Sophie lined the shot up but Gabe obviously thought she could do better. He leaned over her right shoulder and wrapped his arms around her as he corrected the angle of her shot, and Sophie thought she'd perhaps been too hasty in her dislike of all sports. She might learn to enjoy pool. 'Don't hit it too hard, just try to push it down the table towards the back pocket.'

Somehow she managed to pull off the shot and the yellow ball tumbled into the pocket. 'Good work!' Gabe said, and he high-fived her, but her new-found enjoyment of the game slowly dissipated as the rest of her balls languished on the table while Andrew sank three more.

'I don't think this is my game.'

'Don't worry. Andrew's clearing the table. It'll make it easier for you.' Gabe laughed.

Andrew had sunk five of his balls before Sophie got another one in. In a burst of excitement and delight she threw her arms around Gabe's neck and hugged him. He lifted her off her feet. 'Well done. I knew you'd get the hang of this.'

But that was the end of her success. Once Gabe released her she couldn't focus at all. Having Gabe's arms around her had put her into a spin. She felt giddy and off balance but in a good way. She felt excited and desirable. Alive.

The spark wasn't adrenalin. It wasn't circumstances or her imagination. There was most definitely chemistry. But while it made her feel good, she didn't think she could, or should, do anything about it. She wasn't ready for that.

She missed everything from that point on and Andrew wasted no time in finishing off the game. She stayed to watch Gabe as he challenged Andrew next. He wasn't doing any better than she had—well, he did sink more balls but still not enough to win—but she was only vaguely aware of how he'd done as she'd been completely distracted by the sight of his bum in his jeans as he'd leant over the table. She occasionally remembered to watch Andrew or turn her attention to the darts contest but her eye was constantly returning to Gabe.

She was lonely, she knew it, and while she didn't plan on being alone for the rest of her life, that was different than mistaking loneliness for attraction. She didn't want to make a mistake just because she was lonely.

In the background she was aware of Liam's music continuing. She recognised the opening notes of 'Danny Boy' and then Dom joined in with the lyrics.

This had been their song, hers and Danny's, and she hadn't listened to it in seven months.

She'd always loved this song, she'd used to sing it to Danny but now she found the haunting, lilting strains sorrowful as memories of Danny flooded back to her. She knew she wouldn't be able to listen to this song now without crying, and she definitely didn't want to cry in front of everyone. She escaped to her room, leaving Gabe and Andrew to finish their game.

Back in her donga Sophie rebooted her laptop. She needed to see Danny's face. Thinking about Danny made her feel guilty for the attraction she felt towards Gabe because if she closed her eyes right now it wasn't Danny's face she saw. Semi-naked, smiling Gabe was still the vision that sprang to mind. She'd had that image in her head for the past couple of days and bending over the pool table with

Gabe's arms around her was doing nothing to tone it down. She needed to see Danny. To reconnect.

Before the computer could come to life there was a knock on her door. Sophie glanced in the mirror. She looked a mess. Her eyes were watery and her nose was red. She quickly blew her nose before opening the door.

Gabe stood in front of her. 'You all right, Doc?'

Perhaps she looked worse than she'd thought. She wasn't all right but she nodded anyway and started to make excuses. 'I'm not normally such a basket case but that song reminded me of Danny.'

'Your husband?'

She nodded and stepped back, giving Gabe space to enter her room. She didn't want to talk about Danny while standing in the doorway. Did she want to talk about him at all?

Her donga, all the dongas, were small and she was very aware of Gabe and how much room he filled. She sat cross-legged at the head of her bed to give herself some breathing space. Gabe sat at the opposite end. There wasn't anywhere for him *to* sit other than the small chair at her desk and she had clothes draped all over that.

'Are you sure you're okay?' he asked again.

She shook her head. 'I'm fine. Just every now and then something will catch me unawares. I just felt a little bit sad.'

'Is that Danny?'

Her laptop had finally decided to wake up and her screensaver showed the photo of Danny. He was watching them with his goofy smile on his face.

Sophie didn't want him watching them. She didn't want him to watch Gabe sitting on her bed. She reached out and closed the lid.

'Do you want to talk about him?'

'Why?'

'If you're missing him, it might be nice to have someone to talk to about him. Why don't you tell me something? How did you meet?'

Perhaps it would help to talk about him. Perhaps it would make his memory clearer. Maybe it would lessen her guilt.

Was she finally healing or was she forgetting?

She wasn't sure but wasn't this what she'd wanted? A chance to start over? Could she do this? Could she talk about Danny to the only other man who took her breath away?

She met Gabe's brown gaze and prepared to give it a go.

'I'd known Danny practically all my life. We met on the first day of high school when we were assigned each other as lab partners in science class. Danny wanted to test the boundaries even back then and I had to rein him in to stop him from blowing us all to smithereens. That set the pattern for our relationship right from the start. He was always on the go, experimenting, trying different things, I was always the conservative one who followed the rules, but he did encourage me to test my own limits.

'I don't really remember not knowing him. I don't remember what I was like before I met him and that's why it's been so hard to find myself now that he's gone. So much of me is tied up with Danny and I'm not really sure who I am without him.

'He was so fearless. He never doubted himself. He never thought there was something he couldn't do and he made me feel the same way. He gave me the confidence to test myself.'

That was something she'd noticed in Gabe too. Both men seemed to have the ability to bolster her self-confidence. On a couple of occasions when she'd been nervous or out of her depth all Gabe had needed to do had been look at her with his dark brown eyes and she'd instantly felt more capable. But she was talking about Danny now.

'He gave me confidence and I kept him safe. Until one day I couldn't.'

'You couldn't? I thought he died in a road accident.'

Gabe's comment surprised her. She hadn't realised he would be privy to that information.

'It's a note in your file,' he explained apologetically.

'He was bike riding when a reckless driver crashed into him, but if I hadn't taken an extra shift at work to cover for someone who called in sick he would have been home with me. He would have been safe. But instead our lives were changed in an instant.'

'It wasn't your fault.'

'Wasn't it?' She still grappled with the guilt and she thought she might always feel that way. She didn't know how to get past that feeling.

'Is that when you applied to come here? After he died?'

She nodded. 'I'd been working at the AMU for a while but hadn't thought about actually coming to Antarctica until Danny was killed. Danny had sparked my sense of adventure and I decided that coming to the ice would be a good goal to focus on. Getting here gave me something to strive for, a reason to keep going. Because of Dr John's situation it all happened a bit faster than I expected but I have no regrets. It's what I wanted to do, it's where I want to be.

'Back in Hobart every day someone would ask how I was doing. People seemed to expect me not to cope. It was like I was expected to be in a permanent state of grief. It wasn't healthy. It felt like I wasn't allowed to get on with my life. It made me feel guilty for wanting to move on and that was on top of the guilt I already felt over the accident. I needed to get away and when the opportunity came up to relieve John down here I jumped at it. It was my chance to leave my old life for a while, a chance to start afresh. I wanted to be where people didn't know about my history. Being here is about me starting over again.'

Gabe was smiling and immediately Sophie could feel her sadness lifting. 'That's why most people come here,' he said. 'To get away from everyday life. Antarctica is the last frontier. We're like the Australian explorers in the eighteen hundreds or the American pioneers. But a lot of us bring our problems with us. It's not easy to run away completely.'

'I'm not running away but I can't stay in the past. Life goes on. Danny would be the first person to tell me that I need to keep living. I thought coming here would give me a chance to move on. I thought that by being somewhere where no one knew me as one half of Danny and Sophie I would cope better. I didn't expect to have reminders of Danny here. I don't want to forget about him but I can't live the rest of my life mourning him.'

'You're willing to have another go?'

'At love?'

Gabe nodded.

'Yes. I don't believe there's only one person for everybody. I know there's not. I'd planned to spend the rest of my life with Danny and that isn't how things have turned out, but I don't believe that's it for me. I refuse to believe it. I'm thirty-one, I don't want to be on my own for the rest of my life. I came here to learn how to be on my own again but I don't want to be on my own for ever.' She shrugged. 'I have to hope love comes along again one day. Do you see things differently? Do you think people have one soul mate and one only?'

'I have no idea how it works.'

'Have you ever been in love?' she asked.

'Not very successfully.'

'What does that mean?'

'It means I'm better off alone.'

'No one is better off alone,' she argued. 'Not for ever.'

'I am.'

'Gee, someone really did a number on you.' She wondered what his story was. 'Were you married?'

'No.' Gabe was shaking his head. 'But she was.'

'She was married? And you didn't know?'

'Of course not.'

'Ouch.' Sophie didn't know if Gabe was deliberately trying to distract her by redirecting the conversation but he was doing a pretty good job. Her curiosity was piqued. 'When was this?'

'A long time ago.'

'And you've been on your own ever since?'

'No man is an island,' he replied with a grin, 'but I have avoided anything serious since then and I've found I'm quite happy with the alternative.'

'Don't you get lonely? Don't you want to find your other half? The person who really understands you and knows you intimately and loves you anyway?'

'I don't believe in all that. Exposing yourself to another person like that makes you vulnerable. You open yourself up to a world of pain.'

'What exactly did this woman do to you!? What happened that made you so pessimistic about true love?'

'Apart from lying about her marital status, you mean?'

'Apart from that.' Sophie smiled. 'I get why you might take umbrage at being lied to but you can't tar all women with the same brush. We're not all scheming liars. I can't imagine you'd let that put you off ever dating seriously again.'

'You're right. But that wasn't the only thing she was

lying about. She wasn't single or divorced or even separated, she was still very much married, which she'd neglected to mention, and she told me that she spent her weeks off helping her sister care for elderly parents.'

'Another lie?'

Gabe nodded.

'How did she keep her other life a secret?' Sophie asked.

'It was easy, I guess. This was when I was working on the mines and so was she. She worked the same roster as me, two weeks on, two off.'

'And how did you find out the truth?'

'After we'd been dating a while I suggested that we spend our fortnight off together. I'd go with her to meet her parents. She argued against it but I thought I'd surprise her anyway. Turned out I was the one who was surprised. There were no elderly parents but there was a husband—'

'And she never had any intention of leaving him?' Sophie interrupted.

'I don't know. I didn't hang around to find out.'

'You gave up without a fight?' That didn't fit with the Gabe she saw. She liked to imagine him fighting for something he believed in.

'Zara had a husband and a couple of kids. There was no way I was going to be responsible for splitting up a family. My father had an affair when I was quite young. He broke my mother's heart and broke our family apart. Mum never recovered and I didn't want to be the guy who would do that to another family. I didn't want to be my father.'

His story began to make a little more sense now. 'So what did you do?'

'I quit the mine, moved here and tried to put it as far behind me as I could. I told you most of us are running away from something, and that includes me. I'm the last one to give advice on how you need to process what has happened to you and how you should be feeling, so are you sure you don't want me to arrange for you to talk to someone?'

'Talk to someone? Like a psychiatrist, you mean?' Sophie smiled. Maybe Gabe really thought she had lost the plot.

'I was thinking more along the lines of a counsellor.'

'No,' she said, shaking her head. 'Thank you, but I'll be okay. Just remind me to stay away from the red wine while I'm here. Two glasses is obviously making me a bit emotional.'

'Well, if you don't need a counsellor but you just need a friendly hug, I'm here, all right?'

Gabe stood up and Sophie felt like taking him up on his offer right then and there. She could use another one of his hugs but she knew it was dangerous. It was too much too soon and she didn't want to make a mistake. She couldn't afford to fan the spark of attraction just yet. She didn't think she was ready to cope with the consequences.

'Thank you, I'll remember that,' she said, as she saw him to her door.

He'd offered to listen but she didn't think he was ready to hear all her innermost secrets. But she needed to talk to someone. She lifted the lid of her laptop, waking it from its slumber. 'What should I do?' she asked Danny's photo. 'I don't want to forget you, I *won't* forget you, but it felt good to be in Gabe's arms. Is that wrong?'

She picked up the computer and sat it on her lap on her bed. 'Is it too soon to have thoughts like this? Am I reading more into this than I should? What do you think, Danny? Would you like him? I certainly hope I'm not on my own for the rest of my life but should I jump in?'

Danny smiled silently back at her.

'I'm being foolish, aren't I? Gabe hasn't asked me to

jump anywhere. But you would tell me that life goes on. That's something I know you would say. But how soon?'

Sophie shook her head. 'You can't decide for me, can you? It's up to me. I can do whatever I want but I guess if I'm asking for your opinion then maybe I'm not ready. Being here is enough of an adventure. I don't need to complicate things.'

She sighed and shut the laptop. This stint in Antarctica was about her starting again. As a single woman. But when she climbed into bed and closed her eyes it wasn't Danny's goofy smile that she saw. It was a smiling, semi-naked Gabe who kissed her goodnight.

CHAPTER EIGHT

Date: April 1st
Temperature: -15°C
Hours of sunlight: 10.9

To Sophie's dismay, the weather had been declared perfect for the April Fools' Day swim by Gabe, Alex and Michelle, the station's resident meteorologist. Sophie had been hoping it would be delayed as she still wasn't convinced this was a fun, safe, team-bonding activity. It seemed like the sort of silly thing men dreamed up when they were bored, but she had learnt to keep her opinion to herself. Nobody was going to listen to her and unless she declared them all unfit the challenge would take place at some point, if not today then the next perfect day.

She packed up the medical equipment she would need ready to be transported down to the swimming hole at the harbour.

It was a glorious day. Crisp and clear with blue skies and no wind. Goggles were not required but sunglasses were a must. She wore her cold-weather jacket, as had become her habit, but even she didn't need the hood. Either she was acclimatising or the weather was magnificent.

She had checked out the swimming hole a few days earlier to familiarise herself with the situation but she barely recognised it today. Someone had been busy. Inflatable palm trees stood like sentinels at one end and a ladder emerged from the sea water at the opposite end. Folding, plastic beach chairs had been lined up along one edge for the spectators and there was even an inflatable polar bear reclining in one of the chairs. Dom was flipping eggs on the barbecue for bacon and egg muffins and Michelle was making hot chocolate. Anyone who wasn't crazy enough to be taking part in the swim was there to cheer on the hardy souls. There was a celebratory feeling in the air and Sophie found her mood lifting. It was hard to be completely serious when everyone else was getting into the spirit of the occasion.

Alex was the official safety officer and he was stationed by the edge of the hole.

'At least you're sensible,' Sophie said to him.

'Nah, it's just my turn to sit this one out. Someone has to take charge,' he told her in his strong Aussie accent, and Sophie rolled her eyes and decided she was the only sane one in the medical team.

'Just relax, Doc, everything is under control,' he continued, as he picked up a rope and started knotting a loop into one end.

'What's that for?' she asked.

'Before anyone jumps in, I have to tie a rope around them in case I need to pull them out in an emergency. It also means there's no danger of them getting pulled under the ice by any currents or tides.'

The swimming hole looked so much like a pool that Sophie had forgotten it was actually part of the ocean. Her tension kicked up again as she imagined someone being swept out to sea, but before she could voice any concern Alex distracted her.

'Here they come,' he said, and Sophie turned to see a

motley assortment of expeditioners emerging from the temporary hut to parade down to the pool. She'd done a quick, second health check earlier that morning, but the guys had obviously spent the intervening time getting dressed up for the occasion. Finn was wearing board shorts, flippers, a mask and snorkel, Gabe had on a Hawaiian shirt with floral shorts and rubber flip-flops, but Liam took the cake with his mankini outfit. They looked completely ridiculous, so much so that Sophie actually relaxed enough to smile. They looked as though they were headed for the Sydney Mardi Gras, not an icy swim at the bottom of the world.

Finn was first up and he didn't waste any time slipping Alex's rope under his arms and around his chest and jumping in.

'How's the water?' someone called out.

'Friggin' freezing,' came his reply, before he ducked his head under and quickly scrambled out of the pool. One by one they all took their turns and Sophie relaxed more and more as the swims progressed without any disasters.

Finally, only Gabe and Andrew remained.

'You haven't changed your mind, Doc?' Gabe asked, as Andrew stripped down to his shorts.

'About what?'

'The swim. Did you want to join in?'

'Are you kidding?' she said, as Alex tightened the rope around Andrew's chest. 'I'm all for living in the moment but I'm not crazy.'

Andrew jumped into the swimming hole, ducked his head under the water and surfaced beside the ladder. It looked as though he would set the record for the fastest swim of the day but before he could climb out a second head bobbed up out of the water right in front of the ladder.

There was a collective gasp from the crowd as they saw that a Weddell seal had decided to join in the fun.

Andrew turned to grab hold of the ladder and came face to face with the seal. Both the animal and Andrew were equally surprised. The seal dived under the water as Andrew threw himself backwards. He swallowed a mouthful of sea water in the process and sank under the ice.

Alex didn't give him a chance to resurface in his own time. He tugged forcefully on the rope and pulled him back into the swimming hole, clear of the icy shelf. Andrew came out of the water, coughing and spluttering, as Alex hauled him over to the ladder. He managed to get himself out of the pool but he was shivering violently and Sophie wasted no time in hustling him back to the hut to check his obs and get him warmed up again.

Gabe followed them. He wrapped two space blankets around Andrew as Sophie checked his temperature, pulse and blood pressure.

'He's fine,' she told Gabe. 'You'd better go and have your turn before you chicken out.'

By the time Gabe returned from his swim she had sent Andrew back to the red shed to warm up properly.

'How was it?' she asked.

'Cold,' he said, but he was grinning widely and didn't look too uncomfortable. He certainly looked as though he'd fared better than Andrew. He grabbed a towel and Sophie was fascinated by the flexing of his muscles in his chest and arms as he vigorously rubbed himself dry. His wet shorts clung to his legs, showcasing the length and muscle tone. This was the most Sophie had seen of him but she was about to see some more.

He stripped off his shorts to reveal a pair of black trunks that moulded to his sculpted butt. He wrapped his towel around his waist and put his shirt back on, followed by his cold-weather jacket, before swapping his towel for tracksuit pants, until suddenly he was covered up again.

'You look like you enjoyed yourself,' she said, as he sat down beside her to pull on his boots. 'I'm almost sorry I've missed the opportunity. It feels like I might have missed a chance to have a real Antarctic experience.'

'We do another swim in midwinter, on the solstice, you could stay for that.'

Sophie laughed and shook her head. 'I said I was *almost* sorry I missed it. Besides, I won't be here then. You probably haven't had time to check but there was an email from John this morning, confirming that Marianna's surgery was successful and he's planning on returning to Carey on the *Explorer Australis*. He'll be back in three or four weeks.'

Sophie had been disappointed to read John's email. She felt as though she'd barely arrived and she was worried she wasn't going to have time to really experience the ice. She needed to go home a different person.

'So, you're on the downhill stretch?'

'Mmm-hmm.'

'Well, I might have a solution for part of your problem. I'm heading back to the shed for a spa. Why don't you join me? It'll be the closest thing you'll get to the swim.'

'There's really a spa?' She could remember Gabe mentioning it but she couldn't recall seeing one.

'Yep. It's outdoors, just like the swim but the good news is it's heated. It gets fired up on special occasions and this might be your only chance so it would be a shame to miss out on that too. It's quite relaxing.'

Sophie didn't know about relaxing. She was finding it hard to let go when she was wearing almost nothing and sitting mere inches from Gabe, who was also wearing the bare minimum. Even though she'd used all of her fifty-five-kilogram luggage allowance, she hadn't thought to pack bathers so she was wearing a singlet top and a pair of black knickers. She'd tucked her necklace and wedding rings inside the singlet—out of sight, out of mind—but she needn't have bothered. She didn't have room in her head for too many thoughts. Gabe had put his shorts back on but she was very aware of him. It was hard not to be when he took up so much space in the small spa and their knees kept bumping into each other.

Sophie tried to keep to her side of the circular spa but the bubbles and jets had a tendency to push her towards Gabe. Eventually she decided to stop fighting it and let her knees rest against his.

'Are you still regretting missing out on the swim?' he asked her.

'Not really,' she admitted. 'I'm not convinced I would have handled it but there are other things I'd really like to do before I leave. Do you think I'll have a chance to see something away from the station?'

Even though Alex had given his approval for her to operate a quad bike, she still hadn't had time or the opportunity to get out and about.

'The forecast for this week looks good. I have to check a couple of huts before winter really sets in so why don't you come with me?'

The words were out of his mouth before he'd had time to think about what he was asking. He could have easily sent Duncan, the carpenter. In fact, he'd normally send Duncan and one of the mechanics together, but he knew why he was offering—he wanted to spend some time alone with Sophie. Knowing she was now on the countdown to the end of her time in Antarctica made him think about not missing his opportunities. That thought, plus the sensation of her knee against his, made him throw his normal caution to the wind.

He watched her, waiting for her reply. She had piled her hair on top of her head to stop it from getting wet but some tendrils had escaped from the messy bun and the heat of the spa made them curl around her face. She looked young. And beautiful. He'd thought that the first time he'd laid eyes on her too but he'd had other concerns that day. He'd been worried that the AAP were sending him a novice and he knew that he'd judged a book by its cover then. She had been too thin, too beautiful and too young and he had feared the worst. But she'd proved him wrong, showing skills and resilience he hadn't expected and intriguing him along the way. She'd bewitched him with her dimples and her strength of character.

Because of Sophie he'd changed his mind about a lot of things over the past three and a half weeks. Time had become divided in his head to time spent with Sophie and time spent without her. He was normally so cautious but he felt comfortable with her and he could feel her getting under his guard. He knew he should walk away but he couldn't bring himself to do it.

'You look less than impressed, Doc. Doesn't that sound tempting?' he asked, when she didn't immediately jump at his offer.

'I don't want to seem ungrateful but I was hoping for more of an experience, something a bit more…'

'Exciting?'

She looked up at him, lifting her chin and elongating her elegant neck. She was smiling as she replied, 'Interesting.'

She lengthened the word as she ran her eyes over him and he could swear he felt the pressure of her knee increase ever so slightly against his. Was she flirting with him?

'My company's not enough?' he replied, as he fought the urge to pull her towards him and kiss her rosy lips.

'I could have your company at dinner every night without trekking out to look at some huts.'

Yes, she could, and to his ears that sounded pretty enticing, but perhaps she needed more of an incentive. He wanted to spend time with her but that didn't mean that she felt the same way.

'What if I told you that the hut is quite close to a penguin colony and if we're lucky they won't have headed out to sea for the winter yet?'

'That sounds more like it.' She smiled and her dimples winked at him, making him feel like he'd just been awarded a prize. He didn't even worry that he'd made a spur-of-the-moment decision he was so convinced it was the right one.

For the first time in three years he wanted to get to know someone. He wanted to see what would happen.

He couldn't walk away from her. Not any more.

She was skimming her hand across the surface of the water. Backwards and forwards in long sweeping arcs. Her delicate fingers just missed grazing his chest each time she reached past him.

He gave in.

He reached out one hand, blocking her path. His fingers closed around hers and he pulled her towards him. Her knee slid between his and her thigh brushed against him as he tugged her off her seat and onto his lap. Shock waves sparked through his body and a rush of blood flooded his groin. He heard her catch her breath in a little gasp as her breast flattened against his chest.

He waited for her to protest against his actions but she made no other sound.

His erection pressed against the outside of her leg and

her eyes were enormous as she met his gaze. His hand stretched up her back, ready to pull her closer. He needed her closer. He wanted to kiss her. He needed to taste her.

Sophie bent her head and he waited. He wanted her to meet him halfway, he didn't want her to have any regrets. He needed her to want this as much as he did.

But the kiss never came.

Voices drifted across the snow towards them.

'Looks as though we have company,' she said.

She slid off his lap as Finn and Alex came into view. As much as Gabe enjoyed their company, he could quite happily see them both banished to the opposite pole right about now.

Sophie picked up her towel and treated him to a very nice view of her shapely bottom as she climbed out of the spa. But that wasn't enough. Not barely. But that was all he was going to get.

He watched her go. He couldn't follow. He needed to wait for his excitement to subside.

He groaned in frustration but he knew now that it was only a matter of time before the fire that was building between them would consume them both.

CHAPTER NINE

Date: April 5th
Temperature: -11°C
Hours of sunlight: 10.4

SOPHIE GRIPPED THE handles of the quad bike as she concentrated on trying to stay in Gabe's tracks, but she was constantly distracted by the scenery and finding it hard to contain her excitement. Gabe was keeping his promise and the weather had kept her side of the bargain too and Sophie was actually out, with Gabe, exploring the icy continent.

There was only the two of them. She had Gabe to herself for the day. She didn't know what she was more excited about—seeing something of Antarctica or the possibility that she and Gabe might actually cross over the line they'd been dancing on for days. She wasn't going to make the first move, she could never imagine doing that, but if the opportunity presented itself she was going to make sure that she got the kiss she'd been dreaming about. Life was short. She didn't want any more regrets.

The icy plateau stretched for miles on either side of them, flat for the most part, although she could see some distant hills, but the scenery was far from boring. The ice looked smooth but she could feel the swells under her tyres where the wind had formed ripples in the snow that had then frozen into icy waves. The sunlight bounced off the ice, turning the waves a beautiful shade of pale blue, like a shallow tropical sea.

Despite the sunshine and her helmet, gloves and balaclava, her fingers and cheeks were getting cold by the time they stopped at the first hut. Sophie had pictured wooden huts, like in the days of the old explorers, but, of course, it was just another shipping container. Red, naturally. She thought she would remember the colours of Antarctica as being red, white and blue for ever. Red vehicles, red clothing, red sheds and red S&R pods against a blue and white landscape.

The hut was a smaller version of the buildings at Carey Station. Inside was a small kitchen, a couple of bunk beds and lots of shelving holding loads of crates. Sophie was seeing a different side to life on the ice—a more primitive existence but not one without some comforts, but she didn't care. She wouldn't have minded if Gabe had been showing her the garbage collection centre as long as she was getting out and about.

As the station doctor she hadn't expected to have a lot of free time, she had a job to do, but she'd hated to think she might not see anything of her new surroundings before it was time to leave. This was the real Antarctica. The wilderness. The search and rescue had been exciting but she hadn't had time to take in her surroundings. Between the weather conditions obscuring the landscape and the fact that all her concentration and focus had been on her patients and the situation, that day was just a blur in her memory and she wanted to make sure she soaked up every little piece of today.

'There's a check list of things to be done. It's going to take a while,' Gabe said, as he pushed open the door.

The check list was on the wall of the hut, just inside the door. Sophie scanned it. It was a long list.

'Can I help with anything?' She didn't want to miss a minute of the day, and whether it was riding in Gabe's wake, ticking things off a checklist or observing the penguins she was determined to enjoy every minute of the experience.

'Actually, yes. If you want to check the first-aid box, I need a list of any out-of-date items and there should be a list of contents inside the box so see if anything is missing.'

Gabe was moving around the hut, opening and closing vents and examining the structure for any signs of damage. He checked the gas lines, fire extinguishers and tested equipment as Sophie checked the supplies stored in the plastic containers.

Finally they had finished, which meant they could continue on to the penguins. As they crested a ridge Sophie could see a little cove, and filling the icy beach were more penguins than she ever could have imagined. They were huddled together, a huge, seething, dark mass against the ice.

'There must be hundreds of them,' Sophie said, as Gabe switched off his bike and removed his helmet.

'I think it's probably closer to thousands,' he said as he waved her forward. 'Come on.'

Sophie rested her helmet on the seat of her quad bike and said, 'Where are we going?'

'Closer.'

'Won't we frighten them?' They were only a hundred metres or so from the birds now and Sophie wondered how much closer they could get.

Gabe shook his head. 'They're quite fearless and not really fussed about people at any time. The adult penguins need to protect their eggs and newborn chicks from the skua gulls but now that the chicks are so big they don't have any land predators. Leopard seals are their biggest threat and they don't come onto the ice unless they're desperate.'

Having seen how suddenly the Weddell seal had popped up at the swimming hole a few days ago, Sophie wasn't keen on coming face to face with a leopard seal. She moved a little closer to Gabe.

As they got nearer to the colony the mass of black and white gradually separated into more distinguishing features and Sophie was able to make out individual birds. Each penguin had a white shirt front, a black back and black tuxedo tail feathers. At this distance Sophie could see that their beaks were a reddish colour with a black tip—more red!—and they each had a white ring around each eye.

There were thousands of penguins, all identical in their evening finery. They were also taller than she first thought, standing about two feet tall, somewhere in between Emperor penguins and Little penguins, which were the species she was more familiar with. 'What type of penguins are they?'

'Adelie penguins. There are seventeen species of penguins in total but only five call Antarctica home, and you won't see the Adelie anywhere else in the world, only here.'

'Really?'

'Really.'

'Wow.' Sophie thought that was amazing and it made the day even more special.

Gabe stopped by a flat rock only a few metres from the birds, and they sat down to watch. Sophie couldn't believe they could be so close. At this distance the penguins were incredibly loud. They sounded a bit like pigeons crossed with seagulls, cooing and squawking. They were unbelievably loud *and* smelly.

'They look so smart in their feathered tuxedo but they don't smell so great,' she said.

'We're downwind. They've been nesting here since November. That's a lot of penguin poo.'

Sophie laughed. 'That would explain it.'

Amongst the penguins she could see piles of rocks. 'Are those their nests? Those rocks?'

Gabe nodded. 'They build their nests out of rocks, there's quite an art to collecting the best rocks and they like to steal pebbles from each other's nests.'

While that sounded amusing, Sophie thought the finished product looked awfully cold and uncomfortable. A rocky nest sitting on a bed of ice would be cold and difficult to incubate, she imagined. She'd seen Little penguins in Bicheno in Tasmania, and she knew they nested in the grasses on the sand dunes, which seemed far more civilised. She couldn't imagine living on the ice for months at a time.

'The chicks hatch in December,' Gabe explained. 'By February they have their adult feathers and by late March most of the chicks can swim and the penguins will leave the rookery for the pack ice and icebergs and the sea, leaving behind the stone nest. We're lucky to see so many of them still here. By this time next week they could all be gone.'

'You mean you invited me out here, not knowing if they'd still be around?'

Gabe smiled. 'I had to offer you something to get you to keep me company. You weren't too keen on just seeing the hut.'

'You wanted my company?' The idea pleased her, probably more than it should.

'You know the rules, no one goes out alone.'

'Oh.' Sophie was crestfallen. He hadn't needed her specifically. Anyone would have done.

'Relax, I'm joking. I'm glad I got to bring you with me.'

'I'm glad, too,' she admitted. 'I would have hated to miss this.' She pulled her camera out of her pocket and snapped a few photos, before deciding to just enjoy the spectacle and Gabe's company. Who knew when she would have another chance to spend some time alone with him? This was a chance to find out more about him and one of the reasons why she'd been so keen to explore with him today. She looked around her, trying to commit the scene to memory. 'This is just what I imagined Antarctica would be like.'

'The penguins?' Gabe asked.

'All of it—the penguins, the weather, the scenery. It's picture perfect. And untamed. No people around, I feel completely free. It's just what I need.'

It was incredible. She hadn't expected that she could feel so comfortable and relaxed so far from civilisation. It was liberating.

'Would you like to have some time by yourself to take it all in?'

'No. I don't want to be completely alone. If I don't share it with someone then later on it might feel like it wasn't real. I need someone to be able to talk about it with.' That's what she had been missing, someone to share things with. 'I want to share this with you,' she told him. 'Thank you for bringing me here.'

Suddenly, with a lot of squawking, the birds were on the move. Thousands of them. Somehow they all got a simultaneous message that had them heading for the water.

'Can we go closer to the sea?' Sophie asked.

'Sure,' Gabe said as he stood, offered his hand and pulled her to her feet. 'But slowly, okay?'

He led the way and Sophie assumed his caution was to ensure they didn't frighten the birds, but he wasn't paying the penguins any attention. He was looking closely at the ground and she realised he was checking for crevasses and fissures. She hadn't even considered the dangers of crossing the ice. She had been far too caught up in the excitement of the moment. She hadn't expected Gabe to keep her safe, she hadn't even considered that he needed to, but that was exactly what he was doing, and she realised that she wasn't mentally ready for Antarctica and her perils. The excitement of the extraordinary had made her lose focus on the dangers. She was lucky he was with her.

Gabe led her to another rocky outcrop, from where they could watch the penguins dive into the sea. They were moving en masse, the chicks trailing in the wake of their parents. They waddled on their short legs, flapping their wings to maintain their balance on the ice before diving into the ocean. Lots of the chicks hesitated on the shoreline before eventually following the lead of the older birds and plunging into the sea. Sophie could see them skipping through the water, bobbing and diving as they headed out to feed.

By the time the last lot were heading out some were already returning. Most of them shot out of the water and slid along on their bellies several metres before standing up. They walked for a bit and when they grew tired they flopped onto their bellies again and slid forward, pushing themselves along with their feet like little black and white self-propelling skateboards.

They looked hilarious. She pulled her camera out again as she tried to get the perfect photo.

'I could watch them all day,' she said as she turned to

Gabe, only to find out he wasn't beside her. She had a moment of panic before she realised he wouldn't have left her.

She turned further around and found him standing a short distance away on top of a small ridge, facing into the wind. He was standing perfectly still, in profile to her, and she snapped a quick picture of him before a closer look at his expression told her something wasn't right. She looked around her to see if she could pick up any problems. The wind had picked up slightly and the tang of the penguin poo seemed to have lessened. Had she got used to their odour or had the wind direction shifted?

She stood up and went to Gabe. 'What's the matter?'

'I'm not sure. It feels like the temperature has dropped and the wind speed has picked up,' he replied. 'It's probably nothing but I'm just going to put a call in to the station to check the forecast.'

Together they walked back to the quad bikes and Sophie listened while he made the call. A storm was coming. It was headed their way.

'Have they being trying to reach us?'

Gabe shook his head. 'No. We're not due to check in yet and Alex assumed we'd be on our way back by now.'

'Have I held us up?' Sophie had completely lost track of time, she'd been so fascinated by the penguins, and she was concerned that she'd put them in danger.

'No, if it wasn't for the storm we'd have plenty of time, but now it's unlikely we'll make it back to the station. It's too dangerous to try.'

'What will we do?'

'We should have time to make it back to the hut, we can overnight there.'

The intensity of the wind had increased even further and the sun was low on the horizon by the time they reached the hut. Sophie had thought the hut had seemed basic when they'd stopped there earlier, but now that it was their only option she was more than happy to call it home for the night.

Gabe made dinner for them, using a combination of supplies he found in the hut and the contents of the 'rat packs' that they carried in their survival kits. The packs included dried meat, dried vegetables, rice, pasta, soup, chocolate and dried fruit. None of it looked particularly appetising, especially in light of the meals Sophie had grown accustomed to at the station, so she was amazed when Gabe served her a hot three-course dinner. As the wind howled around the hut they feasted by gas lamplight on pumpkin soup with added cumin and dried chives then fried rice with defrosted prawns and veggies, followed by chocolate pudding.

'I wasn't expecting a gourmet meal out here,' she said. 'I can't quite believe that I'm sitting at the bottom of the world, thousands of miles from civilisation as I've always known it, eating a three-course meal. I'm impressed.'

'I aim to please.'

'You never did tell me how you became a chef.'

'Didn't I?'

'No. What got you interested in cooking? It's not a huge secret, is it?' she asked, as she wondered if he was going to stall her again.

'No, it's no secret, it's just not that interesting a story.'

Sophie shrugged. 'We've got all night, and no other entertainment. We may as well tell some stories.'

'Both of us?'

'Yep, but you're going first.' She wasn't going to let him off the hook again. It was time he shared something with her. 'So, come on, spill the beans. Was your mum a good cook?'

* * *

Gabe could think of plenty of other ways to pass the time that didn't involve telling stories but he couldn't suggest most of them. And it looked as though he wasn't going to be able to avoid her questions this time, but he supposed that it would at least get his mind off Sophie. Talking about his mother would remind him of why he was better off alone.

'Cooking wasn't my mum's strong point.' In fact, he couldn't remember his mother cooking anything other than very basic meals—eggs, baked beans on toast, meatloaf. He'd had to learn to feed himself at a young age and he'd started with beans and toast. 'When I was a teenager she had a waitressing job in the local pub. I used to hang out in the kitchen after school and football training and, being a fairly typical teenage boy, I was always hungry. The cook told me that if I wanted to eat I should learn how to cook. It all started there. I didn't love school but I loved cooking. I loved the immediate results and I loved experimenting. I found I had a knack for it and I ended up becoming an apprentice.'

That wasn't the full story but it was enough for now. He didn't think Sophie was ready for the full story, it was something only a few people, including Alex, knew. 'It was just you and your mum?'

'Yep. My father left when I was six and I never saw him again.'

'Never?'

'No.'

'Do you know where he is?'

'No.'

'You haven't tried to find him?'

'He walked out on us. I think I told you before he had an affair?'

Sophie nodded.

'When I was six he chose his girlfriend over his wife and his son. I don't want to find him. There is nothing he and I would have in common. There is nothing I want to have in common with him.' But he knew he always worried that maybe he did share some of his father's traits. Or his mother's. Which would make him either unlovable or a cad. Neither of which were appealing. Both of which confirmed his belief that he was better off alone.

But he didn't want to think or talk about his mother or his father. He preferred to think about Sophie.

'Not everyone has a happy childhood. I certainly didn't and I try not to think about it too much. It's all behind me now.' He said as he steered the conversation back to her family. As he'd hoped, Sophie let the topic lie then and he successfully managed to avoid any further discussion about his past for the rest of the evening.

Gabe woke suddenly. He was disoriented and unsure why he'd woken. It took a moment to get his bearings. The shape of the furniture was wrong and the ceiling was too close to his head. The room was bathed in a pale green light. He turned his head to his left, looking for the time and expecting to see the display of his docking station. There was a green glow but it was different from the LED light from his docking station, and then he remembered. He was in the hut. With Sophie. He was on the top bunk and the green light wasn't coming from an electrical source but through the window.

He knew what it was but he also knew it wasn't the glow that had woken him. It was the absence of noise. The wind had dropped completely. There wasn't a sound except for Sophie's breathing. The weather had cleared, leaving behind the silence that only a world blanketed in snow had.

He got up and pulled his clothes on before waking Sophie.

'Doc?'

Sophie stirred. 'What is it? What's wrong?'

'Nothing. There's something I want you to see.'

'It's the middle of the night,' she said, rubbing her eyes.

'I know. Get dressed. You'll want to see this.'

'What's that light?'

'If you get dressed I'll show you.'

He tried not to watch as she swung her legs out of the bed. She'd been sleeping in her thermal leggings and a T-shirt. It was definitely not sexy lingerie but somehow she managed to make it look hot. She had undone her plaits and her hair fell over her shoulders in dark waves. He could see the swell of her breasts under the thin wool of her top. The hut was warm but the air in the room was obviously colder than the air in her sleeping bag and he saw her nipples peak as her body registered the change in temperature.

He moved away and occupied himself by putting the kettle on while she got dressed, but he was still only inches away from her and her scent filled the hut. Warm and sweet. It was intoxicating. Sophie had really turned his world upside down. He hadn't expected her and having her so close and without anyone else around was proving torturous. He needed to keep some perspective. He needed to remember that he'd lost everyone he'd ever cared about and he was better off alone.

But that didn't stop him from thinking about her. It didn't stop him from imagining the lines of her body, the softness of her skin, the touch of her fingers.

He heard her feet hit the floor as she stood up from the bottom bunk and he imagined he could feel the air moving as she pulled on her clothes.

He opened the door as she finished putting her boots on and together they stepped outside. The sky glowed green and Gabe heard Sophie's intake of breath as she looked up and stretched out a hand as if to touch the lights that danced above their heads. From one edge of the night sky to the other long fingers of light shimmered and glowed. The dark night sky had been overtaken by rich emerald green swirls tinged with sapphire blue and gold.

The lights were bright enough to obscure the stars, which were dulled by the magnificence of the aurora australis.

Sophie turned in a circle to follow the lights as they danced across the sky. 'It looks like the world has been turned upside down. I've seen these colours in the ocean but never in the sky.' The colours were crisp and clear, translucent, and she lifted her hand again as if to reach out to touch them. 'They are so beautiful.' They shone like phosphorescence, splitting the darkness like laser beams. A curtain of coloured smoke wafting across the sky. 'You've seen the lights before?'

'Yes, but every time they're different. So every time is like the first time.' He knew he wouldn't forget seeing the lights tonight but it was the company that made them special.

'It's amazing.'

'Do you want to get your camera?'

She shook her head. 'No. I don't think I could do it justice. I just want to sit and enjoy it.'

Gabe brought cushions from the hut and put them side by side on the steps. The steps were narrow and Sophie was pressed up against him as they watched the display.

He could feel the length of her thigh against his and he imagined he could feel her body heat even through the thick insulated suits. Indecent thoughts had been running through his head ever since he had enticed her out of bed and now that she was practically sitting in his lap his thoughts were getting more and more R-rated. Despite the fact they were both bundled up in myriad layers of clothing, he could picture her shape and he could see her face under the emerald glow of the Southern Lights and that was enough to keep his blood boiling.

'What causes the lights?' she asked him, and her question focussed his attention but also gave him a reason to look at her. She had left her hair loose and the dark curls were poking out from beneath her beanie, spilling over the front of her red suit like a chocolate fountain.

He resisted the urge to reach out and lift the weight of her hair in his hands as he replied, 'How technical do you want me to be, Doc?'

He added her title deliberately to remind himself of who she was. She was a colleague, a fellow expeditioner, she wasn't a random woman who he'd met in a bar and could spend the weekend with. He couldn't afford to indulge his fantasies. He needed to remind himself of who she was and where they were. Having Sophie around was making him rethink his self-imposed rule of not fooling around with colleagues but no matter how much he might want to test the boundaries he couldn't pretend that it would be a good idea, for either of them, but particularly for her. He couldn't imagine that she was emotionally ready for any sort of relationship other than a platonic one.

'I'm a science geek. Give me your best.' She smiled and her dimples flashed and almost destroyed his resolve.

He was sorely tempted to give her his best but he thought it might not end as he wished. Instead, he looked up at the sky, making sure to keep temptation out of sight, as he answered her. 'There are millions of particles in the galaxy; debris, magnetic waves, radiation; which together are generally called a solar wind. They stream off the sun and are drawn to the Earth's magnetic poles.'

'So that's why you see them at the poles? Because of the magnetic fields?'

'Yes, but we only see the lights here in winter because there's too much sunlight during the rest of the year.'

'What makes the different colours?'

'The particles energise the gases in our atmosphere and cause them to release colours of light. The different gases release different colours. When the particles collide with oxygen you'll see yellow and green, while nitrogen will produce red, violet and blue.'

'I think you might be a secret science geek too,' Sophie laughed.

'Why do you say that?'

'You used to cook for a living—cooking can be quite a scientific process—and you had all those penguin facts on the tip of your tongue today, and now this lesson on the universe. You're definitely a science geek.'

'You have to admit penguins are fascinating. I made it my business to learn about them but I suppose there's some merit to your argument. If I'd been more interested in schoolwork then science might have been my thing, but I ended up in a kitchen.'

'And now you're here.' Sophie waved one arm expansively towards the dark horizon and the green sky above them. 'I can see how being here could become addictive. There's nowhere else quite like it, is there?'

'No, it's hard to give up,' he agreed. He missed the ice whenever he left for a break. He was attracted to the wildness and the freedom of Antarctica. It really was the last frontier. Of course, there were rules, particularly in terms of safety, but the expeditioners were a little community at the bottom of the earth, remote and separate from the rest of the world, and that was one of the things he relished.

Sophie was still gazing heavenward as the display continued in all its spectacular glory. 'It's almost impossible to believe that the lights are naturally occurring. Looking up at this sky, I can understand why people believe in extra-terrestrials and alien life forms.'

'There are lots of superstitions associated with the lights. The Northern Lights were thought to be an omen of war or destruction.'

'But they're so beautiful,' she sighed. 'I had the impression that Antarctica was red, white and blue, but now I'll remember it as emerald and gold.'

He felt her leg twitch as she shivered. 'Are you cold?'

'A little.'

'Do you want to go inside?'

'I don't think I can leave yet.'

He knew how she felt. The first experience with the lights was truly magical and he didn't want to break the spell by putting an end to the night. 'Stand up and move around then, get your blood pumping, and I'll bring you something warm to drink.'

Sophie followed Gabe into the hut. She had decided to fetch her camera. If she was going to have a few moments alone she thought she'd try to capture the display. She snapped a few photos but it wasn't long before her batteries succumbed to the cold and the camera was useless. She slipped it into her pocket as Gabe returned with hot drinks and blankets.

He handed her a mug of steaming hot chocolate before wrapping the blanket around her shoulders. She held it in place with one hand as Gabe sat beside her and wrapped the other end around his back. The blanket brought them closer together and now not only was her thigh pressed against his but she was leaning her shoulder against his too.

She sipped the hot chocolate and tried to ignore the feeling of intimacy that sitting so close to Gabe evoked. She could feel the firmness of his body and she could smell a hint of cinnamon underlying the chocolate smell. Was that Gabe? She'd never noticed that before.

'This tastes amazing.' The hot chocolate was unlike anything she'd ever tasted. Was it the location, the experience or the circumstances that was making it taste so heavenly?

'It's my secret ingredient,' he told her.

'What did you put in it?'

'If I told you it wouldn't be a secret any more, would it?'

'I promise not to tell a soul.'

He grinned. 'In that case, it's chilli and cinnamon powders.'

'Really? You're caving in that easily? You're not even going to make me beg?'

'What can I say? I'm a sucker for a pretty face.'

Sophie was slightly disappointed to hear that the cinnamon smell was coming from the drink and not from Gabe but his comment perked her up.

'Did you get any good photos?' he asked.

'I doubt it. It's impossible to do the sky justice but I had to try to capture it. It's a bit like the penguins today. I'm worried that once I leave and no one else I know has seen this it will seem less real. I wanted to try to capture it because if I'm not going to have anyone to share it with I want some way of remembering. I came to the ice to figure out how to be on my own again and this is one of those times when it hits home that I really am alone. But I'll be okay. Given time.'

She wasn't here to forget but to move on. She wanted to make a new start. She wanted new memories and sitting under the Southern Lights, drinking hot chocolate, was exactly the type of new memory she wanted. She would never see this anywhere else and now, whenever she thought of the Southern Lights, she would associate them with Gabe. Tonight would be a perfect memory.

Gabe stood up as they finished their drinks and reached for her hand. 'Time to get warm,' he said, as he pulled her to her feet.

They were standing almost chest to chest and Sophie tipped her head back to look up at him. 'Thank you,' she said. 'It's been a perfect day.'

Gabe's eyes were dark. He wasn't smiling but he was watching her so intensely that she could feel a yearning in her belly as though a fire was being stoked. She leant towards him as if she was the aurora and he was the South Pole. She was powerless to resist the pull of attraction. She put her hands on his chest and even through his thick jacket she could feel his strength. He felt solid and dependable and masculine.

She felt his arms wrap around her as he pulled her in even closer. He bent his head.

'Sophie.'

Her name was a whisper on his lips.

It was the first time in weeks she had been called anything other than 'Doc' and she liked the way her name sounded when he said it. It made her heart sing.

And then the whisper was gone as his lips covered hers.

His beard was rough against her cheek but the contrast between the coarseness of his beard and the softness of his lips was incredible. Her breath escaped in a sigh as she closed her eyes and opened her mouth to him.

He tasted of cinnamon and chocolate and she knew she would always associate those flavours with Gabe.

It was amazing to kiss someone when the only thing you could feel was their mouth. Her hands were on his chest but because of all their layers the only exposed parts of them were their noses and lips. It concentrated her senses and sharpened her focus. Everything she could touch and feel was going into the kiss. Everything she could touch and feel was happening through her lips.

She melted into him, unable to tell where she stopped and he started. This was the kiss she'd been dreaming of but it was better than she'd imagined. Gabe's lips were soft but his tongue was searching and as he explored her mouth a rush of heat shot from her chest to her belly and all the way to her toes. It was intense, powerful and all-consuming. It was an incredible feeling, but did that make it right?

Sophie wasn't sure. She pulled away, pushing her hands against his chest until their lips came apart.

'What's wrong?'

'I didn't mean to kiss you.'

'I think you'll find I kissed you,' he replied without a trace of apology in his voice. 'And I meant to. I'm sorry if I made you feel uncomfortable but you looked so beautiful that I couldn't help it. It seemed like a perfect way to end a perfect day.'

'Don't apologise.' Sophie shook her head, even though she agreed with him. It had felt perfect. 'You didn't make me feel uncomfortable. I enjoyed it, that's not the problem. If I'm honest I've been thinking about what it would be like to kiss you for days.'

'So we're on the same page.' He grinned. 'That's good news.'

'Except that technically you could be considered my patient.'

'I don't think the same rules apply in Antarctica.'

'All the staff are potentially my patients and I shouldn't overstep the boundaries. It's part of the oath I took.'

'I promise not to get sick while you're here. If you're not treating me for anything then surely that's okay?'

It was a flimsy argument but Sophie was tempted to go with it.

'I'm not sure.' The kiss had been so lovely it was going to be hard to stop. It had made her feel alive again. It had made her happy. She wasn't sure how ready she was for this but it felt perfect. They were in a world of their own. A world away from everything else. It was just the two of them and it was very tempting to ignore protocol. After all, who would ever know?

Gabe bent his head. 'I promise I won't tell anyone.' She could feel his words caress her cheek, making her knees go weak. 'But I don't want you to have any regrets. This has to be your decision.'

She didn't want to resist.

'And there's only one decision you need to make,' Gabe continued. 'Either you want to explore this thing between us or you don't. But you don't need to make that decision tonight. I'm not going anywhere but you do need to go to bed. I can stop now but if you don't go inside and go to bed I might not be able to stop again.'

Sophie lay her in bunk underneath Gabe's, trying to breathe quietly. Trying to sleep. But it was going to be impossible. Her mind kept replaying that kiss.

She'd expected to feel guilty but there was no denying she had wanted to kiss him. That she'd wanted to for days.

It wasn't wrong and she wasn't going to feel guilty about something that felt so right. She was done feeling guilty.

Sitting under that magical sky had made her feel small and insignificant. It had put things into perspective for her and reminded her that they were all temporary. The lights would be there long after she and everyone else she knew had gone. The lights would bathe the world in their colours for eternity but she only had the here and now. She only had one chance at life and she needed to live it.

Life was short. She needed to be brave.

She wanted to be fearless. She needed to take a chance and live each moment. She didn't know how many she had left and she didn't want to waste any of them.

He'd said it was her decision.

She wanted to feel alive. She wanted to feel happy.

She wanted to share this night with Gabe.

She wanted to live her life without regrets.

It was her decision and she was willing to take a chance.

Sophie tugged her necklace over her head. She stuffed the chain and her wedding rings into the pocket of her fleece and whispered to Gabe, 'Are you awake?'

CHAPTER TEN

Date: April 6th
Temperature: -12°C
Hours of sunlight: 10.3

SOPHIE HUGGED HER memories of last night to her like a secret. Coming to Antarctica had been the right decision. She felt like the old Sophie. Happy. Light. Floating. Free.

She coasted through the morning. The return trip to the station passed by in a blur. Not even the scenery could distract her from her thoughts, which were filled with memories of last night, snapshots of a day in her life. A day she wasn't going to forget in a hurry, if ever. The spectacle of the lights, the colours of the universe and the stillness of the early morning when all she'd been able to hear had been the sound of Gabe's breathing.

The heat of Gabe's kisses and the touch of his embrace had set her free from the past. She wasn't going to forget Danny but she knew now that she would be able to move on.

Gabe was only the second man she'd ever slept with, and while she'd expected it to be different she hadn't really thought about it being better. But in many ways it had been. She'd got more than she'd bargained for but she wasn't complaining. Perhaps the anticipation had made it all the more sweet or perhaps Gabe's experience had been the difference. She'd been smouldering for days, on edge as she'd tried to ignore their attraction, all while hoping she'd eventually have a chance to explore it, and Gabe's kisses had been the spark that had stoked her fire and set her alight. Her skin tingled with the memory of his touch and her muscles ached from the exercise.

Back at the station she turned on her laptop, ready to download her photos. Danny's photo popped up on the screensaver, his goofy smile filling the screen.

'I'm sorry, Danny, it just felt right. Can you understand?'

She didn't really feel as though she needed to apologise for being happy, and she didn't want to dwell on Danny so she clicked an icon to open a program and the screensaver and Danny's photo disappeared from view.

She loaded her photos and scrolled through them, searching for one that she could use as a new screensaver. There were a couple of good ones of the penguins, a gorgeous one of Gabe in profile that she'd snapped just before the storm warning and one sensational shot of the Southern Lights. She chose that one. It reminded her of Gabe, without actually being him. She wasn't ready to replace Danny's photo with one of Gabe, it was far too early for such an extreme measure, but she didn't want to see Danny smiling at her if she was thinking about someone else. Danny would always be in her heart but he was only a memory now. Gabe was living, breathing, warm and real. His arms could hold her and touch her and she missed the touch of another person.

Her email was flashing, indicating new messages. She clicked on her inbox and found a message from Luke. She waited for a stab of guilt as she read his email but she felt nothing but happiness. She was done feeling guilty. Guilt wasn't going to bring Danny back.

She sent Luke a quick, innocuous reply and attached her two best penguin photos. She thought about attaching one of the Southern Lights but decided she didn't want to share that moment with anyone other than Gabe. That was their thing. She knew there wouldn't be too many things she would share with him, there wasn't time. She was due to leave in three weeks and she wanted to keep something of Gabe just for herself.

CHAPTER ELEVEN

Date: April 19th
Temperature: -6°C
Hours of sunlight: 8.7

SOPHIE WAS HAPPY. Antarctica had given her back her old self. It had given her Gabe and she had spent the past fortnight making memories with him that would sustain her through any dark moments.

She had to make memories, that was all she would be taking with her when she left. Gabe hadn't made her any promises. She knew how he felt about serious relationships. He didn't do commitment and that was fine with her. She wasn't ready for anything more either. She would have been happy with one incredible night but they'd had two weeks. She hadn't expected to find such happiness down here but she was going to grab it with both hands. She had blossomed under Gabe's touch. She was happy again She laughed, she ate, she sang in the shower and walked around with a silly smile on her face. She knew that by the time she left she would be well on her way to healing. She knew she'd be able to move on. Gabe had shown her that, he was the proof she needed.

But he was her secret. She wasn't ready to share what they had with anyone else on the station. She didn't need to share him and it was easy to keep their status private. They were the only two who had their dongas on the ground floor of the red shed and being side by side meant it wasn't difficult to move between their rooms. The only difficulty was squeezing two of them into the narrow bed but, as Gabe had said, where there's a will there's a way, and Sophie enjoyed having to snuggle against him to avoid tumbling out of bed. They fitted together well and she loved being in his arms.

Over the past two weeks she had stopped thinking about everything in contrast to Danny. Life at Carey had become about her and Gabe. Danny wasn't constantly in her thoughts any more. She was surviving without him. She could look to the future again and it no longer seemed quite so bleak.

When she hadn't been sneaking into Gabe's room she had been kept busy with routine medical procedures and examinations. A foreign body in an eye, a back strain, an episode of chest pain, which had thankfully turned out to be indigestion, and stitches in Liam's chin. As she had stitched him up yesterday she'd realised that by the time the stitches would need removing she would be gone. Dr John would be the one to take them out. Her time was flying past. The supply ship, the *Explorer Australis*, was well on its way, making its last voyage down south before winter really closed in. The ship had left Douglas Station and was on her way to Carey. Sophie was into her last week.

She snuggled closer to Gabe, tucking her leg over his, seeking his warmth, as she began to make the most of one of her last mornings.

Gabe was lying in bed, watching her get dressed. She was standing in her underwear and had just pulled a T-shirt over her head when Gabe's door flew open and Finn burst in to the room.

'Gabe, there's been an accident—' Sophie saw Finn's double-take when he saw her standing semi-naked in the middle of the floor but he recovered quickly. 'Doc, good you're here. I need you too.' He might have made a quick recovery but she didn't miss the quizzical look he gave Gabe.

Gabe didn't bother explaining. There were more important things to worry about. He threw back the covers and grabbed a pair of boxer shorts as he asked, 'How bad?'

'One casualty. It's Alex.'

Sophie noticed Gabe's slight hesitation and his hand was shaking as he pulled his shorts up. Sophie knew how close he and Alex were. They were like brothers. Gabe looked at Finn.

'He's alive but unconscious,' Finn said. 'A forklift reversed into some shelving in the storage shed, knocking it down onto Alex.' Finn looked at Sophie. 'We're lifting it off but we don't want to move him.'

Sophie sprang into action. This was her department now. 'I need a spinal board and my emergency kit. Come with me,' she directed Finn.

She collected everything she thought she might need, threw on her cold-weather jacket and pants and followed Finn to the storage shed. Gabe had beaten them there and was overseeing the logistics of removing a heavy metal storage unit that had crushed Alex.

Alex was lying on his back. The shelving unit had fallen across his chest and left shoulder, pinning him to the floor. Sophie knelt beside him and put her hand gently on his right shoulder.

'Alex?' There was no response. He was still unconscious and she could see a pool of blood under his head. But he was breathing.

Gabe and the other men had cleared away the debris that had fallen from the shelves and were looking at her, waiting for her okay to move the toppled unit. She nodded. She knew it had to be done, she just hoped it wasn't going to present her with more problems.

Time was of the essence and she worked quickly once the area was clear. Alex's pupils reacted equally to torchlight, his blood pressure was low and his heart rate was elevated, but nothing too worrying. Carefully she fixed a cervical collar around his neck before getting Gabe and Finn to help her assemble the spinal board around him. Then they made their way slowly and cautiously back to the red shed.

Gabe refused to leave Alex's side, choosing instead to remain in the clinic while Sophie took X-rays and tried her best to assess the extent of his injuries.

'Is he going to be all right?'

'I can't tell you. I have to develop the X-rays and it depends how long he takes to regain consciousness. His pupils are reacting equally so I don't think there's any intracranial bleeding. We can be thankful that the blood is flowing out, not in. I'm sorry but we'll just have to wait and see.' She knew that wasn't what Gabe wanted to hear but it was all she could tell him at the moment.

'Alex is like family to me.'

'I know, and I'll do everything I can.'

'I've lost everyone I've ever cared about.'

Sophie was shaving some of Alex's blond curls so she could stitch his head wound, but she paused briefly to squeeze Gabe's hand. She wanted to stop what she was doing to comfort Gabe but she couldn't. She had to take care of Alex first.

'Everyone?' she asked.

'My father and my mother.'

Sophie knew his father had walked out when Gabe had been young but she hadn't realised he'd lost his mother too. They had been spending every spare minute together but she realised that while she knew him intimately in a physical sense there was a lot he hadn't shared with her. She had tried to get him to open up but he was very adept at changing the subject. She wondered what had happened. He knew her whole life story and she still knew almost nothing about him.

'Do you want to talk about it? You listened to me unload about Danny, it's my turn to listen now.'

'It's a long story.'

'I'm not going anywhere.'

'I'm not really sure exactly where it starts.'

Gabe paused and Sophie thought that he wasn't going to say anything more. She kept stitching, giving him some time, and he eventually continued.

'There are lots of interwoven events and one of them must have come first but I think I was too young to know which one that was. I remember my father coming and going, but only vaguely, when I was a pre-schooler. I don't know if he was around a lot when I was younger but he walked out for good when I was six. I found out years later he'd had an affair. More than one. Mum suffered from depression but I don't know whether that started before or after the affairs. She might have been difficult to live with but that didn't give him the right to be unfaithful. Mum made him choose between us and his latest girlfriend and he didn't pick us. That was the end of our family.'

Sophie's heart ached for the six-year-old Gabe. 'And your mum? What happened to her?' She knew he felt as though his father had abandoned him and she had to agree but surely his mother had been there for him? If not, it would explain a lot more about him. She continued to stitch Alex's head wound, taking her time now, not because it was difficult but because she was worried that if she stopped she might break Gabe's concentration. It was almost as though he was talking to himself, as though he'd forgotten she was there, and she didn't want to interrupt his train of thought.

'Mum struggled to cope after that and when I was seven I was put into foster-care for the first time. When Mum felt like she had things under control again I was sent back to live with her and that pattern kept repeating right through to my teenage years. I was in and out of foster-care and I hated it. I became an angry, rebellious teenager. As far as I could see, there wasn't any point to anything. School, friendships, everything could change in an instant. Sometimes it would be Mum's decision, she'd just pack us up and leave, convinced that starting somewhere new would be the answer, and other times I'd change schools depending on which foster-family I was sent to. I had a very unsettled existence, physically and emotionally, and I think I was heading for big trouble.

'If it wasn't for one particular teacher I had when I was fourteen, I know I wouldn't have made it. That teacher got me into football and it was around that time that Mum got the job waitressing in the pub. It wasn't an exceptional job but her boss was fantastic. I got to hang out in the kitchen after school and football training. I loved being in the kitchen and I loved cooking, but it was the attention and time that Mum's boss gave me that made the difference. He owned the pub but food was his passion and he was the chef. He taught me how to cook. Cooking and football gave me a purpose.'

Sophie had heard part of this story before but Gabe had

certainly kept a lot of the detail from her the first time. He'd made it sound so simple and straightforward and commonplace that night in the hut.

'I was happy but too wrapped up in my own teenage world to notice that Mum was unhappy. When I was sixteen she took her own life. I lost it then for a while. I was sixteen and on my own. All my family were gone.'

Sophie bit back tears as her heart broke for Gabe. 'What did you do?'

'I dropped out of school. But Mum's boss stepped in. He offered me an apprenticeship in the pub, along with lodgings, and because I was sixteen I was allowed to live independently. That was my chance and I took it. I've been on my own ever since.'

'What about Zara?' Sophie knew he'd been invested in that relationship. It hadn't worked out but he *had* made an effort to have a relationship, he hadn't always been alone.

'Zara just confirmed it for me. Relationships aren't worth it. Someone always loses. It was my mother and then me.'

'Maybe you just haven't found the right person yet.'

Gabe shook his head. 'I'm better off on my own.'

Sophie was bandaging Alex's wound. 'No one is better off alone.'

Gabe's words were upsetting her. It wasn't the first time he'd mentioned being better off alone. His childhood experiences went a long way to explain why he felt the way he did, but surely he couldn't think it meant he should spend the rest of his life on his own? He couldn't really mean it, could he? Her relationship with Danny hadn't worked out as she'd expected, but she'd rather have loved Danny than not, and she was positive she would find love again. What was the point in living your life alone?

She was upset but she tried not to show it. Even though

she should have known better, she realised she'd been thinking about the future, a future with Gabe. She had fallen hard and fast but she could see she was being unrealistic, given the fact that she would be leaving soon and Gabe had said nothing about a future together. It was obvious now how different his intentions were from hers but she still needed to look forward. She didn't plan on being on her own for ever, even if Gabe did.

But he had shown her that she could be happy again. That she could love and laugh. He didn't see the same future but there was still one out there for her. She no longer thought in terms of years—her days of making three-year plans were over—but she was feeling better about what was ahead, even if Gabe wouldn't be there to share it with her. She would take little steps, a day, a week, a month at a time, and she would start again when she got home.

She felt confident about returning to the real world. Hopefully, the real world was ready for her.

Date: April 20th
Temperature: -5°C
Hours of sunlight: 8.6

'Well, well, if it isn't the dark horse himself.'

Alex was lying flat on his back in the hospital bed but his greeting to Gabe was robust.

'You're feeling better, I take it,' Gabe said, as he pulled a chair to the side of the bed and sat down.

'Battered and bruised with a bit of a headache, but I'm an old rugby player with a noggin like a brick. It takes more than a collapsed shelf to knock me off. But I reckon there's more interesting things to discuss than the state of my head.'

'Like?'

'Like what's the deal with you and Sophie? How long has that been going on?'

'A couple of weeks.'

Alex raised an eyebrow. 'When were you going to tell me?'

'Dunno. It's no big deal.' Alex was like a brother to Gabe, they'd formed a close friendship on the ice, and no topic, including women, was normally off-limits between them. But Gabe felt differently about Sophie. Their relationship was private and he would have preferred it if it had stayed that way. It was his way of protecting his emotional investment. In his opinion, the fewer people who knew about the relationship the better. It would hurt less if he wasn't expected to talk about his feelings when it ended. 'It just happened.'

'Nice try, Romeo. I think you're forgetting who you're talking to. I know you. Nothing just happens with you. So what's next?'

'Nothing. She's leaving with the ship in a few days.'

'You're letting her go?'

Gabe shrugged.

'You're kidding!'

'What other option do I have?'

'Ask her to stay.'

'I can't.'

'Can't or won't?'

'Won't.'

'Reason?'

'She's said she needs to learn to be on her own.'

'And you're happy to leave it at that? There's enough heat between the two of you to power this place if our generators went down, it was only a matter of time before one of you had to make a move. I can't believe you're happy to let her walk away.'

'It's not up to me. It's her decision.'

Gabe didn't want to say goodbye. Their relationship had begun simply enough. Sophie was aware of his penchant for short-term involvement, his aversion to commitment, and she'd said it was all she wanted at this stage in her life too. There wasn't any other option. Her time on the ice was finite. It was short and sweet or nothing. The problem was that his vision of his future had changed since meeting her. He could picture a future with her and it seemed far less bleak and solitary than any other future he could imagine. But he wasn't sure if now was the right time to tell her that, and he couldn't risk putting his heart on the line. Not yet. He didn't think Sophie was ready to hear how he was feeling. She'd said she needed to learn to be on her own and he didn't think she was there yet. He was just temporary in her life.

But it was rather ironic that this was the one time when he wished that temporary wasn't an option.

CHAPTER TWELVE

Date: April 23rd
Temperature: -11°C
Hours of sunlight: 8.3

SOPHIE HAD BEEN packed and ready to leave for the past two days, but neither she nor Gabe had spoken about what happened next. It was almost as if, by ignoring the inevitable, they could pretend it wasn't real. And that was how their relationship felt to Gabe. Like a fairy-tale.

But it looked as if the fairy-tale would last a little longer. The *Explorer Australis* had been due to dock at Carey yesterday but it was stuck in pack ice off the coast. Gabe didn't mind. It meant he would have the pleasure of Sophie's company for another day but any longer than a few more days without the ship and they would need to put other plans in place. The ship would need to start its return journey before winter really closed in, but the station was waiting on vital supplies and a dozen expeditioners, including Sophie, were waiting to leave. If the ship couldn't get any closer, arrangements would have to be made to chopper supplies in and people out. The ship had picked up helicopters from Douglas Station, they would spend winter on the mainland, but at least that gave them an alternative transport option. Gabe needed to discuss the weather forecast with Michelle. If the ship wasn't going to be able to break through the ice they needed to find a window of favourable weather in which to fly the choppers.

But their resident meteorologist couldn't give Gabe the forecast he wanted. 'There's a big storm front coming,' Michelle told him. 'More cold weather and strong winds. There's no chance of flying the choppers for the next twenty-four hours. The winds are likely to increase and could be in excess of one hundred and fifty kilometres an hour. I think we need to batten down the hatches here and prepare to wait this one out. No one is going anywhere.'

'How long have we got before it hits?'

'Another hour before it starts, another hour after that before it really cranks up.'

'All right, I need to call everyone back to the red shed.' Fortunately, everyone was at the station, they'd been doing the final pack up in preparation for winter so everyone was close to hand, but Gabe wanted them all together. He needed to know they were all safe and accounted for.

He spent the next hour organising for the station to be storm-proofed. Anything that wasn't required was packed away or tied down until one by one everyone had finished and had assembled in the mess hall, but when he did a head count Sophie was missing.

'Does anyone know where she is?'

'If she's not in her clinic then most likely in the hydroponics shed,' came Dom's reply.

'I'm going to get her,' Gabe said. 'No one is to leave the shed.'

Sophie was his responsibility. He needed to see her. He needed to keep her safe.

She was picking lettuces when he found her.

'Soph.' He no longer called her 'Doc'. He had stopped

thinking about her as the doctor, she had taken on a whole new meaning for him. 'There's a big storm coming, we need to get back to the red shed.'

She didn't argue and he waited while she packed away her gardening tools, but when he opened the door he found that the weather had turned in the few minutes he'd been inside the shed. The wind had picked up and was howling between the buildings. The snow was swirling, making whiteout conditions, and the red shed was no longer visible. He shut the door and turned to Sophie. She had pulled on her cold-weather jacket and gloves but had no eye protection.

'Do you have your goggles with you?' he asked.

'No.' She shook her head. 'Just sunglasses.'

Sunglasses weren't going to cut it. Not in these conditions. He opened the first-aid cabinet that was fixed to the wall beside the door and rummaged around for a spare pair. He handed them to her.

'Put these on. The weather's deteriorated. Pull your neck warmer up too,' he said, as he pulled the hood of her jacket over her head and tightened it around her face until all that could be seen of her was her nose. He kissed the tip of her nose before opening the door and reaching for the guide rope. He took her hand and wrapped it around the rope. 'That leads to the red shed. Don't let go of it.' He could see a look of uncertainty and nervousness in her green eyes as her fingers tightened around the rope. 'It's okay,' he reassured her, 'I'll be right behind you.'

The wind was ferocious and even Gabe struggled to keep his feet as they stepped out from the shelter of the building. He made sure he stayed only inches from Sophie, worried he would lose sight of her. They had their heads bent as they leant into the wind. He was almost doubled over and he wondered if they should have clipped themselves to the guide rope. Station policy stated that they just needed to hold on but he couldn't recall ever encountering such strong winds before.

He could taste the saltiness of the ocean in the ice that stung his cheeks and melted on his tongue. The wind was blowing straight off the harbour, lifting the water off the tops of the waves and freezing it as it blew it over the land.

Sophie slipped on the ice and Gabe grabbed her around the waist with one arm, struggling to keep his balance and at the same time trying to help her stay on her feet without completely letting go of the rope. She regained her footing and they battled on. They were only halfway there but Gabe could feel his legs becoming fatigued, it was exhausting. And that was when the mistake was made.

He saw Sophie lift her head, which exposed her chest to the wind. It was the wrong thing to do but before he could tell her to tuck her head down the wind blasted into her and knocked her feet out from under her. Although the scene seemed to play out in slow motion Gabe's reaction time wasn't fast enough and he watched helplessly as the wind ripped the rope from her hands.

'Sophie!'

Her name was torn from his lips and flung away on the wind. He let go of the rope, reaching out for her instinctively, and suddenly there was nothing.

The wind took him too and flung him across the ice. He was tumbling. He was falling. He had no way of knowing which way was up and which was down. He had no sense of direction. He had nothing.

No Sophie. No station. Nothing.

In a split second they had been torn apart.

In the blink of an eye they had both vanished.

Sophie cried out as she felt the rope tear from her grasp but she never heard the words as the wind ripped them straight from her lips and flung them away. Her words were no match for the force of the wind. Neither was she.

The wind took her as well. She spun through the air before crashing onto the ice. She could hear her suit scraping on the ice as she was blown backwards. She tumbled over and over as she flung her arms out, desperately seeking for something to grab hold of even though she knew there was nothing there.

She lost all sense of time and space. The world was white. To her dizzy brain there was no way of discerning between the ice and the sky. It was all the same.

There was nothing she could do. There was no way of stopping. She knew there was nothing out here. Nothing but a vast, icy plateau. She'd seen it.

So this was it.

This was how it was all going to end.

She would become just another soul lost at the bottom of the world.

'Where are they?' Alex peered over Finn's shoulder, searching for a glimpse of Gabe and Sophie. They were taking longer than he'd expected to make their way back to the red shed and he was starting to worry.

'I see them,' Finn said, as the red of Sophie's jacket came into view through the sleet.

Alex could see her now. He could see her struggling to keep her balance. He held his breath as she stumbled and he saw Gabe grab her around the waist to steady her.

He saw her lift her head and watched in slow motion as her feet were blown out from underneath her, but this time Gabe didn't have a chance to grab her. Alex watched, horrified, as the wind whipped her away. He saw Gabe reach for her but he was too late and suddenly they had both disappeared from view.

'No!'

Alex swore under his breath. This was an absolute disaster.

What the hell were they supposed to do now?

But he knew what he had to do. He had to organise S&R. He needed to send out a search party.

He mobilised the team—Finn, Liam, Duncan and himself—but an S&R effort was useless without a plan. Where did they start the search? There was nothing out there. Miles and miles of nothing. Gabe and the doc could be anywhere and to complicate things further, chances were high that they weren't even together. There was no way of knowing where the wind might have taken them.

He consulted with Michelle to try to work out where they might have ended up.

'The wind gust peaked at one hundred and eighty-three kilometres an hour,' Michelle said. 'They could be miles away. Your best bet is to start the search in this area,' she said, pointing to an area south-east of the station.

A decision was made to map out a grid that could then be searched in a zig-zag pattern, but it was all based on an educated guess at best. But he had no other option.

Alex sent Finn to gather medical supplies, while Liam and Duncan fetched two Hägglunds from the machinery shed. 'Make sure you clip yourselves onto the guide ropes and put a portable GPS unit in your pocket just in case,' he instructed. If Gabe and Sophie had GPS trackers on them it would make this S&R much easier, but while that had been discussed in OH&S meetings, it wasn't a policy. Not yet.

Somehow, eventually, Sophie managed to stop tumbling. She got herself onto her back and stayed there. She was hoping her clothing would protect her from the abrasive ice but she had very little time to think. Her brain shut down—she didn't want to think about what was happening.

The wind continued to push her across the ice. She had no idea how long she had been at the mercy of the wind. Seconds or minutes? There was no way of knowing.

She just hoped the wind would give up its hold on her eventually, although she had no idea what she would do then. Then, without warning, she slammed against something solid. The force was so great that the air was knocked out of her lungs but at least she was no longer being hurled across the ice. Something had blocked her path and forced the wind to let her go.

She was struggling to breathe. *Relax, relax,* she told herself, until finally she was able to take a shallow breath in and she felt her dizziness recede.

There was a flash of red as the wind carried something past her. She could only assume it was Gabe. She turned her head in time to see him smack against the same obstruction that had stopped her flight and she heard the air whoosh out of his lungs.

They had crashed against a rocky outcrop. She had been thrown against an icy slope that acted as a buffer between her and the rocks, but she could see that Gabe had come to rest against exposed rocks.

Gingerly, she tested her limbs and was relieved to find everything in working order, although she knew she would be black and blue from the force of the impact.

The wind continued to blow. Through the sleet she could just make out Gabe's red jacket. He hadn't moved. Was he still catching his breath or was he in trouble?

Sophie crawled around the rock, trying to keep as low as possible, trying to make herself as small as she could. She didn't want to give the wind another chance to grab her.

Gabe was lying very still and awkwardly. The rocks on

this side were all sharp angles, with no protective layer of ice and snow to soften the collision. He was conscious but she could tell by the look in his eyes that he was hurt.

'Does it hurt to breathe?' she asked.

He nodded and Sophie took some small comfort from seeing that he could move his head without difficulty.

'Where does it hurt? In your chest?' Looking at the sharp edges of these rocks, it was quite likely that he had sustained major damage.

'No. Lower.' His breaths were shallow, making his speech laboured and difficult. Each word was an effort. It was more than just having the wind knocked out of him. His skin was pale and she could see sweat forming on his brow even in these conditions. She knew she was okay, battered and bruised but basically intact, but Gabe was a different story. He was injured but she didn't know how badly.

The rocks were jagged and sharp and he had been slammed against them with considerable force. He weighed close to ninety kilograms so he would have hit hard.

She needed to determine the nature of his injuries. 'Can you wriggle your fingers? What about your feet?' That he could do but when he tried to bend a knee he cried out in pain.

'Is it your leg?'

Gabe shook his head and put his hand against the left side of his stomach. Sophie could see a large tear in the fabric. She slid her hand inside his jacket. She pressed gently on his ribs and abdomen and around to his back as far as she could reach. She heard his sharp intake of breath as she pressed on his ribs and she could feel them grating under her fingers. The colour drained from his face and she prayed he didn't have a pneumothorax, but while she suspected internal injuries she had no way of knowing. She couldn't listen to his chest. She couldn't check for a pneumothorax. All she could do was palpate and feel his pulse.

She would have liked to have moved him behind the shelter of the rock and out of the direct path of the wind but that wasn't going to happen. Even if she was strong enough to move him she couldn't risk it and it was obvious he wasn't going to be able to move himself, but at least up against the rocks he wasn't going to be blown any further.

His jacket was ripped and the legs of her trousers were torn. She remembered Alex drumming into her that exposure to the wind could be fatal and she knew she needed to find, or build, some sort of shelter. Alex would have told her to build an ice cave but the ice was frozen solid and she had nothing but her hands to dig with. When Alex had shown her what to do they'd had a saw from the survival kit that he'd used to make ice blocks. She had nothing now.

She started scraping at the ice with her hands anyway, even though she knew it was futile. All that would achieve would be to put holes in her gloves. She had to think of another way.

She crawled around the rocks and found a couple of smaller stones. She began scraping at the ice and snow but still felt she was getting nowhere. This was ridiculous. Her eyesight was blurry, making it difficult to see what she was doing. She lifted her goggles to rub her eyes and it was then she realised she was crying. She could taste the salty tears as they ran down to her lips before freezing on her face. She had no idea what to do, she had no clue. The whole exercise felt pointless but she had to try something. Gabe was depending on her.

She was starting to sweat. She could feel perspiration running down between her breasts and she remembered Alex talking about the dangers of sweating and then cooling down in the frigid conditions. She removed her jacket and tucked it around Gabe while she kept digging and tried not to think about how the hole looked like a shallow grave. She piled up the icy snow that she excavated to form a windbreak in front of Gabe. She wasn't going to risk moving him, she just hoped a snow wall would afford enough protection.

With the windbreak finally finished, she put her jacket back on and squeezed in between the ice and Gabe. She hugged him to her, trying to keep him warm. He was shivering. His pulse was weak and thready and she knew he was in shock, and she also suspected he was bleeding internally.

'I'm here, Gabe. I've got you.'

Sophie could feel the temperature dropping. She hoped it was just because she had stopped her physical activity but when she checked her watch she saw it was four in the afternoon. The sun was starting to set and she knew that Gabe's chances would decline dramatically once the temperature fell further. She had no other way of keeping him warm.

If they weren't found soon…

She couldn't afford to think like that. She had to stay positive. She was fighting for them both.

'It'll be okay, someone will come. Alex will find us,' she said, hoping he couldn't hear the lie in her voice. Lying on this frozen, inhospitable ground, it seemed very likely that help would come too late, if at all.

She was surviving without Danny, she was stronger than she'd thought, but she didn't know if she'd survive if she lost Gabe too. He had brought her back to life, he had got her heart beating again but she wasn't sure if it would keep going without him.

And that was when she realised she had fallen hard and fast. That was when she knew she was in love with Gabe.

Was life going to be cruel to her again? Was her next chance at happiness about to be ripped away from her?

She couldn't let that happen. He would never give up and she couldn't either. Gabe made her feel stronger, more confident and more capable, and he needed her to be all those things now. She was all he had.

'Sophie?'

'I'm here.'

'Don't leave me.' His voice was becoming faint.

'I won't leave you.'

'Promise me you'll stay.'

'I promise.' There was nothing else she could say. There was nothing else she could do.

No. There was one more thing.

Unless they were found soon, he wasn't going to make it. He needed proper medical care. He needed blood. And he needed to know how she felt.

She had to tell him. She couldn't wait. She might never get another chance.

'I'm right here,' she whispered. 'I'm not going anywhere. I love you.'

She didn't care if he wanted to be alone for ever. That didn't matter. What mattered was that he knew he was loved.

He didn't respond and Sophie felt a flash of panic. Was he still breathing? She put her cheek against his nose and felt a soft puff of air. She breathed a sigh of relief. He was still alive but he'd lost consciousness. His pulse was weaker still. Had they run out of time?

She wanted to believe they would be ok but she took some comfort in the thought that if they weren't than at least they would be together until the end. She wasn't going to be alone and neither was he.

She hugged him to her as the wind continued to moan

and whistle through the rocks. It was a sad, forlorn sound but Sophie thought she could hear another noise now too, a deeper noise. Engine noise? With a sense of urgency she wriggled out of the ice break, taking care not to move Gabe. She needed to know.

She deliberately kept her back to the rocks, terrified of getting blown away again. The snow and ice were still swirling, making visibility difficult. She couldn't see further than a few metres. There was nothing but white. She listened carefully but the sound, if it had ever existed, had stopped.

It would soon be dark.

This was it.

It was over.

She was turning around to crawl back to Gabe when she caught a flash of red in the corner of her eye. She turned back, almost too scared to look in case she was imagining things, but there it was again. A glimpse of red in the ice and snow.

She waved her arms and burst into tears as two square, boxy Hägglunds emerged from the blizzard.

CHAPTER THIRTEEN

Date: April 24th
Temperature: -14°C
Hours of sunlight: 8.0

'GOOD MORNING.'

Gabe tried to open his eyes but they felt as though they had lead weights strapped to his eyelids. He was dazed and groggy but he could hear Sophie's voice.

'Soph?'

'I'm here.'

He felt her fingers wrap around his hand and give him a gentle squeeze. He tried to open his eyes again and this time he managed it but only briefly. The lights were far too bright. He felt like his eyes were burning. 'Where am I?'

'In the clinic. Do you remember what happened?'

What was the last thing he remembered? 'The storm.' The storm had blown Sophie away. He turned his head and opened his eyes. He needed to see her. 'I thought I'd lost you.'

'Alex found us.'

'Are you all right?'

'I'm fine.' She leant over the bed and kissed him on the lips. 'It's you we were worried about.'

'Me?'

She was nodding. 'We weren't sure if you were going to make it.'

'What happened?' He wriggled his fingers and toes. One finger felt thick and he glanced down and saw an oxygen monitor clamped to it and various leads and tubes hanging off him. The movement hurt his neck but his limbs appeared to be working although he ached all over. He'd obviously been caught up in the storm too but his memory was sketchy.

'I have good news and bad news,' Sophie told him. 'The first bit of good news is you're alive.'

He managed a smile. That didn't hurt too much. 'That is good news.'

'Bad news—we had to operate. Good news—the weather cleared and we managed to get Dr John off the ship. He was choppered in and we operated together. More good news—your injuries weren't as bad as I first feared. You have some busted ribs and you ruptured your spleen.'

'My spleen?' He was too groggy to recall if that was a vital organ or not.

Sophie was nodding. 'We had to remove your spleen but you can live without it.'

'Okay. I think what you're telling me is that there's more good news than bad?'

'Pretty much. It was touch and go for a while but you're going to be fine.' Her dimples flashed at him as she grinned and her green eyes were shining. He didn't think she'd ever looked more beautiful.

'Are you up to seeing Alex?' she asked. 'I know he's hovering anxiously somewhere.'

Gabe shook his head. 'In a bit. I want to talk to you first.'

'What about?'

'What happens next.'

'Next?'

His memory might be hazy but he could vaguely recall some snippets of conversation but he wasn't sure if they were real or imagined. He hoped he hadn't been dreaming but he had to know. 'You promised me you would stay. Did you mean it?'

'I would have promised you anything, I was terrified I was going to lose you.'

'But did you mean it?' he repeated.

'I did.'

He thought that was the best news of all but Sophie hadn't finished.

'But it's not possible, is it?'

'Anything is possible.' That was something he knew for certain now.

'It's time for me to go and there's no reason for me to stay. You don't need two doctors.'

'The station may not need two doctors but I need you.' He was certain of that. 'I could find you something to do. I don't want to say goodbye. I want you with me.'

Sophie stood up and started rearranging his blankets, and he wondered why she was avoiding eye contact. 'This isn't goodbye. Not for another three weeks.'

'I don't understand.'

'The *Explorer Australis* leaves tomorrow and you'll be on it.'

'I can't leave!'

'You have to. It's just a precaution but we're worried about the risk of infection now that you've got no spleen to fight it. You need to be closer to specialised medical care until you've recovered from the surgery so you're going home for winter.'

'Will I be allowed back?'

'Yes.'

'And will you still be here?'

'No,' She was shaking her head. 'I'm leaving too. So this isn't goodbye but it is the end. You'll come back but I won't. But that's okay. It's time for me to leave. You've made me whole and I'll always be grateful to you for that. I'm ready for the real world again. I'm ready to be Sophie Thompson again. This has to be the end.'

'No, it doesn't,' he argued. He was prepared to argue for as long as it took to convince her. 'It's not over. This is just the beginning.'

'The beginning of what? You don't do commitment, remember? You don't want a proper relationship. But I do. I want to be in love again.'

'And are you?'

'It will pass,' she said.

Hope flared in his chest, making him forget his aches and pains. 'I don't want it to pass. I need you. I—'

'Please, don't say anything you're going to regret later,' she interrupted. 'We both agreed this was a short-term thing. A bit of fun until it was time for me to leave. And now it's time.'

'Not yet. Please, this is important. I need you to listen to me. I know I said I was meant to be alone but I wasn't expecting to find you and I'm not going to let you go without a fight. If I've made you whole again you've done the same for me. I want a future with you, Soph. I'm in love with you. Don't you see,' he reached out and took her other hand, ignoring his muscles as they fought against every little movement, 'The way you feel about me, that's how I feel about you. I love you and I want to spend the rest of my life with you.'

'I don't think now is the time to make major decisions. Not when they contradict everything you've ever told me.

You've just suffered a major trauma, had an anaesthetic and undergone surgery, now isn't the time.'

This wasn't going at all as he'd planned. Maybe he wasn't in the best shape to be proposing but he had to tell her how he felt. She had to know. Nothing and no one had ever been as important to him.

'I know exactly what I'm saying. I want to marry you. It might seem like a major decision but it's the easiest one I've ever made. But if you're worried about my state of mind I agree to spend the next three weeks, or however long it takes, convincing you. I have never been more serious about anything in my life. Please, just tell me you'll give me that chance. I know you're happy being Sophie Thompson but I want to know if you could be happy being Sophie Sullivan? I want you to be my wife. Will you marry me?'

EPILOGUE

Date: October 28th
Temperature: -5°C
Hours of sunlight: 16.6

SOPHIE HESITATED IN the doorway of the plane as she remembered a day a little over seven months ago when she'd stood on these same steps. She couldn't believe how different the past seven months had been from the seven before. She couldn't believe how different she was now. Then she'd been apprehensive, excited and searching for her own identity. Now she was happy, excited and secure.

'Ready?'

She turned her head and nodded at the man standing beside her. The man who had helped her to laugh and love again. The man who loved her.

'No regrets?' Gabe asked.

'None.'

'How about all those days you wasted by making me propose three times?'

'I don't regret those at all,' she replied with a wide smile. 'I loved every single one of your proposals.'

Gabe shook his head. 'I knew you were trouble the minute I laid eyes on you.'

'But am I worth it?'

'Most definitely.' He grinned, pulled her in close and kissed her mouth.

Sophie kissed him back. Hard.

'I love you, Soph,' he told her when they came up for air. 'More than you can possibly imagine. You have changed my life and I cannot imagine living without you.'

'I love you too,' she said, as she looked at the man whom she'd promised to stay with for ever and always. She slipped her gloved hand into his and started down the steps to where Alex was waiting, his blond ringlets shining in the sunlight.

'Mr and Mrs Sullivan,' he greeted them with an enormous grin, 'Welcome back to Antarctica.'

'It's good to be home,' Sophie said as Alex wrapped them both in his massive embrace.

And this would be home for the next five and a half months. Home was wherever Gabe was. She'd had to come to the end of the earth to find him but he was worth every mile. She had been given a second chance and she was going to live life without regrets and make every moment count. Starting right now.

She turned to Gabe and whispered. 'Together for ever and always.'

* * * * *

TEMPTED BY HER ITALIAN SURGEON

BY

LOUISA GEORGE

Published in Great Britain 2015
by Mills & Boon, an imprint of Harlequin (UK) Limited,
Eton House, 18-24 Paradise Road, Richmond, Surrey, TW9 1SR

ISBN: 978-0-263-24706-0

Harlequin (UK) Limited's policy is to use papers that are natural, renewable and recyclable products and made from wood grown in sustainable forests. The logging and manufacturing processes conform to the legal environmental regulations of the country of origin.

Printed and bound in Spain
by CPI, Barcelona

Dear Reader,

Thank you so much for picking up Matteo and Ivy's story.

The idea for this book came from a news article I read about a doctor getting into trouble for commenting about a case on social media. The dos and don'ts of stepping into that very public place the internet as a professional person intrigued me. What if someone did something silly and inadvertently brought their place of work into the glare of the media? What would the ramifications be? How do medical providers deal with social media platforms? And, best of all, how would a very English uptight hospital lawyer deal with a super-sexy, rule-breaking Italian man?

These two professionals with very different approaches to life have no idea what's about to hit them when Ivy summons Matteo to her office for a dressing-down!

Both of them have been hurt before, and neither wants to trust anyone any time soon—but having to live a little in each other's world opens them up to the potential of letting their guards down and falling in love. And they fight it every step of the way.

Matteo and Ivy were such fun to write about—possibly my favourite characters so far (although I always think that!). But what's not to like about a handsome Italian surgeon and a good old feisty Yorkshire lass? (I'm slightly biased, I know…)

For all my writing news and release dates visit me at www.louisageorge.com

Happy reading!

Louisa x

Books by Louisa George

A Baby on Her Christmas List
200 Harley Street: The Shameless Maverick
How to Resist a Heartbreaker
The Last Doctor She Should Ever Date
The War Hero's Locked-Away Heart
Waking Up With His Runaway Bride
One Month to Become a Mum

Visit the author profile page at millsandboon.co.uk for more titles

Praise for Louisa George:

'*How to Resist a Heartbreaker* keeps you hooked from beginning to end, but make sure you have a tissue handy, for this one will break your heart only to heal it in the end.'

—*HarlequinJunkie*

'A moving, uplifting and feel-good romance, this is packed with witty dialogue, intense emotion and sizzling love scenes. Louisa George once again brings an emotional and poignant story of past hurts, dealing with grief and new beginnings which will keep a reader turning pages with its captivating blend of medical drama, family dynamics and romance.'

—*GoodReads* on *How to Resist a Heartbreaker*

'Louisa George is a bright star at Mills & Boon®, and I can highly recommend this book to those who believe romance rocks the world.'

—*GoodReads* reader review on *How to Resist a Heartbreaker*

CHAPTER ONE

'WHAT ON EARTH...?' Ivy Leigh blinked at the image downloading to her inbox, pixel by tiny pixel.

A...bottom?

A beautiful perfectly formed, tanned, bare bottom. Two toned thighs, a sculpted back...a naked male body, in what looked like a men's locker room. A tagline next to the pert backside read: *Dr Delicious. As perfect as a peach. Go on...take a bite.*

She swallowed. And again. Fanned her hot cheeks. She might have imposed a strict dating hiatus but she still had an appreciation of what was fine when she saw it. But why on earth would her work computer be the recipient of such a thing?

Maybe the spam screens on the hospital intranet server weren't up to scratch. Adding a new note to her smartphone to-do list—*Call IT*—she let out a heat-infused sigh that had nothing to do with sexual frustration and everything to do with this new job. Two weeks in and yet another department she needed to pull into order. Still, she'd been employed here to drag this hospital into the twenty-first century and that was what she was going to do, no matter how many toes she trod on.

Twisting in her chair to hide the offending but not remotely offensive bottom from anyone who might walk past her open office door, she sneaked a closer look at the image, her gaze landing on a pile of what looked like discarded clothes on a bench. No, not clothes as such…

Scrubs?

Please, no.

Dark green scrubs bearing the embroidered name of St Carmen's Hospital. She gasped, and whatever vague interest she'd had dissolved into a puddle of professional anxiety…her bordering-on-average day was fast turning bad.

So who? What? Why? *Why me?*

She slammed her eyelids shut and refused to look at the accompanying email message.

Okay, big girls' pants.

Opening one eye, she took a deep breath and read.

From Albert Pinkney. St Carmen's Hospital Chairman. His formidable perfectly English pronunciation shone through his words. 'Miss Leigh, what in heaven's name is this? Our new marketing campaign? Since when did St Carmen's turn into some sort of smutty cabaret show? This is all over the internet like a rash and is not synonymous with the image we want to present. The benefactors are baying for blood. We are a children's hospital. You're the lawyer—do something. Make it disappear. Fix it.'

Because she was probably the only person who could solve this—when all else failed call in the lawyer to shut it down, or drag some antiquated law out and hit the offender with it.

And, damn it, fix it she would. Although making it disappear would be a little harder. Didn't Pinkney know that once something was out on the net, it was there for ever? Clearly he was another candidate to add to her social media awareness classes.

First, find out who this…specimen belonged to. Now, that was going to be an interesting task. 'Becca! Becca!'

'Yes, Miss Leigh?' Her legal assistant arrived in the doorway and flashed her usual over-enthusiastic grin. 'What can I help you with?'

'Delicate issue… You've been here a while and have your ear to the ground. You must know pretty much all of the staff by now. Have you any idea who this…might belong to?' Ivy twisted away and made a *ta-da* motion with her hands towards her computer screen.

'Oh, my…' Becca fanned her face with the stack of manila folders in her hand. 'Take a bite? I'm suddenly very hungry.'

Me, too. 'That is so not the point. Can you see our logo? Right there. We can't have this sort of thing happening, it's very bad for our reputation.'

'Not unless we're trying to attract a whole tranche of new nurses… No? Wrong response? Sorry.' Becca gave a little shrug that said she wasn't sorry at all and that, in fact, she was really quite impressed. 'It's very nice. It is kind of perfect. And it says it belongs to a doctor so we can narrow it down. We could do one of those police line-ups, get the main suspects against the wall and…' She looked back at the picture, her voice breathy and high-pitched. 'I'm happy to organise that.'

'Get in line.' But, seriously, how many years at law school? For this? This was what she'd studied so hard for? This was why she'd hibernated away from any kind of social life? Her plan had always been to get into a position where she could safeguard others from what she'd had to endure, to prevent mistakes that cost people their happiness. Not chastise a naked man about impropriety. Still, no one could say her job didn't have variety. 'I don't want to narrow it down, Becca, I want it gone. We need to send out a stack of take-down notices, get the PR team onto damage limitation. And whoever put this out there is going to learn what it's like to feel the wrath of Ivy Leigh.'

It was late. The cadaver transplant he'd just finished on a ten-year-old boy had been difficult and long, but successful, with a good prognosis. He had a planned surgery list lined up for tomorrow and a lot of prep to work up. A ward round. And now this—an urgent summons to a part of the hospital he had not even known existed. Or, for that matter, cared about. The legal team? At six-thirty in the evening? Wouldn't all the pen-pushers have gone home? Matteo Finelli's mood was fading fast. He rapped on the closed door. Didn't wait to hear a response, and walked right in. 'You wanted to see me?'

'Yes.' The woman in front of him sat up straight behind an expensive-looking wide mahogany desk that was flanked by two filing cabinets. Beyond that a large window gave a view over the busy central London street. It was sunny out there and he imagined sitting in a small bar or café with the sun on his back as he downed a cold beer. Instead of being in here, doing this.

Apart from a calendar on the desk there was nothing else anywhere in the room. Nothing personalised, no photos, no pens, stapler...anything. She either had a bad case of OCD or had just moved in. Which would explain why he had not heard of her or seen her around. She ran a hand through short blonde hair that made her look younger than he'd imagined she must be to have achieved such a status and such a large office.

Cool green eyes stared at him. The blouse she wore was a similar colour—and why he'd even noticed he couldn't say. Her mouth, although some would say was pretty, was in a tight thin line. She looked buttoned-up and tautly wound and as if she had never had a moment of pleasure in her life. She met his anger with equal force. 'Mr Finelli, I presume? Please, take a seat.'

He didn't. 'I have not time. I was told you needed to see me immediately… What is the problem?'

'Okay, no pleasantries. Fine by me. I'll cut to the chase. Tell me…' The eyes narrowed a little. Her throat jumped as she swallowed. Emerald-tipped fingers tapped on a keyboard and an image flickered onto the screen. 'Is this you?'

There was no point in concealing his laugh. Whoever had taken the photo had held the lens at a damned fine angle. He looked good. More than good. He whistled on an out breath. 'You like it?'

'That's not the point.' But her pupils flared and heat hit her cheeks.

'You do like it? It is impressive, yes? And you summoned me all the way to the other side of the hospital for a slide show of naked bodies…interesting.' He turned to go. 'Now, I can leave? I have work to do.'

'Not so fast, Mr Finelli.'

Ma che diavolo? 'Call me Matteo, please.'

The woman blinked. 'Mr Finelli, why did you post this picture on the internet? Were you hoping for it to go completely viral, because, congratulations, it did. It seems that cyberspace can't get enough of your…assets. Have you any idea what damage you have caused the hospital by posing for this with the St Carmen's logo available for the world to see?'

'Everybody calls me Matteo, I do not answer to Mr Finelli—too formal. Too…English. I did not post that picture anywhere. And with all due respect, Miss…' His eyes roved over her face—which was turning from a quite attractive pink to a dark shade of red—then to her name badge. Her left hand. No wedding band. Definitely Miss. 'Miss Ivy Leigh. I was not posing.'

'Do you deny this is your bott…er…*gluteus maximus*?'

It wasn't fair to smile again. But he did. 'Of course I don't deny it. I've already agreed that it is mine. But clearly I did not take the picture and I did not pose. It looks to me like I'd had a shower, I was stretching to get my clothes out of the locker, with my back to the lens, you cannot see my face. I can't take a photo of the back of my head from that distance, can I? Besides which I am a very busy doctor and I do not have time to sit around playing on the internet like some people.' *Like you*, he thought. But he let that accusation hover in the silence. 'I don't know for sure who took the picture, but I can guess.'

'Oh? Who?' She leant forward, her eyes fixed on his face, eyebrows arched. In another lifetime it might have been fun to play a little more with her. To see where her soft edges were, if she had any. But not in this life.

'Ged Peterson.' *Touché, my man. You win this round.* 'My registrar, he loves playing pranks.'

'Peterson. Peterson. Ged? Short for Gerard?' Those green-tipped fingers tapped into some database on the computer. 'He doesn't work here.'

'No. But he did. Until last month when he went to work in Australia. He said he was going to give me a leaving present. I didn't realise it would be this.' Matteo stepped back, primed to leave. 'And now we have solved the mystery I must go.'

'Absolutely not. Stay right there.'

That got his attention. No woman had ever spoken to him like that before. It was…well, it was interesting. 'Why?'

'Again, I ask you; have you any idea of the damage you have caused? Lady Margaret has withdrawn her funding for the new family rooms in protest already. Parents are complaining that this is not what they expect from an institution responsible for their children's lives. Surgeons who complain about being overworked and underpaid and yet have time to flaunt their bodies make us look ridiculous. It's not professional.'

'Everyone needs to stop overreacting. It is nothing.'

With a disdainful look that suggested he was in way over his pretty little head, she shook hers. 'Image is everything, Mr Finelli. In this technological age it's all about the message we send out to gain trust and respect. We need people on side to volunteer, raise funds, hit targets. We do not need some jumped-up surgeon flashing his backside with our logo in the picture.'

He strode forward and leaned towards her, pointing at the picture getting a nose full of honeysuckle scent in the process. Overly officious she might be, but she smelt damned good. He edged away from the perfume because it was strangely addictive and he didn't need any more distractions today. This was enough and he still had a few hours' work ahead of him. 'If you are worried about funding I have an idea…why not take another eleven pictures of me and make some calendars you hospital administrators all seem to love so much? Sell me?'

'I am a lawyer.' As if that explained anything. Actually, it explained a lot. With one brother already qualified and another working his way through college, Matteo knew that law school was just as rigorous as med school. That those dark shadows under her eyes weren't from late nights drinking in bars but from studying into the early hours. That this woman had worked diligently amidst strong competition. Along with her English-rose complexion and porcelain skin, it also explained that she'd probably spent the best part of her life cooped up indoors with her nose in a book, not exploring the world, not simply lying in the last rays of a relaxing afternoon letting the sun heat your skin. It explained why she was so damned coiled.

She shook her head. 'The money you've already lost us is in the thousands, possibly hundreds of thousands, Mr Finelli. Calendars only make a few pounds per copy.'

'With my backside on them it would make a lot more.'

'You really do have a high opinion of yourself, don't you?' Her voice had deepened and he got the feeling she was trying very hard to be calm.

Good, because that meant he was niggling her, probably not as much as she was niggling him…but, well, he had more important things to do. Like go check on the transplant patient. 'Sure. Why not?'

In what he could only describe as a power play she stood up and walked around the desk. If he wasn't mistaken it took her a moment to steady herself, then she grabbed a file from a filing cabinet and slammed it shut with finesse and flair. She sat back down again, but not before he'd taken a good long look at the cinched-in waist, curve-enhancing, slim-legged trousers and wedge heels.

Even more interesting…

Opening what he now realised was his employment file, she gave him a cold stare. 'Look, Mr Finelli, it's obvious you are not taking this issue seriously. I need to make sure you are aware of the consequences of having your naked body sprawled over the internet with our name and logo on it. I have discussed the issue with the HR department and the chairman and we are all in agreement that we need to instigate some courses for the staff on the whys and wherefores of social media etiquette. These will be mandatory for every—'

'Because of this? I did nothing wrong.'

'Because of this. Because we can't run risks with people's lives, or be distracted from our true purpose as a hospital. Because we can't make mistakes. Distraction causes death or damage.' This was clearly very important to her—personal, maybe, judging by the passion in her eyes and the slight shake in her hands.

She took a sip of water from a glass next to her elbow. And didn't, he noticed, offer him anything to drink. She waited a moment and seemed to settle herself before continuing. 'We have to control how we are seen, and this episode has just cemented my point. I ran the classes very successfully at my last place of employment and am starting them here on Thursday. You will be required to attend.'

No way. 'I operate on Thursdays.'

'And Tuesdays and Fridays. I know. There are only four sessions. You will be expected to attend them all, like every other person in this hospital, then no more will be said about the matter.'

Dio santo. She was serious. 'Have you any idea how precious operating theatre time is to a surgeon?'

She looked away and her eyes flickered closed for a moment. Then she gathered herself together. 'I have some understanding, yes.'

'And if I refuse?'

She tapped his folder. 'You will have to face a disciplinary hearing. Then there will be no operating time at all. It will be time-consuming and messy. There may even be a stand-down period. Who can say?'

Now the niggling descended into outright anger. 'On what grounds?'

'Bringing the organisation into disrepute. Refusing mandatory training. It's all quite clear in the employment contract…expected behaviour, training requirements, dress code, et cetera. Mr Finelli, many hospital boards don't allow their physicians to have a public face on social media. We are not unusual in wanting to protect ourselves.'

Round one to Ivy Leigh. Ivy…wasn't there a plant…poison ivy? *Sommaco velenoso.* It described her perfectly. He just needed a counter argument to bring Poison Ivy down a peg or two. 'Perhaps I could sue you too.'

Now her eyes widened with a flicker of nervousness. 'What the hell for?'

'Breach of my privacy. I could suggest that I did not give my permission for my body to be used in such a poorly contrived advert.'

She laughed and it was surprisingly soft and feminine. 'Go on and indulge yourself in any fantasy you like. But you and I both know this was not an advert. You have no grounds, but I do. In fact, section three of the Workplace—'

'Forget it. I'm not listening any more. I will not attend your sessions.'

'Okay. Your choice.' She reminded him of his younger sister, Liliana, who would not give up. Ever. Arguing with her was like arguing with a brick wall. 'Then I will have to invite you to attend a meeting with our human relations director first thing tomorrow morning.'

'No.' Take more time out of his work schedule?

Maybe Mike would swap his cardiac roster from a Wednesday for one week just to make this insufferable woman go away?

'Mr Finelli, we are both on the same side.'

'Like hell we are.' But he did not have any more time to waste on this. Better to get it over and done with. 'You leave me with no choice. I'll do the four sessions.'

'Then it's sorted. After that you won't hear anything more from me on this matter. Thank you for your time.' She put out her hand and, grimly, he shook it. It was warm and firm and confident. And a little something reverberated through his body at her touch—which he steadfastly ignored. Clearly she felt none of it as her voice remained calm and cool, like her eyes. 'I'm sure you'll find the sessions most interesting.'

'I'm sure I won't. Now I need to rearrange my day. Four sessions shouldn't take up much time. I will be free from what time? Lunch?'

Amusement flashed across her features, as if she'd won a well-fought victory. 'Oh, sorry, didn't I make myself clear? By four sessions I meant four days.'

'Four days? No. No way. I'm not doing it.'

'But you agreed. And we shook hands. Is an Italian man's word as good as his honour?'

He held her gaze. His honour was fine and intact, unlike others he could name. He would never betray anyone the way he had once been betrayed. 'It is. But I have one condition.'

'Oh, yes?' Her expression told him she thought he was not well placed to be making conditions.

'For every minute I have to spend in your ridiculous class you have to spend an equal amount of time with me, doing my work. The work this hospital is so famous for doing. Saving lives. Then perhaps you'll see just how badly you have wasted my time.' He held her gaze. Saw the flicker of anxiety stamped down by determined resolve as she nodded.

'Okay.' Her smile was like condensed milk—way too sweet. 'Seeing as I'm new to the hospital, I have to familiarise myself with each department anyway. And it'll give me invaluable insights into the specific kind of legal issues that could arise there and a chance to review policy. This way I'll be killing two birds with one stone.'

How had he thought it might be fun to play with her?

Fun was over. This was war. 'Believe me, Miss Leigh, the only killing going on in my OR is of your determination to make a damned fool of me. Goodbye.'

CHAPTER TWO

He wasn't going to come.

Ivy surveyed the conference room filled with porters, nursing staff, ward clerks and doctors, all chattering and drinking copious cups of coffee before the first session started in less than two minutes. And why the heck, with a room full of attendees who looked interested and invested in learning about social media, she was shamefully disappointed that she couldn't see Mr Finelli's famous backside in the foray, she couldn't fathom. Only that she now appeared to be locked in some sort of battle of wills with the doctor and she'd been looking forward to showcasing her side and proving her very valid points. The man may have been infuriatingly narcissistic but she'd believed him a worthy adversary. Clearly not. Typical that he hadn't bothered to turn up.

Mind you, with those dark Mediterranean eyes, that proud haughty jaw and thoughts of what was under those scrubs, it was probably a good thing. And it would be hard to concentrate on her talk with that glower searing a hole in her soul.

'Okay, Miss Leigh…' Becca handed her the folders of hand-outs for the participants. 'One each and a few to spare. Morning tea's at ten-thirty. Catering will deliver at about ten-fifteen.'

'And lunch? You know how these things go. If they don't get regularly fed and watered they get grouchy.'

'One o'clock. In the Steadman Room. Oh, and the laptop's all set up with the projector, you're good to go. Good luck.'

Excellent. Everything was running perfectly, apart from a niggle of a headache. 'Thanks, and, Becca, please, please, drop the formality and call me Ivy. I know the last incumbent had you calling him sir, but I do things differently.'

'Okay. If you're su…' Her assistant's face grew a deep shade of puce as her gaze fixed on something over Ivy's shoulder. 'Oh… Just, oh.'

'Are you okay?'

'Oh, yes. Just *peachy.* Such a shame he's a break-your-heart bad boy.' Becca grinned, and moved forward as if levitated and as if breaking your heart was some kind of spectator sport and he was the *numero uno* world champion title-holder. Which he probably was. 'Mr Finelli, please grab a coffee first and then take a seat. Let me show you where the cups are.'

Great. For some reason Ivy's heart jigged a little. First-time nerves, probably. She was always jittery at the beginning of a workshop. There was so much to think about… technology not working, correct air-conditioning levels—too hot and everyone fell asleep, too cold and no one could concentrate—snacks arriving on time, holding everyone's attention, keeping track…

Suddenly he was walking towards her. She imagined Becca would think him hot, all brooding chocolate-fudge eyes and unruly dark hair. But Ivy had switched off her sexy radar years ago when she'd learned that men wanted their women perfect, and that she didn't fit that bill. Since then she'd watched her flatmates have their hearts broken and her mother reduced…just less, diminished somehow…

because of a man—and Ivy had decided she wasn't going there. Give her books and her career any day. There was something perfect about a beginning, a middle and an end of a novel—a whole. Complete. And, truth be told, reading was just about all she had the energy to do after a day's work.

Unlike the other consultants, he'd adopted informal dress—no suit and tie for Dr Delicious of peachy-bottom fame. Just a white T-shirt over formidable shoulders, with dark jeans hugging slender hips. The same uniform she'd seen on every youth in Florence when she'd been there on a weekend break. She imagined him with dark aviator sunglasses on, perched on a moped like something out of a nineteen-fifties movie. Then her mind wandered back to that picture of him naked, and the knowledge of exactly what was under that uniform made her feel strangely uncomfortable. Heat shimmied through her. It was unseasonably warm in here—a spring heatwave, perhaps? Too many bodies in such a small room? She must ask someone to fiddle with the air-con at once.

Where was she? Ah, yes, keeping…what? Keeping track. *Focus.*

'Good morning, Miss Leigh. And so it begins.' Oh…and then there was the accent. Kind of cute, she supposed. If you were Becca and easily taken in by deep honeyed tones melting over your skin. She let it wash right over her, along with the irritated vibe that emanated from his every pore.

'Mr Finelli, glad you could eventually join us. I hear you kicked up a bit of a fuss about it all, though.'

A frown appeared underneath the dark curls that fell over his forehead. 'The HR director is as enthusiastic about this as you are, it seems. Does no one in this hospital have any common sense, Miss Leigh?'

'That is exactly what I'm trying to engender with this

course, but some of our staff seem to want to flaunt themselves at every opportunity. And, please, call me Ivy.'

'Ivy, ah, yes. But only if you call me Matteo. Or if you can't manage that, Matt will do. *Ivy.*' He smiled as if something other than this conversation was amusing him. He took a sip of black coffee and winced. '*Dio,* more poison. Why is coffee so bad here?'

More poison? What in hell did that mean.? Uh-oh, she could guess. 'Poison ivy? Really? Is that the best you can do? I've been hearing that since I was in kindergarten. I expected better…more…from you, Mr Finelli. Oh, sorry, Matteo. Please, do try harder.'

He put the cup into his saucer, clearly much more insulted by his drink than her words. 'I was just seeing what it would take to wind you up—not a lot, it seems.'

She played it cool, ignoring the fluster in her gut. 'Oh, make no mistake, I'm not wound up. Just disappointed by your performance so far.'

The smile he gave her was wicked and it tickled her deep inside. 'Oh, trust me, Miss Leigh, no woman has ever been disappointed by my performance.'

Heat hit her cheeks as she realised she'd been drawn in and chewed up—worse, he was flirting and she could barely admit to herself that she was a little intrigued by someone so sure of himself. Her heart beat wildly in her chest and she willed it to slow. This sort of battleground tactic was way out of her league—flirting wasn't something she was used to. A cold, hard stare and feigned disinterest had always been enough to keep any potential lovers at bay, that and her refusal to undress in anything other than darkness. Plus a side helping of reservation had helped, and a desire to not end up like her mother.

No way would she let a man have any kind of effect

on her…no way would she let *this* man have any kind of effect on her.

What she needed was to put him on side and a little off balance. She looked at his cup and wondered…maybe if she let him in on her little coffee secret he might just be so taken aback he'd sit quietly at the back of the class and listen, instead of— She could only imagine what he had in store. Creating merry hell about her subject matter. What better way to derail him than by being friendly? She leaned a little closer and whispered, 'There's a coffee shop down the road on the corner, Enrico's, great coffee. I always make sure I get one on my way into work, it keeps me going. I don't like to offend the catering staff here so I decant it into one of their cups.'

'And now we have a secret shared. Me, too. And who would have thought you could be so subversive? Maybe there is more to you than I thought.' His eyes widened and then he winked. 'Enrico's a friend, and, yes, his coffee is the best this side of the English Channel. Although that isn't hard.'

'No. I guess not.' Subversive? *Subversive?* And to her chagrin that thought made her feel damned good. Although it was a stretch even for her imagination—she'd spent the better part of her life working hard and toeing every line she found. Her gaze roved over his face, all swarthy and handsome…no, beautiful, if you were the sort to get carried away by tall, dark and breathtaking. She wasn't.

Then she caught his eye. For a second, or two, maybe more, he looked at her, those dark brown eyes reaching into her soul and tugging a little. There was something about him that was deeper than she'd imagined…something more… She was caught by the hints of honey and gold in his irises, his scent of cleanness and man, and out of the two of them she realised that she was the one a little off balance. So not the plan.

The chatter in the room seemed to dull a little and he turned away, the connection broken. Ivy took a breath. For a moment he'd almost seemed human. But then he turned back, all trace of the friendliness she'd thought she'd seen wiped clear.

His voice lowered. 'So, I am keeping my side of the bargain and here I am. I'm losing valuable operating hours so you'd better blow my damned socks off with this. I'm looking forward to you joining us tomorrow. We have a double whammy for you. In theatre one we have a live donor retrieval. And next door, in theatre two, we will be performing, for your delight and delectation, a renal—*that means kidney*—transplant on a twelve-year-old girl. I hope you've got stamina as well as balls because you're going to need it. It's going to be a long day.'

He thought she had balls? Was that a compliment? Or did he just see her as an equally worthy opponent? She hoped so. 'I am well aware of what renal means, and cardio, hepatology and orthopaedic… Throw me a word, Mr Finelli, and I'm pretty sure I'd be able to translate from medico to legal to layman and back again—I aced Latin and my mother's a GP. I won my high school creative writing prize five years in a row and my favourite subject was Classics, so I think I cover all linguistic challenges. And I've got a lot more stamina than most.' She just wasn't going to mention the teeny-weeny little fact that she was also a fully paid-up member of the hemophobia club. One speck of blood and she was on her back.

So far in her hospital career she'd been able to avoid any incidents by making sure she was never in the wrong place at the wrong time—or always getting out quickly. No way would she admit to being nervous or in any way intimidated at the prospect of watching an operation—no, two operations. A real baptism of fire. 'Actually, I'm looking forward to it.'

'Me, too.' His mouth curled into a smile that was at once mesmerising and irritating. Heat swirled in her chest and she felt an unfamiliar prickling over her skin. Maybe her sexy radar had flickered back into life?

She brushed that thought away immediately. She had more important things to deal with than wayward, unsatisfied hormones.

Because somehow between now and tomorrow she was going to have to overcome her fear of blood. Maybe a quick phone call to Mum for some anti-anxiety drugs? Hypnotherapy? Although she'd heard the best way to deal with phobias was immersion therapy, she just hadn't ever put her hand up for it.

She also had to work out how she was going to stand for eight hours straight when her doctors had distinctly advised her against doing any such thing. Never mind. That was tomorrow. Today she had another hurdle to jump.

Stepping away from him, she nodded across the room to Becca, who rang a bell, drawing everyone's attention.

'Good morning, everyone.' Ivy made sure the room was silent before she continued and stepped up to the raised area. 'Thank you so much for coming today. I have what I hope will be an enlightening presentation that will entertain you as well as teach you something. I hope you don't mind if I take a seat every now and then up here on the stage—it means you get to see the slides and informative videos and not me, which I'm sure you'll all agree is preferable.'

In keeping with the presentations skills she'd honed over the years she ensured she made eye contact with as many people as possible. When her gaze landed on Matteo he looked straight back at her from his front-row seat, teasing and daring lighting up his eyes, but she had no idea what was going through his mind. She had no way of reading him, but she got the distinct impression he was weighing her up, his scrutinising gaze making her catch her breath.

Bring it on, Matteo Finelli, she tried to tell him right back. She was ready for this. *Bring it on.*

This was just the beginning.

'To recap, we have a social media policy for three main reasons: protecting patient confidentiality; protecting and promoting our brand; and protecting our staff. Be very sure that what you say is how you want to be seen, and remember that if something you put up on networking sites can be connected with St Carmen's or our patients in any way then that may result in disciplinary action. There is a lot of chatter out there and how we present ourselves is extremely important; it's very hard to erase a message or a footprint once it's out. These things have a habit of coming back to bite us in the proverbial behind.'

Matteo watched as Ivy's eyes flicked to him and he felt the sting of her retort. Okay, so having his behind out there for all the world to see hadn't been the wisest idea his friend had had, and Matteo was starting to understand a little of the ruckus it had caused. St Carmen's had a solid reputation for putting children first and he could see that having a connection with a naked man may well have done some damage. But, really, four sessions to get that message across? What in hell could next week's workshop be about?

Poison Ivy was certainly passionate about her job, he'd give her that. And her presentation skills had been first rate. He got the impression that public speaking was something she could do with finesse but that she didn't exactly love it. Her voice was endlessly enthusiastic, and he caught a hint of an accent...although not being native to England he couldn't quite place it. She certainly looked the part with another smart dark trouser suit and silk blouse—today it was a deep cobalt blue that had him reminiscing about the summer skies back home. And he felt another sting—sharp enough to remind him of the folly of thinking too hard and investing too much. And that love, in its many forms, could cut deeply.

But Ivy's ballsy forthrightness coupled with the curve-enhancing trousers and form-fitting blouse had piqued his imagination. Although why, he didn't know, she was the exact opposite of everything he usually liked in a woman. He went for tall women, and she was petite. He had a track record of tousled brunettes, and she was blonde with a... what was it? Yes, a pixie cut. He liked to entertain and enthral and she showed nothing but disinterest bordering on contempt. He wasn't usually spurned—spurning was his role. Ah, no—he never led a woman to believe he would give any more than a good time. Until the good times became more one-sidedly meaningful—and that was the signal to get out.

Putting this sudden interest down to the thrill of the chase, he nodded to her, raising his eyebrows. *Do go on.*

She gave him a disinterested smile and looked at someone else. 'I hope you've all enjoyed our journey into cyberspace and an overview of social media opportunities—as you can see, they are many and varied and more are exploding onto our screens and into our homes every day. Now that we've highlighted our hospital policy, I hope you can see how and when mistakes can be made, even from the comfort of your own sofa when you think you're engaging in a private conversation. Nothing is ever private on the internet. Next week we'll be talking about the good, the bad and the very ugly of social networking sites. In the meantime, in the words of someone much wiser than me…when it comes to the World Wide Web, don't be that person with the smartphone making dumb mistakes.'

And everyone around him seemed to have enjoyed themselves immensely. She gave a shy smile at their applause and then concentrated on logging off the laptop and clearing away her papers.

He followed the queue to the door but before he'd made it out he heard her voice. 'Mr Finelli?'

'Yes?'

She stepped down from the small stage and walked towards him, trying hard but not quite managing to hide the limp that now, at the end of a day when she'd mostly been standing, clearly gave her pain. 'I hope that was insightful?'

'It could have been a lot quicker.'

'Not everyone is as quick thinking as you.' She bit her bottom lip as if trying to hold back a smile. 'Besides, we have some very recalcitrant staff members who insist they know better than we do on these matters. I need to make sure I hammer out our message loud and clear.'

Remembering her barb, he gave her a smile back. 'I felt the hammer.'

'Good. My job here is done. I hope in future you'll be contemplating how to send positive messages that reflect the nature of our business. Or, indeed, not sending messages at all.'

'The only positive messages I need to send are in the numbers of children I and the renal department save. And in how many families don't have to endure suffering or loss of life.'

She studied him. 'Well, maybe a bit of help in drumming up support for your unit is in order? You could harness the wave, do some awareness campaigns and get… what? What is on your wish list?'

He didn't need to think twice about this—the same thing every transplant unit across the world wanted. 'More organ donors, more people willing to sign up to donate when they die. More dialysis machines. More research.'

'So put your thinking hat on and see if you can come up with a way of reaching out to people across the internet. Without taking your clothes off? There are plenty of people here in London wanting to help a good cause…but many more reaching out across the internet. Just imagine… Well, have a good evening, I'll see you in the morning. Bright and breezy.' Then she gave him a real smile. An honest to God, big smile that lit up her face. And, *Mio Dio*, the green in her eyes was intense and mesmerising. Her mouth an impish curl that invited him to join her in whatever had amused her. And something in his chest tugged. It was unbalancing and yet steadying at the same time.

'Where are you from?' For some reason his longing-to-leave brain had been outsmarted by his wanting-to-stay mouth.

Her smile melted away. 'I'm sorry?'

'Your accent. I'm not used to all the different ones yet. Other people say Landan…you say Lundun.'

Gathering all her gear together, she shovelled folders under one arm and carried a laptop in her hand. With a hitch of her shoulder she switched the lights out and then indicated for him to leave the conference room ahead of her while she pressed numbers into a keypad that sent the area into lockdown. 'York. I'm from York, it's in the north. A long way away. Three and a half hours' drive—on a good day.'

'Of course I have heard of it.' He noticed a slight narrowing of her eyes and her voice had dropped a little. 'And that makes you sad, being away from family?'

She shrugged. 'No. Well…yes, I suppose. You know how it is. You do miss the familiar.'

'I suppose you do.' Maybe others did. He hadn't been able to leave quickly enough and trips back home had been sporadic. Betrayal and hurt could do that to a man.

They neared the elevators and she paused, put her bag on the floor and pressed the 'up' button. 'And you? You must feel a long way from home. Which is?'

'A small village near Siena. Nothing special.'

Her eyebrows rose. 'You're joking, right? Every Tuscan village is special.'

His village was. The inhabitants, on the other hand, not so much. 'How do you know? Have you visited there?'

'Florence, that's all, just a quick weekend trip. It was lovely.' Her ribcage twisted as she tried to hitch the now falling papers back under her arm.

He reached for them, his hand brushing against her blouse, sending a shiver through his gut. Strange how his body was reacting to her. Very strange. 'Let me take those papers from you.'

'I can manage.' She stopped short and shook her head with determination and resolve, obviously trying to be strong when she didn't need to be. He got the feeling that Ivy Leigh put a brave face on a lot—to hide what? Some perceived weakness? Something that was more than a problem with her foot.

'I know you can manage. But you have too many things to carry and I have nothing. Let me take them.' Without waiting for her to answer, he took the folders and slipped them under his arm, wondering what the hell the point of this was. She was on the other side—the annoying, bureaucratic, meddling middle-men side.

Talking with the enemy, helping the enemy, whatever next? Sleeping with the enemy? Pah! As if he would do anything so foolish.

And she obviously had a full appreciation of that. 'I know what you're doing, Matteo. You're trying to get me on side and then you're going to strike. Pounce…or something. Try to catch me unawares, try to convince me to set you free from my course and then hit me where it hurts.'

'Never. I would never hit anyone.' There had been a few times when he'd come close—okay, once when he'd stepped over that line and with good reason. But never again.

She looked confused. 'Don't panic, it's a turn of phrase. I didn't mean you'd really hit me. I know you wouldn't do that.'

'Good. And, actually, I was just being nice.'

'Well, that is unexpected. Who knew you could be?'

The fleeting anger at the memories melted into humour. Ivy Leigh was good at sparring. He admired that. Always good to respect the enemy. Laughter bubbled from his chest. 'Strange, yes, considering we are on opposite sides. The next thing we know we'll be doing something ridiculous like going for a drink.'

'Oh, no. I can't do that.' She jabbed the lift button again and tsked. 'I never mix business with pleasure.'

'I'm intrigued that you think having a drink with me would be pleasurable?'

Again there was a smile, but it belied a look in her eyes that was…half wistful, half anxious. 'I'm sure the *drink* would be very pleasurable indeed. I'm very partial to a decent red. But, as I say, it's not something I do.'

'Neither do I.'

'Then I'm glad that we agree on something.' But that wistful look remained, until she turned away.

There was no one else around. The place was silent. The conference area had all closed down for the night so it was just him and her and a buzz in the air between them that was so fierce it was almost tangible. 'And you are going where now?'

She shrugged. 'Back to the fifth floor, if this lift ever arrives. I have work to do.'

'After five o'clock? All the other paper-pushers have long gone.'

Her lips curled into a smirk. 'Pen. It's pen-pushers not paper-pushers.'

'I know, I know. I apologise. I'm still getting used to your idioms.' And she was stunning when she smiled. Which, it appeared, made him tongue-tied too. Really? What in hell was wrong with him?

'Where the hell is this lift?' Jab-jab on the button with those emerald fingernails. 'I don't think about the time I put in. I just do what's needed, and if that keeps me here all hours then so be it. Like most lawyers, I expect to work hard.'

'Then you'd make a fine doctor too.'

'Believe me, I wouldn't.' She gave a visible shudder and he wondered whether she'd been hurt at some point. Maybe a doctor had broken that well-protected heart of hers. And, again, why that was remotely relevant to anything, he didn't know.

'You don't like doctors? A hospital is a strange place to work, then.'

'Most doctors are fine. In fact, my mum's one.' Finally the lift arrived with a jolt and the doors swished open. Taking the folders from his hand, she fixed her gaze on him. 'Only a few of them ruin the reputation for the majority…'

What? As she stepped into the lift he put a hand out to stop the doors from closing. 'You mean me? *I* have a reputation?' He laughed. 'Good to know. Let me guess how that goes… I am too outspoken. I am a maverick. I am too committed to my job. Worse, I leave broken hearts in my wake…'

'Apparently so.' Her fingers tapped against the cold steel of the wall panel. 'And a lot more that I couldn't possibly say…'

'I am also very attentive to detail. Some would say passionate. I have a sense of humour. I play very hard indeed…' His gaze drifted over her face. The detail there was stunning. The eyes that gave away her emotions regardless of how hard she tried to keep them locked away. That mouth, the keeper of barbs and insults and a perfect smile. Those lips… How would it feel if he were to kiss her? How would Miss Prim and Proper react then? Would she let him see a little of what was under that hard surface? Because, dammit, he knew there was more to her. A softer side—a passionate side. Just waiting to be set free. Lucky man who ever achieved that.

The door jolted against his back, reminding him that this was neither the time nor the place to be kissing Ivy Leigh. And yet…he reached a hand to her cheek and he could have sworn he saw heat flicker across her eyes, just enough to mist them and to tell him that he was not the only one struggling with this wildly strange scenario. Her mouth opened a little, he could see her breathing had quickened, and her eyes fluttered closed for a microsecond. Enough to show he had an effect on her…and she liked it. Didn't want it, not at all, but she liked it.

She pulled away. 'So. I'll see you tomorrow. Show me what you've got, Mr Finelli, I'm expecting to be very impressed.'

He felt strongly that he could show Miss Leigh a thing or two and she'd be very impressed indeed. *Work. Work.*

Reminding himself of what was truly the most important thing in his life, he took a step back too. *Che stupido.* 'Do not bring me back to that issue again. Those damned workshops. This social media thing. Miss Leigh, you make my blood boil sometimes.'

'I try my best. All part of the service.'

With that she gave him a very satisfied smile that he imagined would grace her lips at the end of a particularly heavy lovemaking session. For a fleeting second he imagined her naked and on his sheets. Spent and glowing.

'Goodbye, Mr Finelli.'

He watched the lift door swish closed, thanking the god of good timing that she'd had the good sense to put a stop to whatever dangerous game had been about to play out. She made his blood boil indeed, the heat between them had been off the scale. No woman had made him so infuriated and so turned on at the same time. He spoke to the metal doors as the lift lurched upwards. 'Goodbye, Ivy.'

Then he turned to walk up the stairs and back to the surgical suite. A ward round beckoned, then some prep, allaying the fears of his patients and their parents...then a quick gym session, a decent meal, some sleep.

He needed to be ready for tomorrow, for Ivy and for round two.

CHAPTER THREE

This is your job, for goodness' sake. Pull yourself together.

As long as Ivy focused on that she'd be fine. She'd put everything on the line for her job her whole adult life and had got exactly where she wanted to be: Director of Legal at a fabulous, age-old and well-respected institution. So this was just another hurdle. Just an incy-wincy hurdle that she would jump with ease.

If only for two little things…

Shut up. Blood and a bloody-minded man would not get to her. She dragged the scrubs top over her head and straightened it, leaned in to the mirror and watched her hands shake as she slid the paper hairnet hat thing over her hair, squashing her fringe in the process. *Great look, girlfriend.*

Then she took a little more notice of her surroundings. The scrubs with the St Carmen's logo and the locker room reminded her of the photo… Would she be for ever condemned to remember that image for as long as she lived?

Half of her hoped so. The other half tried to blot it from her mind.

'Hey, Miss Leigh, are you ready?' Nancy, the OR assistant, called through the door. 'We're going in now, the surgeon's here.'

And she so hadn't needed to hear that. 'Just a second,

I'm almost there.' *Okay. Breathe. Deeply. In. Out. In. Out. You can do this.* It was just a case of mind over matter. She was in control of this.

She didn't know what she was dreading most: the red stuff or the man she'd had the dirtiest dream about last night. The man she'd almost grabbed in the lift and planted a kiss on those too smug lips of his. Who she'd spent an hour trying to describe to her flatmate and had ended up with *annoyingly sexy.*

So, yes, she thought he was sexy. Just as Becca did, and, frankly, the same as all the women in the hospital did. So she was just proving she had working hormones—*nothing else to see here, move right along.* The man who was out to make her look a fool but, God knew, he might not need to try too hard, because if things didn't go as planned she'd be managing that quite well all on her own.

Popping two more herbal rescue sweets into her mouth and sucking for all she was worth, she took a couple of extra-long deep breaths and steadied her rampaging heart. Give her a sticky mediation case, two ornery barristers and an angry, justice-seeking client any day. Words…that was her thing. Words, debate, the power of vocabulary. Not medicine. Not blood. Not internal stuff. Exactly why she hadn't followed in her mother's footsteps.

Here we go.

The smell hit her first. Sharp, tangy and clinical, filling her nostrils, and she thought it might have something to do with the brown stuff a man in scrubs and face mask was painting onto the abdomen of an anaesthetised woman. Then the bright white light of the room hit her, the noise. She'd thought it would be silent—remembered only a quiet efficiency from those endless surgeries, but someone had put classical music on the speakers. It was the only soothing thing in the place.

So much for the rescue sweets. Her heart bumped along, merrily oblivious to the discomfort it was causing her, and now her hands were starting to sweat too. Someone sat at the head of the woman and fiddled with tubes. The anaesthetist, Ivy knew. She had enough experience to be able to identify most of the people in here. Another woman smiled at her and bustled past with a tray of instruments that looked like torture devices…hooks and clamps. Ivy shuddered and hovered on the periphery, not knowing what to do and feeling more and more like a spare part. Should she stand closer? But that would mean she'd get a bird's-eye view of the action.

The man painting the brown stuff raised his head and she realised it was Matteo. Matteo—she'd got to thinking of him like that. Not Mr Finelli. Not something over there and out of reach. But someone here…someone personal. Matteo. Someone she'd almost kissed, for the first time in what felt like a thousand years. All she could see of his face were those eyes, piercing, dark and direct as he looked at her. 'Ah. Miss Leigh. You're here. Come closer, please. Glad you could tear yourself away from your paper pushing.'

'Good to be here.' *Liar.*

'Nancy got you some scrubs. Good. We don't want to get your lovely office suits messed up with bodily fluids. Do come and get a better view of the procedure, my team will make space for you. I'm sorry we didn't reserve the gold-tier seating. And it's a little crowded as I need to teach as well as operate. Perhaps one day you'll be able to help us raise money for a decent viewing room? That would make all of our lives easier.'

She gave him a sarcastic smile, which she knew he couldn't see behind her mask so she stuck her tongue out instead. Then levelled her voice. 'You know very well that

I'm a lawyer, not a fundraiser. However, I'll add it to your wish-list. Which is getting longer by the day.'

'I know. We surgeons are so demanding, yes? You'd think we were wanting to save lives or something.' For a moment he regarded her with humour, but it was gentle and not rude, and then he became very focused and professional. 'Okay. This patient is Emily. She's donating her left kidney to her daughter, who is twelve years old and suffers from polycystic kidney disease. Emily is a perfect match in tissue type and blood type. She's a very active lady with no medical history of any note. With one kidney she is giving her daughter the chance to have a normal life. That is, of course, as long as her body doesn't reject it, although live donors are generally better tolerated than cadaver ones. Once the kidney has been removed, I, and a team of other surgeons, will…' He paused and looked over at Ivy. 'Are you okay, standing there?'

'Yes, thanks. I'm fine.' Shifting the weight from her left foot, she eased more heavily onto her right. And then realised he was still watching her.

His eyes flicked to her feet and then back to her face. 'This is a long procedure—in fact, it's going to be a long day. Would…er…anyone like a seat?' His voice, she noted, had softened, the jokey teasing quite gone. Which was not what she wanted or expected from him. He must have noticed her limp. Goddamn. When had that been? She didn't want anyone's pity; she could hold her own as well as the next person. He called out to the orderly, 'Eric…? Do we have any chairs?'

And look weak in front of all these people. In front of her colleagues? Him? No way. She shook her head vehemently.

Matteo paused with a large green sheet in his hand. 'If you're sure? Everyone?' But she knew he meant just her.

'This is your last chance. We're going to start imminently and then we all need to concentrate.'

Oh, God. *Objection!* she wanted to shout. *Stop!* But instead she fisted her fingers into her palms, dug deep to distract herself from her raging heartbeat. 'I'm fine. Please, just do the operation.'

'As you like.' He nodded to her, the scalpel now in his hand catching the light and glinting ominously. 'Here we go, everyone. One laparoscopic donor nephrectomy begins.'

An hour later and Ivy had run out of places to look other than at the patient and risk the chance of seeing blood. She knew the right-hand corner of the room intimately now and could have recited the words on the warning sign above the electrical sockets blindfolded. The ECG monitoring machine bleeped and she focused once again on the LED display. Lots of squiggly lines and numbers. A niggly pain lodged in her lower back and her legs were starting to ache. She didn't even have anything to lean against—that would have been helpful. So she stood rooted to the spot, trying to blot out the chatter, the music, the smell. Words like tubular…renal ligament…haemo…blood. She knew that. And sorely wished she didn't.

But while her heartbeat was jigging off the scale it was clear that Matteo's wasn't. As he worked three probes jutting out from the woman's abdomen while watching his handiwork on a large TV screen, his voice was measured and calm. For all his macho Italian remonstrating, the man was a damned fine surgeon, she'd give him that. He was also a decent teacher, taking time to explain to everyone exactly what he was doing—which really was amazing. Keyhole surgery was detailed, precise and very, very clever.

Okay, so she'd misjudged him. He was not narcissistic

when it mattered, he was giving of himself to his patients and to the assistants. But he was still annoying. And sexy. And had she mentioned annoying? 'We need to divide the adrenal vein so it is the optimal length for transplantation…'

She focused on the music because his running commentary was making her feel slightly woozy. Or maybe it was the heat in the room. Her gaze drifted over to him again, down his mask-covered face to his throat. The V of skin visible on his broad chest was suntanned, his forearm muscles contracting and stretching as he worked.

He stopped and arched his back, checked the screen, and, as he dipped his head to resume his work, he caught her eye. She could tell by the crinkles at his temples that he was smiling—what kind of a smile it was, she didn't know. She didn't want to. Just one look at those eyes made her gut contract in a sizzling, heat-filled clutch. She wondered what it would be like to wake up to those eyes, that skin… Or what would have happened in that lift yesterday if she hadn't pulled away.

She was darned glad she had pulled away…frustrated, but glad.

But what if she hadn't? Would he have kissed her? And why? Why her when there were so many beautiful women for him to kiss?

My God. Her mouth dried. She couldn't be thinking like that. She couldn't be imagining what it would be like to have Matteo touch her. To kiss him… Not when someone's life was on the line—although, thank goodness, not in her hands.

Not at all. She wasn't the kind of girl to have flings and she didn't want anything else. Didn't even want a fling… unless…

No. Not a fling. Not with Matteo damned Finelli.

She felt her cheeks heat, shook her head to clear her mind and realised it took longer than normal for her vision to catch up. Nausea ripped through her, rising up her gut. She focused on his hands. Hands that were red with blood now. Thick and red…and… The heat in the room was toxic…and she felt cold and hot…and she could feel the blood drain from her face…

'So you are with us again? That is good.' Matteo tapped Ivy's hand with as little force as he dared muster, but enough that she'd at least open her eyes. She looked so pale, so young lying on the trolley covered with a blanket. And as she was his responsibility in the OR he'd deemed it only right to check on her. That's what he told himself anyway as she stared at him, her cheeks reddening. She started to sit up but he coaxed her back down. 'Lie still. Your blood pressure dropped and you fainted. Are you feeling okay?'

'Oh, I'm so sorry. Please, go in and finish the operation. Leave me here.' Her eyelids fluttered closed, more, he figured, out of embarrassment than feeling faint again.

People fainted in the OR on a regular basis. Nothing extraordinary. Except that this time had been the first and only time he'd felt a need to barge in and carry the victim out. But even though he had stood there helplessly as she'd fallen to the floor he'd known that he was not in a position to run to her—no matter what. His patient was his first priority. 'It is all done—it takes more than a vaso-vagal to make me leave someone on the table. You were well cared for by the recovery nurses?'

She gave him a smile. 'Yes. And I'm so sorry I took up their valuable time. It wasn't necessary and neither is this visit. You're busy.'

'Nonsense. I have ten minutes before I go into the transplant. I thought I'd better check on my unexpected patient.'

She twisted to sit up, ignoring any attempt to keep her out of harm's way. 'You didn't need to. Honestly. No one should have looked after me. I'd have been fine.'

'Oh, yes, we always leave the sick ones scattered across the OR floor like the battlefield wounded. We just step over them, like little human hurdles whenever we need to move around the room. Did you have breakfast this morning?'

'Yes.' Which was contrary to what he'd assumed and didn't explain why a strong woman like Ivy would faint. 'A little.'

'So you fell over. Why?'

She shrugged. 'It was hot.'

'We were all hot, it gets like that. The air-conditioning is faulty—just another thing to add to my wish-list.' Maybe it had had something to do with her leg. Maybe she'd been in pain? *Pazzo*, he berated himself. Idiot. There he'd been playing games with her and she'd been unable to stand for so long. Physically unable to, for whatever reason. And he didn't want to pry into something that wasn't his business. But… 'It was something more, I think.'

She looked like she was debating how to answer. 'Okay. Yes.'

He waited for her to elucidate. 'And…?'

'I think I overdosed on rescue sweets.'

'What?' He had not been expecting that. He held back a laugh because he could see she was serious. 'Rescue sweets? Really? You were nervous about the operation? And be honest. You have the kind of face that gives away all your emotions.'

'That is not what someone of my profession wants to hear.' She seemed to fold a little. 'It's not my usual workplace, is it?'

'Which isn't an admission of nerves, just a statement of fact.' Ever the lawyer. 'Were you scared?'

'No comment.' But her eyes dipped down and he knew he had her answer.

'So yes. What of?'

'No comment.'

'Which might work in the courts, Ivy, but won't stop me asking the questions. This is my domain now, not yours. You have a phobia? Needles? Blood? People?' *Me?* That thought made him smile even more. Because he had no doubt that Ivy believed him to be her equal. Maybe it was the buzz between them that she was afraid of. Of what that might lead to unless they both held themselves in check.

The way she pursed her lips reminded him of his sister Liliana again—reluctant to admit any kind of weakness. She'd started to look less fragile, stronger, back to her fighting self. Almost—but was that a little humility there too? 'Okay, if you must know, yes, I get a little woozy with blood…'

'Aha, so you are afraid of something. Interesting…' He'd found a weak spot. Excellent. Although seeing a young woman so pale wasn't excellent at all. Fainting in front of a group of colleagues was pretty embarrassing too, and made anyone feel washed out and often came with a thumping headache. And now he felt compelled to help her. Again. It was becoming a habit. An unusual habit that he needed to shake off. 'Okay, we'll talk about it later. I may have some suggestions to help you with that. Now, I must go and see my next client.'

'Wait. Matteo. Please.' She reached a hand to his arm and a thousand jolts rattled through him. He knew exactly what that was. Chemistry. Physics. And basic biology. There was a connection between them that overrode sense. That ignored his brain and went beyond any interest he'd felt for a woman before. What was it about Ivy Leigh that had him reacting so strongly? Why did he want to help her? What was going on with his body that this attraction was so intense, so fierce?

He wanted answers so he could stop it and get back to normal. He'd never become so interested in a woman that he'd thought about snatching a kiss at work, in an elevator. That was the stuff of romance books and definitely not for a sane, level-headed scientist like himself. He liked to have control in who he kissed…not some sort of urgent, frenzied need. Because he knew exactly where that kind of wild, irrational love got a man. And he wasn't going there ever again.

Her smile broadened. 'Thank you for your concern. But what about the transplant? I'd like to watch…from a safe distance.'

Drawing his arm away from her touch, he shook his head. 'You have nothing to prove, really. But you have to be able to hold your own in there, otherwise you become a liability, and perhaps today is a little soon for you to try to conquer your fears. So, no. You can't come in and watch. I need to make sure you are strong enough—'

'Strong? Of course I am…I was just a little overcome.'

'We don't need that kind of distraction in there. Try again next week?' By which time he'd have this snagging interest in her under control. 'I'll try to find something less intrusive for you to watch.'

Jolting upright, she fixed him with those dark green eyes. 'Damn it, I can do this.'

'Not today and that decision is final.'

Shaking her head, she lay back down on the trolley and covered her eyes with her forearm. 'So you won in the end.' She sounded disappointed but retaliatory.

'This round, yes.' Although there was less satisfaction in that fact than he'd imagined there would be.

Nancy arrived and handed Ivy a plastic cup filled with water. 'You're fine to get up now, Miss Leigh. Your blood pressure is back to normal. Why don't you have a drink first, then pop along to the locker rooms and get changed.' His OR assistant turned to him. 'Matteo, I'm sorry to interrupt, but just wanted to remind you we're having Friday night drinks tonight. Will you be coming along?'

'Of course.'

Nancy's eyes flicked over to Ivy. 'Oh, and Miss Leigh, of course. You must come too.'

Matteo guessed Nancy was playing the polite card because generally the department was pretty tight, but it would be rude not to ask her when this conversation was going on within her earshot. He ignored a little leap in his stomach at the thought of seeing her again. If that was how his body was reacting then maybe he wouldn't go tonight if she was going to be there. It was better not to fuel this attraction any further. Bad enough she'd been the first thing he'd thought about when he'd woken up this morning.

'Why does everyone insist on calling me Miss Leigh? It makes me feel like I'm a ninety-year-old spinster. Please, it's Ivy…' Ivy shook her head vehemently. 'And thanks for the offer but, no. I can't come tonight.'

Nancy chipped in. 'But we all go, every Friday, across the road to the Dragon, straight after work. It's tradition. If you work in OR it's mandatory…'

Matteo added with a grin, remembering how forceful Poison Ivy had been about attending her ridiculous course, 'And we all know what that means. No getting out of it.'

Ivy swung her legs over the edge of the trolley and straightened her scrubs, her blonde hair stuck up in little tufts, and she looked very far from the sophisticated, competent lawyer. In fact, she looked pretty damned cute all mussed up. 'But I didn't exactly do any work here, I just made a fool of myself.'

'And now you have me feeling sorry for you all over again.' He leaned closer. Big mistake—a nose full of her fresh scent had his senses zapping into full-on alert. He stepped back again. 'Let me tell you a secret…the first day in Theatre as a medical student, I vomited.'

'In the theatre?' Both Nancy and Ivy asked at the same time.

He shrugged. 'No, in a bin outside. I managed to leave just in time. A coronary bypass—messy. It takes a bit of getting used to. There's a lot of smells and noise and the blood…and looking inside… It's something you learn to live with. You can't expect to be okay with seeing these things on the first day. Luckily, you have another three chances to get up close and personal.'

'Yay. Three.' Ivy's cheeks blazed as she drained the cup and popped it on the table next to the trolley. 'Er…well, yes. Hypnotherapy's good, I hear. Drugs. Total avoidance has been working really well for me for years. But I really do need to apologise to everyone for inconveniencing them.'

'What better place to do it than at the pub?' He couldn't believe he was convincing her to come. 'You said you needed to get to know the departments. People will chat to you more freely with alcohol in their bellies.'

'Yes,' Nancy chimed in. 'Come on, it's usually a good crowd. And if you do come I promise not to let anyone make fun of you.'

Matteo sniffed. 'Apart from me, obviously.'

'Of course, Matteo. Whatever.' With a shake of her head Nancy jabbed him in the ribs and winked at Ivy. 'Don't be taken in by him. He's just a softie really.'

'Nancy, how could you ruin my reputation?'

'Your reputation's already in tatters, my boy. We've all seen the picture… *Bite me*? Yes…oh, yes. Wouldn't we all love to do that.' Laughing, Nancy ducked away down the corridor. Leaving just him and a bed-ready Ivy, who was laughing and not making any attempt to hide it.

He gave her a smile. 'Now I definitely need you to come out tonight to fight my corner, tell them what penance I've had to serve for that damned picture. They'll be merciless.'

'This I have got to see.' Ivy patted his hand and he felt a comforting warmth that, as he looked into her sparkling eyes, transformed into a sizzle running through him. He wanted to kiss her. Right there. To see what that mouth tasted like, how it felt slammed against his. This was a struggle he was already losing. He wanted her. As he watched her she stopped laughing, but the smile remained. 'Sorry, Matteo, it's no more than you deserve. This is one battle you'll have to fight on your own. And I don't think you'll have a hope in hell of winning.'

CHAPTER FOUR

WITH AN UNEXPECTEDLY free afternoon to attack her to-do list, Ivy felt on top of her work for the first time since she'd taken the job. Wanting to purge the embarrassment burning through her, she'd hit the tasks with gusto and now had a new to-do list that contained *complete projects*, as opposed to, *Go through the masses of unfinished stuff the useless last guy left, find out what the outstanding projects are and then complete.*

Now she had a clear idea of where she was headed—until, of course, the next crisis occurred. Because she had no doubt that it would. She could only hope it wasn't more naked photos…because that scenario appeared to get her into hotter water than she wanted to be.

She buzzed through to the next office. 'Becca, would it be possible for you to line up some interviews for me for next week?'

'Sure. Hang on, I'll come through.' Becca appeared in her office, pencil poised and notepad at the ready, as if she was about to take dictation. 'Who, what, why and when? And, please, please, let it be more bottoms to identify… peachy ones, of course.'

Ivy tried to frown, but the thought of that… *Work, girl.* 'You are incorrigible. It's proper work. You remember that? The stuff we get paid to do? Look through my diary—

any time apart from Thursday and Friday. I need to take a brief on the Partridge case. So, I need to speak to…' She scanned down the list of names on the paper in front of her. 'Maggie Taylor and Leslie Anderson from Ward Three.'

Becca tapped her pad. 'That's the med negligence case, right? The feeding tube that became dislodged?'

'Yes. That hearing's coming up in a couple of weeks and I need to be apprised of all the facts.'

'Certainly. I'll organise that for you.' Becca nodded. 'But, you know, we always win anyway. Or we settle beforehand if we don't think we'll win in court.'

'Yes. I know very well how the system works.' Ivy had personal experience on both sides, but that didn't mean she liked it. Not if it meant mistakes were still being made, mistakes that could be avoided.

With this job she'd found herself in a strange place ethically—on the one hand she wanted to ensure the hospital was a safe place for all, and on the other hand she was responsible to the hospital board. Sometimes it was exciting and technically challenging, and other times she just felt stuck between a rock and a hard place. But she loved it nevertheless. There was still a lot to do here, and she'd always been up for a challenge.

She looked at a pile of employment contracts and a thick file regarding a sexual harassment complaint against a catering manager, all ready for her review. Bedtime reading. Geez, bedtimes had never been such fun.

And why, oh, why did an image of a naked Matteo suddenly flit into her head at the mention of bedtimes? It was impossible these days to think of anything without him straying into her thoughts.

She was not going to go to the pub. She was going to stay here and work. Neither was she going to indulge any fantasies about him touching her or kissing her or undressing her in a lift…which was her most recent one… or perhaps something in the on-call room. She'd heard many a tale about that kind of thing happening in hospitals. But, no—it was all out of bounds.

When she eventually looked up again she realised her assistant was watching her while dragging on a coat. 'Yes, Becca?'

'I don't know where your head was right then, but it wasn't here. Maggie's coming in on Monday at two, Leslie will come straight after her shift on Tuesday at three-thirty.' Becca smiled. 'So, you never did tell me why you came back from Theatre so early. Weren't you supposed to be with Dr Delicious all afternoon, you lucky thing?'

Oh. That. The hospital grapevine was alive and kicking and the news was bound to spread fast. She might as well front up to it, take the ribbing and move on. 'You have to promise not to tell a soul. Or laugh. Or anything, at any point.'

With a very serious look on her face Becca drew a cross over her chest. 'My word is my honour.'

'I fainted.'

Becca bit her lips together to hold in a laugh. 'Aha. Hmm. Okay. Understandable.'

'Really? You think? Honestly?' Ivy breathed out a sigh of relief. It seemed the legal personnel had the same approach to bodies as she did. Preferring to look at them from the outside rather than the inside. 'I can't tell you how much better that makes me feel. I was standing up for such a long time and it was very hot in there.'

'Well, he definitely makes me all hot and bothered too.'

'What?' She might have known Becca's answer would be hormone-related. 'Oh, for goodness' sake, I didn't faint because of him, I fainted because the air-conditioning was broken and all my blood was in my feet and, well, I…don't like seeing inside bodies much. Mr Finelli is just a man. He's nothing special. No need to get all giddy.'

'Tell that to your face, Ivy. It's all red and blotchy.'

Ivy threw her assistant a smile. 'You know, I preferred you when you were meek and polite.'

'Sorry. Overstepping a little?'

'Yes. Kind of.' But, truly, Ivy needed some people on her side. After the stuffy atmosphere in the board meetings and the heavy, long hours, which she really deep down didn't mind, sometimes it was nice to have a little girl time. Usually by the time she got home after a long day her flatmate had either gone to bed or had hit the town with her boyfriend. They had a great flatmate arrangement, it worked well and they didn't get under each other's feet, probably because they rarely spent more than an hour a week together. Which meant that Ivy would find herself alone most evenings. Which was fine, given she had so much work to keep her occupied, but sometimes… 'Are you heading off now? Have a good weekend.'

Becca shook her head. 'Actually, I'm heading over to the pub. Everyone goes there on a Friday night. It's—'

As her heart fell Ivy interrupted, 'Oh, you too? Let me guess, tradition, right?'

'Tradition. Yes, most of the admin and support staff go—in fact, a lot of the hospital workers go. It's always good fun and there's karaoke later.'

'All the more reason for me to stay here, then.' Shuffling bits of paper on a Friday night, looking across the road at the lights in the pub. Listening to the laughter. God, she could have her own pity party right here.

Becca frowned right back. 'It's fun. Really. You should come. You don't have to sing.'

It wasn't the singing. It was the company. Certain company that she didn't want to face again today. 'No can do. I'm busy.'

'It'll wait. Turn your computer off.' With a dramatic flourish Becca stepped forward, stacked the files on the desk into a large pile and handed them over. She grinned, with no hint of apology. 'I know…overstepping again, but it's Friday. Take your folders home and read all weekend if you like, but tonight you're coming for a drink. We never did get to celebrate your arrival here. And it's about time we did. I can't tell you what a breath of fresh air you've been in here.'

'But… I… Wait…' To refuse would be rude. But to tell the truth would be embarrassing and refute what she'd just said about Matteo being nothing special. Because, really, he was a teensy bit set apart from other men she'd dated in her dim and distant past. He was attentive and could be gentle and funny in a macho kind of way. Plus, he made her heart skip just a bit. And she was intrigued by him, by a man who could hold her attention longer than any other had. And by that body, which had her pulse racing at the strangest and most inappropriate moments.

Which was exactly why she had no intention of stepping over the threshold of that pub door.

'Really. No. I can't. I'm just going to head right on home.'

'Seriously, you've got this far, don't be embarrassed. You'll be fine, honestly. I bet it happens all the time anyway. People faint, get over it. Come on.' Becca tugged on Ivy's arm as she had been doing almost every step through the hospital corridors in an attempt to bring her down here to the pub, despite every excuse Ivy could think of. In the end she'd had to give in because, it appeared, no one was listening. 'Last one at the bar buys the round.'

'Fine. Just give me a moment.' Ivy watched her assistant's back disappear into the pub and took a deep breath. If she didn't look at him she'd be fine. He'd be in the middle of a group, she'd shimmy past out of eye contact and hide in a dark corner with the rest of the admin staff. *No problemo.*

Taking another breath, she pushed the heavy door open and stepped in. The noise was bearable, people sat in groups and she could make out some familiar faces in the far corner, but as the door swung closed behind her everyone stopped what they were doing and stared at her.

Huh-huh. This was her idea of hell. Even though no one spoke she could almost read their thoughts. *She's the one who fainted. Top lawyer who's deep-down weak.*

But at least Matteo was nowhere to be seen.

At the bar Becca was talking to the barman, and beckoned Ivy over. 'Seeing as you're paying, I'm having the biggest cocktail they do. A jug of Cancun margarita, I think. What would you like, Ivy?'

'A glass of wine, please. Red.' *Make it a big one.*

'They do a nice merlot. Oh, look…' Becca pointed across to the admin crowd, who were grinning and waving back. 'Everyone's so pleased to see you.'

'Or they're laughing at me.'

'So, Miss Ivy Leigh, you decided to brave it out after all?' *Great.* Matteo's voice behind her thrilled down her spine. She couldn't see him but every tiny hair on her body was standing to attention in some sort of annoying hormonal salute to his arrival. Maybe the admin crowd hadn't been waving at her at all, maybe they'd all been giggling and flirting and fluttering their eyelashes at him.

As she turned she controlled her breathing. She would not be impressed. She would not be impressed. She would not… *Wow.* Every time she looked at him his eyes pierced her—so dark and intense. And right now they were sparkling with mischief. The shadows and dips of his cheekbones seemed more acute today and he certainly rocked the swarthy tall, dark and handsome cliché. In a collared black shirt that showed off his broad chest and snug jeans that hugged his legs he looked dangerous and sinful and so out of her league. Not that she had a league or even wanted to be in one. But, it was safe to say, if she did, he would be stratospherically out of it.

'Good evening, Mr Finelli. Yes, I'm here. My assistant insisted and it looks like the whole hospital is here too, so that's good, I'll get the humiliation over and done with in one clean swoop. I'm just showing my face, having a quick drink and then…' She lifted her overloaded workbag, the zipper almost splitting with the contents. 'Work.'

'Ah, yes. It never stops.' Shoving a hand in his pocket, he pulled out a wad of notes and gave them to the barman. 'I'll get these.'

Becca grinned her starstruck thanks and went to join the group in the far corner. *Double great. Thanks a bunch. Leave me here with him, why don't you? Traitor.* Ivy picked up her glass and nodded to him. 'Thanks. I owe you one.' Then she took a step towards her crowd.

'Not so fast.'

'Sorry?' Ignoring the flustered feeling in her chest, she turned back to him, wondering what the Italian for cold shoulder was. Because that was what she intended on giving him. *Freddo shouldero, matey.* 'I'm on my way over to Becca…'

But he didn't take the hint. Instead, he smiled. For a fleeting moment it was almost genuine. 'How are you feeling, Ivy? No ill effects? No more fainting episodes?'

'I'm fine, thanks. Absolutely hunky dory. I'll see you… Thursday? For my workshop?' *Round two.*

'Again with this.' His voice was grim, but his smile was

infectious as he took her arm and gently steered her away from the busy bar to a quieter corner. And, to her chagrin, she went with him. Was it her imagination or could she feel everyone's eyes on her back? 'We're away from work now on neutral ground, and it's the weekend. People just want to relax and have a good evening, me included. How about we drop our guard a little?'

This could be interesting. 'This is where you lull me into a false sense of security then you pounce, right?'

He shrugged. 'I don't need to do that. We could just have a conversation and see where we get to?'

Nancy squeezed past them to get to the bathrooms. 'Hey, Ivy. How are you feeling? Okay? Is Matteo giving you some tips?' She winked. 'He's very good.'

Ivy looked at the curve of his mouth and imagined a million things he'd be good at. Then ignored the flare of heat circling in her gut. 'I'll bet he is.'

'With fainting cures, that is…'

'Obviously.'

As Nancy disappeared into the bathroom Ivy put her bag on the floor, took a long drink and felt the warmth of the wine suffuse her throat. 'She's a stirrer.'

'She's a joker, but she has a good point.' Matteo's smile hadn't dropped. 'How on earth are we going to get you ready to face the scalpel again next week?'

Aha. Plan A. 'I'll be fine. I was going to start by watching a few videos online. Type "kidney transplant" into a search engine and there are hundreds of operations right there to pick from. You get a bird's-eye view, too, and commentary. It's almost as if you're actually there in the room, without all the smells or noises or…' *Without you*, she thought, all large and looming and stealing her breath. So it would be videos all the way until she was inured to the gore, with the sound turned to mute and a decent bottle of wine for Dutch courage. Anything not to lose face again next week.

'Ah, yes. The joys of the web. Amazing what you can find.' His smile glittered teasingly.

She ignored that, too, knowing damned well he was referring to his glorious backside. Which she did not want to see. Or think about. At all. 'Like I told you, some people do actually put useful things up there. It can be very educational.'

'And you are not at work now, so you don't need to give me the chat.' He emphasised *chat* with a sarcastic twitch of his fingers. 'Enjoy whatever you find on the internet… but make sure you take your hands away from your face first. And that you're sitting…no, lying down. You'll have less far to fall.'

'Ha-ha. You really are enjoying this.'

'What's not to like?' he said, in a voice filled with smugness, like the cat that had got the grappa-laced cream. 'But I'm glad you want to come back and see the wager through. You have strength. You have this hard outer shell, but underneath there is a softer side to you. A side you don't always want other people to see.'

That touched a raw nerve. She was only protecting herself, something she'd learnt to do because of experiences with men like him. She'd already lost enough to a selfish, inadequate man who'd wanted to play God, so she intended to keep herself whole and had no desire to fall prey to any guy's wishes. Plus, she'd seen her mother curl up in a ball and weep over someone who she'd given a part of herself to. Watched her crumble until she'd thought she couldn't live without him, couldn't put one step in front of another. Couldn't function. Ivy had no intention of crumbling. 'Don't we all keep a side of us private? I imagine there's more to you than what you show, too, Matteo. It's just how we project ourselves to the world, that's all. We don't have to show all our sides to everyone.'

He looked at her for a moment, his eyebrows raised, then shook his head, clearly perplexed. 'I am me. This is it.'

'Sure it is.' All annoying and smug and profound Italian with raw sex appeal and, she decided, probably not a lot of substance.

He shrugged as if he was reading her mind and he didn't give a jot what she thought. He probably didn't. 'Okay, whatever you think. You have your mind made up, I don't intend wasting my time trying to convince you otherwise. But, seriously, take a few small steps. Watch a video or two and concentrate on your body's response. Make sure you even out your breathing. Make sure it's deep and slow and regular, not jumpy, like it is right now.'

Ivy took a long slow breath in, felt a thump of palpitation in her chest as she willed her heart to slow. 'My breathing is fine.'

'Really? Could have fooled me. Because right now I'd say you were about to hyperventilate.' He reached a hand to her earlobe and checked out her silver hoop earring, ran a finger across the sensitive part of her neck. 'See. When I do that...up it goes. You need to be aware of that.'

Hello, I am very aware. Too aware. Her heart jittered, her hand started to shake again as she rubbed the spot he'd touched. 'I'll bear that in mind.' And, for the record, if she was to have a *thing* with anyone, it wouldn't be with a sexed-up macho surgeon. She would choose someone interested in the kind of things she liked, art, literature, someone with class and sophistication.

Not just a nice ass. And nice hands. And a devastating smile.

The smile spoke. 'And relax. Know your body well enough that you can identify signs of tension and consciously relax. Or, another method if you start to feel light-headed, tense your arms and legs and get the blood flowing well. Wiggle your toes to make sure your venous return is sufficient.'

'Yup. Thanks.'

'And why not just start with watching someone take blood first…move on up to renal transplants in a day or so? You don't want to run before you walk. Yes?'

'No. Yes. Whatever. Thanks for the pep talk.' She tried, but failed, to keep the sarcasm out of her voice. 'You trained in psychology as well as medicine?'

'No.' His eyebrows rose. 'But I had to get back into that theatre on day two somehow.'

'Oh. You were serious earlier about being sick in the OR? I thought you were just saying that to make me feel better.' Something really had rattled the great Dr Delicious once upon a time? 'And even after that you went on and trained to be a surgeon? Why? Why didn't you go into something less gory if it made you throw up?'

'Because that wasn't my dream. My dream was to be a renal surgeon. I don't like to do second best.'

She didn't doubt that or that he'd fight tooth and nail for what he wanted. He was the kind of guy who always got what he wanted and was used to snapping out orders—and having them followed. 'Why renal surgery? Why not orthopaedics or plastics, or something else?'

He took a drink from his beer bottle and for a moment looked pensive. 'My sister needed a kidney when she was eleven. She got one, in the end, although it took some time. And I could see the immediate change in her. I got my little sister back, with no pain and a future and so much energy. It was like a miracle. They saved her life. It seemed such a fabulous thing to do that I set my heart on it.'

Again with the surprise. The man could do serious and

personal. This was the side of him she'd thought he hid. But he'd been right—he was up-front and honest. In an irritatingly candid way. Maybe she just hadn't asked him the right questions.

And maybe she'd be better joining Becca right now. But hell if her feet didn't root themselves to the spot. 'Knowing how much demand there is for kidneys, I'd say she was very lucky. You have just the one sister?'

'No. Two sisters and three brothers. Yes, I know. It's a huge family by most standards. Even by Italian standards.'

'Wow. That must have been busy. Are they all like you? Your poor mother.'

'It was challenging, I think. In lots of ways it was hard for her.' His face almost dipped into serious, then he broke out into a smile. 'I am the oldest. I know what you're thinking, yes, they hated me. I'm bossy and organised and like being in charge. There isn't any insult you could call me that I haven't already been called.'

'I don't know, I'm sure I could think of a few.'

'Don't think too hard.' He took another drink. 'And you?'

'Me? No. Not many people have insulted me.' Actually, that was a lie, but it had been the pitying looks that had cut the deepest. No amount of physiotherapy and practice could cut the limp out completely. And with that thought the pain came shooting back up her leg, tripping across the scars. She instinctively shifted her weight, wishing she could change out of her work shoes into something more comfortable.

Matteo looked at her as if waiting for her to explain her sudden reverie. 'Ivy?'

'What?'

'I meant family,' he explained. 'You have brothers and sisters?'

'I'm an only child. I did have a stepbrother once, for a few years, and then there was a divorce—make that the second out of three—and they moved away.' She tilted her head a little to one side and found a smile to try to tell him she was fine with it. Still, it had been nice being part of something bigger. More than nice. And the fallout when Sam had left had been huge in so many ways, losing her stepbrother, Taylor, just one of them. *He's not your real brother, so stop whingeing. Imagine how I feel without my husband. How will I cope without him? How will I survive?* 'Largely it's been just me and my mum.' And a string of unsuccessful relationships.

'The doctor. And you didn't want to follow in her footsteps?' He grinned. 'Ah, no, of course, the fainting thing.'

'That and the fact that I hated hospitals for a long, long time.' And now she'd said too much. Looking for an out, she turned to look over at a commotion on the stage. 'What's happening over there?'

Again he looked at her with a quizzical expression. 'Why did you hate hospitals?'

'Look, I really should go.'

'I'm sorry, I asked you something you didn't want to answer.' His voice softened a little and she was startled and humbled by his honest, straightforward approach. Yes, he had asked. And, no, she didn't want to talk about it and see his pity and later his revulsion. But he continued chatting, undeterred, 'It's charity karaoke. The bar manager lets us have fifty percent of the proceeds if we get the crowd started. Every penny counts. We're fundraising for a new dialysis machine. We're always fundraising for a new dialysis machine. We will never have enough. We can only do so much to make our own miracles.' He picked up her bag and started to walk towards the stage. 'Come watch?'

'Er...will I have to sing?'

'If you want to help us raise money. And you said you did.'

Despite the endless irritation he instilled in her, the thought of spending more time with Matteo really appealed. Really, truly, and she knew it was nothing to do with helping him raise money. Panic took over from the pain in her foot. She could not want to spend more time with Matteo.

She shook her head. 'This wasn't what I had in mind. There's lots of other, bigger ways we can help. Besides, I've already made a fool of myself once today, thank you very much. Singing is definitely not going to help my cause of winning over the hearts and minds of the staff.' She checked her watch. 'I'm going home.'

'Matteo! Matteo!' A guy called over. 'Come on, mate, stop chatting up the ladies and get that famous peach of a backside over here. We're starting.'

Matteo grimaced and raised a finger. 'Give me a minute, Steve.' Then he turned to her and she could have sworn his eyes flicked towards her feet and then back to her face. 'I'm never going to live that picture down. Now, how are you getting home? I'll walk you to the door and get you a cab. Or walk you to the car park.'

'It's fine. My bus stop's just over the road. I can walk across the pub on my own, and, believe me, it'll be a damned sight easier than walking in.'

'But you did it, and no one has said anything at all. Except me. And I have kept you all to myself.' Taking her glass from her hand, he gave her another warm smile. No—not warm. It was possessive. Hot. His hand brushed against hers and heat rippled through her. She tried to shake it off, but it stayed, curling into her, making her hot too. His voice was deeper when he spoke again, and it caressed her insides. 'Ivy, do you have to get back for the boyfriend? The husband?'

'No. I told you, I have work to do. I really do.' *Please, don't ask anything...more.* There was something about him that was different from other men, that connected with her on another level. Something about him… Her gaze slammed up against his, the warm tease now a molten heat. She wanted to…do so many things she'd promised herself not to do again. She didn't want to be beholden to a man. To fall too deeply in love with someone who would have a hold over her emotions and actions. She wanted to stay whole. To be herself, and so much more.

He shook his head. 'Okay. I know I'm going to regret this, but I'll let you go this time. Next week I might not be so lenient.' Was it her imagination or was he flirting again? She didn't know. Panic and heat rose in her gut. The heat overriding the panic, squashing it. No. This was not how she wanted to feel—she didn't want to lose control with him. Knew that if that happened she'd be on a spiral to disaster. She didn't need that in her life, not when she'd finally got where she'd wanted to be. His hand touched her arm. 'You're going to leave me to sing to these people, and I'll end up looking like a fool—as always—but it's worth it for the money. Don't work too hard, Ivy. Enjoy the videos.'

'I will.' *Another lie.* Breathing a huge sigh of relief, she pushed the door open and inhaled the late spring evening air. Thank God for that. What was happening to her insides she did not know, or want to even think about. But she knew she had to put some distance between her and Dr Delicious. Wrapping her coat around her, she began to walk towards the bus stop and realised…

My bag. Damn.

Without it her evening, her whole weekend, would be

lost. Besides, those files held confidential information that she could not lose on any account.

Twirling back round towards the pub, she slammed hard into a wall of muscle. A dark collared shirt. Brooding eyes. A hand holding out her bag. 'Ivy.'

'Oh.' But now she was touching him she didn't want to let go. Should have but didn't. Underneath the soft linen of his shirt she could feel every nuance of muscle, every ripple of movement. And there, underneath her fingers, his heart beat strong and regular. Steady. 'Matteo—'

'Hush.' The bag fell to the ground. Then he placed his palm to the back of her neck, pulled her towards him, and pressed his lips against hers.

It took a moment to register that this was Matteo, this was a kiss—so unexpected, and yet everything that their conversations had been leading up to. His mouth was playful as he nipped across her bottom lip and she could feel his smile against her own. Then she stopped thinking altogether—because thinking would throw up too many barriers, and just for once in her life she wanted to be free, to take what she wanted instead of holding back. To open herself up to...*this*. He tasted exotic, of spice and man, and it set her gut on fire.

Wrapping his arm around her waist and drawing her closer, he set the tone, and took control. His tongue slipped into her mouth and danced a fierce dance with hers. She gripped his shirt, pressed her body against his, took everything he gave her and gave it right back to him. All the fighting and the humiliation and the anger and the deep sexual need she'd experienced since she'd crossed paths with him was in that kiss. So too was a longing and heat that she'd never experienced before.

This was bad.

This was good.

This was the biggest mistake she'd ever made. As reality seeped into her brain she stopped. Fighting for breath, she pulled away. 'My God, Matteo. What the hell was that for?'

'You looked like you needed kissing.' And he was all bravado and outward calm but she could see the slight tremor in his body as he inhaled a breath. So it had been an instinctive unthought-out action and had taken him by surprise too. 'And I was right, you did. Kissing suits you. You should do it more often. Look at you now—alive. Vibrant. No words.'

She daren't imagine how she looked, but that was the least of her problems. 'Well, that's not the way I do things. And now I'm going home.' *Don't even think of asking to come with me.*

'Okay. If you insist.' As he appeared to get used to the idea that smile was back on his mouth. A mouth she'd actually, really, truly just kissed, in the street like a...an out-of-control teenager.

Kissing Matteo! She swiped a hand across her lips to remove all trace of him. What the hell had she been thinking? He was all mouth and smug and... Oh, my God, he was good. And she couldn't find an inch of her body that didn't want to do it again—but her conscience, oh, dear, her conscience was very unhappy with such a strange and unexpected turn of events.

'My bag? Please.' She reached for it.

'Sure. Here you go. Sweet dreams, Ivy.' With that he handed her bag over, turned and disappeared back inside the pub, leaving her breathless and hot and shaking.

Sweet dreams? Not if they were going to be filled with him. *Please, no.* Thanks goodness her bag was stuffed to the gills with papers that would keep her occupied into the early hours, because somehow she was going to have to keep her mind on her work and not on a peachy backside, startling eyes and smug mouth.

Good luck with that.

CHAPTER FIVE

'SERIOUSLY, I HAVE to sit in a circle and discuss hypothetical scenarios? Really? When there are real ones happening two floors down in ER…and an empty OR across the hospital?' Matteo looked around at the other members of the group in disbelief. Two doctors, a ward clerk and a phlebotomist. They were okay with this?

'Okay, then.' Ivy was hovering around them, going from group to group checking on progress, a smile plastered to her face. A smile, he could see, that wasn't comfortable every time her eyes settled on him. 'Why don't you share with everyone what the specific problems are for your department? We could do a brainstorm and set something in motion. It could be a true test of the skills you're learning here on the course.'

Marjorie, the ward clerk from ward three, nodded in agreement, her gaze homing in on Matteo. 'Okay, big-shot bottom, tell us what you need.'

He smothered a grin. That photo had certainly been one way of getting attention, unwanted but nevertheless—people certainly knew him now. 'I need, in simple terms, a new dialysis machine, or funds to buy one.'

'Ball park?' Ivy again.

'Around thirty thousand.'

'That's a lot of calendars you'd have to sell, Mr Finelli.

How about you approach a fund starter website? That would be a great place to start. Some people are seeing amazing results…' Ivy certainly got impassioned and enthusiastic about some things. 'Set up an account and get people to pledge money. Those kinds of forums work because it's a little more personal than just donating. You could have giveaways with each level of pledge—say, a plaque for a platinum sponsor. Plus a brochure and a personalised photograph or something…'

'We've already got a perfect picture for that, eh, Matteo?' It was Marjorie again. His backside had certainly gone viral.

Ivy rolled her eyes. 'That's enough about that picture, please. I am so over it. Really. As I've already explained to Mr Finelli, that's not the sort of image we want associated with St Carmen's—as we can clearly see it distracts us from our purpose. Still, great work. Brainstorming certainly helps.'

One of the other doctors chipped in, 'How about a charity run or a bike ride? A run might work better—around one of the parks? Hyde Park would be good. I know they allow a certain number of small events like that. Or Regent's? Or a skydive?'

Ivy beamed and shot an *I told you so* look at Matteo. 'All of these things can catch the public's eye—given enough warning, they would embrace it. We could get the message out via our usual social media outlets—contact radio stations directly, and get their followers to get involved—it's a chain reaction. A personal message in a public forum often gets huge hits and a better positive response. Something like *Want to fly high for St Carmen's? Charity fundraising skydiving event—have fun and do some good! DM us back for details…* Or something. That's off the top of my head, and you'd need to do it in conjunction with marketing.'

Matteo nodded, impressed with the enthusiasm, although daunted by the amount of time it would need to do all this. 'It sounds like a lot of work.'

'And we're not afraid of that.' Ivy tapped her marker pen against her mouth as she thought. 'It would be a team effort, anyway. Small amounts of time and energy spent efficiently, in the right ways.'

He preferred it, he mused to himself, when that mouth was not talking. When it was kissing him. Who would have thought that was how the evening would pan out? It had been a surprise even to him. More so, the way she'd kissed him back with such hunger had stoked a fierce heat inside him, one that had him wanting more from her in a way that he hadn't wanted someone in a very long time.

Which was warning enough. No more kissing.

The afternoon crawled along and eventually the workshops came to a close, and he wasn't sure whether it was such a coincidence that he was, once again, the last person to be leaving the room. His feet seemed to have started a revolution and were taking their time in walking towards the door.

'Mr Finelli. May I, please, have a word?' She sounded like a schoolteacher. Which made him grin to himself. That kiss had shaken her. And it had probably been wrong of him to have done it—but, *Dio mio*, she had looked so uptight and uncomfortable and after the kiss it had been like looking at a different woman. Her hair had become messed a little and her lips had swollen, her cheeks pink, but her eyes—man, her eyes had been alive. That intense green flecked with gold, and sparkling. Just sparkling.

Despite that, he knew bone deep that it had been a crazy thing to do. He had no business kissing Miss Poison Ivy. They were poles apart in everything, not least that he was a one-night-stand man and she looked, as far as he could see, like a one-man-only woman. No—it wasn't going to happen again.

He turned, but made sure he stayed where he was at the door—all the better to make a quick exit before any more kissing happened. 'Sure. What can I do for you?'

'Nothing. That's exactly it. I don't want you to do anything else. Ever.' She walked towards him, her mouth fixed and determined. Her gait, as always, just the tiniest bit off balance. 'No touching. No kissing. Nothing.'

'The kiss? You want to talk about it? I thought you would almost burn up with the heat. It was good, yes?' Just thinking about it again sent hot, sharp need rippling through him.

She shook her head, holding her workbag against her chest. 'That's not the point.'

'You say that a lot.'

'Say what?'

'"That's not the point."' He removed his hand from the doorhandle and tried not to touch her. 'When you deny how you're feeling, or what you're thinking, you close off a corner of yourself.' And he should learn a lesson from his own words—but, hell, he'd learnt to close himself off to attaching any kind of sentiment to a kiss. It was just human nature. It was lust. It was natural desire, that was all. This time he was in control and calling the shots and, besides, he had no intention of taking it any further. He just couldn't. 'It is exactly *my* point. It is a simple answer, yes? Or no? You liked the kiss?'

'Is not the poi— Oh…' she frowned and he thought for a moment she would stamp her foot in irritation, but instead she gave him a haughty smile. 'You are insufferable.'

'Hey, come on, I was there. I know that you liked it. Try to be honest, Ivy. Your eyes give you away anyway. You liked the kiss and you want to do it again, but you won't.

You have a very strong resolve and kissing won't get you where you want to be. Is that right?'

'Yes. Absolutely.'

'But still you liked it.'

Now she looked like she was trying not to laugh, that pretty mouth curling at the edges, light in the green eyes. 'You are very annoying, Matteo. Okay. If I say yes, will you shut up?'

'Perhaps. Take a chance and see.' He raised his eyebrows and waited. And waited some more as the silence in the room became amplified and the lack of anyone else there became more and more obvious. They were alone and if kissing was on the agenda it could happen here. Now. And no one apart from them would ever know. He perched on the edge of one of the tables. 'And…?'

She glared at him, all humour and frustration and tight-lipped. And eventually she shook her head and tsked. 'God, will you never give up? I liked the kiss, okay?'

As he'd thought. 'Good. You said it and nothing bad happened, so it wasn't so hard to be honest and open, was it? I liked it too, but it wasn't a sensible move.'

'No. It wasn't.'

'And if we do it again?' What was it about her that made him so rash? He wanted to say things to her that he'd never said to anyone else. 'You will slap me with a sexual harassment complaint?'

'Oh, no. I wouldn't do that. I fully acknowledge my part in it.' The smile gave way to a frown. 'It is mighty tempting.'

Indeed it was. Achingly so. And a lesser man might well have tried it again. But Matteo knew the score, he had nothing but respect for her and would not step over a line that she drew. But that didn't mean he couldn't be friends with her, somehow.

Friends? What the hell? A debate began to rage in his head. A man could have female friends, couldn't he? But friends with the woman he'd locked horns with last week? With the woman who enraged and entranced him? He'd find being friends with her very hard indeed. It would have to be work colleagues or nothing. 'So, we won't do it again. But for a moment last week I had a glimpse of what you could be like. You let me see a tiny chink of who the real you is. And then, bam, it was gone, all hidden behind the designer suit and the frumpy blouse.'

Her voice rose as she looked down at her top. 'It is not frumpy. It was exclusive—'

'And you are always so antagonistic, always fighting. Why did you have to learn to be like that?' His chest tightened a little, because he knew damned well that no one was born like that, knew that slamming up defences and fighting your corner was a learnt response. He'd been through that and out the other side, learning to withhold his need to fight back. Because, in the end, all that did was make situations worse.

Except, of course, when it was to do with a mandatory training course. He'd keep on fighting against that.

'I didn't realise. Oh.' Two hot spots blossomed on her cheeks. 'Is that how I come across? Antagonistic?'

Her frown deepened and he immediately regretted what he'd said. 'Maybe only to me.'

'I'm ambitious, I want to do well,' she railed at him. 'And I've earned my stripes, so in certain situations I get to call the shots.'

'I understand.'

She glanced at him as she dragged the door open with her free hand and held it open, leaning against it. 'Do you? Really? You understand how hard it was for someone like me to have achieved what I have?'

'Someone like you? What does that mean?'

'Oh, nothing. Forget it.' With that she stalked out of the room, favouring her left foot as always, and walked down the corridor.

'No. Tell me.' He caught her arm. There was a dare in her, a level that he connected with that was fresh and new and challenging and he liked it. A lot. She had depth, layers. Layers he'd like to unwrap. So, what the hell, he was never one to flinch from a challenge. 'I want to know.'

Her shoulders hitched nonchalantly as she slowed to a halt, surprise lacing her eyes as she looked first at his hand on her arm and then at his face. She was hiding behind bravado that was flimsy and fragile.

'Let's just say I didn't exactly have the most conventional route to getting to where I am now. At times it was a struggle and I had to fight very hard, to push myself. I have high expectations and I expect everyone to have the same. Sadly, they don't. I don't like to call it fighting or antagonistic, I prefer determined. Gutsy. And damned hard work. But, whatever it is, I learnt that to get anywhere you have to be prepared to go further than anyone else. And you always have to do it on your own. Because, in the end, you're the only person you can rely on.'

So, somewhere along the line she had been hurt. He got that now. And a dark feral anger shook through him, the ferocity of it shocking him so much he took a step backwards. But he shook it off. Not his problem. Not his fight. He never allowed himself to get swept up in a woman's dramas.

So he was startled by his reaction, his need to fight on her behalf. To protect her. And by the rush of something that clutched at his chest as he saw the pain in her eyes, and the fight. He dropped his hand from her arm but followed her, picking up her pace. 'They certainly picked the right person for the job here, then. I love St Carmen's but they do need to be brought into the twenty-first century. You'll have a challenge on your hands to do that.'

Once again they found themselves at the lift and she pressed the button. No jab-jab-jab this time; she didn't appear to be in such a hurry to get away from him. 'At least we agree on something. For sure, they do. I don't know when the employee contracts were last brought into line with the most recent laws, or the sexual harassment policies, not to mention the complaints procedures, but it wasn't this side of the millennium. So it's a hard enough job as it is, without having to be sidetracked by some jumped-up surgeon's bottom.'

'Touché, Ivy. Touché.' He leaned forward and whispered, 'That's not Italian for "You can touch it," by the way.'

'Ha! In your dreams, Finelli.' She flung him a disdainful sideways glance and shook her head. But he could see, as she hit the lift call button again, that her hands had a tremor. She was all talk of ballsy and brave, but underneath she was bubbling and boiling. 'Now, you must have something more important to be doing?'

More important, undoubtedly, but not as interesting. 'Yes.'

She nodded, all businesslike, as a queue began to form behind them for the lift. 'So, I'll see you tomorrow morning.'

'On Ward Four. Seven-thirty. We'll meet there.'

'Be prepared, Finelli. I've been doing my homework.'

Prepared? Sure. He kept trying to be, but just when he thought he'd got everything under control Ivy Leigh knocked him backwards or sideways or just plain upside down.

* * *

As Ivy stepped onto Ward Four she was consumed by the memories, the smell, the rush-rush of the nurses as they bustled by. The fear. That was it, the place smelt of fear. And no doubt that had not been the intention of the interior designer who'd recently been appointed to cheer the place up. Sure, they'd done a great job with the bright primary-coloured walls and the jungle-animal theme.

But it still smelt of fear.

Or maybe that was just her impression. Surely it was, because the kids she could see were cheerful and smiling and the parents too. It was just her and her memories. Of learning to walk again. Of the pain. And the loss. Of not knowing who was going to turn up to take her home. If, indeed, she had a home to go to.

Brushing those memories away, she fixed on a smile and headed towards the huddle of medics standing around a bed. As she closed in on them she heard Matteo's voice, soft and soothing, chatting to a little boy who was wearing Spiderman pyjamas and sitting up in front of a giraffe mural, with more tubes coming out of him than she'd ever seen.

Matteo stroked the kid's blond hair back from his eyes. Eyes that were dark and sunken and ringed and skin that was tinged with the grey pallor of sickness. 'So, Joey, what's so special about Spiderman? I mean, he can jump a bit, right? But that's all.'

'*Fly.* He can fly, silly. And he saves everyone. The whole world.' The boy's face was animated as he spoke, but depleted of energy, like a deflated balloon. 'He's very cool.'

An anxious-looking woman, whom Ivy presumed was the boy's mother, sitting on the bed next to Joey, smiled and said, 'Like Matteo? He's going to give you a new kidney, so he's very cool, too.'

'I do not think I'm all that cool. But maybe I should get a vest saying *Kidney Man!* on it? And a cape? Will that help me fly too? I quite like that idea.' Matteo examined one of the tubes, then grinned, his face boyish but wise. 'But first we have to make you better. And I'm going to do that this morning. We're going to go along and see my friend Mo who's got special medicine that helps you to go to sleep, and when you wake up you'll be feeling a bit sleepy, but much better. And you'll have a new kidney that means you can stop all the dialysis and a lot of the medicine and then we'll just have to see you sometimes and not every week. And soon you'll be able to go back to school and not be tired. How d'you feel about that?'

The boy nodded sagely. 'Good. Will it hurt?'

'We'll give you special medicine, and if you have any bits that hurt we'll make them all better for you.' As if he sensed Ivy's presence, he glanced over and raised his eyebrows, beckoning her over. 'Hey, this lady works at the hospital. She's new and she's learning how we do things. Is it okay with you all if she watches the operation?'

'Yes. Hello.' The boy stuck out his hand in such an old-fashioned, too grown-up gesture that tears pricked Ivy's eyes. He should be out playing, running around with his friends, getting into mischief, not here in a bed, waiting for the gift of life.

She blinked the tears away—because what use were they to him?—and took his sweaty little hand in hers. She'd never had a broody bone in her body but, heck, she felt everything soften at the faith the boy put in Matteo, and his acceptance of everything. Such trust. And the injustice that someone so little and innocent would even have to go through this. But Matteo was handling it so perfectly Joey didn't appear concerned. 'Hey, Joey. How are you?'

'Okay.'

His mum interrupted, 'He was a bit nervous earlier, but he's fine now Super-Matteo is here, aren't you, Joey?'

Ivy knew exactly how all that felt. The sick feeling in the pit of your stomach, the panic, the fear of the general anaesthetic. The fear of not knowing if she was going to wake up again. The fear of a pain that was uncontrollable. *Run*, she wanted to say, Run! But before she knew what she was doing she stepped forward, her voice low but as friendly and reassuring as she could make it.

'It does feel a bit scary at first, doesn't it? I know, I really do. It's perfectly normal to feel like that, but you'll be fine. Honestly.' She hoped to God he would be. 'Matteo and his friends are really great and you'll be all fixed up.' *And I'll be in there, making damned sure it'll happen.*

And if anything cemented the rightness of her taking this job it was this. Right here. That she was in the perfect place and that she would do her best to make sure everything went exactly to plan, for Joey and kids like him. She couldn't do it for the whole city, or the country, or right the wrongs of the world, but she could do this, make a difference here to these lives. Of course she recognised that Matteo, and his colleagues, were not at all like the surgeon who had operated on her—that these guys were capable and competent and fully aware of their expertise and limitations. And that this child's life and future was in their hands.

She also knew, without a shadow of a doubt, that Matteo would never take a needless risk. And that she would trust him wholeheartedly with her own child's life. And that recognition shuddered through her. She believed in him. Was swept up in the passion with which he attacked his job—and, to her chagrin, the humility too. He may have been the single most irritating man she'd ever met but she trusted him. To do his job properly, at least. Anything more than that was a step too far for her right now.

He was looking at her with a strange expression and she realised she'd given away more than she'd intended. 'Yes, thank you, Ivy. We'd better all get along now. You want to bring anything with you, Joey? A special bear? Teddy?'

'Can Spidey come?' The boy held up a plastic miniature of the superhero, which Matteo took and stuffed into the boy's pyjama pocket. 'Absolutely. Where would we be without him?'

And with that he gave them all a nod, his gaze lingering on her for just a little longer than she felt comfortable with.

Game on.

CHAPTER SIX

SEVEN HOURS AND two operations later Ivy was definitely feeling the effects of standing and tensing and standing and tensing. Trying to stop herself from swaying, she shifted from one foot to the other, ignoring the sharp pain that shivered up her leg, and was so very grateful that she hadn't fallen over or fainted or shown herself up in any way. In fact, she was feeling pretty proud of herself.

At the operating table Matteo was deep in conversation with the medical students, showing them the difference between a renal vein and an adrenal one. She knew that herself, having studied it ad infinitum on the internet—firstly through her fingers and with noise-cancelling headphones. Then, as her confidence had grown and she'd remained upright, with more and more ease. Still not exactly comfortable, but less at risk of falling over. The good thing was that she knew what to expect, what was going to happen, and so knew when to look away or sing a little song in her head to mask the commentary.

Watching him work, she had a full flush of something like nerves, which she knew was all part of the attraction she now admitted she felt for him. And it was rash and stupid and she just wanted it to go and leave her in peace. Because before she'd ever laid eyes on that spectacular pair of buttocks she'd been quite happy. Okay, so maybe she'd been feeling a little like she was missing out on something in her life. But not enough that she'd been bothered to care. Work had been too all-consuming and she'd liked it that way.

But now? Now she wanted to put her hands on him again. To feel that chest fall and rise under her fingertips. To feel his lips pressed against hers.

His voice floated over to her as she focused on the floor and controlled her breathing. 'Yes…thanks for the help, guys. Great job. Now we can go and talk to the boy's parents with an update. Then off to the Dragon for Friday night drinks,' he was saying. 'Not too late for me today as I have to prepare for tomorrow. It's going to be an incredible game. You just wait, we'll give your team a good thrashing.'

'Can't believe you got tickets for Twickenham,' someone answered him. 'How much did you pay for them?'

Matteo laughed. 'I sold my soul. But it will be worth it. This time tomorrow we'll be two tries up, three if we stick to the game plan. Go, Italia! Okay, everyone, let's go.'

So they were finished for the day. Just fine. The OR staff bustled around her as Matteo flicked his gloves into the bin. 'Congratulations, Ivy, you have mastered the art of watching an operation.'

She smiled—not wanting to admit that she'd spent the better part of the time not looking where everyone else had been looking. She knew the floor intimately. 'Well, it hardly warrants congratulations, but I'm feeling pretty elated for the patient and his family after such a long wait and worry. How long will it take Joey to feel better?'

'Almost immediately. He'll be a little groggy, but the cadaver kidney is working—clearly, we need to keep a very close eye on it—but the magic works straight away.' Taking her by the shoulders, he steered her out of the OR and pointed towards a door. 'I need to talk to the parents and my covering on-call staff… I'm not rostered on this weekend but I trust them completely,' he explained. 'Go sit down in there and wait for me. I'll be in shortly to debrief.'

'I should really get back to my desk. I've got an important case coming up next week that I really need to do some work on.'

His eyes darkened as he shook his head. 'And you can work all through the night and every hour of the weekend once you leave here. But, Ivy, it's been a long day. Just go in there and sit for a few minutes. You are allowed to rest. In fact, I insist and I'm the doctor. This is my domain and I call the shots. Go. I'll be in soon.'

'Okay. Okay.' To be honest, she was feeling just a little too exhausted to argue. God only knew how he felt after concentrating so hard for so long, and now he had to pull on a smiling face and meet anxious parents. It had been an emotional day, and a seemingly endless one. 'You can have two whole minutes, but then I do need to go. Cases don't get won by sitting around, doing nothing.' She started to walk towards the door and her heart lifted at the promise of a seat, but she couldn't resist adding, 'But…for the record…'

His eyes flashed with something as he turned back to her. 'Yes?'

'You did really well.'

'I know.' His shoulders relaxed and he laughed. 'Praise from you? Wow, what can I say?' He patted his heart and with a sarcastic grin said, 'It means so much.'

'It should. I don't give it lightly.'

She slipped into the staffroom, slumped onto the sofa and kicked her shoes off. *Wow.* That felt good. Rubbing her left foot with both hands, she massaged the gnarls and dips and scars and eventually managed to get the blood flowing properly, and gradually the numbness started to ease. What they'd achieved in there had been truly amazing. In Matteo's words, they'd given Joey a future. That was something to be proud of. But how could he do this, day in, day out? How could they all? It was exhilarating but so emotionally draining.

One thing she knew—he'd been right when he'd suggested she live a little in his world. Now she felt she understood that it was intense and necessary and so, so important.

But so was hers. Behind-the-scenes stuff that kept them all focused and kept everyone away from harm. They both had their roles to play.

But now…exhaustion dropped over her as she laid her head back and closed her eyes, just for a moment…

'Hey, Ivy.'

Was it a dream? A dark, soothing voice that worked magic over her skin. 'Ivy?'

Not a dream. Actually, here in person. Better than a dream. Or worse. She was here. He was here. Alone. And…hell, she was sleeping. That was so not the way she wanted people to see her, especially people like him.

Her eyelids shot open. He was close, kneeling on the floor next to her, an easy, teasing smile on his lips. 'Ivy? Are you okay?'

'Oh. Hello, Matteo. I…er…' She sat bolt upright, shoving her feet back into her shoes. Had he seen? 'Whoa, how long was I asleep for? I should be getting back to work.'

'No. Wait. Here.' He handed her a hospital-issue white porcelain cup with something that smelled like heaven in it. 'Drink this first. I smuggled it in from Enrico's so don't breathe a word to anyone.'

He'd brought her coffee? Staring at the cup, she grimaced. 'Did you put poison in?'

'Me? Poison the enemy? I wouldn't stoop so low. Besides, I get the feeling I've won this part of the battle.'

'I think I'm starting to see things a little from your point of view. But that doesn't mean I'm backing down or admitting a darned thing.' She took a sip and smiled, leaning her head back against the lumpy cushions. He'd brought her coffee? She didn't want to read anything into that. 'It's perfect. Thank you. How did you know what I liked? Guesswork?'

'When I described you to Enrico he said you always have the *caffe lungo. Americano… Grande…*whatever you all call it here. Strong and black.'

She didn't know what to say. 'Thank you. That's very nice of you.'

When he'd stormed into her office that first day she hadn't imagined he could be like this. She'd jumped to the conclusion that he was all mucho macho Italiano. And, yes, he was. But he was so much more than that. So much more that she was trying hard to resist. And he was making it harder by the minute.

'Ivy.' His eyes shot to her foot and back again, his voice softer. 'What happened?'

Oh, wow again. Straight to the point. 'That? Nothing much. It was all so long ago.'

'And yet still you try to hide it.' Slipping her shoe off, he examined her foot, holding it firmly when she tried to wriggle it away. 'An accident? A car? Crush injury or something?'

'A-ha. Or something.' What to say? She took a breath and thought, struggled for a moment. This was too personal, she never spoke of it, never referenced it—had tried to put that experience to the back of her mind—but even so, it fuelled her job every day. Would it matter if she told him? Was that opening up too much of herself?

Yes. 'Look, it's not important. Thanks for an awesome day. I'll get going now.'

His hand closed over her foot. It was warm. It was safe. The safest she'd felt for a long time. 'I'm not going to let you walk out of here until I know what caused this. I know that's hard for you. I know you don't understand the need to be open. But it will be fine to talk of it. It will help. Maybe. I want to know. For you.'

For you. God, what did that mean? But trying not to talk about it would make it seem like an even bigger issue—and, really, she wanted to downplay it.

'I…er…' She didn't know where to start, so she just started at the beginning. 'I was four. My stepdad was new to us, not married to my mum yet, in fact they'd not long met, and he was trying to show off—to *bond*. He had me by the feet and was swinging me round and round and at first I was enjoying it. But his grip was so, so tight and I was going too fast and too high and no matter what I said he just kept on doing it to impress my mum. I started to panic and wriggled out of his grip. Hit the floor. Broke my ankle.'

'Ouch.'

'Yep. Mum didn't believe it hurt as badly as it did so I tried to walk on it. A few days later it was just so swollen and painful I talked her into taking me to the hospital. Turned out it was broken in a couple of places and had started to heal badly. The orthopaedic surgeon was new and…well, let's say he wasn't in the right head space to be working. He attached an external metal frame to fix it—but he didn't do it properly. The upshot was I ended up with a badly deformed foot and twelve more surgeries to try to fix it.'

'When you say not in the right head space…?'

The all-too-familiar anger rippled through her. 'Drunk. On whisky and power.'

'Oh.' He started to stroke over the scars that snaked round her foot, her ankle, her calf, the knobbly, mottled skin more sensitive to his touch. And again she tried to pull away. How many men had flinched at the sight of it? How many had laughed at her? How long had she endured the teasing at school and beyond? The revulsion? His eyes widened. 'That's a real shame. I'm so sorry.'

'Don't be. It's in the past.'

He let her foot down then settled himself on the other end of the couch. Lifted her foot again and continued to stroke it as if it was the most normal thing he'd ever done. He smelt of dark brown Betadine, that distinctive hospital smell, but over-laced with his own particular scent of spice and pure raw man. 'But you are still affected by it, Ivy, I can see.'

'Plenty of people have worse than this, you only have to spend a day in this hospital to see that. It doesn't hurt much.' Actually, it did. Not a day or an hour went by without pain, but talking about it made it worse. What had hurt much more had been the reaction from everyone else. *Cripple. Ugly. Time-waster.* Her own mother hadn't been bothered enough to listen, to care, to fight.

'But that's why you're here, doing this job.'

'Yes.' She twisted round and leant back on the arm of the sofa to get comfortable. As if having a man like Matteo touching her skin would ever be a comfortable experience. It was terrifying. It was lovely. 'Sure, that's my calling. Righting the wrongs. Capturing the evildoers and taking them to task. Saving the world. Maybe I should get a cape too. Super-Lawyer.'

'Sure, you'd look cute in Lycra. We could be a dynamic duo. But now I understand a lot more about you.'

He paused, waited until the smile had faded. 'And he apologised, this man?'

'The surgeon? Never. But he was eventually struck off after he got caught doing a similar thing—maybe six years later. Turns out he was a serial drunk and had hurt a lot of people over the years.'

'And the man who was swinging you round and round?' His face darkened. 'You went through too much because of him.'

She thought about how much to say. Did it matter? Was she breaking any of her own cardinal rules by just talking to Matteo? It was only words. She could do words easily. She just didn't have such a great handle on emotions. Especially not these new ones—desire, lust, need.

'My mum married him. They all said it was my fault for wriggling while he was swinging me. Said he thought my screams were because I was having fun, not because I was frightened. And Mum was so bowled over by him she believed anything he said. She wasn't interested in my version of events, or in seeking any recompense from the surgeon, or to try make sure he didn't maim anyone else's kid.' It was all too much trouble.

'So that's why you distrust people too. Ah, you are textbook.' He raised his eyebrows and wagged a finger at her.

She grabbed it and twisted slightly. 'Glad I'm so transparent when I thought I was much more complex.'

'And twelve more surgeries?'

She shrugged, trying at the same time to shrug off the memory and the pain she'd endured time after time after time. And learning to walk. Over and over. 'Yep. Internal fixations, pins, plates. Infected wound debriding... You could say I was more of an in-patient than an out-patient for a lot of my growing up. It got to the point that I used to take myself to my out-patient appointments on the bus on my own.'

'As a child?'

'As a young girl. A teenager. Mum wasn't very good at the parenting details of being a mother. There were always too many other things for her to do...' Or, rather, men to pursue. Relationships to sort out. Dramas. Lots and lots of dramas. Unfortunately, not one of them had involved looking after the only child she'd ever had. 'It was just easier to do it on my own than try to rely on her. Although, obviously, she had to come to sign the consent forms for the surgeries, but she didn't tend to hang around much.'

It had always felt as if it had been just too much of a hassle for her. That her needs had been a hindrance to her mother's social life. Until, that was, every time her mother's life had imploded, and then she'd clung to Ivy the way she'd clung to her husbands—with the desperate, all-consuming need that they all learned to despise in the end. The need that Ivy had seen once too often in her friends—the need for a man that overwhelmed them.

So she'd vowed never to be like that. Ever. Never to let a man take over, to take so much of her that there was too little left. But she didn't feel in any danger of that happening with Dr Delicious here—she knew exactly the score with him. He was the kind of guy who didn't offer any promises, and that was just fine, because she didn't want any.

The stroking of his hands had become more intense, the sensation he instilled reaching more than just her leg. It was travelling through her, heating every part of her. He nodded. 'So this is why you're so independent and argumentative? Because you want justice. And because you need to be heard. Because your mum let you down.'

She thought about it, and, yes, he was probably right, but she didn't want him to know that. Like a lot of things, it was easier to shove them deep down than face them. 'I suppose you could say that my relationship with my mother is as broken as my foot.' In fact, the thought of even discussing anything other than the weather with her mum brought Ivy out in hives. As far as she was concerned, it was better to be on her own than risk her heart again. A girl could only take so much emotional fallout.

'Thanks for the psychology lecture. But I'm just who I am, Poison Ivy, who won't tolerate defective people thinking they're immune to the law or to recrimination. Or surgeons who think they're God. Or people who don't take me seriously. Okay, so I've learnt to be like this, but I'm not ashamed of it.'

'You are Ivy. Yes. And you are stronger for your experiences.'

'And do you know, I don't think I've ever really talked about them before.' Not in so much detail. So God only knew what the hell that meant. That she'd exposed her weakness, not only allowed him to see her scars but discussed them too.

Suddenly she felt a little vulnerable. She shrugged her foot from out of his hand and scuttled her feet under her bum as she sat up, inadvertently shuffling closer to him as she resettled herself. 'So, please, please, don't say anything to anyone, I don't really want this to be hospital gossip. Every surgeon's going to think I'm on some kind of witch hunt and I'm not at all. I just want to do my job to the best of my ability, and scuttling out dodgy surgeons is only a tiny part of it. The rest is to put systems in place to prevent these things happening again.'

He frowned. 'Of course. But the scarring and the injury are hardly something you should be ashamed of.'

'If you'd seen the cruel reaction of the kids I grew up

with, and then the men I dated who wanted tabloid perfect, you wouldn't be saying that.'

'Then they are all idiots.'

Yes. Maybe they were. And so was she for being taken in by his words. By his touch. By the way he sounded so unlike every man she'd ever dated—his words like a salve to her wounds. By the little dimple in the cleft of his chin. And by that tiny frozen part of her that had started to thaw, just a little, leaving her open and vulnerable.

She did not want this. Did not have space in her life for this. And, really, she should have stood up and left, but she reached to him anyway, placed her hand over his. Because it seemed a perfectly natural thing to do. 'Thank you. That was a nice thing to say.'

'My pleasure.' His hand cupped her face and he looked at her with such intensity that her heart beat a wild staccato against her ribcage. 'So don't be so hard on yourself.'

He was just being kind in that Italian way of his. He was being gallant and it was so nice to actually be on the receiving end of something like that. Just for once in her life. And he was so close. Looking down with a heated gaze that stoked something deep inside her. Something that answered the question in his eyes.

Then, unable to stop herself, she lifted her face and pressed her lips to his.

What kind of madness was this? Matteo mused in a barely coherent thought process as his hands curled around her, dragging her onto his lap and returning the kiss like a starving man. He was jaded and cynical and not able to offer anything more than this.

Her fingers spiked his hair and she moaned his name, her voice tinged with that cute accent that was so different and refreshing and intriguing and haughty. She tasted delicious. Of risk and freedom and the melting of barriers. Of layers and depth and heat. And wetness.

Her tongue slipped into his mouth and meshed with his, dancing an age-old dance that fired an intense need within him. He pulled her against him, relishing her soft body against his, and then, unable to wait any longer, he slipped his hand underneath the scrub top to her bra. With one easy flick of his fingers he'd undone it and palmed a hand over warm silken flesh and the tight bud of a nipple.

At his touch she moaned again, wriggling her backside against his erection, slowly gyrating on his lap. She was driving him crazy. Wild with desire. That clever mouth that kissed as well as it shot out smart retorts. This achingly sexy body with the softest skin and the scars of a history that made his gut clench. And that drive deep within her that had elevated her from her experiences and made her so much more. He wanted to do anything to erase that hurt.

But wait.

Taking her in the staffroom? That was not his plan. She was worth more than that, deserved more. What kind of madness indeed. But he wasn't thinking straight. It had been a long, hard day and she was just so irresistible. Such a bundle of contrasts, and so damned hot. And he did not know what any of it meant, what this need that drove him was about, that he dreamt about her. But he knew it was intense. That it was something he should be afraid of, yet at the same time he was intrigued and, *mio Dio*, he just couldn't keep away.

A vibrating whirr and a tinny sound had her jumping off him, swiping a hand across her mouth and straightening her top. She reached into her pocket, pulled out a phone and frowned. 'Oh. Er…strange? I should probably get this.'

'Sure.' It would give him time to calm down a little and get things into perspective. Actually, to man up and put a stop to this fooling around in a public place. *Said the guy with his ass hanging out over the internet.* The more he thought about that, the more he realised what a stupid prank it had been. But he wasn't about to admit that to Ivy.

She turned away from him, her shoulders rising up to her ears as she talked. 'Oh. Okay. I see. When? Where?'

A silence stretched as she listened. The longer she stood there the more her body tensed, her hand slowly moving up to her mouth. And, as if in harmony with her, Matteo's heart clutched too. Clearly there was a problem and it went deeper than a work issue.

'Of course,' she said finally, her voice weak and wobbly. 'I'll be there as soon as I can. Please, tell her to… I don't know… Tell her to hold on.'

As she slung the phone back into her pocket she turned to him, her face pale now, all traces of their passion erased. 'I have to go back to York. My mum's sick. She's had a heart attack…they think, they're running tests as we speak. Er…she's asking for me.'

'Of course. You must go.' But there was something about her hesitation that gave him pause too. After all, it hadn't sounded like she had the best relationship with her mother. And he knew how being angry and disillusioned with family could affect someone. 'You think that's the right thing to do?'

She raised her head enough to hold his gaze, and in her darkened, hooded eyes he saw fear and sadness and determination. Her voice was calm. 'Just because she's a lousy mother, it doesn't mean I have to be a lousy daughter. If she needs me, I'll be there for her.'

'Of course, and you shall go. Do you need help organising things?'

'Oh. Well, I guess I need to either hire a car or get the train. Driving's crap on a Friday, but it means I'll be able to go see her straight away, and also pop home for things she might need. But I think the train might be quicker…but…I don't know…' She took a step forward, then back. Almost as if she didn't know how or where to start. For the first time since he'd met her she seemed totally out of her depth. Blindsided.

And he needed to step up.

Didn't want to—because that would make things infinitesimally more complicated. But it wasn't about him. Or this. It was about her and healing things with her *mamma*. 'I'll take you.'

'What? No. No. No, don't be silly. It's fine. I can drive. I just need…' she fished her phone out again '…to call a decent car hire place…or something.'

Wrapping his arms around her, he took the phone from her hands, gave her a hug that she clearly didn't know what to do with but accepted anyway. And he was probably doing this all wrong and sending the wrong message, but he couldn't stand here and watch her sink. She was too proud for that. 'You are upset. Look, you're shaking. You shouldn't drive. Let me take you?'

She shook her head vehemently. 'No, it's too much to ask anyone. This is my problem, not yours. Besides, it's a hell of a long way, a good four hours' drive on a Friday night—more, probably, the traffic's usually a nightmare. You can't do it there and back in one go, not after a long day. And don't you have plans for tomorrow? A rugby game you sold your soul to the devil for or something?'

He hugged her to him, as he would have any friend who was suffering, trying through his actions to say what he wasn't yet ready to say in words. Hell, he didn't know what he was trying to say.

'It's rugby. We will win. It will be over in eighty minutes. This is more important.' *You* are more important, was what he actually thought. The shock of that shuddered through him. He didn't know her. He didn't like her, goddamn. Okay. So he could probably admit to liking her when she wasn't being a prim lawyer chasing his ass. Literally.

She spun out of his arms, looking embarrassed and flustered and about as far from a prim lawyer as anyone could get. 'And what about Joey and your other patients? They need you here.'

'I told you, the on-call team is fabulous—the best in the city. In fact, Dave Marshall taught me everything I know about renal surgery. So they're all in the best hands. It is fine. Really. I'm not due at work until Monday as it is, and I'm only a phone call away.' And he should have heeded the warning bells again then, but he didn't. Should have remembered the last time he'd allowed a woman to invade his life and his heart—and then plundered it and smashed it into tiny pieces and thrown it into the trash. The betrayal. The double whammy of hurt.

But this was different. Ivy needed help and he could give it to her. What kind of a man did otherwise?

CHAPTER SEVEN

IT WAS LATE and dark when they arrived at the hospital, after a long journey where Ivy had felt herself withdraw into her worries. But Matteo had kept a constant stream of trivial conversation to dredge an occasional smile and for that she was grateful.

Now she knew he liked rugby more than football. That he preferred bottled beer to wine. That he'd had his wisdom teeth removed when he was twenty. Nothing deeper than that. But it had been enough. More than enough to keep her from going out of her mind with concern.

He pulled up outside the entrance, a hand on her knee as he spoke. 'I'll find a parking spot. You go in, I'll find you.'

'She'll be in the cardiac ward, I imagine. Or High Dependency or something…I'll ask at Reception. Perhaps I should text you?' She went for her phone in her bag. Did she have his number?

He put his hand on hers and gave her a smile that went bone deep. 'Ivy, I know my way around a hospital. I'll find you. Go.'

'Of course. Yes. Yes.' What was wrong with her? One stolen kiss and she'd been reduced to fluff. Her brain wasn't functioning. Maybe it was the worry about her mum…

After she watched him pull away she went to find her

mother, feeling empty and bewildered, her own heart bruised and broken enough too. There was so much between them that needed to be said, that she wanted to fix but wanted to avoid at all costs.

The hospital corridors were silent as she walked to the reception desk, a grey-haired lady pointing her in the direction of Cardiac Care. Darkness outside the windows penetrated her heart. She'd been talking about her mum and then something bad had happened. What did that mean?

She didn't want to rail at her, to blame her for the crappy upbringing she'd had—it was too late for that. All Ivy had ever wanted was recognition that she was important in her mother's life. But, in the end, she supposed, it didn't matter a jot. Ivy's mother was important to her and if love only went one way, then so be it. It was too late for recriminations.

One of the nurses greeted her and showed her to her mother's bed with a stern warning to be quick and quiet.

'Ivy.' Her mum looked frail and old, lying on pale green sheets that leached colour from her cheeks. Tubes and wires stuck out from under the blanket, attached to a monitor that bleeped at reassuringly regular intervals. A tube piped oxygen into her nostrils, but she sucked in air too, pain etched across her features. 'Thank you for coming, I said not to bother you. I know you're busy—too busy to have to come all this way to see your old mum.'

'Mum, you've had a heart attack—since when was that not enough to bring me to see you?' Guilt ripped through Ivy, as she'd known it would. It was what happened every time she saw her mum—whatever Ivy had done it had never been enough to make her mother love her and she just didn't know how to make things better. She gave her a hug, which was always difficult, and this time it was hindered by the tubes. Movement made her mother's monitor beep, and consequently made Ivy's heart pound—loudly—and so she quickly let go. The space between them seemed to stretch.

'How are you feeling?'

'Lousy.' Breathless and wheezing, her mum settled back down and the beeping stopped. 'I had…an angioplasty. They've cleared the occlusion…put in a stent…so I just need a short stay in here…then do some rehab…as an out-patient.'

It was fixable. Just faulty plumbing. Relief flooded through her as she held her mum's hand. But once again she felt very much like their roles had been reversed, that she was the one taking the care, being the parent. 'That's great news. I was…I was worried about you.'

'Thanks, love. I'm glad you came. You're all I've got now. Can you stay…you know, a while?'

Responsibility tugged Ivy in every direction. Her job, everything, could be put on hold. Couldn't it? She'd only been there a few weeks—but they'd understand. Wouldn't they? She had a nagging sensation that things weren't going to be easy, that she'd have to fight to take time off—time she hadn't yet earned. And she had that upcoming sexual harassment case that was so important for everyone involved. She needed to be in London all clued up for that.

And she needed to be here with her mum. Someone who had never been there for *her*. Maybe she could trust the case to a junior? Maybe she could teleconference with them all. Maybe, *surely*, they'd understand? What would happen if they didn't? She didn't want to contemplate that. She'd finally got her dream job, and now… She looked at her mum, frail and anxious. 'I'll stay here with you as long as you need, Mum.'

'I'd appreciate it. I don't have anyone else.'

'You have me.' Even though it had never seemed enough. 'Is there anything you need? Once they have you settled...'

'I've been thinking, Ivy. About everything... We need to talk. *I* need to...' Her mum's eyes drifted to a spot just behind Ivy and as her skin prickled in response to an external stimulus, also known as Dr Delicious, she turned. Her mum's voice suddenly sounded a lot more healthy. 'Who's this?'

'Oh. Yes. Mum, this is Matteo, my...' What the hell was he? Other than a giant pain in the backside and a damned fine kisser? And, okay, so he was wearing her down a little with his huge generosity of spirit and the four hours' of driving on a soggy spring evening through interminable traffic on a motorway that had been as clogged as her mother's arteries. He was also messing with her head. 'He's my colleague at St Carmen's. He drove me here.'

'All the way from London? Lucky you.'

'Yes, well...' She'd never introduced a man friend to her mother before. 'He's just helping me out.'

Ivy shot Matteo a look that she hoped would silence any other kind of response. Because it was late and she was frazzled, her mum was sick and this wasn't the time or place for explanations. *I met his bottom first, the rest came later, and I have no idea what any of it means.*

And, truth be told, I'm scared. Right now, of everything. Of you dying. Of him becoming too much to me. Of losing myself in either grief or love.

Of not being able to let go.

The nurse bustled over and fiddled with an IV line attached to a large bag of fluid. 'Hello, there. Look, I know you've come a long way and I hope you don't mind me saying this, but visiting hours finished a long time ago. I let you sit with her for a while but, really, she needs to get her rest and so do my other patients...'

'It's okay, Ivy. You go.' Her mum's eyes were already closed, but she squeezed Ivy's hand. A gesture that was the simplest and yet most profound thing Ivy had received from her mum in a very long time. Tears pricked her eyes.

'Of course. Yes. Of course. I'm so sorry. I'll be back tomorrow, Mum.'

'Good. Bring me some toiletries, will you? A night-gown. Make-up.'

'Make-up? What for?'

'Standards, darling.' Typical Mum. But it did make Ivy smile—she couldn't be at the far end of danger if she wanted to put on mascara.

'Let's go, Ivy.' Matteo touched her arm and he drew her away from the ward and out into the silent corridor of eternal half-night. That was how hospitals felt to her—places where reality hovered in the background, and time ticked slowly in an ethereal way.

It was good to have him there, despite the strange unbidden feelings he provoked. Emotions washed through her—elation that her mum wasn't going to die, sadness about the gulf between them, and then, interlaced with all of this, the comfort of being with Matteo. A comfort that pulsed with excitement and sexual attraction. Which seemed really inappropriate and out of place right now. But there it was. Maybe she just needed another human being to metaphorically cling to. There was, after all, a first time for everything.

He waited until they were outside before he spoke. 'So it's good news, then? She's going to be okay?'

A long breath escaped her lungs. 'Yes, it would seem so. She's had an MI and angioplasty and the outlook's good.'

'So why the sad face?'

She tried to find him a smile, because it was good news.

'I don't know… I'm really pleased she's okay. I just feel terrible for saying those awful things about her, for thinking bad things when she was so sick. She could have died and I'd never have forgiven myself.'

He stopped short and looked at her. 'Ivy, her only job was to love you. If she didn't do that then you're right to be angry at her.'

She got the feeling that he was talking from personal experience, that there was something that had happened to him. That he understood what she felt because he'd felt it too. 'Matteo, do you have a good relationship with your family? Were things okay when you were growing up?' It was so not her way to ask direct questions like this—to go deeper than she ever wanted to go herself—but maybe learning how other people coped with things could help.

And she'd quite like to feel she wasn't the only one around here who'd got issues.

At a time like this, in the dark, late at night, with worry hovering around the edges, maybe it was the best time to talk about these things. The things that really mattered.

He shrugged, sucking in the cool fresh northern air. 'My mum could only be described as wanting to love us all to death. She's your typical Italian mother—overfeeding, over-smothering and over-loving us.'

'And your father?'

He shrugged. Opening the car door, his demeanour changed, his voice took on a forced jolly tone. 'Now, we need to eat something half-decent that isn't wrapped in plastic packaging and sold for a fortune in a motorway service station, and you need to get some serious sleep. It has been a long day.'

'Matteo…' She wanted him to continue talking about

his family. This was the guy who believed in openness and honesty. But only, it seemed, when he felt like it.

'No, Ivy. It's too late for talking. Now, show me the way to your house.'

The emotions didn't wane as she shakily put the key in the lock of her mum's central York Georgian townhouse. It had been a long time since she'd been here—too long. And that last time they'd argued—but that was nothing new. Ivy couldn't even remember what it had been about. It didn't matter, it could have been one of a zillion things, as there'd always been an undercurrent of dissatisfaction between them. But she did remember that she'd left in a storm. And now she was back because her mum had nearly died.

They were immediately greeted by the smell of coffee—that was one thing she had inherited from her mum, a love of decent coffee. Then the warm press of Hugo, the fat ginger cat, who purred as he rubbed himself against her legs, preventing a step forward or backwards.

'Hey, cat.' Matteo took a sidestep through the front door, carrying Ivy's suitcase, a small overnight bag of his own and two large brown paper carriers. He walked through to the kitchen, knowing exactly where to go as if he had homing radar, and plonked them all on the floor. Looking around at the modern granite surfaces and white cupboards in a house that was over two hundred years old, he smiled. 'Very English. Nice. My mum would be green with envy if she saw this place. She's been talking about having a new kitchen since I was born.'

It felt strange, having him here in her space—her old space. It wasn't as if it felt like home any more and yet it was filled with so many familiar things and smells that gave her strange sensations of hurt and loss and loneliness.

She'd always envied her friends who'd had happy chaos at home, whereas hers had been all bound up with suffering of one kind or another.

'So what's your home like, Matteo?'

'I guess you'd call it quaint. Old. Small. Traditional. Stone walls, dark wooden cupboards, terracotta tiles, in a village where everyone knows everyone and everyone tries to outdo each other. That's why I like London, you don't have to live in each other's pockets.' He nodded to the bags. 'Okay, so I got what I could from the little supermarket next to the hospital after I parked. It wasn't great, but it had the basics. I have some chicken breasts, pesto sauce and mozzarella cheese. A plastic bag of something the label refers to as salad but which appears to be just leaves. Olives. Bread. And red wine.'

'I thought you said you preferred beer.'

Not hiding his smile, he started to unpack the carriers. 'So you were listening? I thought you were nodding your head in time to the music as you stared out of the window at something no one else could see.'

'I was listening.' It wasn't a lie. She'd been half occupied with dreary thoughts, and half enthralled by the thought of being with him for the next few hours. Alone. 'Well, thank you. I like red wine.'

'I know.' He rustled in the cupboards and fished out a frying pan, some bowls, a chopping board, two glasses and a knife. Then he opened the wine, filled two glasses and handed her one, gently pushing her to sit at the breakfast bar. 'Drink this while I cook.'

She did as she was told, enjoying having someone to look after her for a change but simultaneously feeling a little ill at ease. 'Why are you being like this? So kind and helpful?'

Slicing the chicken, he threw it into the pan and tossed

it around in garlic-infused oil, then emptied the leaves into a bowl. 'Because you looked like you needed a helping hand.'

She thought about that. With his explanation it all seemed so obvious and easy. It wasn't. 'You once said, too, that I looked like I *needed* kissing. Do you always presume things, Matteo? Make up your own reality to suit yourself?'

He stopped chopping for a moment, the knife held in mid-air. 'As you appear not to be able to express your wants and needs, but to repress them and create barriers instead, in some sort of stiff-upper-lip thing, I have to go by gut instinct. Women! You should say what you want. Be honest. Ask and we'll help. Hinting and hiding stuff just confuses us. Pretending to be okay when you're not doesn't help anyone in the end. And definitely not men…' He pushed the olives towards her. 'We're easily confused.'

'Poor men.' She shot him a sympathetic grimace. 'How did you get so knowledgeable about women?'

'I have two sisters, remember? You learn a lot rubbing shoulders with them twenty-four hours a day.'

'And girlfriends?'

His forehead creased into a little frown and he paused, this time the hand in mid-air holding a bowl of olives. 'Of course. I'm a man. We have few desires, but some of them do involve having a woman around.'

Oh, yes, she could see that he was man, thank you very much. In dangerous proximity. And she had no idea why she was taking the conversation down this particular track. 'Anyone…serious…ever?'

'Not really…' He shook his head, eyes guarded. 'No. I'm an emotional Neanderthal, apparently. Selfish. Unfeeling. Because I like to put work first, because I devote myself to my patients.'

'Poor you.' She leaned forward and gave him a kiss. A gentle one, on the cheek.

He rubbed the spot her lips had touched. 'What was that for?'

Shrugging, she threw him a smile. 'You looked like you needed kissing.'

His eyebrows rose and he laughed, full and heartily. 'Round three to Miss Ivy.'

She hardly knew him—and yet there was something soul deep that attracted her to him, a peace and yet a disturbing excitement. It felt natural to talk to him, and the silences were comfortable. She couldn't remember having had that before with a man. She'd spent a lot of time in previous relationships trying to be perfect, to make up for her leg and her limp and her over-officious use of words, her weird sense of humour, trying to give a little of what she held so precious. In the end it had all been hugely disappointing and not worth the trouble.

But Matteo wasn't like that. He was fun to be around. Plus he was pretty damned useful in the kitchen. With a nice bum. Or maybe he was just Mr Too Good To Be True? She flashed him a smile. 'Round three? Are we battling again? Why, when you know you won't win?'

'I will win. Just wait and see.'

She took an olive and popped it into her mouth. Swallowed. Thought a little more about Matteo, who was stir-frying with gusto. 'I suspect this "not really" woman broke your heart?'

'No.'

'Come on.' She narrowed her eyes. 'I thought you were all about being honest and open.'

His frown stuck in place as he emptied the frying-pan contents onto a plate, which he pushed into the centre of the breakfast bar. With a swirl of salt and a crackle of black pepper he finished the presentation with flair. Then carved a few thick slices of fresh white bread and loaded them onto side plates with the mozzarella, handing one to Ivy. 'In truth, she broke my trust and that's worse.'

'Oh, yes. Indeed. I understand that.' So there had been someone significant. And why that knowledge made her heart beat a little faster she didn't want to know. The way the colour had drained from his face told her he'd been hurt badly. That deep down he kept some truths to himself.

He stuck his fork into a piece of chicken and nudged her to do the same. 'Come on. Eat. It's getting cold.'

She didn't miss the fact he'd changed the subject. Or that he hadn't said he was happily looking for The One. But, then again, neither was she.

For that matter, she wasn't looking for anything—fling or attachment, or the whole wedding catastrophe. She was looking for peace of mind and a lifetime doing her own bidding. Of reaching her full potential. Of being the person she was destined to be. Without a man in tow. Without giving anything up. Without losing any of herself.

But a little fun on the side might be nice.

That wine was going to her head. She pushed the bottle away from her. No more. 'I think I'll make a start on the washing up.'

'Let me. It's past midnight, you look exhausted. Go to bed.' He reached for her dirty plate and his hand brushed against hers. They both froze as the connection, the electricity between them, blazed again, bright. He frowned. 'Go. Go to bed, Ivy. I'll sleep down here on the sofa.'

'You don't need to, there's a spare room upstairs. I'll make it up for you—give me a couple of minutes. First door on the right.'

'Okay. If you want.'

What she wanted was for him to sleep in her bed.

My God. She didn't?

She did. And to wake up to that gorgeous smile tomorrow. Preferably with all her current worries wiped clean and her sense of self intact. She wanted to sleep with him and to have no ramifications. No angsty emotions. To be freed up enough to trust him. To trust herself to not be like her mother.

Like that was going to happen.

'Matteo…' She didn't know what she wanted to say. Well, actually, she did, but she didn't know *how* to say it. Or what saying it would mean for both of them. So she chickened out. 'Thank you. For everything. You've been very sweet.'

'My pleasure.' He ran his thumb down her cheek, his eyes kind and startling and misted. She caught his gaze and they stood for a few moments just looking at each other. So much was being unsaid, so many needs and wants. Eventually he dragged his gaze away. 'Now go.'

'But—'

'Please.' He must have known what she was going to ask, knew what she was thinking of offering him—it was written in her eyes, in her body language, in every word, in every gesture. But instead of reaching for her he shook his head. 'Ivy, it's late and it's been an emotional day. First the surgery, then your mum. Don't let's get things mixed up. Don't do something you'd regret.'

I wouldn't regret it.

But, then again, he was probably right. She had enough problems already without adding him to the list.

CHAPTER EIGHT

SOMETHING WARM AND heavy and very noisy pressed against Matteo's chest. Gingerly opening one eye, he came nose to nose with a fat cat that was purring so loudly it sounded like a dentist's drill. 'Hugo? *Ma, che sei grullo.* Eh? You *are* joking? A beautiful woman next door and this is the only offer of bedtime action that I get?'

Matteo wiggled and jiggled his torso but the cat didn't move. He just stretched a lazy leg, gave it a lick, then resumed the loud drill noise. 'Go, cat. Go.'

Purr. Purr. Another lazy lick.

'Okay. Stay there. See if I care. Because I don't.' It was six-thirteen in the morning. He was in bed with a cat. At Ivy's house. She, however, was sleeping elsewhere. That cross mouth and taut, hot body under covers in another room in a house that felt like it was the furthest thing from a home that he'd ever known. There were few pictures on the walls, nothing to say that a family lived here. Or a proud mother. Nothing like the chaos of his home, where you couldn't move for people and things. And the comparison made his heart ache for Ivy and what she hadn't had, growing up.

It had been a mistake to come here, that he knew with certainty.

He'd been so close last night to suggesting things that

would have taken them way beyond this strange relationship they had right now. But just because he'd kept silent didn't mean he was happy about it. Or that he wanted her any less. But he was stuck here for the next few hours at least—he'd promised to take her back to the hospital to see her mum, which meant he had a period of being here… alone with Ivy. He could manage a few hours. Just. Then he would get the hell out and back to the sanitised sanity of his chaotic but uncomplicated life.

In the meantime, he had to make the most of this unexpected downtime. Inching his way from underneath the soggy furball, crawling out of bed and shrugging on some running gear, he left the house in silence to explore what wonders York had to offer. A leafy path opposite the front door headed off next to a slow flowing river, towards what looked like the business centre. What better way to put a woman out of your mind than by sprinting through a new city?

The air was fresh and crisp and rich with something sweet—something delicious, like sugar candy. It made his gut curl with hunger. But again, as with thoughts of Ivy, he put everything aside and focused his effort into each footfall. Few people were out and about this early so he was able to up his pace and circumnavigate what appeared to be an old city surrounded by ancient, crumbling walls and lush greenery.

Weak sunshine fought its way through light grey clouds. It was quiet, the cobbled streets were deserted, and his mind began to settle a little with the rhythmic thud of each step.

An hour later, and much calmer, he found her in the lounge curled up on a window seat that overlooked a typical country garden filled with the fragrant blooms of spring flowers. Her laptop was open and files were scattered around her feet. She was wearing dark blue pyjamas and had wrapped a thick cream woollen cardigan around herself, and his heart clutched a little to see her working so early. Seemed the woman had so much to prove. Too much.

Even though she'd been out of his head briefly while he'd pondered some historical ruins likely put there by some old Roman ancestor of his, she settled firmly back into it the moment he set eyes on her again.

She jumped a little as she realised he was watching her, her eyes narrowing, breath quickening. 'Matteo! Gosh, you must have been up early.'

'*Buongiorno*. I had a strange companion with his own quirky alarm.' If he went to her he might just kiss her good morning. So he stayed exactly where he was, at the door.

'Ah. Yes. Hugo. Sorry about him. He's a freeloader and body heat is his catnip. You should have just kicked him off and turned over.'

'The cat wasn't for kicking.'

'No, you're probably right. He's like you. Stubborn and wilful. Now, there's coffee in the press. Just put a light under it. Actually…' She slapped the lid of her laptop down and swivelled to a stand. Her toes were painted a bright pink that matched her cheeks. And why he noticed such a small, innocuous detail he couldn't say. 'I can finish up for a few minutes if you like. Make you some breakfast. It's the least I can do for you. Where did you get to on your run?'

Sticking firmly to the wall, he tried to remember a route that he hadn't paid a great deal of attention to. 'I stuck to the river path into town, took a detour to see some of the old black and white buildings with the overhanging top storeys and the sagging middles, had a look at the ruined walls, and went down past the railway museum. Pretty place all in all.'

'Well, that at least means I don't have to worry about showing you round, apart from the Minster and a proper walk through the Shambles—you've got to go see them, everyone else does. You can't come here and not see all the most famous bits.' She smiled and it was like sunshine, warming and welcome. He cringed internally at that thought. He was getting too soft. All that work at hardening his heart and she had to start melting it.

No.

It wasn't going to happen. 'You don't have to worry about me. You're here for your mum. I've got calls to make as it is—I need to check up on Joey.'

Busily stacking her files into a pile, she looked up at him. 'Oh, yes. Let me know how he's doing. And you're going to miss your game. I feel very guilty.'

'Don't waste your energy. Stay where you are, you're working. I can fix myself something.'

'I feel guilty about that too. And about not getting enough work done. I'd planned to get through so much this weekend. I've just phoned the ward to see how Mum's doing and the nurse said she was comfortable and asking for some breakfast.' She walked through to the kitchen, flicked the heat under a stovetop coffeepot. Then turned to him, biting her bottom lip.

'Matteo, how am I going to manage to work while I'm here? I know this sounds really mean and very selfish, but I need to be in London. And I need to be here for my mum. I can't do both. How do people juggle these things?'

His eyebrows rose. 'It's very important, this sexual harassment case?'

'It is to the three women making it. And to the guy who could lose his job and reputation if it turns out he's been falsely accused—although I doubt it. It's a delicate issue and I need to be there.'

'Work, work, work. You have to learn to put yourself first. Put family first.' God forgive him for that. Because when it came to family he chose not to be there too. 'Is there anyone else who could fill in?'

The coffee fizzed and spluttered and she decanted it into two cups. 'I have a junior, but he's still very inexperienced. Becca's my assistant, but I don't really know her strengths as yet and this is too important to get wrong. I'd wanted to go through it all with her, have her watch how I do things. Besides, work is me. I am work. And that sounds really sad. But at least it's clear cut. There's nothing confusing about getting up every morning and heading in to the office. No room for anything else, like extraneous distractions.'

No room for a life. And that was the way he liked it too, although he was starting to wonder just what he was missing. He trotted out the line he gave his overworked junior staff. 'Life's all about the stuff that's not work, too. No wonder you end up so strung out. Ivy, there is so much more, you just have to give yourself a chance. Couldn't you postpone the case?' When she didn't answer he touched her arm. 'Ivy? Couldn't they put it off? How long do you think you need to be here?'

She shrugged. 'You're the doctor. How long does she need?'

'You're the daughter. Same question.' It was a challenge that seemed to hit home, but she didn't show that she understood his inference. It wasn't his place to tell her what was important in her life. *Mio Dio*, who was he to judge?

Her smile was genuine. 'Did anyone ever tell you that you're a giant insufferable pain in the backside?'

'All the time.'

'Does it make a difference?'

He fluttered his eyelashes at her. 'What do you think?'

'That you make me crazy.' She threw her hands in the air in an exasperated gesture that was more Italian than English. He liked it. She made him laugh. She turned him on. Plain and simple.

None of this was simple, he was realising. 'I think you were crazy long before you met me.'

'You, Matteo, are everything I hate about men. You're bossy and…well, bossy. And, well, let's just say you annoy me. A lot.'

So funny, because she was very definitely not annoyed right now. She was hot and sweet and looking like she needed kissing again. He caught her chin between his thumb and forefinger and pulled her to look at him. 'Aha. But still you kissed me. And not just once.'

'I was trying you out. Sizing you up.' This close to that pouting mouth he was very tempted to do it again.

'And what?'

'And nothing. Absolutely nothing.' She flapped a hand at his chest and it struck ever so lightly against his skin. He caught her wrist and she turned full into him, so close he caught her scent mingling with the smell of her shampoo. Saw the dark green of her eyes, the honeyed flecks, all golden and melting. God, she was breathtaking. He wanted to kiss her. To have her, right now, here on the kitchen table. Wanted to be inside her. He wanted her with a passion he'd never had for anyone, ever.

A little dalliance would be fun, but then what? At what cost to both of them? Neither wanted…*anything* from anyone else. They were two islands of independence with a large ocean of complication between them.

So he tried to make it playful, dropped her hand, gave her a smile. 'Okay, so take me out for breakfast. And I want to see the Minster that everyone's so keen on showing me.'

She stepped back and held her wrist—not in pain, no,

he hadn't hurt her—but she just held it close to her chest. Her voice was sultry and shaky, as if she'd just had the best sex of her life—or wanted to. 'Yes. Good idea, let's go outside. First, phone about Joey?'

Matteo looked down at his running gear. 'No. First a shower. I need to get out of these things.'

'A shower. Okay. Shower…water…over your body…' Her gaze scanned his face slowly from his eyes to his mouth, where it lingered. The memories of those kisses hovered in the silence. Heat rose within him. Need curled through the kitchen, thick and heavy and tangible.

He took a step back. 'I'll go now.'

'Yes. Do.'

This thing was getting more intense, like a flame that had suddenly erupted into life and was consuming everything in its path, blazing a trail between them. He needed to get away from her before he did something stupid. Like kiss her again. If he didn't douse himself in cold water he wouldn't be able to function around her.

'Wait!' She walked towards him, the cardigan slipping from her shoulders and falling to the floor. Without a word she walked up the stairs and he followed her, hungry to see what she was doing. Was she going to…? Did she want…? A shower? With him? Was this the beginning?

His heart began a strange thumping against his ribcage and for the first time in his life he felt less than sure of his next move.

She stopped short at a door, turned to look at him and gave him a smile, eyebrows cocked. Then she dragged the door open, reached in and pulled out… 'Towels, Matteo. I forgot to give them to you last night.'

Mio Dio. He'd thought he was going to have a heart attack. And now she was so close to him he wanted to touch her. To run his fingers through her hair. To feel that soft skin against his. He was hot and hard for her. Every part of him strained for her.

Holding the towels at hip level, he cursed the flimsy running shorts. 'Thanks. I'll go. Now...'

'Just so you know, the shower's a bit temperamental. Turn the cold water on first then adjust the hot to suit you. That is...' Glancing towards his nether regions, she gave him a wry but cheeky smile that was so not the buttoned-up Ivy he knew—but was a whole lot more of the Ivy he wanted to get to know. 'If you want hot at all.'

The cardiac care ward was locked. Ivy pressed the intercom button and waited. And waited some more. Inside she could see a blur of people running along the corridor. *Running.* To the blare of a siren. *Crap.* Her hand hit her mouth as her heart developed a fast, jerky rhythm. 'What's happening? What is it?'

She knew what it was.

Matteo's hand slipped into hers. 'It's an emergency. Crash call, I imagine. It's okay, Ivy. They're all experts.'

'Do you think...?' *It's my mum?* She couldn't get the words out. Pain crushed her chest as she held her breath.

'Try not to think at all.' With a gentle smile that shone through his eyes he cradled her head against his chest and she inhaled his now familiar scent, which steadied her nerves. He was solid and strong and she felt safe with him. Apart from the fact that there was an emergency in there. And she was out here. That pain intensified. 'Put your arms around me,' he said softly.

'No.' She didn't know whether she'd be able to let go. Whether holding on tight was giving him the wrong message. So, digging deep inside herself, she steadied her reactions. She'd managed this far in her life without needing anyone else. She could manage some more.

He shook his head and took her hand. 'Don't think about it, just do it. Hold on.'

'Oh.' Her defences worn down, her grip on her mum's bag lessened. The bag dropped to the floor. Ivy did as she was told, wriggling her arms round his waist, feeling the breadth of him, his warmth. 'I'm scared.'

'I know.' He didn't give her any pithy pep talks about how fine she would be, how everything would be okay, he just held her. And for that she was grateful. She just took strength from him. Leaning against him, she felt the regular beat of his heart, the unrushed intake of breath. The safety net that she knew would be willing to hold her up if she needed it.

And she wondered what it would be like to be part of something. To be a half of a whole. If that could even happen. All that *you complete me* stuff wasn't real, was it? It was something her mum had been looking for her whole life, and had never found. All those wasted years of chasing a ghost.

No, maybe it wasn't real. But it felt damned nice to be held like this in her worst moments. She'd never had that—not from anyone. Someone to be with her and focus just on her. Someone who seemed to know what she needed without her having to tell them, without her having to strive for their attention.

Eventually the alarm stopped. The rushing slowed and after a few minutes a smiling doctor came to the door. 'Oh, were you waiting? So sorry. Come on in.'

An air of calm pervaded the place. It was as if the running hadn't happened. Or as if the doctor took everything in his stride. Like Matteo. So Ivy tried to stop herself from running too. 'If something bad had happened they'd have stopped me from coming in, right? Surely? They'd take me to one side?'

Matteo nodded. 'Of course. You think too much, like you expect something bad to happen.'

'Well, I just want to be prepared if it does.' Her mum was standing, in an old faded hospital nightie and dressing gown, at the side of her bed, smiling and chatting to a man about her age. Ivy almost ran to her in relief. 'Hey, Mum. Thank God. You look a lot better today, up and about even.'

Her mum's face brightened as she gave a hesitant smile. 'Oh, yes, well, you always look better when they get rid of some of the tubes. This is Richard. He's visiting my neighbour in bed eight. Funnily enough, he lives on West Mews, just round the corner from us.'

From you. Ivy didn't live there any more. It wasn't home. Hadn't ever been, really. And what now? Her mum chatting someone up already—she really was getting back to normal. 'Hi, Richard. Mum, what was going on before? That alarm? All those doctors rushing around? That wasn't...that wasn't for you?'

'Oh, that. It was someone in the first bay. Poor chap. I'll be happy when they move me off here.'

So will I.

'Hello, Mrs Leigh.' Matteo stepped forward and Ivy realised she was still holding his hand and that her mum was looking at her strangely.

Her mum's eyebrows rose. 'Montgomery. Actually, it's Dr Montgomery. But that's okay, you can call me Angela. Everyone does. Has Ivy shown you around the town?'

'Yes. And he was impressed with the Minster, but it's not as beautiful as Siena Duomo, apparently. As if. It's a darned sight older. Or at least the foundations are.' Ivy felt the smile in her voice. She just couldn't help it. Cathedral wars, really? Seemed they had to differ on most things, or rather they both had opinions they liked to air.

But it was a good challenge. Kept her on her toes. 'The man's a philistine.'

'I said it was impressive. It is,' he clarified. 'I liked it, truly. It just doesn't have the romance of the Duomo's structure.'

Angela gave him an interested smile, her lips twitching. 'You're right, there. I did love all that marble.' Then she turned back to Ivy. 'Did you bring my things? I need to freshen up.'

'Sure.' Ivy proffered the bag while taking in the plethora of tubes attached to her mum. 'Do you need any help?'

'Okay. Yes.' Angela's eyes flitted between Ivy and Matteo, and Ivy sensed a mother-daughter talk or something was brewing. Which would be novel. 'Actually, that would be great.'

As her mum hobbled off towards the bathroom, IV stand in tow, Matteo squeezed Ivy's hand and she realised she didn't want to let it go. It was nice to have someone on her side. Which was a whole crock of crazy considering that a couple of weeks ago they'd been at loggerheads. But he gave her a gentle push. 'Off you go. Start now.'

'Start what?'

'Fixing things.'

'What if she doesn't want to?'

He rolled his eyes. 'Would you ever want to look back and regret that you didn't give it a go? Just be honest.'

'She might not want to hear it.'

'How else can you work things through, without honesty?'

'Okay. I s'pose.' He was right. He was often right, goddamn him. Not always...but enough to annoy her just a little bit more. She hid her smile.

As she followed her mum towards the ladies' bathroom she felt his gaze on her back, realising that for the first time in years she hadn't been conscious of her limp—that she was rarely self-conscious when she was with him.

Sensing him still watching her, she injected her gait with a jaunty swing of her bottom. It felt good. Mischievous, and out of character. Or maybe she had a part of her that she'd repressed? Maybe there was a part of her psyche that did want the trappings, the sex, the man? A part that she'd chosen to deny?

Wow. That was an eye-opening thought. But not one she was going to pay any more attention to. She hadn't come this far in her life to give it all up for a life of compromise and dependency.

As if to remind her of that, her mum's bag handle dug into her palm. Ivy tried to ignore those feelings of regret and…well, fear. Fear of feeling things. Of hurting. Of being let down. Of rejection all over again. She'd spent a good deal of her life closing herself off to people. But if Matteo was right, she needed to stop being scared. At least where her mum was concerned.

Let her in.

Let her in.

Let her in.

And she wanted to. She did. She wanted a chance.

'How do I look?' Angela was looking in the mirror and patting her hair, which was matted and flattened at the back. In truth, she looked tired and washed out and old. Blue-red bruises bloomed on her papery skin and her eyes were clouded.

'Like I said, you look great, all things considered, and getting better every day. You've just had a life-saving operation, you're not meant to look like something out of a magazine.' Lifting her mum's arm, threading the IV bag up through her nightgown sleeve and then hanging the fluid bag on the stand, Ivy gave her a smile. 'I was so worried about you.'

'Don't be. I'm fine. Listen, Ivy, I need to talk to you.'

Ivy spoke to her mum's reflection in the mirror. 'Mum, you're healing, you have to take it easy.'

'There's something I need to say.'

'Save it for another time.' Matteo's big honest kick could wait until her mum was feeling better. 'This isn't the time or the place. You're not well.'

'But I need to talk about this.' Angela nodded, still breathless, still pale, but clearly trying to act normal. Whatever that was. 'I know I haven't been easy to live with, Ivy. Things have been hard over the years. Depression has clouded so much, it was so disabling at times. But this scare has made me take stock of things. I want to put things right.'

'Depression?' Ivy had considered that over the years, but her mum had always seemed so content with a man and so unhappy without one that Ivy had thought her mum's moods had been linked entirely with her relationship status at the time. Guilt shook through her again, but sadness too. 'I didn't realise. I should have, but I didn't.'

'You were too busy just being a girl, Ivy. I didn't want to bother you with my problems. But I suspect you lived them anyway?'

Her childhood had been no fairy-tale. She hadn't exactly been shielded from the dramas, especially when her step-family had been ripped away from her. She'd lost her normal, and had been plunged into her mum's darkest moments, borne the brunt of her insecurities.

Even though this conversation was the last thing Ivy wanted, she nodded. If Angela felt up to saying this—and she really did seem to want to talk—then Ivy needed to let her say it.

Angela looked genuinely sorry. 'I'm sorry. I wasn't very good at all that. I know you got caught in the cross-fire and I leaned on you a lot at times. But I was grateful to have you.'

It never felt like it.

Hurt surged through her. This truth gig wasn't pleasant. In fact, it was downright painful. Ivy didn't want to relive everything that had happened, she just wanted things to be different going forward. Why drag over the old pain? Why not just try to fix things from now? 'I'm sure you did your best.'

'I don't know… Now that I look back, I can see so many mistakes.' Holding onto the sink rim, Angela looked down at her thin hands, then back at Ivy. 'I don't know if we can make things better. Just a little? I don't know…'

'Me neither.' Was it too late for them? Ivy didn't know. What she did know was that she didn't want her mother to die—that had to mean something. Stepping forward, she stroked a hand on Angela's shoulder. 'We could try.' Whatever that meant. There was no blueprint for the next steps they were going to take. Did her mum really mean it? Or would she revert to her old ways once she'd regained some strength?

It was a risk Ivy was willing to take. She pushed away the dark cloud hovering at the back of her mind. Things would be better now. Surely?

Her mum's smile was a little wobbly. 'Yes, I think we should try, Ivy. I'd like to. I'm so glad you're here to stay for a while, we can do some nice mother-daughter things together.'

But, despite wanting to fix everything, Ivy's heart lurched. And, yes, she knew it was terribly self-absorbed to be thinking of herself, but if she stayed too long in York and lost her job then everything she'd worked for would be gone. She'd have no security.

And no seeing Matteo.

That thought bothered her more than she'd thought it would. Over the last couple of days he'd become more than a colleague. Despite his annoying ways. Despite every barrier she'd put up.

But, on the other hand, how could she leave her mum?

Would this time to heal be any different from the rest?

It was the first time they'd ever been so open with each other, that they'd acknowledged out loud that there had been problems. It felt scary. Strange, kind of wobbly, but hopeful. Angela looped her arm into Ivy's as they made their way slowly out of the bathroom, dragging the IV stand with them. 'Your man seems nice.'

'He's not my man.' Ivy lowered her voice—even though he was metres away. Healing the rift with her mother was one thing, but she hadn't envisaged diving straight into confidences about her personal life. 'He's just a friend.'

Angela threw her a sideways look. 'Yes, I hold hands with my male friends too. All the time. And the way you look at him—that's not the way a friend looks at another friend.'

'Oh, no. Really? *Eurgh*. Really?' Was it obvious to everyone? Somewhere along the line he'd wriggled his way under her skin. She cared for him. A fierce panic gripped her chest. 'Great. Brilliant. It's so not the right thing to do.'

Her mum looked at her as if she'd gone mad. 'Calm down. It's not a crime to have a bit of fun.'

'That's just it, Mum. I haven't really done this before and I don't know what to do.' Was she really asking relationship advice from the serial divorcee? Apparently so. 'I don't want anything from him, I don't want a relationship. I just want to do my job and to be left in peace.'

But I do want him. That's the damned problem.

'Hey, don't overthink it like I do—that's the kiss of death to any relationship. Just enjoy it. That's what I'm going to do with Richard, anyway.'

'Richard? Really? You've only just met him.' Ivy came to a halt so the men couldn't hear her. What was her mum saying? She was unbelievable. She hadn't changed a bit, she was the same old lady saying the same old things, doing the same old routine. She'd spent the best part of her working life as a doctor fixing people, but in the end the only person she'd failed to fix was herself.

She's fragile, Ivy reminded herself. She's had a scare and is reaching out for comfort.

Or was she just up to her old tricks again? Her mum needed people around her, she couldn't function on her own, and regardless of anything Ivy did or said, she couldn't change that. Happiness was fleeting, she'd learnt. And if Richard made Angela happy, even for a short while, who was she to interfere?

But she needed to say how she felt, just to know that she'd tried to protect her mum from yet another relationship disaster. 'You're in hospital. You had a heart scare. A serious medical problem. You can't start flirting with someone's visitor.'

'Ah, there you go again, overthinking. To tell you the truth, Ivy, I'm lonely, I need a little companionship. It's not as if you're living next door, popping round for sugar every other day. You're miles away and I never get to see you.' Angela gave Ivy's hand a pat. 'And that's you through and through, always so independent, doing your own thing, forging your way in the world. You never accepted any help from being about four years old. I have no idea where you got that from.'

Necessity. 'My dream job is in London, Mum, I have

to go where the work is. I'm sorry I can't be here all the time, but that doesn't mean you have to jump into a… friendship…with the first person you meet. You need to be careful. Remember what happened with the others…' The tears, the drama.

'Of course I'll be careful, dear. But I need to do what I need to do, too. I just want some company. It's not a lot to ask for after everything I've been through. Really, darling, I know we've never done the heart-to-heart thing, but when you're ready I can listen. Mind you, don't ask my advice. I'm useless with men.'

'Oh?' Ivy threw her a smile. There was only so much she could say or do to stop her mum following her well-trodden path. Angela seemed undeterred. 'I hadn't noticed.'

When they arrived back at the bed Matteo and Richard were discussing something to do with an article in an open newspaper on the table. Matteo looked up as she arrived, helped her settle her mum back in bed, all concern and interest and polite nodding.

He'd been so nice Ivy wanted to give something back, even if it meant sacrificing something for herself. Drawing him to one side, she whispered, 'Matteo, I know you're probably thinking about heading off back to London soon, but I wondered—when we've done here, could we go to the pub? Watch the game on TV? What do you think?'

Those dark stubborn eyes glinted. 'I was going to listen to it on the sports radio on the drive back.'

'Oh. Well, that's okay, then.' Disappointment rattled through her. She had an insane desire to spend just a few more minutes with him. 'I feel as if the last two days have been all about me. You've sacrificed your days off to be here, I just thought it would be a way of saying thank you. It's not… I don't want you to get the wrong impression. It's just a pub, maybe some food. The game. I'm not offering any more than that.'

Was it her imagination, or did he look just a little relieved? 'Well, I would prefer to watch it than listen to it. But what about your work? I thought you had too much to do already?'

She shrugged. 'So maybe I can take a little time off? Just a couple of hours.'

His eyebrows rose in surprise. 'Whoa. Watch out, Ivy Leigh, you might get into the habit of relaxing. Then what would happen?'

Staring into his eyes, his heated gaze focused on her, she felt relaxed and excited and scared and comfortable all at the same time. This man was too easy to fall for and she was tumbling deeper and deeper. But she could handle it. She'd laid out the parameters. 'I can't imagine, Matteo. I just can't imagine.'

CHAPTER NINE

'COME ON, ENGLAND! Yes! Yes! Yes! Go!'

So this was the unleashed version of Ivy Leigh? Matteo laughed as she stood, eyes glued to the huge wall-hung TV in the sports pub, body tensed and fists punching the air. 'God,' he groaned into his pint. 'This is terrible. Less than an hour ago you did not know a thing about rugby. Now look at you—England's most fervent fan.'

High-fiving the two open-mouthed English supporters at the next table, she beamed. 'This is fun. We're beating you, Matteo, that's all that matters.'

'There's time yet.' He shrugged, far more entertained by her reactions than the game.

'You think? In the history of the Six Nations championship there have been over twenty games between England and Italy, and England have won them all. Your chances are zero, Mr Hero.'

'Twenty games—how the hell…? Since when did you know that?'

'The wonders of the internet. You just have to know where to look.' She winked at him. 'I did my research. You didn't think I'd invite you to watch a game we had the remotest chance of losing, did you?' On-field action caught her attention again, she paused, breathing heavily as her eyes glued themselves to the game. 'Come on, mate. Pass it. Yes. Yes!'

Thank God for half-time. She sat down, all flushed and hot-cheeked, her chest heaving with excitement. 'This is brilliant. Why did no one ever tell me that watching sport was such fun?'

He drained his glass and put it back on the table. The fun was in watching her watching the game. 'It is when you're winning. And I have to say you are very entertaining.'

She patted his arm condescendingly. 'Poor pet, you're a very sore loser. But still glad you came?'

'To watch you beat us? No.' *Yes.* But he was confused as all hell now. He should have gone when he'd had a chance, instead of being drawn in by those large green eyes sparkling so coyly at him, offering *no more* than a game of rugby. And despite every brain cell screaming at him to climb into the car and head down the motorway, he'd grabbed the chance for a couple more hours with her, like a starving man thrown paltry crumbs.

Her tongue darted out to moisten her lips and he was mesmerised by the action, every part of him wanting to taste her. She gave him a smile. 'I mean, are you glad you came to York? I know it wasn't exactly for your benefit but I hope it hasn't been too bad.'

'What? Spending my non-hospital hours in a hospital, not sleeping with a ginger cat that purrs like a drill? Sure, it has been the best weekend ever.' He felt a laugh rumbling from his throat. Being here with her, on the other hand… 'And now we are losing. It is getting better all the time.'

'I hope it does, for your sake. Although I'm not sure I want to give up that win—so you'll have to find something else to make you smile.'

He let that thought hover for a while, not wanting to

admit the way he was feeling so conflicted about how much she made him smile. 'It's too late, Ivy. The weekend is doomed.'

'Oh, poor sweetheart. Things can only get better. So, tell me, when did you come to live in England, and why?'

He did a quick mental calculation. 'It was about six years ago. I wanted to work with Dave Marshall, he has such a great international reputation—the very best and cutting-edge work in our field—so when we met at a conference in Milan and he invited me to join his team, I jumped at the chance. I haven't looked back.'

'And you already spoke English? I'm impressed.'

'I was pretty rusty. We had learnt it at school from a young age, but even so I was pretty terrible when I first got here. It has been a steep learning curve.'

'I'll bet. Where did you train to be a doctor?'

So she wanted his life history, which was fine by him. He could give her a short version and veer away from anything that might make her ask deeper questions. 'In Florence. Then I went to Milan to specialise, they have a great renal unit there.'

She took another drink of wine. 'You said you don't go home. Why not?'

Straight to the point. Now he wished he hadn't encouraged her to be like this. 'I see you have taken notice of your lawyer training, you have…how do you say it? Cut to the chase. You can do it to me but not for yourself.'

'That, my boy, is called self-preservation.' She twiddled with the stem of the glass then focused her gaze at him again, which made him hot under the collar. 'Now answer my question. Why don't you go home?'

'I'm too busy. Work takes up my time. And there's not a lot there for me.'

'What, a whole load of siblings and parents? That's a lot of reasons to go home.'

Not enough. 'Some of them come here. I see them. Liliana, my little sister with the renal problems, lived with me for a year in London. You can imagine how much fun that was. She is years younger and about five times the trouble of all the others put together.'

'But you love her, I can tell.' Ivy smiled again. It was sweet and soft and real and for a moment he wanted to do nothing but stare at that mouth.

'Of course I love her.' And now he had time to think about it, he did miss the closeness they'd all had, growing up. But betrayal had blown a hole into that that could never be healed. He'd purposely left them all to their lives and chosen disconnectedness. That way he would remain intact, heart and soul. To go home would be to have a constant reminder of what had happened.

But, of course, Ivy did not need to know any of this. Why go deep when this was not that sort of relationship?

This was a weekend for her to be with her family, not for him to get intense about his. Or intense about anything, for that matter, or to lose himself at the whim of emotions that he knew never lasted.

Ivy ran a hand across her blonde hair and fluffed it up nonchalantly. She didn't seem to care that it stuck up in tufts. She had stopped hiding her limp. She was cheering like a madwoman. He was seeing a very different Ivy from the one at work. She was letting her guard down; was that a good sign, or a dangerous one? He had a bad feeling it was the latter. And all he knew was that she was in his head and he couldn't get her out of it.

'Don't you miss it all, though, Matteo? Your family. The sunshine. Decent food. Blue sky. All that wine. Amazing architecture. Art…? Nah, there's nothing there at all for you, is there? God, I'd love to live in Italy.'

'You have a very touristy image of my home.' Which was indeed all the things she'd mentioned but with a large dose of reality. And feuding families. And hurt. 'But now you come to mention it, I guess it does have a few things going for it. Decent coffee, for a start. Although you do have some pretty amazing architecture here too. The Minster is stunning, with its stained glass, and the intricate carving and the history.'

'Yeah, right. Just not marble enough?' After she'd signalled to a glass collector and given a repeat order for beer and wine she turned back to him. 'What do your parents do?'

He shrugged. 'So clichéd. A small taverna. My mum's the…I suppose you'd call it the maitre d'. She makes it work, ruling with a fist of iron. My dad is the chef. We all did our time there, growing up, in the kitchen, waiting tables.'

She eyed him suspiciously, eyes narrowing. 'What's the problem with your dad?'

'What do you mean?' But he was aware that he had become tense and tried to loosen his shoulders.

'Your voice changed, you paused. Your eyes narrowed. Your shoulders are trying to break for freedom. You're not the only one who can ace elementary psychology. You have father issues.'

No, he'd solved them years ago and never looked back. 'He's not worth wasting your time over. None of it is. Live in the now, Ivy. Oh, look, the game's beginning again.'

Her eyes flicked to the TV screen and back to him again. 'Sod the game.'

Forcing a smile he shook his head. 'Ivy, Ivy, you are

too…what is the word?…fickle. I thought you were the world's biggest rugby convert?'

'Not when there are more interesting things to talk about.'

Thankfully the waiter brought their drinks, buying Matteo some time. He took a long drink and tried to watch the game. But he'd underestimated her. She nudged him. 'Your dad?'

'Trust me, my past is not interesting.'

'It is to me.'

That was an admission. Her eyes clashed with his and he saw the moment she also realised the enormity of what she had just said.

What the hell was happening here he didn't know. Because he was as shocked as she was. Right when part of him was keeping that door slammed closed there was a part of him that wanted to talk. That wanted out-and-out openness. It wasn't that he had made a solemn vow never to talk about it, he just hadn't ever wanted to expose so much of his damaged past.

This was neither the right time nor the right place. 'You need to focus on yourself. On healing things with your mum, on how you're going to do your job next week. And the fact we just scored a try while you weren't paying attention. Now we are drawing. England are on the run.'

She looked at him for a long time. Long enough for Italy to miss the conversion. For them to stay just behind their opponents.

Nothing was said. She didn't push. She didn't nag him, she let him off. Which was the sweetest thing she could do right then, when he didn't want his past interfering with this moment. It seemed she knew when to ask, when to stop. She knew every damned button he had and pressed them all. Too much.

Something shifted in his chest, something momentous. Something real. Something he hadn't been looking for and didn't know if he wanted. In fact, something that scared the hell out of him because he'd felt similar things before and it had ended horribly. He didn't want anything close to that happening again. He needed to get away from here. From her.

He sat back in his seat, putting distance between himself and the woman who he knew was taking up more of his heart and his head than she should. But Ivy didn't seem to notice, fixed her eyes on the game.

She wasn't quiet for long.

'Come on, boys. Come on. That's it. Pass it out. To the left. Yes! *Yes!* We won! You beauty!' She jumped up, turned, squeezed his cheeks between her thumb and forefinger and kissed him on the lips, hard and fast. And another. 'Beat that, Matteo.'

For a second he stilled. He didn't want to touch her.

Could not. Would not.

Who was he kidding? No matter what he thought, his body was hell-bent on betraying him at every turn. He wanted her.

It was a normal, natural attraction. It didn't have to mean more than that. It didn't have to be dangerous. He was worrying over nothing. He'd had sex many times with many women and he'd made sure he'd got out with his heart unscathed. He could do that with Ivy, couldn't he?

He was through thinking about it, he was getting as bad as she was.

'Oh, no, you don't get away that easily.' Yanking her towards him amongst the cheering supporters who had all left their seats, he gripped her waist. Planted another kiss on her lips. Then another. My God, she tasted divine. Heat shimmied through him, heat and need. Hot and hungry.

She wrapped her arms around his neck and deepened the kiss with equal hunger. Her body pressed against his, curling into him. When she wriggled her hips against his erection he felt her sigh. With a dirty smile she pulled away but kept a grip on his arm, her words forced out. 'Sod the game. Sod everything. Matteo, do you have to go home tonight?'

'Typical northern weather.' For an early evening the sky was dark. Heavy clouds loomed overhead, threatening a downpour. Ivy's hands were shaking as she stepped out into the thick raindrops that began to fall. This was so out of her comfort zone. She didn't do this. She didn't straight up ask a man to come back to her place. She didn't have wanton sex. She never made a move, first or otherwise. Her heart jittered as she quickened her pace, more out of a desire not to lose her nerve than anything else. 'Come on, we'll have to hurry or we'll get soaked.'

Matteo was uncharacteristically quiet as they headed down the river path to her mum's house. Slipping his hand into hers, he pulled her against him. Rain fell in relentless waves feeding the swollen river, water dripping in gullies between their layers of clothes.

'Ivy.' His eyes were dark and intense and misted. And she knew from one look that he wanted her, wanted this as much as she did. There was a promise between them, silent and yet overt. Dangerous. Dark. So very sexy. One step over an invisible line. Her tummy danced and curled and tightened as the sexy look in his eyes seemed to reach into her gut and tease.

He ran his thumb down her cheek, traced a path over her bottom lip.

She bit down.

His eyes grew darker, hotter. His body tensed. '*Mi fai impazzire.*'

She groaned. 'What are you saying? Please, tell me that means come to bed.'

'Almost. It means you make me crazy.'

'It could mean *two tickets to Leeds, please,* and I swear I wouldn't care, I just love how you sound. Say more...'

'*Sei cosa bella. Due biglietti per Leeds, per favore.*'

'Yes. Yes. Anything you want.' Without thinking further than this moment, she pulled him towards her, fixed her mouth on his and tasted him again. Maybe it was the wine that had relaxed her reserve but she felt tipsy with desire, filled with a need that seemed to become more intense, more breathtaking every time she looked at him.

As she heard a moan coming from her throat she was shocked by the spiralling need at her core. She wanted this man. So much. Too much. Her hands circled his waist, palm flattening against that famous backside. With a sudden rush of excitement she pressed herself against him. She wanted to feel every inch of him against her. Naked. Wet.

She began to explore the taut ridges of his back, hands running over wet linen that stuck to a body she'd dreamt about, that she'd seen butt naked on a screen. Until now out of reach, but still stalking her thoughts. Now it was real. It was real and she wasn't going to think too deeply about it. She was going to do what her mother said...she was going to enjoy it. She was going to not overthink it.

Her mother...good God. Ivy felt her body shut down.

No way in hell.

Her heart pounding fast and hard, Ivy turned away from him, away from the path, and strode towards the road. It was slippery and cold and she tried to concentrate on putting her weight onto her right foot but her head was filled with Matteo and his kisses and the wrongness and the rightness. And she was so torn and muddled. The only thing she knew with any clarity was that she wanted to kiss him. To hold him. And that, for so many reasons, seemed the worst course of action.

'Ivy?' His voice was behind her.

'I'm sorry, Matteo. I just need to go home.' She knew she was being a jerk. But she couldn't do this. Not with him. Not if it meant she was following in her mother's footsteps. She had to take some time out to think about what the hell she was doing at all. If she was going to do anything, she'd do it on her own terms.

'Wait. Ivy. Stop! Sto—!'

She kept her head down and eyes fixed forward.

'Ivy!'

It was fear, not anger she could hear in his voice. Fear? What the—? 'What's wrong?'

As she turned she felt a thump against her body, and at the same time she heard a screech and a scream. Then pain seared through her leg. Someone flew across her path. A whirr of wheels filled the air and a crash. A bicycle? A man on a bicycle?

Off now. On the ground. Shouting at her. Her leg hurt.

Blood was starting to drip from his knee. His face was scrunched up. There was blood. Uh-oh. What did she have to do? Breathe? Tense? Relax? She couldn't remember.

Breathe.

Matteo? Where was Matteo?

Strong, warm arms circled her, lifting her off the road as her knees buckled and her vision began to swim.

'Ivy. What the hell? Are you crazy?' Matteo was sitting her down on the kerbside, his hands on her leg, on her foot, ripping her shoe off. She didn't have the energy to stop him. 'Are you okay? Ivy?'

She swallowed the pain and didn't look at the man with the bike. It was her fault.

All her fault. She'd spent her whole life being cautious and this one time…this was her fault. She should have been more careful. Right from the get-go. Right from the second she'd downloaded that picture. She should have been more careful.

She did a mental body scan. Her leg hurt, more than usual, but she wasn't badly injured. 'Yes. Yes, I'm fine. You'd better go and see the man. I didn't see him. He came out of nowhere. He wasn't there and then he was.'

'He didn't have any lights on. In this weather.' Matteo glanced towards the guy on the ground. The whirring of the wheels were slower now. The man groaned. 'Please. Help me.'

Within an instant Matteo was gone from her side, giving her time to take stock. Every time she let herself go just a little, something happened to remind her of the folly of her actions.

'Ivy.' Matteo's voice was the one he used in the operating theatre. 'Ivy. I need you to focus.'

'Y-yes?'

'Call an ambulance. *Now.* Then come here and give me help.'

'Okay.' As rain teemed down and soaked through to her skin she did as she was asked, telling the ambulance receiver their location. Her hands wouldn't stop shaking and her body felt as if it had gone into shock. She tried to take a few breaths to steady herself, her voice, mirroring Matteo's demeanour when in medical scenarios. She would not think about the blood dripping from the man's head. 'What is the injury?' she called over to Matteo. 'Head injury? Broken arm?'

His voice was too casual as he undid his trouser belt and

fashioned a sling around the man's wrist and neck. 'Tell them it looks like a…' He slowed down his speaking so she could understand and repeat his words. 'A displaced clavicle fracture. A bump to his head, a laceration. No loss of consciousness. Tell them it would be really great if they got here pretty soon.' Then he turned to the man. 'Okay, mate. Sit up and take a few deep breaths. The ambulance will be here soon. You'll be fine.'

'It hurts like hell,' the man groaned, as he sat on the opposite kerb to Ivy, Matteo's hands guiding him into place but supporting the elbow and taking it very slowly so as not to jolt his collarbone.

Ivy limped across the road, her left foot bruised and becoming more sore as she put weight on it. The man's collarbone looked misshapen at its mid-point. But it wasn't sticking out, as she'd assumed it might. It looked as if it had buckled in on itself. 'I'm so sorry.'

'Yeah. You should…watch where…you're going.' Their patient heaved out between breaths. 'But I should have… had lights on…I know. I know…'

'Save your energy, both of you.' Matteo interceded. 'What is done is done. We now have to get this fixed. And quickly.'

Something about his tone had Ivy looking over at Matteo. His eyes were darkened and his jaw taut. There was something more here that she didn't understand. But he clearly couldn't discuss it in front of…

'What's your name?' she asked, trying to keep the conversation light, and to keep the man focused on something other than his injury. He grimaced, his eyes fluttering closed as he spoke. 'Pete. Pete O'Donnell.'

'Well, Pete.' She smiled at him, digging as deep as she could into her failing reserves. 'I don't suppose you caught the rugby game today?'

He shook his head. 'No. I was…going home…to watch…it. Win? Or lose?'

'A great seventeen-fifteen win.'

Matteo gave a hollow laugh. 'Depends who you support.'

'He's Italian,' she explained, hoping to keep Pete interested enough to forget a little of his pain and shock. 'And not particularly happy. But, really, they played well. It was touch and go at one point.'

In the distance a siren blared shrill and welcome. It came closer and closer and louder and louder and Ivy could see Pete starting to become agitated. Mixed with her relief was a little bit of panic. 'If you can just hang on a bit longer, they'll have something to help with the pain.'

Pete tried to push her away with his elbow. 'I think I'm going to be sick.'

'Okay.' She rubbed her palm gently up and down his back. 'It's shock setting in. Take some deep breaths. In. That's it…' She watched as he followed her lead. 'Great. Now out. In again…'

Within seconds the paramedics were out of the ambulance and giving him some gas and air to help with the pain. Within minutes they'd stabilised his injury, stemmed the bleeding from his grazed head and loaded him into the ambulance. Within half an hour she was alone again with Matteo, facing the real reason this whole sorry scenario had played out. She'd wanted to kiss him so badly it had frightened her.

Her heart hammered. 'God, that was awful.' Now her hands began to shake again as the images of broken bones and blood flitted back into her brain. 'I wish I'd seen him.'

'It is dark and raining and he had no lights. How can he expect to ride on a cobbled street in those conditions and not get hurt? But…' Matteo took her arm and prised her gently from her seated position to standing. 'He's gone and is going to be fine. But you? Not so much? Tell me what the hell was going on.'

'I was in a hurry to get back.'

'Yes? But because you wanted to get away from me.' His hands clenched and he shook his head. 'One minute you were willing, the next you were running away. I don't understand.'

'Mixed messages. I'm so sorry. That wasn't my intention. I just got a little spooked.'

He shook his head. 'You should have told me what you were feeling. Talked to me, Ivy. Not run out into the road. Especially with your leg being so damaged. It could have been serious for you too.'

'I did not run. I was walking. And I looked before I crossed.' She took his arm and tried not to wince as they turned the corner towards her mum's place. 'I don't care about my leg and neither should you.'

'I don't care about your leg. No, I do care. I mean I don't care about how it looks. But now it hurts and I don't want to see you in pain because of me.' He stopped and took her by the shoulders to face him. 'What is the matter?'

How honest could she be with him without making herself vulnerable? 'I don't know. I panicked, suddenly. I didn't know what I was doing.'

'You were kissing me. And it was good. And now you're shivering and we're both soaked and a man has a potentially life-threatening injury.' His thumb ran across her cheek, and his eyes were concerned as he gazed at her. He wasn't cross, as she'd thought he might be.

Even so, her stomach felt as if it had dropped to her toes. 'Was it really bad? I thought you were worried, I could tell by your voice. But you stayed so calm.'

'And you managed to distract him while I stemmed the

bleeding and stabilised the break. We were a great team. And you didn't flinch at the blood—too much. A major step forward.' His eyebrows rose and did she see just a little pride there simmering in his pupils? 'His collarbone broke inwards—it could have punctured a blood vessel or his sternum. He may have—we don't know. But it was an emergency in any case.'

'Thank God you were there. I feel so bad.' She bit her lip as she thought. How honest should she be? It felt as if the inside of her head was about to explode. How she wanted to be free and open and honest with him, to relax into something good. To tell him all her thoughts and feelings, to lay herself bare metaphorically. Because that was when true and mutual trust happened, she imagined. But she was conflicted, fighting, knowing that by opening her heart she would be gifting him a part of herself—and she didn't know if she could do that. If she dared. Because what else would she be tempted to give him? What else would he take from her? But he did deserve some kind of coherent explanation. 'I was thinking about my mum.'

Confusion flared, mixed with a little humour. 'That is not a good sign. You were thinking about other things when you were kissing me. Is my kissing that bad?'

'No, your kissing is wonderful. But I was thinking about how she does things and how I don't want to end up like her. She's so dependent. So needy. I don't want to be like that.' *I don't want to lose myself.*

He peeled his jacket off and hooked it over her shoulders, rubbing his hands up and down her arms. 'And you aren't. You could never be like her. You shouldn't have been thinking about anything except the kiss. You want to try again?'

Yes! At just seeing the look in his eyes, feeling his heat, despite the cold and the rain, she knew without a shadow of a doubt that most of her wanted to do it again. This was so unfair. She was holding onto a very fragile line of sensibility here. Torn between her heart and her head. Between doing the right thing and doing the very wrong one. Although she knew which one would be the most fun. 'I don't know.'

'You need convincing? You are a woman and I am a man and there are things we could do that will make us feel amazing.' Scudding his fingers through his chestnut-coloured hair, he shook his head. '*Mio Dio*, this is the hardest I have ever had to work to get a woman to kiss me. Ever.'

A surge of pride swelled in her chest now. 'Good.'

'Good? How can it be good if we are losing valuable time? We could have been kissing for the last hour. Instead, you want to dissect everything into tiny pieces. It is like you're at a trial and everything's under examination. You want to pick. Pick. Pick.' His fingers tickled her ribs with every pointed word.

Squirming away from him, she giggled. This was supposed to be serious, and he was making her laugh? 'I don't want to pick. I'm just being careful. I'm—' *I'm a coward.*

'Stop talking. You and your words drive me insane. Sometimes you just have to go with your gut feeling. Yes?' The pale light of a streetlamp illuminated him. He was glorious. Tall. Strong. Dark. His head tipped back with a smile that would light up a million rugby stadiums. Just being under his heated gaze made every part of her light up too. Anticipation of his kiss, of his touch, skittered across her skin, then penetrated her body, heating her inside.

She thought about what he was saying. What he was asking of her. Her gut feeling was that he would be a very good lover. That he would look amazing with no clothes on. That she wanted to kiss him, to lose herself in the pleasure he was promising. He was asking, sure, but she had to answer. Everything from this moment rested with her next decision. If she said no then she would live to regret it. The same could be said if she said yes. But she could allow herself one small regret in her life, couldn't she? She remembered a phrase she'd heard once before… Always regret something you've done, not something you haven't. She made herself say the word. 'Yes.'

'*Buono.*' Sliding his arm underneath her knees, he stooped and picked her up. 'Now stop the talking. Let's get some action happening.'

'Hey, what the hell do you think you're doing?' Although she didn't try to too hard to stop him.

He shrugged as he walked up the path to her house, carrying her as if she was no weight at all. 'You are cold and wet and shivering. You have an injured foot…'

'It's not that bad…'

'Humour me. Perhaps if I take the lead and make you want me so bad you won't think so much?'

'So bad? No, Matteo, the word is bad*ly*.'

With that he stopped short and grimaced. 'Yes, it's official, you will drive me completely insane.'

Then he plastered her mouth with his, whipping her breath away, along with any further thought process. His kiss was greedy. Hard. Long. Everything she imagined a perfect kiss would be. When he pulled away he was grinning, and breathing heavily. 'But I'm quite happy to go mad if it means I can make you moan again.'

CHAPTER TEN

'ER...MATTEO...' SHE was laughing so hard now she could hardly draw breath. 'That's not the bedroom.'

Opening the bathroom door with a single push of his hips, he tipped her onto the tiles, where she landed feet first. He steadied her. 'A shower first? I'm freezing, and it's one way to heat up. And I thought maybe we just need to start again—with a clean slate.'

'Ooh. Are your jokes as bad in Italian as they are in English?' Her heart was pounding, every nerve-ending was on fire. She didn't need heating up—she was already very, very hot.

Flicking on the tap in the walk-in shower area, he grinned. 'Very bad indeed. Come here.' He pulled her closer, one hand covering hers, the other palming the back of her head as he kissed her again. She gasped as heat and need curled inside her. As he dragged the coat and then her soggy cardigan from her arms his eyes never left her face. 'Yesterday I was in here, praying you would join me. Yesterday I thought you might but I was disappointed. Today I am so glad you are here.'

'Me too. If it's any consolation, I almost did come in here. I was trying to do the right thing. It almost killed me,' she admitted. Her hands fisted his T-shirt, running over dips and curves of muscle, across his chest, down his biceps. She stepped into the shower and pulled him in with her, feeling the most liberated she'd ever felt. Warm water sluiced over them, running in rivulets over their shoulders. And she laughed. It sounded brave, new, echoing across the tiles. Wow. She blinked. So that was what freedom sounded like.

Dragging his T-shirt over his head, she sighed at the sight of his naked torso. My God, he was gorgeous—a heady combination of rippled muscle and tanned skin. She followed the contracting muscles down his chest to his belly. Then her fingers made contact with his jeans waistband. His excitement was evident, and it stoked hers. He wanted her and, *God*, she wanted him. She played a little, running feather finger strokes over his zipper. 'Ah, shucks, now everything's wet. You're just going to have to take these off.'

'Of course. But only if you take these off.' Before she could argue about who should go first, he undid the button on her trousers palmed the fabric and pulled them down. When he reached her feet she lifted one foot then the other and he threw the trousers to one side. On his way back up he stopped briefly to kiss her belly button, the underside of her ribs, her throat. 'My God, Ivy. *Sei cosi bella*.'

So beautiful. And she felt it. For the first time in her life she felt like a goddess. But she was distracted by what she could see. He was every bit as amazing as the picture she'd seen that first morning when her life had been about to fundamentally change. When she'd had no idea what was going to happen; never in her wildest dreams had she thought she would be in such achingly close proximity to that body. Lathering some body wash between her hands, she worked up a decent amount of citrus-scented bubbles.

Running them over his chest in slow circles, her hands

kneaded down his abdomen. There were dips there too, a groove she hadn't noticed until now. 'What's this?'

He took her hand and kissed it. 'Nothing. Just an operation scar.'

'Funny place to have an operation.' Looking closer, she found another groove. Across his belly but further down, another. 'They look like bullet holes.'

His laugh reverberated around the room. 'Didn't I teach you anything in my OR? They're laparascope scars. You see? Nothing important.' He took her hand on a journey to each dip then kissed the tips of her fingers. 'You aren't the only one who has lived an interesting life.'

'Mine wasn't interesting. It was just…unusual.' His scars looked pretty. Did he hate them like she hated hers? Did hers look this pretty to him? She doubted that very much. 'From what? What operation?'

'Kiss me again and I'll tell you.' His fingers played over her breasts and for a moment she almost forgot the question. Heat pulsated through her. She wanted to kiss him again. To feel his mouth on hers, to taste him. But she wanted to play too.

'Tell me or I won't kiss you again.'

'Madness. You and your words.' He didn't give her a chance to argue but pushed her against the glass wall and crushed his mouth on hers until she couldn't think straight, until all she wanted to do was touch him. This thing that had been building between them for the last few weeks was so acute, so overpowering. 'I want you, Ivy. I want you too much. You drive me crazy.'

She wasn't going to argue about that. Talking was wasting time. She ran her hands round his waist, grabbed a handful of his bum, making a mental note to ask him later about his scars. Right now she wanted more, she wanted everything he had to offer. With a sharp slap she whacked him on the backside. 'This is the cause of all the trouble. I want to see it. I want to see it right now. I want to see you naked.'

He laughed. 'You already have. The whole world has.'

'Don't I know it.' She pressed herself against him, the water still sluicing over them, the last of the bubbles draining down the plug. 'I want a private audience with your bottom, Mr Finelli. Make it happen.'

'Ah, okay. If you insist.' He turned and began to hum a sexy striptease song as he started to peel his jeans down, a wiggle of the hips, a coy wink, the teasingly slow lowering of his zip. Her mouth watered—every part of her hot. The best private show of her life. *The only one.*

He was the only one.

For a second she hesitated, her heart pounding loud and hard. What did that mean?

She pushed that thought away—no more dissecting things.

Then, her attention firmly back on Matteo's now naked back and…ass…assets, she swallowed. Hard. Her body was simmering. Her core hot. There it was, in all its glory. Peachy indeed. And ripe. God, yes. Extraordinary.

With a quick wiggle he looked over his shoulder, faking the pose from the picture, arms raised against the shower wall. 'Impressive, yes?'

'Hmm, I've seen better.' Oh, holy cow. *If Becca could see me now.* 'Maybe I need a closer look.'

'Feel, I think. Examination is always important. But first…' He turned, fully naked. And she gasped again. He was beautiful. Big. Hard. So damned confident. So dazzling.

Then he, in turn, reached for the shampoo. With slow sensual strokes and in a silence split only by sighs and moans he began to wash her hair, sensually releasing all fear of being here with him, doing this, all shock of the bicycle incident washed away. The shaking that remained came purely from her desire. The quickened breaths only from his touch, from the anticipation of more.

She tried to reach for him through the steam but he shook his head, concentrating on rinsing the shampoo away. Then he started to massage her shoulders, her neck, tantalisingly close to her breasts…nuzzled against her throat, kissing a trail to her collarbone, down to her bra. Which he undid with supreme ease. The man was clearly used to seducing women.

His fingers went lower, caressing her abdomen, her bottom…and he removed her panties… Every part of her strained for his touch. Heat spiralled through her.

Every part of her thrummed with desire. She felt dizzy. To steady herself she grabbed onto his shoulders, reaching, on tiptoe, to give him another kiss. But he had other ideas for his mouth.

When his lips closed around her nipple she thought she had died and gone to heaven. When his fingers slid between her thighs she knew she was definitely there. *Floating.* 'Oh, Matteo. That is…amazing.' She wrapped a leg round his as his stroking became more intense. She wanted him inside her. Wanted him now. Desperation and urgency began to claw through her gut. She was losing… losing all control to his expert touch.

Losing herself…

She could feel his erection against her thigh. Hard and hot. Her fingers closed around it. Now it was his turn to gasp. *'Mio Dio.'*

'Matteo. I need you.' He was so tantalisingly close. 'I need you inside me.'

His forehead rested against hers as his fingers slowed. 'Not yet. Not yet.'

'Now, Matteo. Please. I want you.' She found his mouth again, kissed him hard in a flurry of wet hunger. She bucked against his hand, faster.

'Oh, God.' His eyes shifted from the shower to the door, and back to her. 'Condom…we need…'

Noooooooooo. Don't stop. 'I don't have any.' For a moment she almost didn't care.

The water came to an abrupt stop. He was already out of the shower area. 'In my bag. In the bedroom.'

Shoving past him, she grabbed his hand. 'What are we waiting for?'

'We are all wet.'

'I don't care, Matteo. I just need you.'

That was a thought.

She pushed that away too.

The journey to the bedroom was too long. The faffing with the condom was really too long. But then he was lowering her onto the bed that already smelt of him, and she wanted to sink deep into it and never re-emerge.

'Yeeeogh!'

'What the hell…?' She followed Matteo's jump from the bed as a ginger furball streaked across the room, yowling.

'Your damned cat. My damned butt.' He was peering over his shoulder and rubbing a cheek.

'Oh. No! Not picture perfect any more? It's his bed, I'm afraid. You're just trespassing as far as he's concerned.' Looking at the claw marks indenting those perfect cheeks, she bit back a smile. 'Oh. Goodness. But thank God it was the backside and not the front. Come here and let me kiss it better.'

Eyeing an unrepentant Hugo sitting smugly in the corner, washing one leg with no care in the world, Matteo hissed. 'I do not like making love with an audience.'

Making love. It was too soon, too immense a thing to

imagine that that was some place they'd reached. 'I think he wants to show you who is the alpha male.'

'No contest. Hands down. I win. Every time.'

Yes, he did. No argument there. She opened the door and shooed the cat out, then came back to Matteo, spiralling fingers through his hair. 'But I think you have to prove it. I might need some convincing, because up until now Hugo's been the only significant male in my life. Show me how alpha you are.'

'Pah. I have nothing to prove. I'm not fluffy. I'm not fat. And I would never, ever hurt you.' Matteo pulled her to him and smothered her mouth with his and she let herself believe him. Let his fingers work magic, let the doubt fairies creep back into the dark place they'd come from. This time the kiss was slow and deeply sensual. His eyes fixed on hers, so dark and misted and full of something… something deep and honest and true. She couldn't look away. Needed to watch him, to see in his eyes what she knew was mirrored in hers. This was pure. Real. Profound.

The stroke of his tongue against hers sent shockwaves through her, stoking the heat again. Bringing her to fever pitch. 'Matteo.' She didn't know what to say, couldn't find enough words to describe the emotions rippling through her. Enough that everything she thought, everything she felt came down to one word. 'Matteo.'

'Ivy. Ivy...' He wanted her. He called her name. He was losing control. This amazing, accomplished, sexy man was here. With her. For her.

He laid her down on to the bed. Then he was sliding inside her in one deep thrust. And she felt the initial stretch and an intense sharp sting that melted into need. But she still kept watching him, watching that beautiful face showing every nuance of emotion. The intensity of pleasure.

The pain of ecstasy. The wonder of such honesty. And she felt every bit as he did. She was raw. Open.

As he increased the pace she went with him. As he began to shake she went with him. Then as he moaned her name over and over again into her mouth she was crashing and flying and soaring with him. And her heart felt as if it had cracked wide open, shifting, making space, letting him in. That last piece of her that wanted to hold back shook loose—tumbling over and over and away until it was barely there, out of reach, so far away, then nothing at all. For a moment panic gripped her. And so she forced herself to look deeper into his eyes, because there, surely, she'd find an answer.

Then she couldn't think at all. She just went with him, giving herself up to this feeling. Losing herself in him.

It was a few minutes before Matteo really had himself under control.

Pah! He wasn't in any kind of control at all. Never had he had such an intense experience. Never had he been so wholly under the spell of a woman. He didn't know what to make of it all, what this feeling in his heart was. It was like a long slow fall into something exciting yet comfortable. To familiarity, and yet a whole new experience of learning. It was exquisite and unique. It was beautiful.

And it scared the hell out of him.

He gave her a soft gentle kiss, his heart lighter when she responded. Cupping her cheek to look at her, he finally managed some words. 'Okay, good, you're still breathing.'

'Only just.'

'That was intense.'

She hesitated before she spoke again. Gathering her breath and, he imagined, her thoughts. What was going through her head? He wondered whether it was messed-up crazy thoughts like his. The pull of intimacy and the push of fear.

Wriggling out from underneath him, she snuggled into the crook of his arm, her head on his chest, blonde hair tickling his nose. 'Yes. That was…just amazing, Matteo. Just amazing.'

'Yes. It was…amazing.' His heart was too full to find any more words to describe what had just happened.

Normally he'd start his leaving routine about now. Faking tiredness, faking a reason to go. Because staying the night, actually sleeping with a woman was a commitment too far that gave too many messages, meant too many things that he did not or could not feel. And, with his head swimming in and out of rationality, distance would have probably been a good thing right now.

Should he leave? How could he leave? A better man would leave when there was no possible future for them. No long-term promises doomed to fail. She was warm, so beautiful. Anchoring him in a place he wanted to stay a while.

An insane man would leave.

Her fingers tiptoed down his chest. 'Oh. I just remembered, you were going to tell me about the scars.'

'Not this again. They are nothing.' His heart began to thud. Not from the memory of the operation—that had been like child's play in comparison—but because of the associations, the ramifications of his time in hospital. But he never talked about this. Especially not after something so intimate that had made him off balance. 'It is time to sleep.'

'Matteo, it's still early. I'm wired…' She shifted over him and he could feel her heart beating against his stomach. Tender kisses across his abdomen.

He gave her backside a gentle tap and tried to play,

to distract her from what felt like her only conversation choice. 'You know, you have a peachy bum too, Miss Leigh. Maybe we could do his and hers calendars. That would raise a bit of money for the hospital.'

'Matteo! That's hysterical. It would raise a lot of eyebrows, and knowing the board it would probably lose me my job. If I don't lose it anyway when I don't turn up for work on Monday.'

A tremor of irritation rippled through him. It was supposed to have been a joke. 'Always your job…it's like it's the only thing that matters.' He got it. It was what he'd always prided himself on too. But now…?

No. Now it was still the same. Nothing had changed. He was still the same Matteo, she was still the hospital lawyer who he happened to be in bed with. Nothing more.

At least, that was what he was trying to convince himself.

She gave him a confused look. 'It's not the only thing that's important. Surely you know that about me now? I'm here, aren't I? I mean…here, for my mum, of course.' Her eyes had flitted away from his face and he had no idea what she was thinking—perhaps, like him, she was surprised at how quickly things had moved from the pub to the bed. The intensity of emotions.

She ran fingertips across the top of his pubic bone. Her voice had been serious for a moment, but now it was lighter. 'So, you have four laparoscopy scars and a longer one here, stretching across your abdomen. That looks…' Levering herself up onto one elbow, she looked straight at him. 'Wait a minute…am I right? Did you…no? Matteo? Did you donate one of your kidneys?'

That was so obvious he couldn't lie. 'Elementary, Miss Leigh. You can be my number-one student. So don't ever ask me to give you a kidney, because now I don't have any to spare.'

'But why?' Her eyes darkened. A stormy sea. 'Who did you give it to? Wait...let me guess. Oh, my God. It was you. You gave the kidney to your sister?'

'Very good.'

She jerked upright, grasping the sheet and wrapping it round her breasts. It looked like she was settling in for a long talk. 'You donated your kidney. My God, when? How old were you?'

He didn't need to lay his life out to her. But he knew she would not stop asking. And this one act he had done he was proud of. 'Eighteen. It was one of the first laparoscopic transplants in Milan.'

'You saved her life.'

Not wanting to see any more questions in Ivy's eyes, he laid his head on her lap and looked up at the ceiling. 'I gave her more time. Transplants can last for ten, twenty years. Sometimes up to forty—after that we just don't know.'

'Wow. You must have been such a hero to your family.'

'It was the easiest decision I've ever had to make. Ever. No one else was such a close match.' That time...those memories. Without being able to control it, the tension rose through him.

She must have sensed it too because her voice lowered, a hand went to his shoulder. 'What? What happened?'

'It is too long ago.'

'Let me see...' Drumming her fingers on his ribcage, she thought for a few minutes. 'Your sister...and... It's something to do with your father. Let's examine the evidence.'

Per l'amor di Dio. It was so long ago and yet the pain still lingered—not overtly but under the surface. A stark reminder of why he never trusted his heart to anyone. Why he never could.

Ivy needed to know that, especially now. 'Okay. Okay. I was engaged to be married. Elizabetta. She lived in the same village as me. Her family were like our family too. We grew up together. We fell in love at eight years old. Our lives were planned in the cradle.'

'What has this got to do with these?' She popped a finger into the dip of each of the faded round scars. 'I don't understand.'

'We...we were always "we" from as far back as I can remember. We had plans—big plans—fuelled by my father, who saw the village as a tie and the restaurant as a failing burden with no future. He filled our heads with dreams, to go to Florence to study medicine, to conquer the world. So that was my life. Study. Working in the restaurant. Elizabetta. It was all leading up to us escaping the small closed-in village and exploring the world.'

Ivy looked at him as if she'd never had those kinds of dreams. Then he realised that escape for her had meant just getting out of hospital. Escape had meant being able to put one foot in front of the other. Escape was knowing there was someone who cared about her enough to help her fight the injustices she'd faced.

Maybe if he'd narrowed his world down to such singular things then he wouldn't have run the risk he had. But he'd had no choice in the end.

'Then my sister got sick. It was sudden and irreversible and she was going to die without a transplant. Dialysis could only help her for so long. We were all tested and I was the lucky one who went off to Milan with her and we had more tests and were away for a few weeks with sporadic contact with our families.' He gave a hollow laugh.

'Who knows, if we'd had your fabulous social media back then, things might have been different.'

He felt Ivy's quiet laugh against his chest.

If things had been different he wouldn't be here, doing this. He wouldn't have found her. A twist of fate that meant his life was more now, richer.

'When we eventually came home Elizabetta had changed. She was quiet and distant—one minute she was loving, the next she couldn't bear to look at me. Eventually she told me she was pregnant. That she had to stay in the village, that we had to change our plans. So I…what do you say?…*sucked* it up. I put my plans aside. I stopped studying. I missed the start of the medical school course. I started to build a life there, working for my father—who berated me every day for giving up on my dream so easily. For not escaping as he'd wanted to do. He laughed at me. Said I should go far away and take Elizabetta with me.'

'Easy for him to say.'

But hard to watch his son throw his life away, Matteo guessed. Hindsight was a wonderful thing. How would he have reacted if he'd watched his son give up his dreams? 'I had made the same mistake he had—got a girl pregnant—and he could see the same pattern happening. He was angry and disappointed. And so, deep down, was I. Everything started to crowd into my head. It was a dark time. I had no future that I wanted and a fiancée who hardly spoke to me. But I tried to make the best of it and grew to love the child inside the woman I wasn't sure loved me any more. This was my problem and I was dealing with it.'

She had started to stroke his hair. It was comforting. Sweet. 'Big decisions at such a young age.'

And he'd thought himself such a man. How wrong he'd been. 'One day I was out walking, trying to piece my life together, when I caught her and Rafaele together in the fields. Something they'd apparently been doing since I'd gone to Milan. And probably before.'

'Rafaele?'

'A friend.' He could barely even say the word because it did not describe how Matteo felt about Rafaele. Not at all. 'When I confronted them Elizabetta admitted she loved us both, that she was torn between us. And that she hadn't known how to tell me. That the baby I'd given my future up for wasn't even mine. Rafaele just stood there. Silent. He had nothing to say.'

'What did you do?'

Matteo shrugged. 'She'd lied to me. He'd lied to me, too, and there he was, not defending himself. Not saying anything. He had insulted me and any honour or pride I had. So I hit him. Then I told Elizabetta that I would make the decision easy for her and went to pack my things. Back at the house my father laughed in my face. Told me I'd been taken for a ride, that I'd given up my future for nothing. That I was worth nothing. Thank God I didn't hit him too. But I wanted to. I so very nearly did. In the end I just walked away.'

It was the first time he'd ever spoken about this. It was at once cathartic and yet disturbing to relive it again. But the anger wasn't as intense as it had been. It felt like the dark stain on his heart had finally begun to fade. Ivy's soothing voice encouraged him to go on. 'I don't blame you. It sounds very messed up.'

'They have four children now. They have the life I had been prepared to have, in the village where we all grew up.'

Ivy's fingers massaged the tops of his shoulders now. 'Which explains why you don't want to go back. I understand now. And why you insist on honesty. Because you had your trust broken completely. I get that. But you have an amazing life now. Look at all the good you do.'

It was, he realised, an empty life that he filled with work. A life like Ivy's. They were the same, the two of them. Trying to convince themselves that they were okay. That they were living just fine. Because that way they didn't have to risk any part of themselves. They were scared, underneath it all. Scared.

'But it stays with you. Even just a little bit, no matter how much you try to let it all go. Lies can ruin lives. But not as much as love does.'

CHAPTER ELEVEN

SCRATCH. SCRATCH. SCRATCH.

Ivy opened her eyes and tried to work out where the noise was coming from. For that matter, what the noise was. And where the hell *she* was.

Scratch. Meow.

Hugo. Of course. The spare room. With… Wriggling a foot to the other side of the bed, she tested the temperature. Cold. He was long gone. She was in the spare room and *not* with Matteo.

But his scent remained, and, with it the memories of a wonderful night of lovemaking. Of intense emotion. Of discovering that part of him that he held back. The reason he had his famous reputation of non-commitment. It wasn't hard to see why. His history was punctuated with hurt and betrayal and she knew how that felt.

Like right now. When she wanted so much to believe in the fairy-tale ending, and yet he had already disappeared into the night like a guilty gigolo. It would have been nice if he'd had the decency to at least say goodbye. It wasn't as if she hadn't known this would happen, especially after his words last night, but what surprised her was how much it hurt.

Getting out of bed, she pushed the negativity away. It had been a wonderful weekend, and she had begun to feel things she'd never thought possible. She'd laughed and worried and held onto him, exposed her inner fears and experienced such intense joy. He'd made her feel important and special and worthy.

And that, she realised, was the problem.

Downstairs in the kitchen Hugo wound around her feet as if she was the last person alive on earth. In danger of being knocked off balance between her dodgy foot and a starving, needy cat, she picked him up. 'At least someone's pleased to see me.'

Snuggling her face into his fur, she got some comfort from a warm, beating heart under her fingers and the purr that sounded, indeed, like a drill. So what if it was all cupboard love? She was under absolutely no pretences with the cat. Shame she couldn't say the same about her own love life.

And there it was again. That feeling of panic. It wasn't love. It had been one night, the only thing they could ever share. She knew that, they both did. It would be ludicrous to want otherwise.

Plopping Hugo back on the floor, she turned to the fridge. 'Hold on, buster. Here's some food—'

Whoa. A magnet with a pretty terrible amateurish painting of Scarborough beach held a handwritten note on the fridge door:

Ivy

Joey is sick. I have gone back to London in a hurry. I will phone you.

Matteo x

She was disappointed at how much her heart soared at those few words. At the hope she imbued into the one tiny letter at the end of the note. What was wrong with her? Instead of worrying about that poor boy, she'd been buoyed by the thought that Matteo had not run away but had left because of an emergency. She'd never been like this before—living in hope of a word, a caress. Been desperate for a man's touch, a kiss. It was infusing everything she did. Infecting her thoughts. Making her feel anxious and excitable.

So being here helping her mum to recuperate had come at the right time. It meant she didn't have to face Matteo right now, she could hunker down and get on top of her wayward emotions, work out a way of avoiding him when she got back, and then she'd back to her normal self.

Talking of which... Ivy glanced at the oven clock. Damn. She was late.

Two hours later she bundled her mum—and Richard, which was a strange turn of events, but, really, not so surprising after all—out of the taxi and back into the house. 'Okay, sit down, Mum, and...er...Richard.'

'Thank you, Ivy. Shoo. Shoo.' Richard pushed Hugo roughly from the sofa, sat down and got a hiss in return. 'Oh, and, please, you can call me—'

'Right. Okay...so...' *Please, don't do that* you can call me dad *routine.* She'd been through too many dads all in all. And they had all turned out like her real one—absent. Picking up Hugo, she gave him a conciliatory stroke. 'I'll pop the kettle on, make a pot of tea and start on lunch.'

Angela gave her a weary smile that was irritated or exasperated or something that Ivy couldn't put her finger on. But was all too familiar. 'That's very kind of you, darling, especially when I know how much you need to be getting back to your important job. Are you packed yet? What time's the train? Should we call you a taxi?'

What? Train? Taxi? 'I was going to stay a few days,

make sure you're okay. You know, like we agreed.' *Mum and daughter time.* 'I want to make sure you're okay.' *That we're okay.*

'Oh, don't worry about that. Richard said he'd cook me dinner tonight, and he's going to pop in every day to check up on me.' Her mother reached out and gave Richard's hand a squeeze, and then left her hand there, tight in his fist, and they looked comfortable and settled—how had they done that in such a short space of time? How had they given themselves up to this, whatever it was. For as long as it lasted. 'Every day, he says. So I'll be fine. Don't feel like you have to stay on my account. We'll be just fine.'

'Oh. Of course, yes, I see.' Ivy didn't know what else to say as she turned away. But she could see very clearly that she wasn't any use now. Richard was going to fill the hole in her mother's life, Ivy could go back to her job, to her other life in London with no need to worry. Except she'd so wanted to fix things with her mum now she was here.

But she didn't want to do it with an audience, and she knew it would need a lot more than the few precious minutes they had right now—and with a mother who had a focus on that and not on another potential husband.

It was yet another example of her mum's erratic behaviour. Her short attention span where Ivy was concerned. And, yes, it hurt.

Damn it, don't cry. She squeezed her eyelids shut and forced back any sign of distress. Maybe leaving was for the best.

She looked back over at her mum and had to admit she did look happy and relaxed, and the best she'd been since her heart scare. Ivy caught a smattering of her conversation with Richard. 'Stay right there,' he was saying in a quietly calm voice. 'I'll get a cushion for you. Wait…wait… I want to make sure you're comfortable.'

The man was certainly attentive, even if he didn't appear to like cats. And who was she to deprive her mum of some happiness? If she'd been suffering from depression for all those years and now she wasn't—if this man made her happy and this was what Angela wanted, then she had to let it go. Regardless of her own misgivings.

'I don't know,' her mother replied, looking up at her new man with a sort of adoration as he plumped a cushion and fussed around her. 'You and your fussing ways, you'll drive me crazy.'

'You'll get used to it. See that my way is best.' Richard gave her mum a smile and Ivy's heart lurched.

You drive me crazy.

They were only words. But she'd used them to Matteo and he'd used them right back. And it was the sentiment, it was the same—you drive me crazy, but that's okay. What's a bit of madness between friends? Losing sanity. It was two people becoming a little less of who they were for the sake of someone else. It was Ivy becoming Angela.

Her hand went to her mouth. Oh, my goodness. Of all the things she'd dreaded. She couldn't let that happen.

But it was too late, Ivy *was* different. He had made her different, he'd made her yearn for more. For more in her life than just work. Which was impossible. Just downright impossible, if she was going to be true to her herself and her years of promises and grit.

If she went back to London tonight she would have to face Matteo again too soon and she didn't know what she would say, or how to act, or how to be the same person she'd been before. Before she'd ever met him.

Truth was, she wasn't sure of anything any more. Of where she fitted in her own life, or in other people's. Fighting back the sting of more tears, she walked into the kitchen. At that same moment her phone rang. She pulled it out of her pocket, unable to see the number for the teary blur, which she scrubbed away as quickly as it arrived.

There was absolutely no point in getting emotional about any of this. She just needed to compartmentalise her feelings and move on, like she always did. 'Hello?'

'Ivy?'

Matteo. She swallowed back the lump in her throat and disregarded the accompanying jittery heart rate at the sound of his voice. She would not show him any reason to feel sorry for her, she would not let him know her feelings. She infused her voice with cheeriness. 'Hello! How's Joey?'

'Good, you saw the note. He's a lot better now. He had a ureteral obstruction, which didn't resolve with a nephrostomy. I operated early this morning.'

'Er...English, Matteo?' Cradling the phone between her ear and her shoulder, she filled the kettle, plonked two teabags into a teapot and tried very hard to act normally.

'I had to take him back to Theatre to unblock a blockage. What is wrong?'

'Nothing. Nothing at all.'

'But your voice isn't right. You are upset?' He knew the timbre of her voice? He knew her so well he could tell when she was upset, without words? He knew her too well. She'd let him in too—she'd let him in and she was going to get hurt. Because that's what happened if she let her guard down. There was a pause she didn't know how to fill. Then he was back again.

'Are you cross because I left? I'm sorry I had to leave so quickly and so early. I didn't want to wake you.' Another pause, then his voice was more serious. 'I need to talk to you.'

Uh-huh. She knew exactly what was coming, but she couldn't do a heart-to-heart, not without understanding what the heck was going on in her head and why her body had become a quivering mess. Why she desperately needed to feel his arms around her when it was the opposite of what she should be needing.

But something had to be said, surely? They'd moved further into something last night. Something tangible and deep and frighteningly wonderful. And so very, very dangerous. A line had been crossed and it couldn't be ignored.

But it could be delayed. Until she'd got a better grip on herself. 'Another time, Matteo. I'm busy… I have too much to do.'

'That is what I mean.'

'Sorry? You're not making sense.'

'I saw the boss today at the hospital. Pinkney. I told him your dilemma and he agreed to a week of compassionate leave. You can stay with your mum and work can wait. I fixed it for you.' He had a smile in his voice and she imagined that wonderful mouth curving upwards, the light in his eyes. And felt a stab of pain in her solar plexus.

You drive me crazy.

And he did. And that was the problem. He drove her wild with desire, he drove her to the edge, he drove her to want things she couldn't have. To dream impossible things. And now he was trying to fix her messed-up life. And it would be so easy to let him do it—so easy, and yet the hardest thing in the world. Because she could not let go of her grip on her life.

'But, you see…I don't want you to do that. I don't need you to fix things for me, I can manage quite well on my own. I don't need you. I don't need anyone.' It was harsh. And it was everything she needed to believe and feel again but didn't, but if she kept on saying it he'd get the message and she wouldn't have to face him. Or this. Or herself.

'I thought that was what you wanted. I was trying to

help.' She could hear the building anger in his voice. And, yes, he'd been kind, as always, and thought he was doing the right thing. But, as it turned out, she hadn't needed him to. Once again she was surplus to Angela's requirements.

'Thank you. But I won't be needing it. Please, don't interfere in things like that again. Not my work. Thank you.'

'Hey! Stop right there. Do not talk to me as if I am just a colleague, as if there is nothing between us. Ivy, we need to talk.'

'I'm not sure there's anything to say.'

His voice was louder, harsher. 'And I think there is. I think that what happened last night meant something. Did it mean nothing to you?'

She could lie, but he'd know. He *knew* her. He knew what had passed between them last night, the startling honesty and the wonder—that wasn't something she could deny. It had been too profound, too…too *much*—and it had shocked them both. She lowered her voice, the truth of her words like glass shards in her gut. 'Yes. Yes. It meant something.'

'So explain to me what is happening here, because I'm confused. You're distant and different from the woman I know. Damn it, Ivy, tell me the truth.'

I'm saying that you mean too much to me. That I have to let you go. 'I'm sorry, really. I do have to go.' Her heart twisted keenly, making her inhale. But her lungs wouldn't work. She forced the words through a closed throat. 'Goodbye, Matteo.'

It was for the best. It was. And one day she'd thank herself for it.

Without waiting another moment, she flicked the phone off and went up to her room to pack. It was time to go home.

Wherever the hell that was. But it wasn't here. And it wasn't in Matteo's arms.

* * *

Round three. Part one.

Matteo circumvented the tasteless coffee table and surreptitiously drank out of his clandestine cup as he mingled with the waiting group. The only saving grace was that Ivy wouldn't be here to tempt him, to confuse him. To drive him mad all over again.

In fact, it was very useful that he'd had to leave in the night to come and see Joey, before he'd had a chance to do anything even more foolish than make love to a woman who was destined to trample all over his heart. She'd proved that enough when she'd answered his attempts at intimacy with silence. Refuted his well-intentioned intervention into her work life—which, for the record, he'd thought was the right thing to do.

But that would never happen again, not if it generated such a response. He could feel his blood pressure rising at the memory of her sharp words and the swiftly ended phone call. The reminder that relationships brought about all kinds of problems that he was better not having.

He took a seat in the front row, glared at the clock. Willed the day to be over so he could get the big fat tick on his attendance sheet and eventually put this whole exercise behind him. Then he wouldn't have any more unreturned calls to Ivy Leigh. Along with the whole bunch of questions and no answers.

The door swung open and her assistant walked in, handed out the day's schedule. And—

In walked Ivy.

Matteo's head pounded. That blood pressure was rising at an alarming rate. Why was she not in York?

'Good morning, everyone.' She was all business and no eye contact. Well, no eye contact with him at any rate. 'Welcome to the third day in our social media course.

Today we are going to expand on branding and why it is important in this technological age to capitalise on it. I'm going to give a few pointers about how we do this as a company, and how you can help…'

He didn't want to help. He wanted it to be over. He wanted to be alone with her. He wanted her. That was the startling, raw, naked truth of it. And at the same time he knew that wanting a woman who did not want him back was the first step to madness.

Two hours later they were split into more infuriating groups to discuss brand statements. Ivy walked over, her limp undiminished—in fact, worse than usual. He put it down to the bicycle accident. She looked tired and frazzled and distant. To stop himself from spending too much time just looking at her, at the proud, straight back, the curve of a breast he knew was lush and sweet, the unintentionally honest green eyes, he started to give his ideas to the group. 'Brand statements… Okay. We help children. We save lives. I know…we save children's lives…er… Children first? Kids first…? *Aargh*. This is pointless. I'm a doctor, not a marketing person. I instinctively know what the brand is, I live the damned thing every day—why do I have to come up with a statement?'

She stopped at his shoulder. 'So that we are all on the same page, Mr Finelli. If we have a mission statement and a brand statement that are symbiotic then we all have a pathway for our work.'

Mr Finelli now, was it? 'I already have one and, I imagine, so does everyone here. It's about doing our best…for everyone. And about being *open* and *honest* about intention.'

Judging by the two hot spots on her cheeks, she took the veiled meaning for what it was. He didn't like playing guessing games. He didn't like hot and cold. He liked to know exactly where he stood. On all things. He didn't like having the phone put down on him when he was trying hard to work things through.

'I...I...understand...' She looked away. 'So—'

'I am not sure you do, Miss Leigh. This hospital is about children, we all know that. Children are not a brand, they are people. Living, breathing, vulnerable and sick people. Show me how branding can really, actually, honestly change a single life more than what we do here every day then I'll be impressed. Until then, well, I just want to do my job in peace. Like you, I presume, with no needless distractions.'

For a moment she stared at him open-mouthed, the two hot-spots spreading across her neck like a rash. And he immediately regretted allowing his frustration to overspill into this public domain.

She gave a quick clap of her hands. 'Okay, everyone, let's break for morning tea.' Then she turned to him and whispered, 'Outside. Now.'

A cruel wind whipped at the side of the red-brick hospital building as they huddled in a disused doorway. She'd made sure they were well away from prying ears and eyes. So typical. Anything to keep the work-life divide real. He cut through the tension. 'Ivy. How come you are here? Your mum?'

'Is fine, it appears. I came back on Sunday. The train...' Her tone was dismissive, not allowing for any more discussion on that subject. 'It's not important.'

'I see.' This was a surprise, especially given the compassionate leave she'd been granted and her stated intention that she wanted to fix things. She clearly wasn't going to expand on this, she was closed off and wound as tight as that first day he'd met her. Was this really the warm-hearted woman who had held him so tightly outside the cardiac care unit? Who had screamed loudly in a pub? Who had laughed heartily at his jokes? Who had gripped him and exposed her fears? Who had lain breathless and spent on his bed after the best lovemaking of his life?

She looked at him now with a taut line of a mouth. With eyes that she clearly hoped were cold and distant but which gave away a traitorous flicker of heat. She would not like to know that, he supposed. 'So work won out in the end? I'm surprised, Ivy. I thought you had changed your priorities a little. What do you want to say to me?'

'Work did not win. My mother simply didn't need me.' That flicker of heat gave way to sadness. Something had happened between her and her mum and she was dealing with it badly. 'Now, I'd be grateful if you could keep our personal life out of the work environment.'

'Since when did I bring it in?'

Her eyes fired up again. 'When you spoke to Pinkney. And with the between-the-lines comments in there. I'm at work. We both are. Please, remember that.'

Leaning against the wall, he looked at her, barely trying to disguise his surprise and growing anger. 'No one knows anything. And since you have refused to speak to me in private I'm stuck with having to put things between the lines. I told you about my life, I told you how much I value honesty. What the hell is going on, Ivy?'

'I…' She shook her head, the tautness of her mouth softening, wobbling slightly, and for a moment he thought she might cry. 'I don't know what to say. Just that I'm sorry, but…'

And it was all well and good being angry with her, but he knew deep down that she was not a hurtful kind of woman. That she was facing challenges that were testing her, pushing her to the limits. That she was warm and funny and with a lot to give and usually had too many words but now had none.

Matteo stepped closer but ignored the need to pull her to him. She was so proud she would never allow that. He kept his voice low. 'Okay. Talk to me. Please, that's all I ask. I will start. This all took me by surprise. Things went from slow to fast in a heartbe—'

'Yes. Yes.' She held her hand up and stopped him from saying more. 'Thank goodness you feel the same. Too fast, Matteo. Too deep. Too quick. I never wanted this. I like being on my own. I like not having to make decisions for someone else. I'm too independent for all this. Last weekend was…nice. And thank you. But we can't… I can't—'

'Nice? Nice? All the words in the world and that's the one you choose. Oh, Ivy. What kind of game are you playing? Because I don't understand your rules. One day you were happy to be with me, and now…this coldness.'

'I'm not playing a game. I'm being serious. I don't want a relationship. I can't…do it. I can't give myself… I don't want to.' She looked down at her watch. 'Damn. Look, I have to go back in and start.'

'Just like that, it is over?'

'Yes. Yes, it is.'

He waited for relief to flood in, but it didn't. Only bitter sadness, a hole in his chest. Which was surprising and startling and bleak. The thought that he'd see her over and over again in the hospital and never get to kiss those lips. To hold her close and stroke her cheek. To be at the end of a smart quip. This was not how he'd envisioned he would feel and he didn't know what to do or say. He was out of his depth here, with feelings swirling inside him. He didn't want them but he couldn't seem to let them go. What did it mean?

Did he love her? Surely he could not have done such

a thing? He had always protected himself from that. Because of the pain. Because of Elizabetta, because he had been so wary to give his heart to a woman and watch her toss it aside. Was Ivy any different from that? He'd hoped so, but now he wasn't so sure.

'No more talking about it? I have no choice?'

'No. Please. Don't make me say anything else. Because I don't know what more to say.' She gave a swift shrug of her shoulder and blinked away what he thought might be tears. 'I really do have to go and finish this workshop.'

'Always your job.'

'Oh, yes, well, you know me. No hard feelings?'

'I thought I did know you, but I was wrong.' He watched as she swivelled on the hard gravel and began to walk back towards the conference room. 'And, no, Ivy, I have no hard feelings. I have no feelings about this at all.'

And that was when he knew that he'd fallen completely for her. That he had given her much, much more than he'd ever intended; he'd given her his heart on a platter and all but invited her to chop it into pieces. Yes, he knew he'd fallen in too deep, because saying he had no feelings was the first real lie he'd ever told.

CHAPTER TWELVE

'BACK FOR MORE, I see? You're a glutton for punishment.' Nancy gave Ivy a little smile as she gave her wet hands a shake and scanned the OR prep-room sinks, looking for the paper towels. 'You've done so well, considering what you were like that first time.'

'Thanks.' It was all Ivy could muster. She was feeling much worse than that first day—she may well have mastered the sight of blood, but mastering the sight of Matteo Finelli was something she would probably never be able to do. She could see him through the glass door in the OR, talking and laughing with the anaesthetist. Her stomach clenched into a tight ball.

She didn't want to face him today, because yesterday she'd felt as if her heart was shattering. She'd summoned every single ounce of strength she'd had to tell him it was over, when it felt like the words had been stuck in her throat, refusing to come out. She'd had no sleep, curled up with Hugo, who she'd rescued from the clutches of *daddy Richard.* And, unsurprisingly, Hugo had been about as helpful with relationship advice as her mother.

And now…well, now she had to stand with Matteo all day and watch him save another life. Watch him laugh and joke and be lovely and warm to all those people and feel her heart beating to the rhythm of his voice, feel the pull of her body towards him, and know that it made no sense to take those steps, no matter how much she was compelled to.

The door swung open and he strode in.

Looking around, she realised Nancy had gone and they were alone. She took a deep breath. 'Matteo, hello.'

'I thought it was Mr Finelli these days.' He wasn't wearing a surgical mask so she felt the full effect of his indifference. No, actually, it was a simmering deep anger that he'd dressed up as indifference. She'd hurt him and that had not been her intention.

'Matteo, please—'

He shook his head. 'Miss Leigh, I can honestly say that I have no problem whatsoever about bowing out of our petty little war. I'm even happy to admit you to be the winner—in truth, it makes no difference to me. So you have no need to be here.' He came a little closer, not close enough that she could touch him but enough that she felt the magnetic pull towards him, and feel, too, the venom in his words. 'In fact, I'm asking you leave.'

'To leave? But—why?'

His eyes bored into her, stern, angry, righteous. 'Because having you here distracts me. I need to be fully focused on my work. It is better if you're not here, particularly for the patient. And that, after all, is the full focus of *your* job, right?'

'Matteo, please—'

This time he held up his hand and she shut up immediately. 'Did you really think I would let you in? What an idea! When you don't let anyone in yourself? When you don't even know how?'

'I can't. I tried, but I can't.' Because the second she'd let him in she'd started to be someone else. She hadn't been

Ivy Leigh any more…and she didn't want that. She wanted to keep herself intact.

'Things might have worked if we'd both wanted to try.'

'But…' She finally found the words to admit how she was feeling. 'I don't want to lose myself.'

'I know. I understand that. Who does? Have you ever thought that perhaps, just perhaps, we could have had a… what did you call it?…symbiotic pathway? Walk it together? Be ourselves and yet part of something?'

She thought of her mum and her flatmate and of the weekend and of how desperately she'd ached for Matteo when he hadn't been there. How he had become the focus of her thoughts. 'Everything I've ever seen has shown me that independence becomes interdependence and then dependence. I don't want to depend on anyone. That wouldn't be me. I don't want to be like that.'

He huffed out an exasperated breath. 'It doesn't have to be like that. I know plenty of people who have managed to have happy relationships. You don't even want to take the risk.'

Please, don't ask again. Because I might just say yes. 'No, Matteo. I don't. For both of our sakes. It wouldn't be fair.' She turned away from him, unable to keep looking at those dark eyes that drew her in so deep. 'Okay. I'll go, if you insist. But I won't say I've won. I don't even want to think about that.' This was no victory at all. 'I think we've both won. And lost. And now I'm talking in circles. I'll just go.'

'Yes. Please.'

She went to leave, biting back the shout, *I want you. Please, don't do this.* Fighting back tears, knowing that stopping this before it became too intense, too hard to handle, too overpowering was the very right thing to do, even though her heart told her otherwise. But she hadn't achieved all those amazing things in her life by listening to her heart. So it had no right to interfere now.

Her head bobbed a little as she leaned towards the door. She was going.

'Ivy. Stop.' Matteo felt the blood boiling through his veins. This was not the best way to start a difficult day in the OR. This was not how he had planned this conversation to go. He had been going to ban her from the theatre, yes, but he hadn't wanted to see her look so accepting of his rejection. So vulnerable. 'This…this is… Just listen, you're making me say things I don't mean. You're making me crazy.'

She turned a little, her eyes brighter. Her mouth made a tentative attempt at a smile, but it just looked sad. 'I know, and that's the biggest problem of all. Apparently it doesn't get any better with age. So my mum says, and she should know.'

'She is better now?'

'She's exactly the same as always. With a slightly damaged heart. But haven't we all?'

He laughed. He actually laughed. Right in the middle of this…break-up of something that wasn't even a whole of anything. He laughed. Because she was impressive, this woman. She was more than impressive. She had shown up today knowing that it would be the hardest thing to face him, but she had done it anyway. She had kept her sorrows to herself. She had hidden her emotions and kept on working. It was either admirable or downright destructive. Or both.

And no matter what words came out of his mouth the feelings remained the same. He was awash with anger at her decision, with joy at knowing the real woman underneath the hard veneer, with a frustration that she was so damned private. With pride that she'd chosen him to take to bed, to tell her secrets to when she'd been ready. With a yearning for more and more and more, and he didn't know what any of that meant.

And then he did. The pieces began to slip into place.

He had fallen in love with her. Of all the women in the damned hospital, in the damned city, in the whole damned world to fall in love with, he had chosen the most complicated, stubborn, uptight one of all. And now she was walking away and there was nothing he could do or say to make her stop because she didn't believe she could do it. She didn't believe that love could happen for her.

And so this was what he was left with: he loved her and he didn't know what to do with it. He didn't want to love her. He didn't want to like her even. Because, *oh, mio Dio,* she could be very difficult and all she cared about was her work.

Like him. Like he used to be.

He turned away and tried to steady himself. Panic swirled in his gut. He had protected himself for years against this. But, it seemed, it was something you could not fight in the end.

'*Ciao*, Matteo. And thank you for everything. It was a hell of a lot better than nice.' She was going. Leaving, because he had made her go. His mind began to swirl too. Why this? Why now? Why, in hell, *her*? But the only answers were right in front of his eyes.

'Wait.'

Taking too many steps closer to her, he touched her cheek. Pulled her to him. And he felt hesitation. For a moment he thought she might push him away, but instead she dragged him to her, clamped her mouth hard against his.

'Matteo…'

She was in his arms and the emotions filled his chest thick and heavy and yet weightless, and he tried to hold them back but they just kept coming, rising and filling him with this urgent need. 'Ivy, *ti amo*.'

And he hoped she did not understand or hear him, because the moment he'd said those words he'd known it was the wrong thing to say. The last thing he should do was open his heart to her.

Then he was kissing her again. A rough, hard kiss filled with every damned ounce of emotion he had in him, and she was kissing him back with just as much. With anger. With joy and frustration that they just wouldn't work, because she didn't want them to.

And because that had been the one startlingly honest thing she had said, he kissed her some more.

'Okay, people, let's get going. Oh. God. Sorry. Oops. Bad timing.'

It was Nancy. Matteo winced. Now, to add humiliation to Ivy's list of worries, their privately public display would definitely be hospital gossip.

Ivy jerked away, the space where she'd been in his arms now just a heavy emptiness. She was swiping her hand across her mouth. Then she was gone. Along with his hope.

He looked around for something to kick, to hit, to assuage these feelings of hurt and anger and…this new feeling of love. But there was a surge of people into the adjoining room. A child who needed an operation. A family waiting for his skills. A team needing to be led. So he just balled his hands into fists and took a minute to let the emotions wash through him.

His heart was as empty as his arms. Because he knew, with certainty, that she would never come back. That he had lost her. Because she had never known such a thing as love and she was so desperately in need of it but, oh, so afraid. And now he had lost it too.

* * *

'Well done. You were great in there! Scary, but great.' Becca gave Ivy a high five as they walked away from the sexual harassment tribunal. The wind had dropped and the afternoon was promising to be unseasonably warm. They took the shortcut through Regent's Park back towards the hospital, dodging what appeared to be some kind of kiddie fun run event as they walked. 'You knew exactly what you were doing, and you wiped the floor with his defence.'

Ivy smiled. Ah, the naivety of the inexperienced. 'I just let the evidence speak for itself. There really wasn't anything he could say in the face of three witnesses.' But Becca was right. She had felt like a fight this morning. In fact, she had felt like a fight quite a lot recently. She put it down to lack of sleep. Which in turn was a result of... She wouldn't think about it. She wouldn't think about him any more. It was too exhausting. Too damaging to ache and want and dream, and need someone so badly. She just needed to focus on work some more and he'd be gone from her brain soon. He would.

The trouble was, almost a week on and he was still there, looming large inside her head.

'But you just kept on. You were epic. I started to feel a bit sorry for him by the end. You needled and needled until he admitted everything.' Becca put her hand on Ivy's arm. 'Girl crush alert. I think I'd like to be you when I grow up.'

'Oh, no, you wouldn't. Believe me. I do everything wrong.'

Becca shook her head. 'What? You just won a case, you did that right. You want to celebrate?' They'd stopped outside a café, the smell of strong dark coffee irresistible. And, for some reason, Ivy felt like staying a while, not rushing back. The thought of her stuffy office was nothing compared to the fresh air, the kids' squeals and cheers as they crossed the finishing line. Ivy envied them their innocence.

'Okay. A quick one.'

Ivy placed the order and found Becca sitting at an outside table, swatting a large bee away. 'I asked them to be quick. Shouldn't be too long.'

'Doesn't matter if it is. To be honest, with the hours you've put in this week you're owed a small break and... Oh, don't they look pretty? So fresh and gorgeous.' Becca was pointing towards a carpet of red and white flowers. 'Tulips? I never know the names of flowers.'

Ivy pulled out her notepad. 'So, about tomorrow's course. Are you sure you can handle it? You know the schedule?'

Becca rolled her eyes. 'We've been over and over this. Yes, I can handle it. It's only the wrap-up, question time and feedback. It won't be hard. But, you know, I did just point out that absolutely stunning tulip bed over there, and can you smell that divine smell? There are some seriously beautiful plants here but you don't appear to notice them. Or anything out of the confines of your office.'

Becca inhaled and looked a little apprehensive. 'I wasn't going to say anything, but I can't let you go on like this. I know you're not running tomorrow's social media course because Dr Peachy Bum will be there...but I don't know why. What on earth happened?'

'Becca. Please.' Ivy didn't need this. She was coping just fine, and would continue to do so as long as she didn't have to speak about it. Or think about him. 'I have an unavoidable meeting with the board tomorrow, you know that.'

'You could have rearranged it. Said you had an important previous appointment. And, yes, I'm overstepping again, but I'm worried about you. Seriously. You've been head down all week, locked in your office until all hours—and I know you think we all believe you're working, but I can see straight through you. There's not much more done than this time last week.'

'There is. I would never let anything interfere with my work.' Had she? Had she spent time staring out the window? Yes. But that had been critical thinking time. Had she thought about Matteo at all?

Okay, yes. She'd thought about little else. She missed him. Missed having his arms wrapped around her, missed feeling able to tell him anything. Missed his smile and his laugh and…okay, yes. She missed his bum too.

Becca tapped her finger on the tabletop. 'Besides, there are doodles…incriminating doodles…'

'What?'

'In your bin. Words, doodles, hearts. Tearstained hearts…'

And Ivy had thought she'd managed to hide them away at the bottom of the rubbish bin. Hearts. Yeah, right. It was all fluff and nonsense and wishful thinking. 'You are seriously deranged. Either that or you'll go far in this profession—observation and attention to detail are key.' For a moment Ivy thought Becca might explode with such an admission of excited suspicion. 'But sorry to disappoint you, there weren't any tears, I just spilled my water—'

Becca's voice dropped and softened. 'Something happened, something momentous, and you think you can hide it all. But you can't. Guess what? You're human, Ivy, and you're allowed to bleed.'

Sure, but what if it never stops? 'It wasn't… I didn't…'

'What happened?'

'Nothing.'

The coffee came and it was satisfactory, but not as nice as the one Matteo had bought for her that day he'd kissed her in the staffroom. Seemed she couldn't do the most mundane of things without thinking about him. *Fade, please, memory. Fade.* But it didn't fade, it just sent shooting pains to her chest instead. 'I can't talk about it.'

Replacing her cup in its saucer, Becca shook her head. 'Okay. Fine. Spend all your days solving everyone else's problems just so you don't have to think about your own.'

Like her mother? 'That's not why I do this job.'

Her assistant's eyebrows rose. 'Really?'

'No. I do it because I want everyone to get a fair go. I love this job.' Although recently it hadn't held her attention quite as much as it always had. And she knew the reason. She just wasn't ready to admit it. She wanted more in her life than files and injunctions and other people's messes. She wanted a chance at her own happy mess. Hugo had filled a little space, but she ached for more.

For Matteo.

Becca ran her finger round the froth in her cup and licked. 'You love being needed here. Does it...does it stop you from needing something else? Love? A peachy—?'

'Stop it. I should fire you for insubordination.'

'Well, you could, but that would mean you'd have to do tomorrow's course on your own.'

Panic twisted in her stomach. 'I can't see him, Becca. I just can't.'

Becca breathed out and smiled reassuringly. 'Sure you can.'

'I can?' Yes, of course she could. He was just a man. She was fine. 'I don't think I can.'

'So you had a thing?'

Oh, what was the point in denying it? She knew any secrets shared would stay with Becca. She shrugged. 'A small one.'

'Wait, though, you look crushed. You've been so hyped

up recently. Oh, Ivy…it wasn't small at all. Was it? Not for you.' Her hand slid across the table to Ivy's shaking one. 'You've fallen in love with him?'

Do not cry. Do not cry. Do not cry. 'I haven't got time to do anything like that. I have a busy job—'

'You do. You love him.'

'And there are a lot of long hours involved. I have to review all the employment contracts starting from next Monday—'

Becca patted her hand. 'It's okay, you know. It's okay to be frightened. It's okay to meet someone halfway. You don't have to give all this up. You can do both. People do both.'

'And then…' Ivy stopped talking. Simply because there was a rock in her throat that she couldn't squeeze words past. But she thought about her life. How she'd been forging forward her whole life because she so wanted people to take her seriously. Wanted people to notice her for the right reasons, and not because she couldn't walk properly. And he had. Matteo had plucked her from the three billion women on the planet and had made her feel important. He'd given her the one thing she'd craved all her life. And it scared her so much. That responsibility, just taking what he was offering, it was overwhelming… Man, she was so scared. 'Yes.'

'Yes, what?'

And she thought about her sleepless nights, and about how much she missed him. How she had never wanted to believe all that *you complete me* guff, but she could see how it could be possible that one person could make you more whole, better, stronger than before. That plenty of people weren't like her mum, plenty of people had happy stable lives that they shared very successfully. It was a question of finding the right person for you.

That person was Matteo. Her heart softened a little at the thought of him. And then filled with panic at the thought that she'd lost him already. 'Yes. I think I love him. I don't know for sure, but I think I could. I'd like to try.' And that scared her the most.

'Hallelujah. Great. Finally, we have a breakthrough.' Becca raised her hands to the sky and cheered. 'But does he love you back?'

'I sincerely doubt it after everything I've said and done to stop that happening. He thinks I'm selfish and self-centred and only think about my work.'

'Hmm, clearly the man's a good judge of character.' Becca flashed a smile. 'Seriously, though, did he ever do anything that might make you think he felt the same?'

Ivy thought about the kisses and the night of lovemaking, and driving her all that way home in the rain, and just the simple, sweet look in his eyes when he talked to her. The kisses, though—they couldn't lie about the way he felt. No one could kiss like that and not mean it. 'Yes. Lots and lots.'

'So show him that you're all of those things and so much more. You're driven and dedicated and passionate. Italians like that.'

'He does.' And for the first time in for ever Ivy began to feel a little glimmer of hope blooming in her chest. She breathed deeply, the gorgeous scent of some exotic plant catching in her throat. He was right, there was so much more to life than work. There was him, Matteo Finelli. And her, Poison Ivy. Maybe they could try to be part of something. Something together. 'But I really messed up. I just need to find a way to convince him.'

Becca punched the air. 'Yes! If anyone can, you can. Why don't you just march right up to him and tell him?'

Because she wasn't that brave. 'Because he's the kind of

man who judges by actions. I know him, Becca, he's tired of all my words. He was hurt badly once by a girl who said she loved him but acted otherwise. She broke his heart and he's waited all this time to take a chance on someone else. And when he did it backfired and he's retreated to lick his wounds. It's enough for me to accept that I love him, but I need to work out a way to prove it to him.'

CHAPTER THIRTEEN

IT WAS LATE. The transplant he'd just finished on a thirteen-year-old girl had been very difficult but she was recovering well. He had pre-op blood results to go through for the list tomorrow and an informal ward round to complete. He had a headache. And heartache. And he wanted to go to bed.

But to top off the day from hell, someone had organised a night walk through Regent's Park to raise money for the department. Tonight. For a dialysis machine. So he was duty bound to attend.

'Wow, what's happening?' Regent's Park was one of his usual running spots but as he approached it he was surprised at the size of the crowd. Everywhere he looked he saw people; adults, kids, baby strollers, all dressed up in green, a surging emerald sea. Getting closer, he heard clapping start. Quietly at first, but with every step he took it got louder and louder. And then he began to recognise faces. Joey's mum and dad. Portia, who he'd operated on last year, and her family. Mathilde. Ahmed. Benjamin. All these familiar faces greeting him with cheers and smiles. What the hell? Why were they clapping?

Confused and a little humbled, he stopped at the first marquee with a banner reading *'KIDney Kidz—Give a little, save a life.'* He spoke to a nurse from the intensive care unit. 'Hi. I'm Matteo. I need to pay for my ticket. I think I'm a little late. Where's the start?'

She beamed at him. 'Hi, yes, I know who you are. I think everyone does.'

That damned picture again. 'But—'

'Thanks for everything you've done.' She gave a quick nod. 'We're five minutes away from starting—the line's over there.' She pointed down the crowd of people to the right. 'And it's okay, VIPs don't have to pay.'

VIPs? Now he was really confused. Was this another unfunny Ged joke? 'It's for a good cause. I'd like to give something—'

'I think you've given enough, Matteo.'

He froze. That voice. The northern accent. *Ivy.* His heart thumped. Would it ever stop its Pavlovian response to her? Four weeks and he'd managed to keep out of her way. Four long weeks of hell wondering how to fix something that appeared irrevocably broken.

Sucking in a deep breath, he turned. She was dressed in a green T-shirt and shorts, her hair covered by a green baseball cap. She wore a tentative smile. In her hands she had a clipboard and a large net bag stuffed with green fabric. It was good to see her. Good and bad as his gut tumbled over and over. 'Ivy. What are you doing here?'

Her pretty smile faded. 'A fun run, obviously.'

His gaze flitted from that beautiful, heart-breaking mouth to her leg. 'But your foot?'

'Will be fine, I'm sure. It's only ten kilometres.' Although she looked more defiant than convinced. He had no doubt that if anyone would do it, she would. 'Good turnout.'

'I've never seen so many people at one of our events before. It's miraculous.'

Her head dipped a little as she replied, 'No, Matteo. It's called using the internet for what it's good at.'

'You? You did this?' *What the hell is going on?*

'Yes.'

'How?' *Why?* For some reason his voice was croaky, his throat blocked.

Hers clearly wasn't. She was determined and forthright. Vibrant in her passion for what she'd done. 'I sent out a call. I contacted Joey's mum and dad, who are part of the kidney kids support network, who in turn contacted your previous patients, who promoted the idea on all their social network sites. Within twenty-four hours the buzz got picked up by a radio station. That got covered by the local newspaper. That was online and got clicked on by hundreds of people. Like your bottom, my call went viral. It doesn't happen every time, but this seems to have captured people's imaginations. Your patients and their families wanted to do this, for you. Because of what you'd done for them.'

Whoa. That was humbling and affirming at the same time. 'What was your message?'

'I said…and please don't be angry because only you and I really know what happened…' From her clipboard she peeled off a leaflet with his photo on it. His work profile one, not the one in the locker room. Thank goodness for small mercies. 'Dr Matteo gave the gift of life, now you can too. One step at a time. Join us on a night walk. Wear green to be seen. KIDney Kidz: We won't fail them.'

'You make me sound too perfect.'

She grinned and her green eyes shone with a fire he'd only seen once before. When he'd been in bed with her. *Mio Dio*, she was beautiful. She'd broken what had been left of his heart—he understood that now. 'Nah—you're just the pretty face poster-boy. Amazing what you can do, even with clothes on. I thought that there must be a lot of people out there who want to show their thanks, and who want to help others in the same situation. It's amazing how many people said yes as soon as your name was mentioned. You have quite a fan club.'

But the one person he wanted wasn't a member. 'I don't know what to say.'

'"Thank you" will suffice. Oh, and at three thousand people, ten quid a head, you've pretty much got your dialysis machine.' He followed her, walking slowly towards the start line, and they became engulfed with people on all sides, chatting, cheering, patting him on the back.

He still couldn't believe it. 'And you organised this in four weeks?'

'I pulled a few strings. Someone I was at university with knows someone who could make it happen. Becca helped too. We were stuffing the goody bags at three this morning.' Her face lit up as she looked at all the smiling faces around them. And he could see the tired edges of her face and he longed to touch her, but he wouldn't. 'It was worth every second.'

'But why? Why did you do this?'

She turned to look at him, her eyes misting. 'Because you got to me in the end. I believe you need this equipment. I believe you, Matteo, when you say children are vulnerable and not a brand. I believe in you. And I wanted to show you how using the internet for the right things can really pay off.' A loud crack split the sky. 'Oh. Looks like we're starting. Come on.'

She stuffed a T-shirt—green, of course—into his hand and started to walk along the path. If her ankle was hurting she certainly had no intention of showing it. She'd done all this for him? Using her skills and knowledge and pure raw grit.

'No. Stop a minute.' He pulled her off the path for a

moment onto lush, warm grass. 'I was wrong about you. Well, kind of wrong and right at the same time. I suppose I can concede that the internet has its advantages. Look at how many people *you* have helped.'

She shook her head. 'I started to do this for you, Matteo. It would be wrong of me to say otherwise. I wanted to make you happy. But, actually, as the whole thing began to gain traction I got so completely invested in it that I had to make it work. Look at Joey there—you've made such a difference. To all of them.'

What was she saying? That this grand gesture was for him? Why? 'I don't understand you, Ivy. You said it was over. You said you didn't want me. And that's okay. Sad, but okay. We have our own lives.' He didn't want to have this conversation. Enough that it was all over between them, without this prolonged attachment. He watched as people streamed by, green balloons bobbing above their heads in the fading daylight, and felt overwhelming emotion. For them. For this. For him and Ivy. Between them they could have made an excellent team.

But that was useless. She'd been trying to prove a point that she could use social media for a good cause. This wasn't about them. Or about piecing together a broken heart. 'Thank you for doing this—the department will be grateful. I am grateful. We should be going.'

This was not how Ivy had envisaged things going. She'd thought he would be pleased, thrilled enough that she wouldn't have to completely open herself up to him. That he'd accept this whole night run as a sign of how she felt. Which was…overwhelmed. Just being with him again left her breathless and aching for more. To touch him. To kiss him.

Say it.

Bleed if you have to.

She watched him moving quickly in the crowd. 'Matteo. Stop.' Damn. This had not been such a great idea after all. How to declare yourself in front of three thousand runners? *Really?* She doubled her pace, her leg jarring with every footfall, but, damn it, she was going to get through to him, all ten kilometres if she had to—shouting his name all the damned way. 'Matteo! Stop.' He did, finally. 'What I'm trying to say…badly…is that I'm sorry for how I reacted to everything. I didn't want it to end. Not really.'

He began to walk back to her, frowning. 'But you made it very obvious you didn't want me. Are you saying that you do now? You've changed your mind?'

His words were like tiny daggers stabbing at her heart. 'I always wanted you, you idiot. But I was scared. It went from a game, a battle of wills and a point to prove, to very serious, very quickly.' How else could she show him how she felt? Was this not enough?

'Matteo, I've been trying to prove that I'm worth something my whole life—it was hard, bloody hard, and there were times even I didn't believe it. But I learnt to fight for myself, I learnt not to rely on anyone, not to let anyone in because I just knew I'd get hurt in the end. And then you came along and I didn't need to try too hard with you because you seemed to accept me as I was—which was new and weird and exciting. And then I didn't know what to do. You took me by surprise—I needed to make space for you and I didn't want to let go of the safety blanket I'd shrouded myself in. My life was fine before you and your magnificent bottom came along, thank you very much, I wasn't expecting to fall in love with you…'

'You love…?' His eyes widened at her admission.

She placed a finger over his mouth. If she didn't say it all now, she might never say it. 'I felt frightened by the intensity of how I was feeling. My mum…she never wanted me around. Even now I'm of no use to her and I guess I got used to being on my own. But the thing is, I'm lost without you. I'm lost with you too, but that's okay… I'd kind of like us to be lost with each other. If you'll give me a second chance?'

He looked at her for a while. Took her finger from his lips and pressed a kiss onto the tip. 'I'm not lost at all, Ivy. I found you and you are worth more to me than everything else.'

'Oh, so good…'

But he still didn't look convinced. He wasn't. 'How do I know you mean it this time? How do I know you will not throw it all back in my face?'

Oh, so bad. Was he for real? Could he not see the love she knew was in her eyes? Could he not hear it in her voice? 'You want *more* than thirty thousand pounds, a massive show of support and a new dialysis machine? Really? That's not enough? This isn't enough? I'm not enough? I love you, Matteo. I don't know how else to show you. Please, believe me. I'm not Elizabetta. I'm not your father. I won't throw your love back at you. I don't know what else would prove to you how I feel.'

The crowds had all moved along, balloons bobbing in the distance, the park now silent except for the whistle of wind through the trees and a dull buzz from a hovering bee. And she was left standing with Matteo, alone, in a garden that smelt of sunshine and roses. Then she smiled to herself. She'd noticed them. Becca would be proud.

He looked away, at the balloons and the children and the banners. At the posters and the marquee. A slow smile flitted onto his lips as his gaze went from her eyes to her mouth. 'A kiss maybe?'

'Oh. Yes. Of course. Good idea.' She took a step closer, hardly daring to believe that this could be happening. Maybe he did believe her. His arms snaked round her waist and he dragged her to him. She bunched his work shirt into her fists, choking back the tears that were threatening. 'But how do you feel? About me? Us?'

'I love you more than anything. I told you already.'

She blinked, trying to remember. She would have remembered. 'When? When did you say that?'

'Our last kiss. I whispered it to you.'

'I wish I'd heard it.'

His mouth was close to her ear. 'I said, *Ti amo*.'

She tried it, to see how it felt. '*Ti amo,* Matteo. I love you.' Goddamn, it felt great, however she said it. Then she couldn't say anything else because the lump in her throat had got jammed there so tightly she could barely breathe. What little breath she did have left was whipped away by his kiss. A slow, gentle, heart-warming kiss that told her exactly how he felt.

He pulled away, a huge grin on his face. 'No more wars? No more games.'

'None.'

'Good.' His finger stroked the side of her cheek. 'So we have some catching up to do.'

'Oh, yes, the run… We'd better hurry up, we're going to be last.'

He shook his head, those dark eyes blazing with desire, a smile that was at once innocent and dirty. 'I wasn't thinking about that. I want you so bad…'

'*Badly*.' She saw the flicker of a frown then the smile. Then the grimace. 'Oh, whatever, I don't care how you say it. Just keep on saying it… I want you right back.'

'You know, you will drive me crazy.' He held out his hand.

She took it, held on tight, promising to never let go. 'That sounds like a very good plan.'

* * * * *